W9-CAD-926

DETROIT PUBLIC LIBRARY

Browsing Library

DATE DUE

NOV 2 0 1993	
DEC - 1 1993	
MAR 17 1994	
APR 1 3 1994	
APR 2 7 1994	
AUG 2 0 1998	
NOV 2 5 1998	

OCT 2 7 1993

KILLINGS

Also by A. W. *Gray*
BINO
SIZE
IN DEFENSE OF JUDGES
THE MAN OFFSIDE
PRIME SUSPECT

A. W. Gray

KILLINGS

A DUTTON BOOK

DUTTON
Published by the Penguin Group
Penguin Books USA Inc., 375 Hudson Street,
New York, New York 10014, U.S.A.
Penguin Books Ltd, 27 Wrights Lane, London W8 5TZ, England
Penguin Books Australia Ltd, Ringwood, Victoria, Australia
Penguin Books Canada Ltd, 10 Alcorn Avenue,
Toronto, Ontario, Canada M4V 3B2
Penguin Books (N.Z.) Ltd, 182–190 Wairau Road, Auckland 10, New Zealand

Penguin Books Ltd, Registered Offices:
Harmondsworth, Middlesex, England

First published by Dutton, an imprint of New American Library,
a division of Penguin Books USA Inc.
Distributed in Canada by McClelland & Stewart Inc.

First Printing, August, 1993
10 9 8 7 6 5 4 3 2 1

Copyright © A. W. Gray, 1993
All rights reserved.

REGISTERED TRADEMARK—MARCA REGISTRADA

LIBRARY OF CONGRESS CATALOGING IN PUBLICATION DATA

Gray, A. W. (Albert William)
    Killings / A. W. Gray.
        p.   cm.
    ISBN 0-525-93625-4
    I. Title.
    PS3557.R2914K5   1993
    813'.54—dc20   92-42983
                                                        CIP

Printed in the United States of America
Set in Electra

PUBLISHER'S NOTE
This is a work of fiction. Names, characters, places, and incidents either are the
product of the author's imagination or are used fictitiously, and any resemblance to
actual persons, living or dead, events, or locales is entirely coincidental.

Without limiting the rights under copyright reserved above, no part of this publication
may be reproduced, stored in or introduced into a retrieval system, or transmitted, in
any form, or by any means (electronic, mechanical, photocopying, recording, or otherwise), without the prior written permission of both the copyright owner and the above
publisher of this book.

For Thomas Arrington Gray II
March 18, 1938–July 18, 1992
Big Bud.
Oh, to tote your helmet after practice,
Just one more time.

1

A custodian named Herbert Trevino, as he reported for four a.m. duty on the SMU campus, found the second victim under a tree. At five in the morning he told Dallas County Investigator Hardy Cole that the nude body of the girl would have gone unnoticed if it hadn't have been for the noise.

"Wait a minute," Cole said. "This is the first I've heard about any noise." He was lean and angular, with a permanent what-you're-telling-me's-a-lot-of-bullshit set to his mouth, and at the moment was more than a little pissed over the call at his home at four in the morning. He hadn't shaved and had wolfed down a doughnut and a cup of 7-Eleven coffee on his way to the campus.

The custodian said, "That's 'cause this is the first time anybody ask me. All these cops tramping around here don't do nothing 'cept put up them barriers and then stand the fuck around. I try to tell them what happen three or four times, they just say, 'wait a minute,' and then throw some more cigarette butts down for me to clean up after." He wore a gray broadcloth short-sleeved uniform and hard-toed work boots. His thick hair was graying, his weather-creased skin the color of a tamale wrapper.

Cole and Trevino were sitting in the front seat of Cole's gray four-door county-owned Chevy, parked at the curb on Airline Road. Across the way, flashlight beams stabbed here and there as the University Park Police and the Dallas County Sheriff's Department poked among the bushes and shrubs around the Fondren Science Building. In the distance, the dome atop Dallas Hall blotted out a large portion of the northwestern horizon. In another half hour, a late September dawn would streak the darkness with pink and gold.

"Let's get this straight," Cole said. "You understand how important it is for me to get this right, huh?" He was bracing a steno pad on his thigh and had a flashlight clamped between his left arm and his rib cage. The flashlight's beam was directed at the page on which Cole was taking notes.

"I s'pose," Trevino said. "I got some of my people wish them poleez would fuck around like this when they out off Harry Hines Boulevard hassling Mexican brothers."

"I ain't here to talk about that," Cole said. "You're coming to work at four o'clock, right?"

"Quarter to. Twen'y-six year I don't be late a time. My wife, she let me off right over there." Trevino pointed across the street, toward a row of old brick houses with tree-lined yards. The houses were built before World War II, without central air or heat. Most of them had rickety wooden floors which creaked underfoot and, in this Park Cities neighborhood, carried price tags of two hundred grand and up. Cole pictured his own home, a three-bedroom Fox & Jacobs which had run him forty-five thousand ten years earlier, and decided that for the money he'd made a better deal.

"Okay," Cole said. "So you came across Airline and crossed that little asphalt parking lot toward the science building. Notice anything out of line?"

"No, man, not till I go up the walk toward the building. Around them big trees over there."

"And you say you heard a noise?"

"That's what I say, man," Trevino said.

"Well, *man*, what did it sound like?"

"Like somebody giving somebody a blow job," Trevino said.

"Jesus Christ, I can't put *that* in my report," Cole said.

"Well, lick-lick, slurp-slurp, then."

"A slurping noise?"

"Yeah," Trevino said.

Cole held his pencil between his first and middle fingers and tapped it on the steering wheel. The a/c fan was on low; ice-cold air drifted from the vents. "One thing's bothering me, Herbert,"

Cole said. "This naked body was only five feet from the walk, and you say you didn't see it?"

"She was under the blanket," Trevino said.

"I don't have any information on that."

"Man, you don't got no information on chit."

"Listen, you want to talk about this downtown?" Cole said.

"Huh? Well, what you asking about you don't got no information on?"

"Any blanket," Cole said.

"I done told you, man," Trevino said. "Them fucking cops."

"The *police* took the blanket?"

"Yeah. Prob'ly took a nap."

Cole wrote down the information, leaving out the witness's opinion as to what the officers had done with the blanket. "So where were you when you first heard the slurping noise?" Cole said.

"I just turn up the walk and go for the building," Trevino said, pointing. "Maybe twen'y steps."

"Any idea what was making the noise?" Cole said.

"Yeah. The dude under the blanket with the dead gorl."

Cole couldn't say anything for a couple of seconds, then said, "Are you putting me on, Herbert?"

"No, man, I telling you. I thought they was a couple of kids fucking on the lawn."

" 'Engaged in sex,' " Cole said. "That's what I'm writing down."

"Yeah, okay. I go over and I say to the blanket, 'Hey, you can't do that chit around here.' That when the dude jump up and run off."

"Jesus Christ, you *saw* somebody?"

"I told you, man, them fucking cops. They don't listen," Trevino said.

"Well what did he look like?" Cole said.

"I can't tell. Eighty degrees, man, that dude had on a snowsuit. Had dark hair, maybe black or brown. Fucker run like hell."

"Let's get back to the slurping noise," Cole said. "Any idea what it was?"

"Sure," Trevino said. "It was the dude under the blanket. I ain't lying, man, he was under there sucking all over that dead gorl."

Cole's lips twisted as he pictured it, the guy crouched down underneath a blanket hungrily sucking at the lifeless flesh. "Lick-lick, slurp-slurp, huh?" Cole said.

"You got it, man," Herbert Trevino said.

By seven a.m. a meeting had convened at the University Park police station, a red brick, Colonial-style building on McFarlin Boulevard. Ancient elm, sycamore, and weeping willow trees surrounded the building, and up and down the street rolling lawns fronted seventy-five-year-old homes the size of small English castles. Across the street from the station were four tennis courts which belonged to the city of University Park.

The meeting took place in the police conference room adjacent to the municipal courtroom. Present and seated at the conference table were Dallas County Assistant D.A. McIver Strange, Detective Ben Lewis and Captain Will Utley of the University Park police department, and Vernon "Shoesole" Traynor of the Dallas County coroner's office. The last to come in was Hardy Cole, a day's growth of beard on his face, wearing his plaid sport coat and slacks as though he'd rather be dressed in slouchy jeans and a T-shirt. Cole sat down.

"Detective Cole," McIver Strange said. "Glad you could join us. By the way, who's your tailor?" He was wearing a pressed navy suit, a white shirt with a starched collar, was round and soft like a formal penguin.

Cole favored Strange with a shit-eating grin, scooted down in his chair, and propped his knee against the edge of the table. "Hi, Mac," Cole said. "Early, ain't it?"

The two University Park cops exchanged glances. Captain Utley kept his gaze on the table as he said, "We haven't talked to any newspaper people. We have to ask you. Before you do, check with us, huh?" Captain Utley was tall and thin and also wore a navy suit. He had short brown hair, neatly trimmed, with a hint of gray in his sideburns, and wore thick bifocals encased in dark plastic frames.

Cole's chin lifted slightly, then dropped. "Yeah, we know. Park Cities. Allah, Mohammed, and all that shit."

Detective Lewis was short and thick, in his thirties, with a wide face and a thin brown mustache. He folded his hands on the table. "We just work here, Hardy. Something you can't do in this jurisdiction is play the tough monkey."

"Naw," Cole said. "Frank Sinatra already did that. *From Here to Eternity*. Well I don't work here, and what I'm interested in doing is busting one sick son of a bitch. If we got to use the papers, these uppity folks out here are just going to have to lump it."

"The mayor's going to have something to say about that," Lewis said. "He does have a little stroke where you come from."

Cole snorted. "I don't give a fuck about—"

"Hardy." Mac Strange lifted a hand, his eyes half closed as though he were bored. "Just knock it off. We can be here a week with all that. What we need to talk about here is that we've got a real doozy on our hands."

Utley looked relieved, glad to get around the conflict for the time being, at the same time showing by the twitch at the corner of his mouth that he knew the problem would come up again. "No doubt about it," Utley said. "That first one could have been a drifter or somebody pissed off about something. This one makes it look like a bona fide nut case. So. So far, what's anybody got?"

Cole used the forefingers of each hand to rub his eyelids. "Oh, not much. Only that the body was originally under a blanket that nobody seems to know anything about. Oh, yeah, and the custodian that found the body just happened to see the guy, not that anybody bothered to ask him about it until an hour later. Just little shit like that." He tossed a blink in Strange's direction.

"There's a lot going on at a crime scene," Lewis said, his gaze lowered.

Mac Strange opened his mouth as if to say something, but Cole bulled ahead. "Look," Cole said, then held up a hand, palm out, in Strange's direction. "Hear me out, Mac." Then, glancing alternately from Utley to Lewis and back again, "Listen, you guys got some facts to face. This ain't exactly the corner of Oakland and Martin Luther King out here. You people don't get many homicides. What you get is maybe some high school kids shitting in a bag and then setting it on fire and putting it on somebody's front porch and ringing the doorbell. Somebody knocking up somebody's underage daughter, if the guy don't flash his bankroll around and grease a few palms to hush it up. What you're into this time is some heavy bullshit. Well, when the next one comes down, how about calling us first, before your kiddie-cops get out there and mess up the scene. That might step on somebody's toes, but if it does, it does." He settled back with a defiant tilt to his chin.

Captain Utley folded his hands and stuck out his narrow jaw. "We have our people."

Cole rolled his eyes. "Jesus Christ."

Mac Strange pointed a finger. "No more, Hardy, I'm not kidding."

"I ain't kidding either," Cole said. "All this fucking around these people are doing, they're going to wind up with the FBI out here shoving their noses in. That's the next step. You guys probably haven't had the feds fucking with one of your investigations, but Mac and me been through it before."

"Hardy." Strange said.

"Okay." Cole said. He regarded his knee.

"First things first," Strange said. "Any ID on the victim?"

"She was nude," Detective Lewis said. "No belongings or anything. Blond, eighteen to twenty-five"—he took a small notepad from the pocket of his brown suit coat and looked at it—"right at five-six, around a hundred and twenty. Tattoo of a rose on her left cheek."

"Of her ass?" Strange said.

"Yeah. Well-nourished female. Well-built," Lewis said.

"Well-built?" Cole said. "Who came up with that statistic?" He showed another shit-eating grin while Lewis did his best to stare the county investigator down. It didn't work. Lewis dropped his gaze.

Captain Utley leaned forward and said, "No positive identification as yet. We're checking all the dorms to see what female students are missing, but that's pretty much of a bitch. A whole bunch of 'em are missing, all they have to do out there is sign out for the night. Plus a big portion of the student body lives off campus, in apartments."

"Things have changed since I went to college," Strange said.

"Haven't they?" the University Park captain said. "Classes begin at eight, we can narrow it down better when we see who's not in class. But that's not easy, either, everybody doesn't have an eight o'clock. Plus a lot of them cut, and classes don't meet every day. It'll be tomorrow before we get a full roll call."

"If she's a student," Cole said.

Four heads swiveled as one to look at Cole.

"Yeah," Cole said. "Just because you found her on a college campus don't mean she's a student. How about around the body? Any signs that maybe the guy did her someplace else and then dumped her?"

The University Park officers exchanged more looks.

"Well, how 'bout this?" Cole said. "I guess somebody did bother to take some fingerprints."

"Hardy," Strange said.

"That's what I'm talking about, Mac." Cole folded his arms and regarded the ceiling.

"The prints are taken and already shot to Washington," Lewis said. Utley gave Lewis a that's-telling-'em nod.

"Okay," Strange said. "How 'bout it, Shoesole?"

Deputy Coroner Shoesole Traynor had a thick head of graying hair and a good-sized belly, which poked out against the front of his white shin-length smock. He had a Sherlock Holmes–style briar pipe clenched lightly between his teeth. The pipe wasn't lit, but the bowl was filled with tobacco. He'd been listening to the proceedings with the barest hint of a smile. He sat forward, removed the pipe from his mouth, and cupped the bowl in his palm. "No autopsy yet, of course—maybe we'll know more then. All appearances are like the last one, same bite marks, same cuts, same kind of mutilation. Like I said, nothing official till we can slice her open." His smile broadened.

"What mutilation are we talking about?" Cole said.

"You mean there's something you don't know?" University Park detective Lewis said. Alongside him, Captain Utley snickered, then quickly regained his composure.

"The worst one," Traynor said, "that's the peg. A sharpened four-inch hard maple spike, actually, driven into the pelvis bone through the wall of the vagina. On the last victim, the bruise patterns in the flesh show that the guy used a hammer, or something like it. Drove the peg in with series of sharp blows. Odds are we'll find the same thing on this one." He looked down at his pipe, then raised his gaze. "The peg wound on the last one was post mortem. Something like that would almost have to be, given that the victim would have to be lying still."

"I'd think so," Cole said. "Jesus Christ."

"Then there are the same cuts as the last one. Horizontal incisions bisecting the arteries on both sides of the throat. The cuts were made while the last victim was alive." Traynor spoke in a monotone, as though he were speaking into a recorder.

"What in hell killed her?" Cole said.

"Hardy didn't work the last one," Strange said. "He was on vacation."

"Indirectly, it was the cuts," Traynor said. "That last girl was missing almost three pints of blood."

Cole sat bolt upright, his eyebrows lifted. "Well, if she bled to death . . . How much blood was around her, where they found the body?"

"None, or almost none," Traynor said.

"Well, Jesus, that means she got it someplace else," Cole said.

Traynor shook his head. Detective Lewis was grinning openly at Cole while Captain Utley looked as though he were trying not to grin. "Not necessarily," Traynor said. "I said 'indirectly.' Indirectly, the cuts were the cause of death."

Cole frowned. "What the hell are you talking about?"

Traynor put his pipe between his teeth and let it dangle from one corner of his mouth. "Teeth marks around the wounds," he said, "plus the outward swelling of the surrounding tissue would indicate that whoever it was cut the arteries and sucked out the blood."

Cole searched the faces around him. They had to be putting him on.

Finally, Strange nodded. "That's right, Hardy. The guy probably drank it. It seems we got some kind of vampire here."

2

Bino Phillips wondered if the same barber cut all of the federal snitches' hair before they climbed up onto the witness stand. The haircuts damn sure *looked* the same—short and neat, no sideburns to speak of, the guy clean-shaven like he was interviewing for a job. Bino glanced toward the prosecution's table, where Assistant U.S. Attorney Marvin Goldman was saying something to a Drug Enforcement agent. Goldman was talking from the side of his mouth, and the DEA man's hair was cut exactly like the snitch's hair. Jesus, Bino thought, maybe *Goldman* is giving the haircuts.

Bino raised a finger and smiled respectfully toward the bench. "One moment, Your Honor," he said. Judge Hazel Burke Sanderson, her iron-gray hair stiff as papier-mâché, favored Bino with an impatient glare. Her eyes were lumps of smoldering coal.

As Bino retreated to the defense table, Hazel Sanderson's gaze bored holes in his backside. He leaned his six-foot-six over and slid one of his two file folders toward him and turned it right-side up. The folder was about three inches thick and was held together by jumbo rubber bands. Bino snapped the bands off, laid them aside, and rummaged through the file. Behind him, Hazel Sanderson cleared her throat. Two U.S. marshals, both in western-cut coats and cowboy boots, were seated behind the defense table with their chairs tilted back against the railing. The older of the two lurched sideways, almost toppled over, grabbed the rail for support, and righted himself.

Bino found the photo midway down in the file. It was a pretty big picture, a black and white about the size of a sheet of typing paper, a frontal view of a guy with a scraggly beard, a silly grin, and a piercing glare like Manson. Bino scratched his head through his snow-white hair as he glanced at the witness, then looked back at the photo, and finally at the snitch again. Jesus, could this be the same guy? The witness continued to smile earnestly in the direction of the jury box. Bino thought that Goldman had done a pretty good job of rehearsing the snitch—having the guy speak directly to the jurors and show his best I'm-telling-it-like-it-is expression—but Goldman needed to give the witness something to do during time-outs, when he wasn't giving testimony. Maybe lean over and talk to Judge Sanderson or something. Hell, what if everybody went to lunch and left the guy smiling at a bunch of empty chairs? As Bino watched, a couple of the jurors—a guy in a blue sport coat and a woman in a green jumper—shifted nervously and averted their gazes from the witness stand.

Bino carried the picture around the defense table and over to the railing. Then he leaned over and whispered to Dodie Peterson, "Hey, you got some scissors?"

Dodie was seated in the front row of the spectator section, which in a high-profile case like this one was about three-quarters full, with the usual hangers-on present, plus some extra newspaper people from out-of-town rags and both wire services. Dodie wore a white cotton sleeveless sweater along with a navy skirt which rode six or eight inches above crossed shapely knees. Her soft blond hair was done in ringlets and touched her shoulders. She snatched up her purse and dug through it as she murmured, "Wow."

Judge Sanderson said loudly, "This is out of order, sir."

Marvin Goldman said in a stage whisper, "What *is* this?"

Bino grinned weakly at the judge. "Just a few seconds more, please," he said.

Dodie was now holding out a pair of cuticle scissors. As Bino reached over and took them, she said softly, "Are you out of your mind?" He winked at her.

Bino went back to the defense table and spread the picture out, cut off the row of numbers that appeared across the wild-looking guy's chest, then laid the tiny scissors aside. He showed the photo to his client Mickey Stanley, who at the moment was in deep shit. Mickey shrugged.

Over at the prosecution's table, Marvin Goldman rose up and squinted sideways at the photo. Bino left the defense table and approached the witness in a roundabout way. He held the picture between a thumb and forefinger and gave old Marv a flashcard glimpse as he swept past the prosecution's table. Then Bino's detour took him within feet of the jury box, where he managed to give the jurors a look by turning his back and holding the picture out behind him, and finally stalked over to the witness stand and thrust the photo in the snitch's face. "Listen, is this you?" Bino said. The witness cringed and looked fearfully toward Goldman.

Goldman popped to his feet like a marionette on a string. "Objection." The prosecutor was built like a middleweight fighter, had coal-black hair with tiny silver threads showing here and there, and wore a goatee. "This is irrelevant, your honor. The witness has already been identified."

Hazel Sanderson raised her gavel, and for an instant Bino thought the judge was going to lean over the bench and bonk him over the head. But instead she brought the gavel down with a bang that shook the courtroom. "Both counsel approach the bench," she said. She sounded to Bino like Cinderella's stepmother.

Bino took two long strides and stood at attention. Goldman came before the judge and strutted in place, the top of his head on a level with Bino's shoulder. Hazel Sanderson bent forward and said to Bino, "Do you have a good excuse for continuing to try the court's patience? I'm going to tell you that you'd better have."

"Well, I've got a problem, judge," Bino said. "The thing is, I'm looking at a federal witness list with sixty-two names on it. Now we've been doing a lot of preparation for this trial, and part of it has to do with getting ready for each witness. You know, figuring out what to ask them on cross. I've got pictures of all of them over there, mug shots I got from the marshals' office and—"

"You've got mug shots of *all* the federal witnesses?" Hazel Sanderson said.

"Well, except for the DEA agents, and I don't think they can get hired on if they've ever been arrested. Besides, I know what those guys look like. My problem is that this witness doesn't look

like any of the pictures, and so I'll know to ask the right questions
I need to make sure which one he is." Bino smiled hopefully.

"Your Honor, I think Mr. Phillips knows who the witness is."
Goldman half turned and folded his arms, speaking to Bino and
the judge at the same time. "The witness's name is Allan Kilbourne, as he identified himself under oath." Goldman showed a
condescending smirk.

"Yeah," Bino said, looking down at Goldman's spit-shined
shoes, then slowly back up, "but is he 'Twenty-Kilo' Kilbourne,
or 'Ten-Kilo' Kilbourne? They're brothers. Both of them are on
the government's witness list, but I—"

"Mr. Phillips," Judge Sanderson said.

"—can't tell one from the other. Is this the guy that made the
deal for six months probation, or the guy that made the deal for
a year in the country club out at Texarkana Camp? If I'm going
to ask the right questions I need to get my ducks in a—"

"*Mr. Phillips.*" Judge Sanderson sounded like a woman with
asthma. Over by the rail, the older marshal's chair landed on its
front legs with a muted thump on padded carpet. Judge Sanderson
pointed a wavering finger. "Give me that blasted picture," she
said.

Bino shrugged and handed over the photo. Hazel Sanderson
dropped her Martha Washington wire-framed glasses to the tip of
her nose, held the picture at arm's length and peered at it, and
for a moment Bino thought the judge herself was going to burst
out laughing. Be the first time the old heifer ever laughed at
anything, Bino thought. Judge Hazel glanced over at the witness,
then back at the photo. Finally she handed the picture to Bino
over the top of the bench. Bino held the photo by one corner,
facing the jury box. Goldman shuffled quickly sideways to block
the jurors' view.

Judge Sanderson took off her glasses and folded the earpieces.
"Mr. Phillips, do you intend to introduce that picture into
evidence?"

"I hadn't thought about it, Your Honor," Bino said.

"Because if you do," Judge Sanderson said, "you're wasting
your time. It doesn't have anything to do with any testimony here.
And unless it's in evidence, you can't wave it around in front of
the jury. Which you already know, sir. Now, Mr. Phillips, that's
one strike. And this isn't a baseball game. In this courtroom

here"—she pointed her bony finger downward—"you don't get but two strikes. Is that perfectly clear, sir?"

Bino looked at the floor and folded his arms. "I guess it is, judge," he said.

"Now, you carry that picture back over there and slip it into your little file, and let's get on with this. Otherwise your client is going to spend as much time in this courtroom as he is in jail, if he lives long enough. Go on, now, I've had enough of this behavior."

His ears reddening, Bino went back to the defense table and put the picture away while Goldman strutted over and sat down beside the short-haired DEA agent. Mickey Stanley leaned over and touched Bino's arm. "What happened?" Mickey whispered. Bino rolled his eyes.

Judge Sanderson addressed the jurors. "Ladies and gentlemen, sometimes these attorneys are overzealous in their presentation. Now, I'm instructing you to disregard that photo Mr. Phillips was just flashing around, as it has nothing to do with this case. You're simply to pretend you never saw it." She cleared her throat, allowing that to sink in, while a couple of the jurors—a stumpy redhaired woman and a man wearing a hearing aid—exchanged puzzled glances. Then Judge Sanderson said, "Go on with your cross-examination, Mr. Phillips," in a voice like doom.

Bino dusted his hands together, walked confidently over to lean on the rail surrounding the witness, and said in a buddy-buddy tone, "Where did you meet Mr. Stanley, Mr. Kilbourne?" He indicated Mickey, who was sitting attentively upright at the defense table. Mickey Stanley was twenty-six, fresh-faced and clean-shaven, with square shoulders and a big corded neck. Had been one helluva defensive back, All-Southwest Conference, three years running. I didn't have to cut his hair, either, Bino thought.

Allan Kilbourne—"Twenty-Kilo," Bino knew, this was the older of the stoolpigeon duo—was in his mid-thirties, tall and skinny, with a sallow face, scrawny neck, and an Adam's apple the size of a canteloupe. "I ran into him over at Milo's," Kilbourne said.

"Milo Butterfinger's? The nightclub?" Bino said.

"Yeah." Kilbourne glanced quickly at Goldman, whose eyebrows bunched together. "Yes sir," Kilbourne said.

"When was that?"

"Couple of years ago. Eighty-nine."

"And at that meeting, how were you dressed?" Bino said.

Kilbourne swallowed hard. "Huh?"

"How were you dressed? How were you wearing your hair in those days?"

Goldman slowly rose from his chair.

"Tell me," Bino said quickly. "And the jury. Do you have any snapshots of yourself in those good old days?"

"Objection," Goldman said.

"*Mr. Phillips,*" Judge Sanderson said.

From where she was sitting, it looked to Dodie Peterson as though Bino was getting himself in hot water and Mickey Stanley in a worse predicament than he was in already. Of course, Dodie thought, this sure isn't the first time. In the eight years that she'd been his secretary, Dodie had never seen Bino handle *any* case in what could be called a normal manner. Here we go again, she thought as she tucked her tongue into the corner of her mouth and went on with her note-taking. She wrote on her steno pad that Juror Number Three seemed to like Mickey's looks. That was the overweight fortyish woman, top row, second from the left. Little things, most of them not amounting to a hill of beans, but sometimes . . . Dodie jumped slightly as a hand touched her shoulder. She turned around.

A young man with curly brown hair—pretty cute guy at that, Dodie thought—was smiling at her, holding out a folded slip of paper. She took it, glanced down at the folded slip, and then back at the guy. He shrugged and jerked a thumb over his shoulder in the direction of the exit. Dodie raised partway from her seat and craned her neck.

Half-a-Point Harrison, Bino's investigator and friend since childhood, was standing just inside the courtroom. He was skinny as a sick man, with thinning brown hair combed straight back, wearing a black and white checkered sport coat and coal-black slacks, and at the moment, he was frowning. At least he's not carrying a racing form, Dodie thought. She unfolded Half's note and read it. "I need you, little girl. H." She laid her notebook aside, then got up and excuse-me'd her way down the row and into the aisle, marching primly toward the exit, one high-heeled shoe in front of the other in graceful rhythm, as—

*   *   *

Patrick Quarles watched the lovely blond move away up the aisle—watched her hips sway gently under her navy skirt, in time with her walk, her slim bare arms at her sides, her back straight, her soft blond hair in ringlets that touched her shoulders—and smiled to himself, pleased that he had selected one so perfect. The others he had permitted only to gaze at him. But this one . . . this *one* alone would surely unite with him. She and she only would know the whole Truth.

Her name, the silly Dodie-name, wouldn't do, of course. Nor would her proper name, Dora Annette, suit the purpose of the Truth. No, in her union with him she would be called Rebecca, and she would cling to him eagerly even as Rebecca had clung to Isaac and had borne two sons, Jacob the Good and Esau the Fool, who had squandered his birthright for a mess of pottage. Quarles's inner smile now became physical, turning up the corners of his mouth as he pictured his joining with her. Rebecca. Soon she would know.

The razor he'd used to cut the girl last night was in the pocket of his suit, and he shuddered with delight each time his fingers came in contact with the blood-flecked thing. The girl had been such a worthless piece of trash that Quarles had feared contamination from her, and he had said a cleansing prayer before he'd allowed her fluid to come in contact with him. The cleansing was a part of the Truth as well, and was one of the things he would share with Rebecca. She would be washed in the blood even as Quarles himself had been, and then he would annoint her with the oil. For then and only then could she know Quarles's own name under the Truth, and only then could she be set free. As Rebecca—Quarles thought of her as Rebecca even though her time was not yet come—went out the door with the weird thin man, Quarles returned his attention to the front of the courtroom.

And looked upon the white-haired tree of a lawyer for whom Rebecca worked in her current being, the tall one strutting in front of the judge as though he considered himself a god. Quarles wondered whether to kill the White-haired One would become a part of the Truth. As a man, Quarles wouldn't mind killing the White-haired One at all. As a disciple of the Truth, though, Quarles wasn't sure.

           *   *   *

Half led Dodie over by the elevators. "Things ain't good."

She blinked. "Wow, you look like every favorite beat the line or something."

"That ain't what I'm talking about." Half gestured toward the courtroom. "How's it going in there?"

"About what you'd expect. They're not through with the first witness yet, and already Judge Hazel's had him on the carpet twice. Probably three times by now—she looked like she was about to let him have it again." Dodie pressed a shoulder against the wall and crossed her ankles. "What's up?"

Half scratched his forehead. "That witness, Brenda What's-Her-Name. She ain't up. I can't find her anyplace."

"Brenda Milton," Dodie said. "She's a college student, Half, why don't you try looking out at—"

"I know she's a college student, little girl. That's why I been looking for her out at the college. She ain't there. Not in her dorm. Her boyfriend ain't seen her in three days. Her folks down in New Braunfels ain't heard from her. Like I said, she ain't up."

Dodie sighed and lifted her chin toward the ceiling. "Wow, Half, not another one. Bino doesn't have many witnesses to count on as it is."

Half pinched his chin with a thumb and forefinger. "We better hope it ain't another one. One witness having that happen to her, that might be the way the dice come out. But two of 'em? I ain't buying that. No way am I."

Bino decided that if he didn't cool it in Hazel Sanderson's courtroom (at least for the rest of the day—tomorrow would be a different story) one of two things was going to happen. Either Bino was going to have his fanny slapped with a contempt citation and get to spend the night over in the jail with his client, or Hazel Sanderson was going to have a stroke. He wondered which would be worse. The stroke, he guessed, though it was close to a toss-up.

As much as he disliked Hazel Sanderson, and as much as she returned the favor, Bino had to admit that being in front of the old heifer had a few pluses. He'd spent a helluva lot more of his legal career than he liked to remember trying cases in Hazel's court. While she was about as predictable as a Tarrant County thunderstorm, there were a few telltale signs that Bino had learned to pick up on, signs that told him she was on the verge of blowing her stack. The signs that he was seeing now told him he'd better back off. And fast.

As Bino stood in front of the bench, with his head bowed and his hands clasped behind his back, and listened to Goldman's louder-than-necessary breathing close to his right shoulder while Judge Hazel proceeded to read him the riot act, Bino was painfully conscious of sign number one: Judge Hazel's bench-conference stage whisper was a couple of decibels louder than it should have been. Bench conferences were off the record and were supposed to be held so that the jury couldn't hear. But when old Hazel got her dander up, she was a whiz at getting her feelings across to the jury without the risk of having her wrists slapped by the appellate court. As the judge continued to rant and rave, Bino checked the jury box from the corner of his eye. The jurors were forward in their seats with their gazes riveted on the bench. They were hearing, okay.

The second—and most dangerous—sign of all: The judge was cleaning her glasses. As she leaned forward in her chair and gave Bino a Sunday tongue-lashing, old Hazel was holding her Martha Washingtons by an earpiece and wiping the lenses with a handkerchief. Jesus, Hazel Sanderson *never* cleaned her glasses. Normally her lenses were coated with dust and crap so thick that Bino had wondered for years how she made it from her house to downtown without running her car into a telephone pole or fireplug. But here she was, cleaning her glasses. It's a pacifier, Bino thought, she's keeping her hands busy so she won't go bananas.

"Do you, Mr. Phillips?" Hazel Sanderson said.

Bino lifted his head so that his view of his toes was replaced by a straight-on image of the judge. "Huh?" Bino said. "I mean, I beg your pardon?" On his right, Goldman was grinning at him. A juror cleared her throat.

"I asked you if you had a death wish," Hazel Sanderson said. "You certainly act like it."

"Well, of course not," Bino said. He hung his head once more. "To tell you the truth, judge, I don't know what's wrong with me. But the court can rest assured that whatever it is, I'm going to fix it." Now Goldman was staring at Bino as though the big white-haired lawyer had suddenly grown a second head. Bino resisted the urge to giggle.

It was Hazel Sanderson's turn to say "I beg your pardon?"

Bino squared his posture. "Fix it, Your Honor. You're not going to have any more trouble with Bino Phillips, no ma'am. What it is, I think, I've just gotten too wrapped up in this case. I believe too doggone strongly in my client. Plus, you know we've lost a witness."

Hazel's lip twitched. Bino felt guilty about using what had happened to Annette Ray—Jesus, just thinking about Annette made the icicles parade up and down his spine—but knowing Annette and how firmly in Mickey Stanley's corner she'd been, he thought she would have wanted it that way. Bino went on.

"Starting right here and now, I'm going strictly by the book, judge. I hope you'll overlook the way I've been acting," Bino said. Now Goldman put both hands on his hips and snorted.

For just a second, Bino thought Hazel Sanderson was going to drop her glasses. Her jaw lowered a fraction, then snapped closed. Finally she placed her Martha Washingtons on the hump in her nose and said, "Final warning, Mr. Phillips, and I'll tell you that's one more warning than I'd intended to give. Now *please*, let's get on with this trial." She leaned back in her chair.

Bino parted company with Goldman and retreated halfway to the defense table and was so busy patting himself mentally on the back that he nearly forgot where he was. Jesus, he had a witness to cross-examine. Twenty-Kilo Kilbourne—Bino'd nearly forgotten the guy. He was turning on his heel to march back to the witness stand when he caught movement in the corner of his vision. Bino halted in mid-pirouette. From her seat dead center in the spectators' section, Kit Stanley was signaling him.

And there was nothing discreet about it, either. Kit had risen halfway out of her seat and was waving her arm like a lap warning flag on the Indy speedway. Her hair was cut summertime short and was so jet-black that, if he hadn't have known better, Bino would have suspected that Kit used dye. But he *did* know better; had known better, in fact, ever since the days when she'd been Kitty Boston and had tutored him in freshman biology. Just as he did every time he was in the room with both of them, Bino now studied Kit's straight broad nose, wide face, and generous mouth, then glanced quickly at Mickey sitting at the defense table. The family resemblance between Kit and her son was spooky, and Bino wondered briefly what had happened to Teddy Stanley's genes.

The way things had worked out, though, the kid was probably
lucky that he didn't resemble his dad. If he'd looked anything like
Teddy, Mickey would have probably wound up in jail long before
this. In jail or dead, shot by some woman's husband or brother.
Kit had come to court wearing a brown pantsuit. Bino nodded to
her, took a deep breath, and returned to stand before Hazel Sanderson. "I'm not being difficult, Your Honor," Bino said. "Really
I'm not. But I've got to have another brief pause."

Hazel Sanderson's breath came out in an exasperated sigh.
"My goodness. How long this time?"

"Quicker'n a minnow, Your Honor," Bino said. "Really." He
stepped over to the rail before Hazel Sanderson could nix the
delay, and waited with arms folded while Kit wriggled her way
into the aisle and came to meet him.

Kit was far from beautiful—even though she was a long way
from being homely—but what she lacked in looks she'd always
made up for in bouncy enthusiasm. Bino was pretty sure (at least
up to the time *he'd* gone to college—today things were different)
that Kit had been the only single mother in the history of SMU
to get a homecoming queen nomination. Mickey's problems were
taking their toll on her, though. As she drew nearer, the worry
lines were visible through her light blush makeup. She leaned
close and, pointing to the rear of the courtroom, said in a low
voice, "See those four men? Last row, aisle seat and three more
seats to your right?"

Bino did see them. The four guys were decked out in suits
and had short haircuts and could have been lawyers or government
agents. Bino nodded briefly. "Yeah, I got 'em," he said.

Kit shot a quick look over her shoulder, then turned back to
Bino. "They came in after you started your questioning and—I
can't be sure of this—but I think they're the same guys who were
talking to the prosecutor earlier, in the hall. I think they're witnesses. Didn't I hear something about, that witnesses aren't supposed to be in court or something?" She blinked, shot a sideways
glance toward the defense table, and smiled hopefully at her son.
Then she said to Bino, "Is there any problem with them being in
here?"

Bino's eyes narrowed and anger knotted his midsection. Sure,
he'd seen these guys himself. In fact, one of them was none other
than "Ten-Kilo" Kilbourne, whose brother was at the moment

grinning at the jury from the witness stand. And there damn sure was a problem with them being in the courtroom. Hell, Bino had invoked The Rule the moment the trial had begun, before Goldman had made his opening statement. It was such a standard part of procedure that all a lawyer had to say was, "Your Honor, we move that The Rule be invoked," and the judge, without even asking what the lawyer was talking about, would shoo anyone out of the courtroom who was scheduled to testify. The Rule, stated in plain language, meant that witnesses couldn't sit in court and listen to other witnesses testify, and the purpose of The Rule was to see that the witnesses couldn't change their stories to coincide with what the other guy had said. Jesus, Bino thought, Goldman again.

He winked at Kit. "Thanks for being on your toes," Bino said. "I'll handle it." He patted her on the shoulder—thinking briefly that if he ever got in a crack he'd sure like to have Kit in his corner—then made a beeline for the prosecution's table.

Goldman was bent sideways, saying something to the DEA agent, and both men were grinning. Bino stiffened his index finger and gave Goldman's shoulder a poke that Bino hoped would leave a bruise. Goldman's grin became an expression of shock as he turned. Bino leaned over and put his lips about an inch from the prosecutor's ear. "Come on, asshole," Bino whispered. Then, without waiting for Goldman, Bino marched up and stood before the judge. Wincing, rubbing his shoulder where Bino had poked him, Goldman got up and came alongside. His look said that he wasn't sure what was coming, but he didn't think he was going to like it.

"Your Honor, I'm going to move for a mistrial," Bino said.

Hazel Sanderson drummed her fingers and looked at the ceiling. "Oh, my God . . ."

"This isn't any stunt, judge. The Rule is in force, and four of the government's witnesses are sitting in the courtroom. Right back"—Bino pointed toward the exit—"there." He stared at Goldman. Goldman regarded the floor. In the last row of the spectator section, Ten-Kilo Kilbourne looked at his three buddies and smirked.

Hazel Sanderson's gaze followed Bino's direction. "Where?" she said.

"Right back there, judge. Back row, the four guys with the suits and the Dick Tracy haircuts."

The judge blinked and regarded Goldman with a mild curiosity. "Is this true, Mr. Goldman?"

Goldman folded his hands over his stomach and continued to regard the floor. "It's news to me, Your Honor. Perhaps the witnesses didn't have a full understanding of The Rule."

Bino's thoughts paraded through his mind in a high, mimicking, falsetto: *Is this true, Mr. Goldman?* Then, in an answering falsetto like Norman Bates taking on his mother's personality: *It's news to me, Your Honor.* Jesus Christ, if Bino were to pull a stunt like this, Hazel Sanderson would have him *under* the jail. He briefly pictured the judge and Goldman, arm in arm, as they went to the federal bursar's office on payday, picked up their checks and then flipped to see who was buying the drinks.

Bino squared his shoulders and riveted his gaze on a spot just above Hazel Sanderson's head. "Our motion stands, Your Honor," Bino said. "We move for a mistrial."

Judge Sanderson regarded her folded hands and said softly, "Oh, my." Then she stood and raised her voice. "You men in the back row. Back there, you four men with the Dick— You gentlemen dressed in suits."

Ten-Kilo Kilbourne was shorter and blockier than his brother but had the same sallow complexion and big Adam's apple. He stood and cleared his throat. "Yes, ma'am?"

"Excuse me, but aren't the four of you scheduled to testify for the government in this case?"

Kilbourne shifted his gaze to his cohorts on his right, then looked back to the judge. "Yes ma'am," he said again.

Judge Sanderson sank resignedly into her chair. She lowered her voice. "I suppose I'm going to have to clear the courtroom to deal with this." She banged her gavel and addressed the room at large. "You spectators and jurors. We have a sensitive matter here, and this may take a few minutes. It's"—she checked her tiny silver, feminine watch—"about time for lunch anyway, so I'll excuse the jury to eat now. I have a matter to take up with these lawyers."

After the bailiff had escorted a group of puzzled-looking jurors through the back exit into the jury room and had taken Twenty-Kilo Kilbourne to a special witness's waiting area in the hall, and after most of the spectators had left—some of the newspeople stayed, balancing legal pads on their laps, pens held ready and their heads cocked in a listening attitude—only eight people remained in the courtroom's bullpen area: the judge, the court reporter (a clear-complexioned young guy who operated the shorthand machine with his tongue tucked viciously into one corner of his mouth, as though he were writing a horror novel), Bino, Goldman, Mickey Stanley seated at the defense table, the DEA agent seated in one of the prosecution's chairs, and the two marshals who were lounging against the rail (one of whom appeared to be asleep). Hazel Sanderson put her glasses on and folded her hands. "You've heard the defense's motion, Mr. Goldman. Any objections?"

Goldman raised up on the balls of his feet and flexed his muscles under his black courtroom suit. "The government will oppose, Your Honor. The witnesses apparently didn't understand The Rule, and we don't think they've heard anything which would influence their testimony." One corner of the prosecutor's mouth turned up in a smirk. Bino thought that anybody who'd just been called an asshole should be navigating under sort of a limp sail. Not Goldman, though. To Goldman, insults were like a massive dose of vitamin C. Insults actually *strengthened* the guy.

"Our motion continues to stand, Your Honor," Bino said. "There's been testimony about some meetings that took place, and—"

"I've *heard* the testimony, Mr. Phillips," the judge snapped. She regarded Bino like something the cat had dragged in, then appeared deep in thought for a moment. She leaned forward and spoke to the court reporter. "How long before I can get a copy of the testimony transcribed? Just the one witness."

The court reporter hesitated with his hands poised over the keys and withdrew his tongue from the corner of his mouth. "Probably around three o'clock, judge. Sooner if I skip lunch, but that'll cost the government extra." He grinned and waited for someone to laugh at his little joke. No one did. The court reporter's mouth relaxed into a deadpan expression.

Hazel Sanderson reached for the case file before her and opened the jacket to shuffle some papers around. "Three will be fine," she said to the court reporter, then to Bino and Goldman, "You heard the man. I'm going to call it a day, gentlemen. Tonight I'm going to review the law and go over the transcript, and you'll have my ruling on the motion in the morning." She blinked. "Anyone have any questions?"

Bino wanted to ask why they couldn't pay the court reporter a little overtime to get it over with more quickly but decided he'd better not. Neither he nor Goldman said anything.

"Very well, then," Judge Sanderson said. "Have a nice afternoon, gentlemen." She beamed at the prosecutor. "I think you may have a valid point, Mr. Goldman," Hazel Sanderson said.

Patrick Quarles exited the courtroom and brushed so near to his beautiful blond Rebecca that he could feel her warmth, smell the sweetness of her. She was still talking to the skinny man, and she lifted her face to Quarles and smiled. True, it was a brief impersonal smile, but it was such a wondrous smile that Quarles got weak in the knees and practically stumbled. Goodness, but she was the perfect one. And her smile told him what only he could know. She *knew*. Not in the conscious sense as yet, of course, but in spirit she was already one with him. Quarles became so excited that the welts on his chest and belly reddened at once; their warmth penetrated his shirt and caused perspiration to break out on his neck and forehead.

He wanted to reach out and touch the beauty's hair, but he controlled himself, forced himself to behave as he left the group of courtroom spectators and moved down the hallway to the men's room. He walked at a normal pace, though he wanted to run. The need for privacy was so strong that he very nearly did break into a trot, and urgency forced him to take a long running stride as he entered the men's room. Once inside, he permitted his breathing to quicken as he glanced around.

All was silent save for the steady drip of a faucet. A row of gleaming white urinals lined one wall against a backdrop of spotless beige tile. Disinfectant tablets lay in the urinals like dull green pucks.

There was no one in sight. Excitement caused Quarles's full bladder to throb against his groin as he made a quick survey of the water closets, bending to peer under each and every door. Finally satisfied that he was alone, he opened the center water closet, stepped into the stall, and latched the door behind him.

He lowered his trousers and undershorts to his knees and sat on the stool to pee between his legs. Quarles never urinated in the standing position for fear that the filthy piss would splatter from the bowl and touch his body. Above all else, he must keep his body clean. The coat of his brown suit draped over the rear of the stool and the coat's lower hem brushed his outer thighs.

As the stream of urine flowed into the water beneath his buttocks, Quarles reached up underneath his shirt to touch his scars. Until the Truth had come to him he'd been ashamed of the raised welts, but now understood them as a divine mark, just another of many signs which singled him out as a Disciple of Truth. Soon Rebecca would touch the welts, and would come to love them even as he did. He caressed the gristly red marks with his fingers.

When he'd finished urinating he withdrew his hand from under his shirt, then fished in the side pocket of his coat to produce a rubber suction bulb with a plastic cap. Last night he'd filled the bulb with the wench's blood, and he now paused with the bulb inches from his mouth. Was this blood cleansed? He had prayed to cleanse the fluid he'd drained from the wench's body, but had that been before or after he'd filled the bulb? He wasn't sure. Quarles frowned.

He could afford to take no chances. He held the bulb against his forehead and bowed until his face was inches from his knees. "Father," he said in a near whisper, "I pray that Thou wilt bless this communion and make it as pure as the blood of Thine own Son."

Satisfied, he uncapped the bulb and placed the nipple between his lips and squeezed. The salty thick stuff ran over his tongue. Quarles swallowed thirstily, and the strength flowed in his limbs as the blood plunged into the depths of his belly.

A few minutes later, Quarles stood in front of a sink and washed his hands. The bulb was once again in his pocket, and the image that smiled back at him in the mirror was just old Patrick. Not his true image, the image of the Disciple, but just good old Patrick. It was important that he remain Patrick Quarles, that he keep up the *pretense* of being Patrick before the eyes of men until the Truth was completed. Once the Truth had come into being, there would be no more need for Patrick to exist. At that point he could reveal himself to one and all as the Disciple.

There was a spot on Quarles's shirt which was quickly drying to reddish brown. Should anyone question him, he would explain that he must have cut himself shaving. The man who now stood at the adjacent sink was with one of the newspapers, Quarles knew, just as Quarles had made it a point to know something about everyone who regularly attended the trial. In Quarles's meager human occupation it was important to know things like that. The reporter was short and paunchy and had prominent whiskey-inflamed veins around his nose.

"Wouldn't you know it?" the newsman said, turning on the faucet to wet his comb. "They've got more recesses in these fucking things than they've got trial time. Wonder how long this is going to drag on."

Quarles adjusted the knot on his tie and smiled once again at his reflection. "Not long, I hope," Quarles said. "I've got things to do."

After she'd recessed the trial until the following morning, Judge Hazel Sanderson beat a hasty retreat to her chambers. The marshals led Mickey Stanley away through the rear courtroom exit, and Bino made his way out into the hall, giving Goldman a wide berth in the process so that the federal prosecutor wouldn't have a chance to gripe about Bino calling him an asshole.

Dodie stood in the corridor near the bank of pay phones, talking to Kit Stanley. Dodie was showing an encouraging smile while Kit, though she was obviously doing her damnedest to appear cheerful, was fighting to keep her lower lip from quivering. Bino hated to see Kit like this—hated it like hell. If it hadn't have been for Kit he never would have taken Mickey's case to begin with. He went over, touched Dodie's arm, and said, "Where's Half?"

Dodie didn't look directly at him, her gaze instead on his upper lip. "He's out looking for somebody," she said.

He'd never caught Dodie in an out-and-out lie, but it was easy to tell when she was hiding something. "Looking for who?" Bino said.

Dodie said quickly, "Kit's asking about the motion for mistrial. I told her you'd have to explain it."

Bino opened his mouth to repeat, Looking for who? Before he could draw his breath to speak, Kit stepped forward and said, "I was just wondering, Bino. If she calls a mistrial, what happens then?"

Bino's heart sank as he studied the hopeful tilt to Kit's chin. If ever there'd been a time in his law practice that he'd like to bullshit somebody just to make them feel better, the time was now. He took a shallow breath and felt the tightness around his eyes relax in sympathy. "There's not going to be any mistrial, Kit," Bino said. "The judge will deny the motion. The only reason for making it is, we'd like to have a few points to appeal on in case Mickey gets convicted." He cleared his throat. "If it'll make you feel any better, even if she granted the motion the government would just crank the whole thing back up and try Mickey again."

Kit's eyes lowered until she was looking at the floor. "Oh," she said softly. She tugged at the collar of her brown pantsuit.

Bino glanced at Dodie, who stood with her arms folded and one foot slightly in front of the other. He said to her, "Take Kit home, Dode. Those reporters . . ." He gestured toward the knot of men in shirt-sleeves and young women in business dresses who waited expectantly, pads and pens in hand, near the elevators. "You know what to do about them," Bino said.

Dodie nodded, her blond curls bobbing up and down, then took Kit by the arm and led her away. She stayed between Kit and the media people, ignoring their shouted questions, and ushered Kit into an elevator car and pressed a button. The doors began to slide closed.

Bino took a long step forward and raised his voice. "Dodie. Hey, Dode."

She didn't seem to hear him. Dodie and Kit disappeared from view as the portals touched.

Jesus, Bino thought. My own secretary. Dodie had gotten away with it. She'd never answered his question.

Looking for who? Bino thought.

3

Nobody had to tell Half-a-Point Harrison that you couldn't find anything out by asking a bunch of squarejohns. Going around asking a bunch of squarejohns how to find this girl Brenda Milton was like asking a pro football coach how his team was going to do. All the coach knew was what went on in practice. If you really wanted to know about a pro team, you had to ask the guy who was selling steroids to the linemen and cocaine to the pass receivers. The coach only knew what the ballplayers *wanted* him to know.

Brenda Milton's parents were nice people, all right, and her boyfriend—whose name was Roger Norris, and who was a second-year law student—looked to Half as though he ought to have a part on "L.A. Law." Both the parents and the boyfriend were worried sick, and Half didn't blame them. If they'd have known what Half knew about Brenda, they would have worried even more.

There were three pictures of Brenda Milton in the pocket of Half's sport coat. One picture—blond and bright-eyed Brenda in a filmy blue evening gown, a wistful smile on her face and a faraway look in her eyes—had come from Brenda's dormitory room and, Half knew from a long-distance conversation with her father, was a duplicate of the framed studio portrait which sat on her parents' dresser back in New Braunfels, a pretty little painting of a town between Austin and San Antonio. He thought of Brenda's teary-eyed mom and dad, who were at the moment on their way to Dallas because they couldn't stand waiting at home for news of their daughter, and Half was pretty sure that the evening gown photo was, not surprisingly, the way that Brenda's parents had their little girl pegged. Half, though, knew better.

Another picture had come from the boyfriend. Brenda Milton and Roger Norris were supposed to be engaged (from what he was finding out about Brenda, Half doubted that the wedding was ever going to happen), and the photo that Roger had provided was a boy-and-girl-in-love pose taken on the steps of Lawyer's Inn, the law school residence at SMU. In the law school snapshot, Brenda was wearing baggy thigh-length shorts along with a billowy white shirt, and she and Roger had their arms about each other's waists. The picture was from the previous fall's homecoming week, and prominent in the background was a monstrous white banner over the Lawyer's Inn's entrance, a banner with red and blue lettering reading, "LAWYERS SAY, PROSECUTE THE AGGIES." The picture was cute, and Brenda's cheerful pose was even cuter, but the mental image that Half was forming of Brenda Milton had more to do with the third photo which rested in his pocket.

The third picture had come from Mickey Stanley, in a round-about way. Kit Stanley had gone through Mickey's things and come up with the photo just days after the feds had jailed her son. Kit had seemed more worried about invading Mickey's privacy than she had seemed happy to find something that might help. Bino had just taken the case at the time and had been grabbing at any straw to find something to use as ammunition against Goldman's parade of witnesses. As an engaged coed from a prominent family, Brenda had seemed a prime candidate to knuckle under to pressure from Goldman and be a government witness. The third picture Half now carried was one that Bino had intended to use to show that Brenda might not be as lily-white as she was coming across on the witness stand. But as it had turned out, Bino had figured little Brenda dead wrong. She'd been tough as a boot, standing right in there and thumbing her nose at Goldman while agreeing to be a witness for the defense, and the government snitches had turned out to be the guys that Mickey had thought to be his friends. "Federal prosecutions, five millionth verse," Bino had said.

The picture was a beach scene, South Padre Island on spring break, and the background was shoreline-to-beach-road bikini and boxer trunk–clad bodies sprawled on beach towels, playing volleyball in the sand, shaking and shimmying to the music from a thousand ghetto blasters, and generally doing whatever college students did on spring break to make asses out of themselves. The subject of the photo was an old Ford pickup with SOUTH PADRE OR BUST whitewashed across the rear window, and with a group of kids gathered around. Well, not *just* kids. Mickey Stanley was there, seated on the pickup's open tailgate and drinking Lone Star beer, his belly taut and his pectorals bulging with magazine-ad muscle, and a big Our Gang comedy grin on his face. Both Ten-Kilo and Twenty-Kilo Kilbourne were in the picture as well (Half didn't know which was which, and he and Bino had settled with calling the Kilbournes, collectively, the "Kilo turds"), both brothers sporting wild-looking beards and long, unwashed hair, and both smoking hand-rolled cigarettes that were probably—probably, hell, Half thought, you can bet your ass on it—joints. The two drug dealers looked out of place among the college kids but seemed to be having one helluva good time. Two other youngsters were standing in the back of the pickup, also drinking beer, but with Brenda as the centerpiece, everyone else in the photo seemed just part of the background.

Anybody who'd seen the evening gown and the law school pictures might think that somebody had cut out Brenda's head from another photo and pasted it over the girl's face in the beach scene. It was Brenda, all right, the same blue eyes and short blond hair, but Brenda in the Padre Island scene was anything but a campus flower. She wore bikini bottoms and nothing else (Jesus Christ, Half had thought when he'd first seen the picture, what a set of . . .), and the top of her bathing suit hung from her outstretched fingers. One generous hip stuck out at a saucy angle, and sunglasses were perched on top of her head. Her free hand was squeezing one of the Kilbourne brothers' crotches; the dope dealer's head was thrown back and his eyes were closed.

According to Mickey Stanley, on the night after this photo was taken, Brenda had slept in between both Kilo turds on a Brownsville motel bed. Later, in Bino's office, Brenda had admitted to Half and Bino that Mickey's story was true. Demurely, her lashes down, she'd also said that it would kill her folks, not to mention her boyfriend, if the story were to come out at trial. It didn't matter, though, she'd said, if the story would help Mickey, then that was the way the cookie crumbled. The important thing wasn't the sexual threesome between Brenda and the dope dealers, anyway. The important thing was that, the following morning, Brenda had gone with the Kilbournes to a remote stretch of farm-to-market asphalt road about ten miles from Brownsville. There she'd sat in the car while a single-engine plane had buzzed in from Mexico and deposited a cocaine payload with the Kilbournes, and Mickey Stanley had been playing on the Padre Island beach while all of this had been going on. Mickey hadn't known a thing about it. Nonetheless, the South Texas cocaine delivery was one of the conspiracy counts in Mickey's indictment.

Now, keeping the photo and the story behind it in mind, Half told Dodie that he had a couple of more places to go before he gave up on finding Brenda Milton, then left Dodie in the Federal Building hallway and rode the elevator to the lobby. There he hustled onto Commerce Street (Jesus, it was hot—after the coolness of the Federal Building the sidewalk was like a concrete griddle) and crossed to the parking lot where he'd left his four-year-old Plymouth sedan. The Plymouth was two rows of cars from Commerce, between a Bronco and an Eldo. Half paused for a moment with the Plymouth's door open. He fished in his pocket, and had one more look at the beach-scene photo. He scratched his ear and slowly shook his head.

No matter what she'd done, Half had taken a liking to Brenda Milton. So she'd gotten herself hooked on dope. So what? She was still one standup little girl, and her type didn't come along too often. In fact, Brenda reminded him more than a little bit of another girl who'd been strung out on drugs, not so many years ago. Half had just left the other little girl. Dodie Peterson had turned out okay—a helluva lot more than okay, Half thought—and who was to say that Brenda Milton couldn't do the same?

Sighing, muttering under his breath, Half-a-Point Harrison climbed into his Plymouth and drove out of the parking lot, headed east on Commerce Street.

Half-a-Point Harrison thought that bookmakers who went around driving Porsches and Mercedeses, and wearing a bunch of pimpy-looking diamond rings, were just asking for it. Didn't the yo-yos know that the feds were just looking for a guy in a flashy car to follow around and see what he was up to? Half thought that the Plymouth he drove was perfect, just another working man's transportation, and even had a hard time swallowing Bino's driving a white Lincoln Town Car. Bino's Lincoln, though, was something Half put up with, just as he'd put up with Bino ever since they'd been kids together, back in small-town Mesquite.

And the cellular mobile phone that Half had installed in his used Plymouth was something else he didn't like. Guys who drove around talking on car phones, to Half's way of thinking, looked fishy. Pop Harrison used to say "Show me a man with a phone in his car, and I'll show you somebody that's fixing to pull a fast one." Nonetheless, Half needed the phone. If he was going to do a good job investigating Bino's cases—and at the same time keep his and Pop's bookmaking operation afloat—he couldn't do without the damn thing, even if it *did* make him look as if he was a swindler. As he made the turn from Commerce Street onto Central Expressway, headed for North Dallas, Half picked up the receiver. As he punched in Pop's number, Half took his gaze off the road and very nearly sideswiped a gray GMC pickup. The pickup's driver, a beefy guy wearing a Texas Rangers batting helmet, shook his fist at Half and mouthed something that Half probably didn't want to hear. Half pretended not to notice the guy. Pop answered after the third ring.

"Nolan Ryan's shoulder's acting up," Half said. "Guy's as old as I am—my shoulder's not so hot, either. Anyhow, he ain't pitching. What we got on the game?"

Papers rustled and rattled, then Pop said, "Texas you can lay seven to get five, Minnesota you bet five to win six. Where you been, son?"

"I'm working on a case. I'm thinking we need to move that number." Half shifted the receiver from his left shoulder to his right, and in the process let go of the steering wheel. The Plymouth listed dangerously to the left. Half grabbed the wheel and straightened the car's path. "We'll get all Twins action once the word gets out on Ryan."

"Yeah, okay," Pop said. "I been thinking the same thing. Texas six-to-five, Minnesota even, huh?"

"I'm thinking more than that," Half said. "Let's make it, say, six-to-five, pick 'em." Visible over the Plymouth's nose was the

Fitzhugh Avenue exit from the freeway, old tree-lined streets running off to the east. As usual, Central Expressway traffic was bumper-to-bumper, businessmen in four-door cars, mostly, a lot of them talking on cellular phones. Bunch of shysters, Half thought. He gave the Plymouth a little gas; the speedometer needle inched its way up to fifty-five, and stayed there.

"Yeah, okay," Pop said. "Course, we can put it wherever we want to put it, we still won't get no *big* action with you running around town not answering the phone. I only got so many hands and so many ears, you know?"

"You're right," Half said. "But for a few days you're going to have to live with it. Bino's got a trial going on."

"Yeah, well, I got a trial going on myself," Pop said. "I'm trying to keep from going nuts with these phones ringing off the wall."

"Just a little while longer, Pop," Half said. "This case is the one where one of Bino's witnesses got herself butchered up. You remember, huh?"

There was a moment's hesitation. "Yeah," Pop finally said. "The girl."

"Well, now I'm looking for another girl," Half said. "Jesus, I'm hoping . . . Hell, I ain't even going to think about it. Let's just say I'm looking hard for her, okay?"

The Bump 'n' Run was on Yale Boulevard, a block east of Central Expressway, between a lumber yard and a real estate office, and across the street from a UA multicinema that was currently showing *The Silence of the Lambs* along with *The Rocketeer*. You'd never notice the Bump 'n' Run unless you were looking for it. It was set a hundred yards back from the street, facing a long narrow drive which ran alongside the building, and had no sign visible from the front. The place catered to college kids, and since most of them were under the legal drinking age, the Bump 'n' Run wasn't looking for publicity. Normally, Half-a-Point Harrison wouldn't have gone within a mile of the joint. He couldn't stomach the noisy younger crowd, and things went on inside of a college hangout that a man in Half's profession was better off staying away from. But he did make it a point to know about such places.

He inched the Plymouth off the street and up the drive, bumping the curbs a couple of times along the way, and went past the entrance to park in back, hidden from passersby on Yale Boulevard. The Bump 'n' Run's parking lot, Half knew, was invisible from the street by design. Some of the patrons might be cutting class and might not want anyone to see where they'd left their cars. The SMU campus was just a few blocks away, and a lot of the professors used Yale Boulevard as an avenue to and from the school.

He left the Plymouth parked beside a BMW—Jesus Christ, Half thought, anybody buying that auto for their kid to park behind a beer joint has got to have more money than sense—and went around to the entrance and pushed open the door. He went in. A spring creaked, and the door slammed behind him as he stopped in the foyer. One bare bulb, lit, dangled from a cord overhead. Refrigerated air cooled his skin and the odor of cigarette smoke mixed with stale air assaulted his nostrils. Two girls in their late teens or early twenties came from the club's interior and passed him by as they went outside. One of them, a short brunette, wore a Bart Simpson T-shirt. She glanced up at Half and said, "Excuse me, sir." Then the two campus queens went through the creaking door into the parking lot. There was a mirror on Half's right, and he leaned toward it to look at his own narrow face and pencil mustache. "Sir," she called me. Jesus, Half thought, do I look that old? He ran his finger underneath his collar as he moved on into the Bump 'n' Run.

It was dark inside the club, dark as hell. Half collided lightly with the edge of a table, extended his arm to steady himself, and stood still while his pupils dilated. There was a pool table in the far corner, illuminated by a shaded ceiling lamp, and two kids— a big muscular white boy in shorts and a tank top, and a bigger and even more muscular black youngster in a white T-shirt, with his hair waxed up into a High-Top Fade—were playing nine-ball. The black kid broke the rack, then stood back and chalked while the balls banged into one another and ricocheted from the rails with muted thumps. One ball rattled into a corner pocket.

As Half's eyes grew accustomed to the dimness, huddled dark shapes became clearer. At one small table a group of girls drank from tall stemmed glasses while, nearby, three young guys drank beer and shot furtive glances at the girls. Isolated in the far corner, a couple conversed with their faces practically touching. A cigarette glowed hotly, then quickly dimmed. Taped rap music throbbed from stereo speakers. It wasn't going to take long in the Bump 'n' Run for Half to develop one monster of a headache.

The man seated at the bar was anything but a college kid, and ditto for the bartender. The customer had a round bald spot at his crown; the rest of his hair was graying. He wore jeans that were too tight, and rolls of fat poked out over the back of his belt. He also had on a T-shirt and a dark vest. He was drinking a highball, taking small sips, and chomping on handfuls of peanuts from a plastic bowl.

The bartender was completely bald and had a full, neatly trimmed, salt-and-pepper beard. He was as thin as a skeleton, with a scrawny neck and sunken chest, and wore a flowered shirt open to the third button. A thick gold chain was around his neck, supporting a heavy medallion. Half moved over to the bar and sat on a stool five places down from the peanut-eating guy. The bartender had one foot propped up on a beer cooler. He took his foot down, walked a couple of steps in Half's direction, then halted and snapped long fingers.

"Hey," the bartender said. "Hey, I haven't seen you since—hell, whenever."

Half fished in the breast pocket of his sport coat, found a toothpick and dangled it from one corner of his mouth. "Since you had the joint on East Grand Avenue. The Dirty Bop. How you doing, Henry?"

"Yeah. Hey, yeah. Been a while." The bartender laughed a nervous laugh that was more of a squeak. "Well, lemme, hey, lemme get you one on the house. You still don't drink no alcohol, huh? Plain soda with a twist, right?"

One corner of Half's mouth bunched together. "You remember."

"Never forget," Henry said. "Names, sometimes. What a man's drinking, never." He filled a tumbler with ice, squirted plain soda from a liquor gun, twisted a lime rind before dropping it in, and set the drink on a small paper napkin. "So how you like my new joint?"

There was a glass on the bar, filled with hollow plastic stir sticks. Half reached for one and used it to swirl the liquid around in his glass. "I don't," he said.

Henry's grin froze for an instant, then his mouth relaxed. "Listen, I been meaning to call you."

The man wearing the vest shot a quick glance in Half's direction, then returned his attention to his highball and bowl of peanuts. "Sure, you have."

"No kidding," Henry said. "I had some problems."

Half laid his toothpick on the napkin beside his glass, then slowly raised his eyes. Henry was grinning again, but he was faking it. "Henry," Half said. "Let's get that shit out of the way. I wrote you off a long time ago."

Henry leaned on the bar and stabbed the air with a finger. "Nobody writes me off. I never stiffed nobody."

Half snorted. "Naw, you don't stiff nobody. You'd rather owe 'em than beat 'em out of it. You been at this joint a year, Henry— you don't think I coulda come here a long time ago? Couple of thousand you owe me ain't worth it."

Henry's lip curled. "Ain't worth what?"

"Ain't worth chasing any dope peddlers. If I'd have known you was selling dope out of the Dirty Bop, I wouldn't have been taking your action in the first place."

Henry lifted a skinny hand, palm out. "Now hold, I got a bad rap on that thing."

"You didn't get no bad rap, Henry. You sold a bunch of pills to the wrong guy is all. You still on parole, huh?"

Henry regarded the bartop. "Naw, that shit's over with. I couldn't be in the bar business on parole, you know that."

Half glanced around the interior of the Bump 'n' Run, at the kids seated at tables, at the two athletes shooting pool. "Better spot for you, Henry, this place. Rich college kids got money, less likely to see the DEA hanging around."

"What you talking about?" Henry said. "Don't you read the paper? What kind of dope trial you think that is going on right now, that Mickey Stanley deal? All that shit went down in a college bar just like this one. Narcs hang around these joints in droves."

Half considered telling Henry that he knew all about Mickey Stanley's trial, then changed his mind. None of Henry's business. He pulled the beach-scene picture out of his pocket and placed it face-up on the bar. "You know this girl." He made it a statement instead of a question. Henry would lie if he thought he could get away with it.

Henry leaned over and squinted, then picked up a flashlight and shined it on the photo. "One with her titties hanging out?"

"That's the only female in the picture, Henry," Half said. "Unless you want to count the beach bunnies in the background. I know you know this girl." He tapped once again on the photo.

Henry's gaze shifted. "Well, maybe. Yeah, I might."

"She ran a lot with a girl named Annette Ray," Half said. "Annette Ray's the girl got killed."

"Yeah," Henry said, pretending to think about it. "Nasty thing, huh? Well, maybe I seen this girl in the picture. Kids come in and out, you know?"

Half picked up his toothpick and chewed it. "Henry, you can't stand any complaints."

"What complaints?"

Half gestured around the room. "Underage drinking complaints. And I'll lay pretty good that somebody'd find a few joints rolled up in some purses around here, probably more serious shit than that."

Henry pulled nervously on his beard. "You ain't the kind of guy to fuck with somebody. You didn't used to be."

"I'm just looking for a girl, Henry. If somebody don't lie to me, you're right—I got no reason to mess with anybody's business. I tell you, though. Your business I wouldn't feel so bad about messing with." Half tapped the picture a third time. "I bet you a phone call downtown that you know this girl."

Henry lowered his head, and a stray beam of light glinted from his bald scalp. "Who you talking about calling downtown, huh? Maybe downtown like to know about a guy making book, too."

Half cocked his head to one side. "I been downtown, Henry. You want to bet on which one of us stays down there the longest?"

Henry fiddled with his medallion; his fingers trembled slightly. "Okay, well, I seen her a few times."

"Sure you have," Half said. "And Mickey Stanley a few times, and I bet you seen them Kilo turds."

"Kilo *what?*"

"Them Kilbournes, the two guys in the picture. I ain't interested in them. I'm interested in that girl. I bet you know her name's Brenda Milton, and I bet you something else. None of her squarejohn friends seen this girl in three, four days, but I bet during that time she's been in your joint." Half stuck the toothpick between his lips and bit down on it. "You want to bet, Henry?"

Henry glanced nervously at the guy in the vest, who was reaching for more peanuts, then leaned closer to Half and lowered his voice. "There's this guy," Henry said.

"We're getting somewhere, huh?" Half said.

"Can't nobody know it was me talked about this guy."

"Far as I'm concerned," Half said, "I ain't seen you since the Dirty Bop."

"I don't know this guy's name, I swear to God," Henry said. "They call him, they call him Donatello. Like one of the turtles."

"What turtles?" Half said.

"Teenage Mutant Ninja Turtles. You know, Donatello, Michelangelo—"

"Jesus Christ, Henry, I don't know from nothing about cartoon characters. Talk about the guy."

Henry rubbed his palm on the top of his head. "Donatello comes in here. He meets people, you know?"

"Yeah," Half said. "Sells them shit."

"I don't know nothing about that. Maybe he does. Hey, Brenda Milton don't come by so much anymore, since she got mixed up in that Mickey Stanley thing. You know about that?"

Half blinked and nodded, not saying anything.

"But sometimes she does. They can't stay away from dope permanent, not those I seen."

" 'Specially," Half said, "as long as assholes like you got these places for them to go to buy that shit, huh?"

Henry steadied his gaze. "You want to know something or not?"

Half didn't flinch. "You want to go downtown or not?"

Henry lowered his eyes. "Okay, she comes by. Saturday night it was, this Donatello guy was here and got to talking to her. Couple of other girls, too, and this guy I don't know. Kind of a strange dude, tell you the truth. Donatello likes to have parties, you know?"

"So he'll have more than one customer at a time," Half said.

"He don't sell nothing in here. I don't go for that shit in my joint."

"Spare me," Half said.

"So okay, yeah," Henry said. "Closing time Saturday night, Donatello and them people left together."

"All of 'em?"

"Yeah."

"What about the weird guy you're talking about?" Half said.

"Him, too. This guy, I don't see him in here before. Kind of sits around looking at people. Don't say anything, but Donatello knew the guy. Guy had money, you know?"

Half removed the toothpick, then sipped through the swizzle stick. "I bet you know where they were going Henry. Don't tell me no bullshit, now, I ain't got a lot of time."

Henry's shoulders sagged. "Donatello's place. He gives a few late parties."

"Which is where?" Half said.

"I told you, man, can't nobody know I—"

"Which is where, Henry?"

Henry expelled breath in a sigh. "I only been there a couple of times."

"Which means you know where it's at, right?"

Henry put both elbows on the bar and leaned on them. "Village Apartments. Southwestern Boulevard, you know the place?"

"Sure do. Must be ten thousand apartments there, huh?" Half blinked. The Village was the biggest complex in Dallas, acres of garden apartments, swimming pools, tennis courts. It was also where Dodie Peterson lived, but that didn't mean much. If you saw someone in Dallas who wasn't married and guessed that they lived at the Village, you'd be right one time in ten. "So the Village, that don't narrow it down much. Where 'bouts at the Village?"

"Shady Brook Lane," Henry said. "First driveway on your right off Southwestern. Pull in the drive and park in the lot, the apartment's through the breezeway on your left. Last door on your left, right in front of the pool. You can't miss it."

"This Donatello, he got a phone?" Half said.

"Yeah, but he don't answer it. Got one of those recording machines, you know?"

Half shot a quick look at Henry's eyes. Henry was telling the truth about the phone, and it made sense. Guys like this Donatello wouldn't want to talk to anybody unless they knew for sure who was calling. Half stood, reached in his pocket, and dropped a couple of dollars on the bar.

"No," Henry said. "I told you, man, it's on the house."

"*This* house I don't want it to be on, Henry." Half took a couple of steps toward the exit, then paused and turned. "Oh, and Henry. Next time don't give me a lot of double-talk. Things go faster when you get to the point, okay?"

Half was so busy following Henry's directions, turning this way and that in a sea of garden apartments with shingled roofs, clipped lawns, and what seemed like a thousand glistening swimming pools, that he didn't realize until he'd pulled off Shady Brook Lane and gotten his bearings that Donatello lived a whole lot closer to Dodie than Half had thought. Hell, right across the parking lot. As Half sat in his Plymouth with the motor running and the a/c blowing, the breezeway where, according to the bar owner, Donatello's place was located, was about fifty yards to Half's left, and Dodie's ground-floor one-bedroom was approximately the same distance off to the right. Small world, huh? Half drummed his fingers on the dashboard and shook his head.

Half had never had any children—the thought of marrying anybody had always given him the willies—and had been the only kid in his own family. Dodie Peterson was the nearest thing to a daughter or sister that he'd ever run across. He'd told Dodie over and over that she didn't have any business living alone in this kind of a neighborhood, but she'd just say, "*What* kind of a neighborhood?" and then giggle and wrinkle her nose at him. And Half had to admit, the neighborhood didn't look anything like the shithole that it was.

The problem was in the window dressing: perfectly clipped and manicured lawns, pools like aqua jewels set in shaded, spotless patios, lean and suntanned bodies everywhere, walking, jogging, biking, or serving tennis balls. On its surface, the Village was just the place for a sharp and with-it girl like Dodie to live. And for the most part that was just the case. The Village, along with the hundreds of similar complexes in North Dallas, housed up-and-coming single doctors, lawyers, bankers, and all manner of young professional folks. But, Half thought, just ask any patrolman or undercover cop, and they'll tell you there are plenty of assholes around those complexes as well. There was another side to the Village that you'd never spot from the window dressing.

Half's Mesquite neighborhood was old, granted, but in Half's neighborhood everybody knew everybody else. If a stranger appeared on the block, every resident knew at once that person didn't belong, and until newcomers proved themselves, no one was going to have anything to do with them. But in an apartment complex like the Village, people moved in and out every day, and a stranger wasn't going to cause any commotion. Also, it was pretty easy for somebody who didn't live at the Village—might even live way to hell off in Chicago or someplace—to put on walking shorts or a bathing suit and blend in with the crowd, and everyone who saw them would think that person lived in the apartments. And the assholes of the world didn't have much trouble figuring that out, either.

Rapes were common in the Village, and so were muggings and robberies, though the newspapers didn't report crime in the Village with the same enthusiasm as they did crimes in the poorer parts of town. Also there were a lot of dope dealers who rented apartments in the Village, operated for a month or two, and then moved on down the line. Here today, gone tomorrow.

NARCOTICS COP: Who sold you the crack, punk?
PUNK: Dude up in that apartment, man, only he moved a coupla months ago. Don't have no idea what his name is or where he's gone to.

End of investigation.

Half spent a helluva lot more time worrying about Dodie living in the Village than he'd ever let on. He'd tried talking to Bino about it, but Bino had pooh-poohed him and said Half was being an old woman about it. Bino and Half-a-Point were on the same wavelength on most subjects, but the danger of living in luxury singles apartments wasn't one of them. Hell, Bino himself lived in a similar type apartment—the Vapors North—just off LBJ Freeway, and no way could he relate to what Half was talking about. But Jesus, Half thought, who'd want to try to rape *Bino*. Bino spent a lot of time wishing somebody *would* come over and rape him. Bino Phillips would be the easiest score a female rapist ever made.

Shaking his head, mumbling under his breath, Half steered the Plymouth into a parking slot near the breezeway on his left and cut the engine.

If the Donatello guy was home, he wasn't coming to the door. The doorbell was working. Every time Half pressed the button, muffled chimes sounded from within. Knocking didn't do any good, either, even though Half rapped on wood until his knuckles stung. Dope peddlers slept a lot during the day, so before he gave up, Half wanted to make so much racket that a dead man couldn't sleep through the noise. He paused to catch his breath and let his gaze wander through the opening in the breezeway. Visible through the opening, past an iron railing and a clipped two-foot hedge, a young woman sat by the pool on a chaise longue. She wore an orange and white–striped French-cut swimsuit, and she was reading a paperback book. As Half watched, she uncrossed her legs and recrossed them, adjusted her sunglasses on her nose, and turned a page. September would become October in another week or so, and the sunbathing would be over until spring. Half walked through the breezeway, nodded to the girl—who pointedly ignored him—and had a look at the front side of Donatello's apartment.

There was a small patio facing the pool, surrounded by a wooden rail, and a sliding glass door leading from the patio into what Half assumed to be the living room. On one side of the patio was a small hibachi on a tripod, and Half pictured Donatello charcoaling steaks for his best dope customers. He glanced toward the girl, placed a hand on the rail and vaulted over to stand on the patio, then looked toward the girl again. She was absorbed in her book, and Half wondered briefly what she was reading as he moved over to the glass door and peered inside.

It was a living room of sorts and a bedroom of sorts. The couch was folded out into a daybed, and Donatello wasn't a good housekeeper. The sheets were rumpled and one of the pillows was tossed on the floor. There was a cabinet-model TV and a dining table, but the centerpiece of the room was a six-foot wooden cutout of a Teenage Mutant Ninja Turtle. Half seemed to recall an identical cutout in front of a theater where *The Secret of the Ooze* had been showing, a grinning lifesize cartoon of one of the turtles, battle armor and all, brandishing a pair of numchucks. There was cartoon dialog in the picture, an enclosed white background for the words "Awesome, dudes," and a curved pointer extending from the dialog in the general direction of the turtle's mouth. The turtle's free hand hung near his crotch, and someone had painted a crude erect penis which extended from the turtle's pubic area to the hand's palm. Donatello, Half decided, was a classy prince of a guy. He stood on tiptoes, put his nose a quarter-inch from the glass, and looked downward.

The bar that Half expected to see wasn't there. Sliding glass doors were pushovers for burglars, and most garden apartment dwellers wedged a steel bar or broomstick against the sliding portion of the door so that, if the lock were sprung, the door wouldn't move sideways. Of all people, Half would expect a dope dealer to have a bar wedged into the slots, but apparently Donatello hadn't thought of it. Half was just deciding that not only was Donatello a classy guy, he was pretty stupid as well, when his gaze fell on the six-foot length of chrome pipe on the floor at the foot of the daybed. So Donatello *did* have a burglar-resistor, but it wasn't in place. Which meant either that Donatello was home, or that when he'd left he'd forgotten to wedge the bar into place. Half's brow knitted as he rapped loudly on the glass, then waited a full two minutes. Nothing. He fished in his wallet and found his Blockbuster Video membership card, laminated in plastic.

The girl by the pool had now flattened the chaise longue and was lying on her stomach with her face turned away from him, so Half wasn't particularly sneaky about slipping the card inside the crack and disengaging the catch. The door moved sideways with a faint metallic swish. Half entered the apartment to stand on pale green shag carpet. The carpet hadn't been vacuumed in a while; the yarn was mashed down and there was lint on the carpet's surface. Half used his index finger to pull on his collar and let the refrigerated air cool his neck as he stood and listened. He heard nothing save for the distant hum of a refrigerator motor, so he went on in and looked around. An odor that wasn't quite a stink hung in the air. Half had smelled it someplace before. He rattled his brain. Nothing. He'd have to think further about the smell.

Somebody had either been fucking on the daybed, or had had one helluva wrestling match. The gray-grimy bottom sheet was wadded in places, and one corner had been pulled back—*yanked*

back, more than likely, Half thought, by somebody who was getting their rocks off—to reveal the mattress. There were a few coarse
black hairs on the sheets, and a few fine blond hairs as well. On
Half's left was a Formica counter separating the living room from
a tiny kitchen, and directly in front of him was a hallway leading
to the rear of the apartment. Visible in the kitchen, a half-eaten
pizza, still in the box, was on the stove. Crust crumbs were scattered over stained porcelain on top of the stove, and a few of the
crumbs had dropped on one of the cold burners. Make one helluva
stink, Half thought, when somebody gets ready to boil water to
make a little freebase. He took a couple of steps in the direction
of the hallway before his foot collided with something on the floor.
Something solid and heavy. Half stooped to pick the thing up.

He rose holding a mug, a big one, large enough for *two* cups
of coffee. Painted on the side of the mug was another Ninja Turtle, this one riding a motorcycle. Since he'd been doing investigations for Bino, Half had met quite a few dope dealers (neither he
nor Pop would book bets for druggies, that was just asking for
trouble) but not many smart ones. Most dope dealers were hooked
on their own product, and most of their brains were fried. Saturday
morning cartoons would be right up a dope dealer's alley, especially a guy who went around drawing dicks on movie display
cutouts. Half tilted the mug and held it under his nose. The odor
grew stronger.

The mug had been holding something that had coated the
insides and edges reddish brown. Half got down on his haunches
to examine a red-brown stain on the carpet. What was the fucking
smell? He was pretty sure it would come to him. He rose to a
standing position and, walking softly, moved out of the living room
and went down the hall.

Directly in front of him was the bathroom. Half went in and
let the mug dangle by his hip while he looked around. The tile
floor was filthy and the porcelain on the tub a dirty gray. Soap
residue clung to the bottom of a shower curtain that had once
been white but now was the color of cigar ash. Half paused for a
moment to cluck his tongue over the black ring inside the toilet
bowl, then went back out in the hall. A door on his left was
closed. Half tried the handle, opened the door, and peered into
the bedroom.

The curtains were drawn and the room was in darkness. Light

spilling in from the hallway revealed the foot of a bed, more grimy sheets, more reddish brown stain. The odor was now stifling, and Half closed his nasal passages to blot out the smell. He reached around the doorjamb, found a switch, and clicked on the ceiling light.

Half had seen a few dead guys in his time, but the man spreadeagled on the mattress was quite a bit more than dead. He'd been a pudgy, soft-looking guy, and sported a scraggly dope-dealer beard and had flashy dope-dealer rings on his fingers. His mouth was open, his jaw slack, his eyes open wide and staring at the ceiling. He was stark naked, and he was gutted like a fish. The wound ran from just above his pubic area to the point of his breastbone, and his midsection flesh was peeled back to reveal his body cavity. Blood had soaked into the sheets, had pooled around the dead man's sides, and had flowed off the bed onto the carpet. The man's entrails lay beside him like a pile of bloody gray vipers.

Half covered his mouth and gagged, and at the same time raised the coffee mug and looked at it once more. The stuff in the mug had been . . . Jesus, it was . . .

Half threw the mug in disgust. It slammed into the wall and thudded to the floor. He turned, went into the bathroom, and threw up in the toilet. Then he flushed the commode, splashed water on his face at the sink, and retreated down the hall into the living room to sink down on the daybed. A white Princess phone sat on an end table. Half picked up the receiver and punched in 911. As he listened to the rings on the line, his gaze fell on the cutout of the Ninja Turtle. The fucking turtle was grinning at him. Standing there with a cartoon grin on its face, its dick in its hand, and saying in cartoon dialog, "Awesome, dudes."

As there was a click on the line and the operator said, "911, your emergency?" Half raised his foot and kicked the Ninja Turtle over. It fell on its back and continued to grin.

4

After Dodie had successfully dodged his question about Half-a-Point Harrison's whereabouts, and then had left him standing in the Federal Building hallway like a man who'd missed his bus, Bino walked to his office in the Davis Building. Anytime he had a case in federal court, it was his practice to leave his white Lincoln Town Car in the lot across from the office and hoof it. He couldn't walk to court when trying a State of Texas criminal matter. The Frank Crowley Courts Building, the county facility where state cases went to trial, was way to hell and gone on the other side of Reunion Arena. It was a quarter-mile past the spot where Commerce Street ducked under Stemmons Freeway, near the Texas Schoolbook Depository, the site of the Kennedy assassination. The Earle Cabell Federal Building, though, was just blocks from the Davis Building, and walking—in addition to providing awesome views of the mirror-walled canyons of downtown Dallas, as well as some even more awesome views of shapely dimpled knees and pretty thighs beneath wind-billowed skirts—gave Bino time to think.

And today he had a lot to think about. He was beginning to think he'd bitten off more than he could chew in taking on Mickey Stanley's case to begin with. Like every criminal lawyer's, most of Bino's cases were pure dogs. Cops didn't go around arresting innocent bystanders as a rule; generally the client was guilty as hell, and all the lawyer could do was work out the best plea bargain possible for the guy. But if the majority of Bino's other cases were dogs, the Stanley deal was beginning to fall into the Great Dane category, basketball-sized turds and all.

Bino had only taken on the case as a favor to Kit. Jesus, he'd do about anything for Kit, as much as she'd helped him when he was in college. Kit was near starvation status, having spent all of her money raising her son, and Bino hadn't expected much of a fee for representing Mickey. At first the case hadn't seemed to amount to a hill of beans, but now it was growing to mountainous proportions.

There wasn't anything unusual about Mickey's story. He was a star football player in college who for some reason hadn't cut the mustard as a pro cornerback, and who, coddled as an athlete and doted on by his mother, wasn't prepared for anything else in life. Jobless, he'd drifted aimlessly around town, snorted a little cocaine and popped a few steroids, and had fallen in with the dope-peddling crowd. At the time Kit had come to Bino with tears streaming down her cheeks, Mickey was under federal indictment on a misdemeanor possession beef, and all Bino had expected to do was get with Marvin Goldman and work out a plea bargain. Bino should have known better. He and Goldman had been thorns in one another's sides for years, and working out any kind of amicable deal with that fitness nut of a federal prosecutor had been next to impossible. The misdemeanor charge against Mickey, in fact, had been a mere pimple on the ass of what was to come. Mickey's associates, it turned out—particularly the two Kilbourne brothers, along with a couple of out-of-a-job airline pilots—were up to their ears in importing cocaine from Columbia and were also the main dope connection for college students at SMU.

Early on in the investigation, the feds had approached Mickey with an offer. In return for his testimony the government would grant him immunity in the smuggling case plus drop the misdemeanor charge. Mickey had thumbed his nose at the feds, which was a mark in the kid's favor where Bino was concerned; Bino didn't like snitches and wouldn't represent a stoolpigeon for *any* fee.

But if Mickey wouldn't play ball with the feds, the Kilbournes and the pilots were horses of a different color. Before you could say "J. Edgar Hoover"—just two weeks, in fact, after Mickey had

told the DEA to take a hike—Goldman had made the Kilo turds
and the fly-boys full-fledged members of the government team,
and a pretty cute little indictment had come down against Mickey
Stanley. Racketeering, conspiracy, you name it. With one wave
of his magic wand, Goldman had transformed Mickey from a
fringe hanger-on and cocaine snorter into an international thug,
the brains behind the organization. Shazam!

It had now been nine months since the indictment. Mickey
had gone to jail on the day the charges had come down, and he
was yet to come up for air.

Bino suspected—was dead certain, rather—that Mickey's prosecution had a lot to do with the fact that the kid's name was pretty
well known from the sports pages. Goldman, as usual, had used
his media connections to blow the case up big. Rather than cop-
ping his client out for the shortest sentence he could beg, which
had been his plan when he had originally taken on the case, Bino
had found himself knee-deep in reporters and TV newspeople as
he prepared for a full-blown trial. He hadn't bothered to ask Kit
for more money and was pretty sure that she couldn't have afforded
more even if he had. Though it sure as hell didn't put any beans
on the table, the satisfaction of beating Goldman was about all
that Bino was now working for.

Through Mickey's connections (and Kit's effort), Bino had
come up with a couple of watch-charm witnesses, Brenda Milton
and Annette Ray. Both were leggy campus beauties, both were
intelligent and articulate, both were from prominent families, and
both had closet cocaine habits. More important, both girls had
been semi-groupies of the cocaine smugglers, and both could give
bang-up testimony that showed that it was the Kilbournes and not
Mickey Stanley who'd been the main force in smuggling the dope.
Bino had been getting his ducks in a row in preparation for trial
and had even thought about organizing a Beat Goldman Bonfire
and Pep Rally when, in the middle of the proceedings, someone
had decided to brutally murder Annette Ray.

Annette had disappeared in midsummer after she'd testified at
Mickey's bond hearing (one of many; Bino had been trying to get
his client out on bond ever since Mickey had been arrested but
had yet to get to first base). Annette had sat on the witness chair
in prim finishing-school posture, blond hair billowing around her
head, had given her testimony in a cool, slightly crackly alto

voice—once the court reporter had asked her to speak up so that he could accurately get her answers down—and after her appearance had told Bino that she'd see him next week in his office. Then she had walked out of the Federal Building and off the face of the earth. Her disappearance had been front-page news for a few days, then had drifted to the back of section B, and had completely disappeared from the newspaper when, two weeks later, a couple of kids fishing for crawdads in a creek had snagged a line on Annette's ankle. She had been shot in the face, and about half of the blood had been drained from her body.

If Mickey's indictment had gotten media attention before, Annette's killing had turned the case into an absolute circus. Speculation was rampant; theories ranged from the bizarre—that one of the drug smugglers, high on cocaine, had killed Annette in a sexual frenzy—to the impossible—that Mickey had somehow gotten out of jail, done her in himself, and sneaked back into his cell. Personally, Bino doubted that there was any connection to the Stanley case. He thought that Annette had simply been luckless enough to encounter a lunatic on her way home from the Federal Building.

And, Bino thought as he jaywalked across Commerce and hustled up Akard Street on his way to the Davis Building, aside from the stark tragedy of what had happened to Annette, Mickey Stanley now had only one witness in his corner. Mickey's fate now rested solely on the slim athletic shoulders of Brenda Milton. God forbid, Bino thought, that anything should happen to Brenda.

Bino took off his coat and slung it over his shoulder, hooking his index finger through the loop in the back below the collar, and loosened his tie. The temperature was close to ninety degrees, not unusual in Texas for late September, and most of the people he passed on the street were still wearing summer clothes. One of these days—before too long—a blue norther would blow in from the panhandle, and summer would become winter as though some fairy had waved a wand. Early season football in Texas was played in a sauna; later on there'd be a few frostbite cases among the fans.

As Bino turned right on Main to pass in front of One Main Place, a skyscraper of roughened stone on his left, the sculptured lions which guarded the Davis Building's entrance came into view a block ahead. Bino liked the lions, liked the fifty-year-old Davis Building even better, and couldn't help but blink in surprise every day that the ancient structure was still standing. Three years earlier there had been plans to raze the Davis Building—place dynamite at strategic locations inside the old girl and blow her all to hell— to make room for a modern complex complete with moats and fountains, but the economy at the time—a bank failure, plunging real estate prices, and, Bino suspected, more than a little light- fingeredness on the part of the principals involved—had put the developers under before the project had gotten off the ground. To Bino's way of thinking, that had just been marvelous. Old songs and old buildings suited Bino to a tee, always had and always would. He threw a wink at the old woman who was selling little potted plants from a sidewalk counter, slipped a dollar to the un- shaven street-person guy who lurked, dark glasses and all, against the side of a building and held a tin cup in grimy fingers (the guy wasn't blind and Bino knew it, and the street guy *knew* that Bino knew it, which gave the two of them an understanding), and whis- tling the opening bars to "Take It to the Limit" by the Eagles, went through the revolving door into the lobby of the Davis Building.

Even the Davis Building wasn't immune to progress, which was something that Bino didn't particularly like. For fifteen of the sixteen years that he'd officed here, the Davis Building had been the only place left in Dallas—in the whole United States, as far as Bino knew—which had continued to employ elevator operators. Up until the previous spring, Hispanic women in pale green uni- forms had sat on stools which swiveled out of the elevator walls, had asked politely for passengers' floors, and had cranked handles to make the cars go up and down. Something about that, Bino thought, had been neat. But a year earlier, Mama Valdez, who'd run a Davis Building elevator since Eisenhower had been in office, had finally retired, and her niece Veronica had gone to work for the civil service. "Hell, no, Mr. Bino," Veronica had said, "I tired of all these ups and downs alla time. I'm gonna get me some retirement plan." When Mama and Veronica had gone, so had the old elevator cars. The renovation had progressed one shaft at a time, with the passengers allowed to drive themselves up and down in the interim, and had been finished for a couple of months. Now the Davis Building's elevators, just like everyplace else's, operated on lighted panel buttons.

But occasionally, Bino forgot about the change. Today as he entered the elevator car, his mind was still back in the courtroom where he was enduring one of Hazel Sanderson's gravel-voiced tirades. He retreated to the back of the car, set down his briefcase, leaned against the wall, and folded his arms.

In a few seconds a portly gray-haired woman entered the car carrying a shopping bag. She glanced at the lighted panel, then at Bino, and back at the panel again. Finally she said, "Are you waiting for someone?"

Bino snapped out of his trance. "Huh? I mean, I beg your pardon?"

"Waiting for someone," the woman said. "Or is it all right if we go on up?" She sounded as though she was talking to a retard (which, Bino realized with a jolt, she probably thought that he was).

"No, I'm . . ." Bino said, then cleared his throat and said, "Seven. I'm, um, going to seven."

The woman pressed the sixth-floor button, then the seventh, and moved back as the doors rumbled shut. On the ride up, she stood as far from Bino as she could without knocking a hole in the wall, and kept a protective deathlock on her shopping bag.

The name "W. A. PHILLIPS" on Bino's office door probably threw a lot of people, and he'd thought more than once through the years about inserting "BINO" in parentheses. But he'd never gotten around to doing it for several reasons. There wasn't a damn thing wrong with Wendell Arthur. His dad, a Baptist deacon out in Mesquite, had named him for an old-time circuit-riding preacher. And besides, anybody looking for Wendell A. Phillips was likely a salesman or a process server anyhow. The way people pronounced his nickname gave him even more of a problem, because quite a few folks whom he'd just met went around calling him "Beano." He'd considered changing the spelling to "Byno," or even "Bye-no," but had long ago discarded the idea. His nickname came from his snow-white hair and was short for "albino," even though his eyes were blue and he had just enough pigment in his skin to tan pretty nicely during the summer. Bino he had been ever since he'd been a little shaver, and Bino he was going to remain—and anybody who insisted on pronouncing it "Beano" didn't know him very well to begin with.

Since Half was missing—and since he'd sent Dodie to take Kit Stanley home—there wasn't anyone in the office to cover for him. So he approached the door with caution—sneaked up on his own office, actually, opening the door a fraction and peeking through the crack into the reception area. The brown cloth divan was vacant, magazines (*Sports Illustrated* and *Golf Digest,* mostly, which were Bino's only two subscriptions, with an occasional *Better Homes and Gardens* or *Popular Mechanics* left by clients who'd rather bring their own than read the sports garbage) stacked neatly on the end table beside a shaded lamp. Bino shifted his position in the hall like a man peering through a swiveling telescope until Dodie's desk came into view. No one there, either, just Dodie's rolling secretarial chair pushed up flush, a metal file cabinet behind where she sat, pencils, steno pads, and pen set in perfect order on her blotter as though arranged for a display photo. Bino breathed a shallow sigh of relief, swung the door open wide, and breezed on in.

The door to Half's little cubbyhole was ajar, newspapers, racing forms, and sports betting sheets in a jumbled pile, the red private-line phone on the corner of Half's desk like a blistered thumb. Half would have forwarded the bookmaking calls over to Pop's for the day, so the red phone wasn't likely to cause any problems by ringing incessantly the way it did when Half was in. Bino reminded himself—for maybe the hundredth time that month—to have a talk with Half about straightening the mess in there, then stepped over to Half's office and gently closed the door. After a final satisfied look around at the reception area, and a hasty glance into the supply room where the Xerox sat, he strode into his own roomy office and headed for his desk. He was softly singing "Chain-chain-chaaayne, chain of foo-wols" in his off-key baritone and snapping his fingers in time to the music.

A lively male voice behind him said, "Hey, I came on in. I hope you don't mind—nobody was here."

Bino froze in his tracks and did a slow about-face. The guy was seated on the imitation leather sofa beneath the old photo of Bino and his SMU basketball teammates. The visitor had a pleasant round face, wore thick glasses, and looked early forties, around Bino's age. He wore a navy blazer with a few dust motes on its surface and gray cloth slacks whose crease was practically gone, along with black sheenless loafers. His stout legs were crossed and a yellow legal pad rested on his thigh. He was tapping a Bic disposable ballpoint against the pad's edge. Reporter, Bino thought. At the base of his neck, snow-white hackles stirred.

"Well, to tell you the truth," Bino said, "I'd have preferred you wait in the reception room. That's what it's there for—for people to wait."

The guy showed a smile which looked genuine enough. "I sort of forgot myself, looking at your basketball memories. Mind telling me who the other guys are in the picture?" He jerked a fleshy thumb toward the photo behind him.

Bino placed his hands on his waist and didn't say anything.

The newcomer laughed nervously, laid his pen and pad aside, and stood. "Oh, hey, I'm . . ." He reached in his side pocket and handed Bino a business card. "That's me, I'm Nolan Pounds."

Bino parked his rump on the corner of his desk and held the card between his thumb and forefinger. Apparently he was talking to Nolan Pounds, Writer. No address, no phone number. Bino slipped the card in the pocket of his pale blue summer-weight suit coat. "Writer for who?" Bino said.

Nolan Pounds, his smile now a little uncertain, sat back down. He started to pick up his yellow pad, then apparently changed his mind and folded his hands in his lap. "For myself. I do true crime."

"Yeah," Bino said. "So do a lot of my clients." He went around behind his desk, sat, and tilted his high-backed swivel chair.

"No," Pounds said. "I *write* about true crime."

"I figured that's what you meant."

"I do books."

Bino slid his middle drawer open, drew a filtered Camel from a pack and lit it, and placed an ashtray on his desk. He didn't smoke but three or four cigarettes a day, and seldom smoked at all in his office, but at the moment he was hoping that Nolan Pounds was a no-smoking freak and would get the fuck out of there. "That's good, Mr. Pounds. More people should write books. Helps the literacy rate."

A few strands of Pounds's thick brown hair stuck up from the crown of his head like a drab peacock's tail. He fished a Marlboro from his shirt pocket and lit one of his own. "You got another ashtray?"

So much for smoking Pounds away. Jesus, was Dodie ever going to bitch about the smell. It so happened that Bino did have another, a little round glass ashtray that he'd swiped from Joe Miller's Bar. He slid it across the desk without saying anything.

Pounds got the ashtray and set it on the arm of the sofa, then craned his neck at the basketball picture. "That your Final Four season? I could get a roster from the SMU athletic department, I guess."

Bino zeroed in on a cobweb stretched between the ceiling and wall, just above the picture. He needed to mention the web to the cleaning people. "What do you want, Mr. Pounds?" Bino said.

"Right now I want to find out a few things about you, Mr. Phillips." Pounds's smile broadened. "Bino—long *i*, right?"

"You got it."

"Who's the guy with his arm around your shoulders?" Pounds gestured toward the picture, wherein a two-decades-younger Bino, rosy-cheeked and wearing a sixties flattop, held the giant Southwest Conference trophy aloft.

"His name's Barney Dalton. Today he's a golf pro around here, out at Crooked River. What's this all about?" In the photo Barney also wore a flattop, as did the rest of the team, and was standing on tiptoes in order to give Bino a one-armed victory hug.

Pounds briefly picked up the legal pad and (presumably) wrote down Barney's name. He set the pad aside once more. "Well, I'm doing a book about this case you have," Pounds said. "This Stanley narcotics conspiracy. Which wasn't particularly book material, frankly, until what happened to one of the witnesses. The girl, you know?"

Bino ground his cigarette firmly out in the bottom of the ashtray. "Goodbye, Mr. Pounds."

"Don't you think you should think it over?"

"I just did."

"Listen." Pounds raised his right hand like Honest Abe up for election. "Believe me, I understand your position. A lot of people don't like journalists, and I'll tell you up front that I'm not one—strictly a book writer. And to really develop my stories I've got to show both sides. Yours *and* the prosecution's. Besides, like I said, this whole thing has taken on a new slant. I'm not even sure that the smuggling case is the main thrust of the story after what's happened to Miss Annette Ray."

"More sex and gore, huh?" Bino said.

Pounds's chin tilted in a defensive posture. "Well, if you're going to put it that way . . ."

"What books have you written, Mr. Pounds?" Bino intertwined his fingers behind his head.

Pounds rested one thick ankle on his knee and clasped his hands over his shin. "Nothing big, but, you know, everybody hopes. My last one was *The Girl in the Steel Cylinder*. It's about a sex-slave case out in El Paso. Original paperback. Maybe you saw it."

"Jesus Christ," Bino said. "No, I missed that one."

"Look, you mind if I call you Bino?"

"Everybody else does. So, yeah, for what little time you're going to be here, you can call me Bino. I don't mind a bit."

"Well, I'm Nolan."

"I'll try to remember that," Bino said.

"I'll give you my word, Bino. Nothing I do is going to hurt your case. All I want is general information about you, character development stuff. And what the hell, the book won't be out until at least a year after the case is over, long after the jury verdict's in. Even if I *was* doing a hatchet job."

Bino's lips relaxed. He had to admit he'd always been curious about these book writers. "Well, suppose I was to give you an interview, Mr. Pounds—"

"Nolan."

"Yeah, okay, Nolan then. What kind of questions would you be asking me?"

"General background stuff. Your education and whatnot. Your basketball career would be of interest. And, maybe, just a little bit about how you got into this case. The Stanley case." Pounds grinned. "Believe me when I say I don't care if your client smuggled half the dope in Texas. I'm just trying to write a book and make a living."

Bino stabbed the air with a finger in Pounds's direction. "My client's not charged with smuggling dope. He's charged with being the brains behind a ring. There's a big difference."

"I'm sure there is, Bino. I was speaking in generalities."

"Well, to be specific," Bino said, "Mickey Stanley didn't do any organizing of anything. Look, you got a kid here that's been a star athlete all his life, pampered and whatever. Suddenly he doesn't make it in pro ball, and just as suddenly he's a lost soul wandering around."

"He was one of the athletes involved in SMU's recruiting scandal a few years back, wasn't he?" Pounds said. "One of the guys that got 'em the death penalty?"

"I'll acknowledge that he was a scholarship athlete at the time the NCAA put a two-year suspension on the school's football program," Bino said. "Beyond that I'm not saying anything."

Pounds picked up his legal pad and doodled on the page. "I can get information about Mickey Stanley a lot of places. As I said, what I want is information on you. Did you know Annette Ray pretty well?" He asked the question with his eyebrows slightly raised, as though the question was an afterthought.

"I thought you wanted information about me," Bino said. "So how come you're asking about her?"

"Well, let's face it. She's the most newsworthy thing that's happened in the case so far. Until what happened to her, I wasn't even sure I could get a contract to write a book on the deal."

"So what happened to Annette tickled you to death, right?" Bino said.

"Now, I didn't say that." Pounds sat forward on the edge of his chair.

"You didn't have to. To get that out of the way, if you want to know anything about Annette ask the county sheriff's department. Or a guy named Mac Strange at the D.A.'s office, either one. I don't like talking about that kind of stuff."

Pounds looked down at the floor, then slowly back up. "Fair enough. I already knew who to contact at the county, I just thought you might have some background on the young lady that the others don't."

"Well, you can forget—"

"Now, though, about yourself." Pounds gave what Bino assumed to be the writer's version of a disarming grin. Bino didn't feel disarmed. "Local boy, aren't you?" Pounds said.

Bino hesitated. He didn't mind telling a few things about himself, but he intended to keep on his toes with this guy. "Local, if you want to call Mesquite local. About fifteen miles east of here," Bino said.

"And you were a basketball star, right?"

Bino glanced over Pounds's shoulder at the photo. "I'm not sure what you mean by a star," Bino said. "We had a pretty good team, all around."

"Yeah, but . . . Small-town boy made good because of basketball, that's the reading I'm getting," Pounds said.

"Well, I never could have afforded SMU if it hadn't been for my scholarship," Bino said. "So, yeah, I guess you'd have to say if I hadn't played I'd probably still be in Mesquite. Fixing cars or pumping gas or something."

"So, class of '66, right?" Pounds was taking notes in earnest, now, honing in.

"Undergraduate, yeah," Bino said.

"Law school four years after that?"

"Three and a half. I told you I couldn't afford SMU, and after my scholarship ran out I had to go to Houston for law school— South Texas College of Law."

Pounds flipped a page over in his legal pad. "Could have played pro ball if it hadn't been for an injury, right?"

Bino cocked his head. "Yeah, my ankle. Who you been talking to?"

"That kind of stuff is pretty easy to come up with," Pounds said. "You got hurt against UCLA and Kareem Abdul Jabbar, didn't you?"

There was a slight twinge in Bino's ankle, just as there was every time he thought of the three-point landing on L.A.'s Pauley Pavilion hardwood, or pictured Jabbar towering over him, ebony-skinned arms flailing in a powder blue uniform. "He was Lew Alcindor in those days," Bino said. "Before the Muslim stuff."

Pounds hesitated, and the hesitation brought Bino's mental guard up. The guy was probably about to get into something that Bino might not want to answer. "Your old school ties, SMU. That have anything to do with you getting involved in defending Mickey Stanley?" Pounds said. Visible through the open doorway, the lamp in the reception area suddenly went out. Bino couldn't remember whether or not there were spare bulbs in the supply room. He hoped to hell that Dodie returned before long.

"Mickey's mother used to tutor me, she was a couple of years older," Bino said. "And I'll tell you, she's one first-class lady. I'll tell you too, Nolan old boy, if I read anything bad about Kit Stanley in your book, I'm going to know you're full of shit."

"Let's talk about your legal career," Pounds said.

Bino pointed a finger. "I'm not kidding about Kit."

"I know you're not," Pounds said. "And I wouldn't worry too much about that. Won a lot of cases, haven't you?"

"Yeah, a few."

"Defended a federal judge a couple of years ago. Emmett Burns?"

"That case never even went to trial," Bino said.

"I know that. You had it dismissed on a motion hearing. Wasn't there something about his daughter and some guy who'd escaped from prison?"

Yeah, Bino thought, a lovely bastard named Daryl Siminian who damn near killed Dodie on the street in broad daylight. "You can get all that out of the papers," Bino said. "I don't have anything to add other than the newspaper accounts."

"I'll accept that," Pounds said. "Just before that, didn't you get involved in defending one of the guys that assassinated a congressman?"

"Now hold on," Bino said. "I didn't defend the guy for killing Richard Bigelow. All I did was get him to talk about it so he could make a plea-bargain deal. I never would have represented him for killing Richard. That was an unusual circumstance."

"I'll say it was," Pounds said. "Wasn't there something in that case about an affair between you and a lady FBI agent?"

Bino sat bolt upright. "Jesus Christ. You've been talking to Goldman."

"Well, he's the prosecutor. I've got to interview him just like I do you."

"You don't have to ask him questions about *me*," Bino said. "You ask me about old Marv, I might not have anything good to say, either. And I'm not talking about affairs with anybody, that's nobody's business."

Pounds drilled ahead. "What about family? You married?"

Bino pictured Annabelle as she'd looked in college, cheerleader uniform and all, then pictured the day he'd come home from law school classes to find her gone. "Divorced," Bino said.

"So I understand. And your ex-wife, isn't she Mrs. Dante Tirelli? Married to the Mafia guy?"

Bino lowered his chair, propped his elbows on his desk, and rested his square chin on his clenched fists. "I wouldn't go around saying Dante Tirelli's a gangster unless I had proof of it, Mr. Pounds. Nobody's ever even charged him with anything. But, yeah, Annabelle's married to the guy. What else did Goldman tell you?"

Pounds ignored the question. "Let me ask you something else. Would it be fair to say that you've got a reputation as a swinger?"

"Huh? Goldman told you I was AC/DC or something?"

"Not *that* kind of a swinger, Bino. I mean, don't you play a lot of poker, maybe bet a little on the golf course?"

Bino was getting hot under the collar and fought to control himself. "That shit's blown way out of proportion. Listen, Mr. Pounds—Nolan—I got a lot to do."

"Isn't your investigator, the guy working in there"—Pounds jerked a thumb in the direction of Half's office—"isn't he also a bookmaker?"

Bino stood. "Now, I'd watch my ass if I were you. I know something about suing people, and you'd better not be printing any of that kind of shit. What evidence you got that anybody around here's a bookmaker, huh?"

"I'm just asking you," Pounds said.

"Well, you can just *un*ask. I'm not talking to you anymore." Bino jumped slightly as the phone on his desk buzzed.

"Go ahead and get that," Pounds said. "I'll wait."

"My answering service will get it," Bino said. "And there's no point in you waiting for anything." The phone buzzed again.

"Oh, don't get in an uproar. I told you I'm not doing a hatchet job. Just trying to make a living."

"Yeah, I can tell. I'm warning you, Pounds, I'd better not read one word about anybody making book around here. That could damage me."

As Bino glared at the writer and Pounds leaned back in a mild posture, the phone rang two more times. Jesus, what was wrong with the fucking answering service? Bino reached for the phone, then hesitated. He couldn't afford not to answer—hell, it might be a new client or something.

"Look, Nolan," Bino said, "as long as you're going to stick your nose in my affairs, how about making yourself useful and answering that. I'm not here to anybody, but you could take a message. Jesus, a bookmaker. Goldman really knows how to hurt a guy."

Pounds stood, picked up the receiver, and said into the mouthpiece, "Bino Phillips's office." Then he listened and said, "No, he's out. Can I take a message?" Then Pounds listened some more, grinned slightly, and held out the phone in Bino's direction. "Maybe you'd better take this," Pounds said. "It's your buddy, the guy you were talking about from the D.A.'s office, Mac Strange. He says he's got your bookie with him." His grin broadened. "Whatever that means," Pounds said.

5

Bino thought that Mac Strange, outlined against a background of grassy courtyard and glistening aqua swimming pool water, looked pretty grim—which wasn't surprising. What had happened to the guy who lay gutted like a fish in the bedroom was grim as hell. It was just that Bino had never considered Strange to be a particularly gruesome guy. The county prosecutor was, in fact, really funny at times, particularly when he let his hair down and had a few cool ones at Joe Miller's Bar. This wasn't one of those times, though.

Strange was standing in the patio doorway of a flat at the Village Apartments, while two county lab guys went over the place with a fine-tooth comb. One of the lab technicians, a pudgy thirty-year-old in off-white coveralls, was dusting the kitchen counter for fingerprints. The other tech, a slim gray-haired man in slacks and a button-down sport shirt, was vacuuming the carpet, stopping every two minutes or so to remove the bag from the standup Electrolux, carefully mark on it the portion of the carpet from which the debris had come, and add it to a growing pile in the corner. At the moment he was down on his haunches, vacuuming underneath the folded-out daybed with short firm strokes.

Strange said something that Bino couldn't hear over the hum of the vacuum cleaner. Bino gestured toward the cleaner, at the same time pointing at his own ear, and shook his head.

Strange raised his voice. "Harry, turn that goddam thing off."

The gray-haired lab guy thumbed the switch; the noise diminished into silence as the cleaner's outer fabric bag deflated. "How long you want this to take?" Harry said. "I retire in two years."

"Well, couldn't you just . . . ?" Strange said. "Just go vacuum in the bedroom, huh?"

"Shoesole's in there going over the stiff. He told me to vacuum out here." Harry stood and looked morosely at the rumpled daybed.

Assistant Coroner Shoesole Traynor had gone in to examine the body a few minute earlier. He'd been smiling. Bino had gotten a brief glimpse of the corpse, and now, picturing the dead guy, winced as a shudder ran the length of his spine. Half-a-Point Harrison, seated in a chair on Bino's right, looked as if he might throw up again.

"Yeah, well," Strange said, looking from one lab guy to the other. "What the hell, Bino, let's go outside. You can't hear yourself think in here." He led the way out on the patio; Bino gave Half a come-on wave, then followed Strange through the doorway. Half joined Bino and the county prosecutor and slid the glass door behind him. Muted by the glass, the vacuum cleaner began its whining anew.

Strange placed his hands on the iron patio railing and leaned over to regard his shoes. "I'm not getting enough sleep. Everything's bugging me." He raised his head and looked at Bino over his shoulder. His soft round cheeks sagged downward and there were dark circles under his eyes like healing bruises.

"I can tell," Bino said.

Strange looked down once more, between his arms, at his own feet. "I've been up since four-thirty this morning working on stuff just such as this, and it doesn't look like things are going to get any better. Jesus Christ, you see the guy in there?"

"Got a glimpse of him," Bino said.

Strange slowly lifted his head and looked over his shoulder at Half. Half had moseyed to one side and was carefully studying Donatello's hibachi sitting on its tripod. The grill was caked with grease and grit. "So, Mr. Oddsmaker," Strange said, jerking his head in Bino's direction while keeping his gaze on Half. "We've got him here. Called him just like you asked us to. Now. You feel like telling us what you were doing poking around? This boy a bettor or something?"

Half touched the edge of the hibachi and didn't say anything. Bino took a short step toward his investigator. "I'd like to have the answer to that one myself," Bino said. "You don't take action from druggies, so what are you doing in this place?"

Half shrugged. "I was doing what I'm supposed to be doing—trying to find Brenda Milton."

"Wait a minute," Bino said. "What do you mean, trying to find her?"

Half backed away from the hibachi and turned to face Bino and Strange. One corner of Half's mouth was turned down. "Just what I said. Listen, me and Dodie weren't going to tell you till I was sure she wasn't just shacked up someplace."

"Nice of you," Bino said. "Jesus Christ, Half. Her, too?"

Strange stepped away from the railing and dusted his hands together. "Who in hell is Brenda Milton?"

"She's a . . ." Bino paused, thought it over. He couldn't see any reason not to tell Mac. "She's a witness in the case I'm trying. Damn near my only witness."

"Just like the other girl?" Strange said. "Annette Ray?"

Bino sighed. "Yep. Come on, Half, what's the deal?"

"I talked to a guy that had seen her," Half said. "She left a joint the other night with this Donatello guy and a couple more people."

Strange cocked his head to one side as he said to Half, "You're going to tell us all about everything—let's get that out in the open. You give us one bit of bullshit about telling us who's who, you're not going to like it."

Half extended a hand, palm up, in Bino's direction. "He's the Man. Whatever he says," Half said to Strange.

Strange cleared his throat. "Bino—"

"Mac," Bino said. "Cool it. We're not into the evidence covering up business. You ought to know better than to worry about it."

"Yeah," Strange said. "I ought to know better than a lot of things. Currently I've got two dead young ladies who happen to be missing over a gallon of blood between them, and a guy in there looking like somebody was going to stuff him for Thanksgiving. Excuse me if I *do* worry a little, okay? And by the way, what about your buddy over there? Has he got any connection to this?"

Strange was pointing across the rail in the general direction of the swimming pool. Across the courtyard, Nolan Pounds the true-crime guy had moved a lawn chair into shade and was sitting patiently with his legal pad in his lap. When Pounds had finally convinced Bino that, whether Bino liked it or not, Pounds was going to come along, Bino had let the writer ride to the Village in the Linc. A few minutes earlier Strange had admitted Bino to the apartment and told Pounds to wait in the courtyard. Pounds had retreated showing a condescending smile. In the heat of the moment, Bino had forgotten about the guy.

"Him?" Bino shook his head. "He's just a writer. A guy doing a book."

Strange did a double take. "Great. All we need—a guy doing a book."

"Well, I'll tell you that ignoring him won't do any good," Bino said. "I tried that. He'll grind you down until you talk to him. Hey, Mac, you say you got *two* dead girls?"

"Yeah, one on a slab at county medical, found under a tree this morning out at SMU. Cut just like the Ray girl, and with the . . . you know, the *peg*, stuck in the same place. The only difference is, Annette Ray was shot in the head and the new one's shot in the chest. If you want to call that a difference. I've got Hardy Cole and half a squadron running around trying to ID the second girl, but from what I just found out we may have that problem solved."

Bino closed his eyes and gently rubbed the lids with a thumb and forefinger. "Oh, Jesus."

"It doesn't have to be her," Strange said. "But it's worth having somebody that knows her take a look. You, I guess, Bino."

"I can think of one or two things I'd rather do," Bino said.

"I'd rather do a lot of other things myself," Strange said. "But somebody's got to shovel the shit, you know?"

Half stepped hesitantly forward. "Her—" he said, then paused for a breath, then said, "Brenda's folks drove up here from New Braunfels this morning. That's where Dodie is, she was going to get with them after she took Mickey Stanley's mom to her house."

"Well, hey," Bino said, "good to know my people keep me up to date."

Half regarded his shoes and didn't say anything.

Strange lifted the tail of his navy suit coat and shoved his hand in his pocket. "I guess we'd better take the angle, assume that this Stanley case has got a connection. Two girls, both of them witnesses, you know. Both of the victims have been to the federal courthouse. Maybe somebody down there, huh? Some hanger-on or something."

"They're both students at the same college. But that's you people's department," Bino said. "And I got to admit I'm glad it's not mine. But it does sound logical. This is a dope trial; half the people testifying are addicts. Guys get hopped up on crap, they do funny things."

"You tell 'em," Strange said.

"Goldman's witness list looks like Who's Who in Cocaine," Bino said. "Maybe one of those people."

"I damn sure don't relish the idea of asking Goldman for any help," Strange said. "Maybe we could—"

The county prosecutor stopped in midsentence and stared into the apartment through the glass door. Bino turned to follow Strange's gaze. Shoesole Traynor stood in the center of the living room, behind the daybed and beside the fallen cutout of the Teenage Mutant Ninja Turtle. Traynor beckoned. There were reddish streaks on his dirty white smock, and Bino pictured the deputy coroner brushing against the gutted guy in the bedroom. Knowing Traynor, though, the reddish spots might just as likely be catsup or barbecue sauce.

Strange stepped over and slid the glass door aside. "Yeah?"

"I've got a couple of things." The forensics man shifted his gaze away from the prosecutor, then smiled and nodded at Bino. "Hi," Traynor said.

Bino returned the nod. "Shoesole."

From across the pool, Nolan Pounds yelled, "Hey. When you get a minute." He had removed his coat and was standing on stumpy legs.

Strange lifted a palm in Pounds's direction and raised his voice. "Just stay put. We'll get to you." Then, his voice lowered, Strange said to Bino, "Writers. Listen, I guess you'd better be in on this. Come on." The county prosecutor led the way into the apartment, pausing long enough to say over his shoulder, "You, too, Half, I think you both need to hear this. Show you what we're fooling with here." As the three men moved in to stand on mashed-down shag carpet, refrigerated air cooled Bino's cheeks and nose.

Bino and Shoesole Traynor had always gotten along, and in spite of the fact that some of Shoesole's theories were way out in left field, the guy was a pretty good forensics man. And he loved to lecture people, did he ever. Traynor's ever-present Sherlock Holmes pipe dangled from one corner of his mouth. Traynor wore his permanent I'm-letting-you-in-on-a-big-secret expression. As Bino entered the apartment he caught the faintest whiff of formaldehyde. There wasn't any reason for the smell—Jesus, thought Bino, Shoesole hasn't been in the bedroom *embalming* the guy— and Bino had suspected for years that the deputy medical examiner secretly dabbed the stuff on like aftershave. Traynor nodded first to one lab tech, then the other, and indicated the bedroom. The fingerprint man hauled his dusting paraphernalia down the hall while the vacuum-cleaner guy unplugged his Electrolux and followed, dragging the cleaner along by the handle. Bino sat down in a chair and crossed his legs. Half leaned his shoulder against one wall of the living room while Mac Strange folded his arms and stood with one hip slightly higher than the other in an expectant attitude. Heard from the bedroom, the vacuum cleaner whined.

Traynor dug into the bulging side pocket of his smock and brought out two thick paperback books. He handed one to Strange and the other to Bino, and with an apologetic grin said to Half, "I've only got two, but I'm getting more." Then Shoesole went back to his pocket to produce a tobacco pouch and dipped the pipe, bowl first, inside the pouch. While the deputy M.E. filled his pipe, Bino turned the book over in his hands and looked at the cover.

The book was a real supermarket special, raised letters on the cover and all. The title, *Alone with the Devil*, was in fire-engine red, beneath the white-letter lead-in, "A SHOCKING LOOK INSIDE THE MINDS OF AMERICA'S MOST INFAMOUS KILLERS." Running perpendicular down both sides of the cover were photos of some real crazies. One was Manson, hypnotic stare and all, another was Leslie Van Houten. Bino flipped the book over to read the back, and quickly scanned the blurb, "DO THE GUILTY GET AWAY WITH MURDER?" Underneath the blurb was a list of names: Charles "Tex" Watson, Lawrence Butaker, and other lovely folks. Bino thought, Jesus, don't tell me . . . He quickly turned the book over to search for the name of the author. There it was, at the bottom; Ronald Markham, M.D., with Dominick Bosco. Bino breathed a sigh. If this had been one of Nolan Pounds's books, Bino didn't think he could have taken it. He let the book rest on his knee and looked expectantly at Shoesole Traynor.

Traynor applied a disposable butane flamethrower to his pipe, and puffed furiously. Smoke billowed from his mouth and spiraled upward to form a cloud over his head. He snapped the switch on the lighter and the flame disappeared. Then Shoesole put the lighter away and, still puffing, said, "Markham's pretty good, the guy that wrote that. A little offbeat in a couple of places, but still pretty good. He interviewed all those folks so he could give sanity testimony at their trials. Some day I might do a book like that. I could give 'em a few cases that are real doozies."

While Traynor paused and sucked at his pipe, Bino put on an expression that (Bino hoped) said that any book by Shoesole Traynor was bound to be a blockbuster. Bino glanced at Strange, and the prosecutor was also looking as though he thought Shoesole should do a book. It was the way you had to handle Shoesole if you wanted to get anything out of the guy. Bino resisted the impulse to giggle. Traynor went on.

"Now the case in point"—Traynor reached out and tapped Strange's copy of the book with a grimy-nailed index finger— "begins on page 161. We've ordered court records from California, but for now the book's the best we've got. Richard Chase, the Vampire of Sacramento."

Bino flipped to the page in his copy of the book where the vampire tale began, then turned to the photo section in the center to look for Chase's picture. He found it—a black-and-white of a young guy with wild-looking hair, standing handcuffed behind a uniformed cop. Seemed like a really desperate guy. Bino looked up to find Strange flipping rapidly through his copy of the book while Half, who had moved to the center of the room, stood on tiptoes and looked over the prosecutor's shoulder. Like a bunch of men going over the latest *Penthouse*, Bino thought.

"Now, correct me if I'm wrong," Traynor said, "but the FBI's Washington unit is going to get in on this."

Strange said, his gaze still on the pages of the book, "Yeah, they've been called."

"Okay," Traynor said. "What they'll do is try to tell us what makes a guy like this tick. Give you an idea what he might do next, though I've got my doubts anybody can tell you that with any accuracy. As far as I know, the Vampire of Sacramento is the only blood drinker on record that anybody's made a detailed study of."

"Only one I ever heard of," Strange said. "And I've got to admit, I only heard of this one today."

Bino swallowed. "I don't think I've ever met one. Course, I don't go around asking people." He showed a weak grin. None of the other men seemed to get the joke.

"What you'll be looking for," Traynor said, "—and the psychological part of it isn't my job—but what you'll be looking for, if you do get a suspect, is somebody that's background sort of parallels Mr. Chase's there." He touched Strange's copy of the book.

"Wait a minute," Bino said. "I don't know what I've got to do with this. I'm not going to be looking for any suspects, all I'm doing is representing a guy."

Strange and Traynor exchanged glances, then Strange said, "I'll talk to you in private, Bino. Go ahead, Shoesole."

"Right on," Traynor said. "So what I'm saying is, the psychological makeup of this guy I'm leaving up to the D.A.'s office and the FBI. I'm talking physical description of the victim, that's my bailiwick. I suspected we had another Vampire of Sacramento running around here when we found the first girl, and when the second one turned up this morning, I'll say I wasn't surprised. The guy in the bedroom there cinches it, as far as I'm concerned." The deputy coroner bent to pick up the cartoon cutout of the turtle and set it on its pedestal. "Donatello, huh?" Traynor said. "Bet you weren't ready for this one, buddy."

Traynor went over to the kitchen, leaned on the counter for a moment as if deep in thought, then turned to face his audience again. "Opening the midsection up, the removal of the entrails— that's the kind of stuff that Richard Chase did out in California. Read up on it. The clearing out of the body cavity lets the blood drain down and fill the opening. Then he can take a cup or ladle and scoop the blood out like punch out of a bowl."

Bino's stomach churned. Half coughed into his own cupped hand. Mac Strange had an expression on his face like a man watching a scene from *The Texas Chainsaw Massacre*. Traynor, looking slightly amused, took his disposable lighter from his pocket and relit his pipe.

"One thing's certain," Traynor said, "the guy isn't faking. He's got a real taste for blood. Craves it like some people do heroin. I'll lay odds that somewhere in his background, if you ever find the guy, that some animals have been missing close to where he lives. Dogs, cats, any kind of pet. Richard Chase started with animals; about all of these wackos do. There are a few cannibals on record, guys that dismembered people. They all started out by butchering animals—like they were practicing or something."

"As long as you're making everybody's afternoon so pleasant," Bino said, "how about this? How do you know it's a man? As militant as all these women are getting . . . Hell, it's just a thought."

Traynor glanced at Strange, who looked at his own shoes, then clamped his pipe lightly between his teeth. "Because women don't do this kind of thing. Never in history. There've been women serial killers, yeah, but there was always a profit motive. Some old gal knocking off a string of husbands for insurance money, stuff like that. Besides, there's the peg he's used on both of the girls. Phallic symbol, maybe, but a woman just wouldn't do it that way. It's a man you're looking for—that's one thing you can be sure of. Incidentally, our friend shot the guy in the bedroom before going to work on him with the knife. Ought to give ballistics something to work with."

It didn't surprise Bino that Shoesole was coming on like some kind of half-assed psychiatrist, even though he'd said he was going to leave that to the FBI. Shoesole Traynor had a theory on every-thing. Bino didn't want to talk about the peg. He'd gotten the details on the peg when Annette Ray had died, and he hadn't slept a wink for three nights thinking about it. Jesus, but he'd hate to be a homicide cop, dealing with things like this. The air inside the apartment was suddenly stifling. Bino stood. "I hate to cut this short. But didn't you say something about somebody identifying Brenda Milton?" Anything, Bino thought, anything to get away from all this talk about human vampires, and anything to get away from the disemboweled corpse in the bedroom.

"You sure you want to do that?" Strange said. "Half-a-Point said the girl's folks were in town. They're the ones that ought to be doing the ID."

Mac was right, of course. Bino'd never met Brenda Milton's parents—had only talked to Brenda herself a couple of times, in fact—but was pretty sure they were going to need some moral support. Jesus, anybody would. "Where's Dodie meeting them, Half?" Bino said.

"Motel," Half said, shifting his weight from one foot to the other and watching the floor. "Park Cities Inn, right across Hillcrest Avenue from SMU. They were going to stay there as long as it took to find her. Jesus Christ, I don't want to face them people."

"That makes all of us," Bino said, "but they're going to have to know about it sooner or later. I guess we better call out to the Park Cities Inn and get ahold of them. You and Dodie don't do this to me again. I got to know what the hell is going on."

"You were busy," Half said.

"Not *that* busy," Bino said.

From over near the sliding glass door, Mac Strange said, "What about that guy?" He had lifted his coattails and jammed his hands into his back pockets and was looking out across the patio in the general direction of the place where Nolan Pounds sat.

Bino walked over to stand beside Strange. Across the pool, Pounds didn't seemed to have moved a muscle, still sitting patiently in the lawn chair holding his legal pad. Must be what it takes to be a writer, Bino thought. Wait 'em out long enough and eventually somebody's going to break down and talk to you. "Jesus," Bino said. "I forgot about him."

"Well, we can't take him to County Medical," Strange said. "I've got a big picture of that—those poor people just finding out their little girl's dead and this guy running around asking questions." He snapped his fingers. "Wait a minute, I've got an idea." Strange slid the door open and stepped out on the patio. He cupped his hands over his mouth. "Listen, we've got someplace to go for a while. If you want, you can come in and look around as long as you don't touch anything. You can talk to the men from the lab, too."

As Pounds climbed eagerly to his feet and slung his coat over his shoulder, Strange came back into the apartment, went over to the hall and yelled, "Harry, turn that off and come here."

The vacuum cleaner noise slowly died, and in a couple of

seconds the gray-haired lab man came out of the bedroom and said, "Yeah?"

"I'm taking Bino and the bookie on a little drive," Strange said. "There's going to be a guy in here asking questions. Let him have a good look at the corpse, that ought to keep him quiet for a while. Then, when he asks you a question—and believe me, he's going to—when he asks you a question, go ahead and tell him what he wants to know. But just before you answer, turn the vacuum cleaner on. We want to cooperate as much as possible, you know?"

Twenty-five years ago, Bino knew, back before Mac Strange had been a prosecutor, Strange had spent five years as a Dallas patrol cop while going to law school at night. Strange's partner, in fact, had been Hardy Cole, and when Mac had passed the bar exam and gotten on with the D.A.'s staff, one of the first things he'd done had been to hire Hardy away from the city. A quarter-century of working together had made Hardy and Mac quite a team, and the fact that Strange had paid his dues in the trenches gave Bino a lot of respect for the guy.

The problem was that Mac still drove like a squad-car cop. He kept his four-door Buick sedan in the righthand lane at a solid twenty miles an hour, took his sweet time about getting in motion when a light changed from red to green, and sometimes drove with his left wheels in the center lane, hogging the road. A black and white cruiser could get away with driving in that manner because all of the other drivers on the road were scared to death of getting a ticket, and no one was likely to give a police car a ration of shit over hogging the road. Not so with Strange's personal Buick. As they proceeded at a snail's pace across Dallas toward County Medical on Harry Hines Boulevard, with Strange behind the wheel, Bino riding shotgun, and Half-a-Point in the backseat, muttering under his breath, other drivers honked their horns, made nasty faces as they passed on the left, and one beefy guy in a GMC pickup even shot the county prosecutor the finger. If Strange noticed any of the other drivers, he didn't let on. He kept one limp wrist hung over the top of the steering wheel, one arm draped across the back of the seat, and talked nonstop out of the side of his mouth while keeping sleepy-lidded eyes trained on the pavement in front of him.

As they moseyed through the intersection of Lovers Lane and Lemmon Avenue to turn left on Lemmon and proceed along beside Love Field's easternmost runways, Strange said, "Any way you slice it, it's a touchy situation. When you get multiple homicides and you're pretty sure it's the same perpetrator, the first thing you do is look for common grounds. You're assuming they're random killings, but the killer has to choose his victims somewhere. So here, what do our victims have in common? The girls are both college students, right? So you first think maybe somebody at the school. That narrows it down to four thousand guys, right? Plus the faculty and whatnot. Don't worry, we're checking out the school, but that's going to be a long and drawn-out proposition.

"But these two girls have got something else in common," Strange said. "They're both witnesses for the defense in the same federal case, right? And the first murder happens right after one girl testifies in a bond hearing, and the second on the night before the first day of trial. Narrows your choices some, you following me?"

"So far," Bino said, "—Jesus Christ, Mac, look out." The Buick listed to the right; the front wheel hit the curb with a squeal of rubber. Strange steered halfway into the next lane, ignored an angry honk from a woman in a Volvo, and kept on truckin'.

"So I'm thinking it probably doesn't have anything to do with the college," Strange said. "I'm thinking more than likely that our asshole saw the girls somewhere down around that federal court. In the hallways, in the courtroom, you name it. Our guy could be a janitor or something. Lawyer. Hell, who knows?—even a judge. Which brings us to you."

Bino jammed an imaginary brake pedal to the floorboard as the Buick made the wide curve to the right where Lemmon Avenue blended into the westbound traffic on Mockingbird Lane. Strange steered the Buick in between a Chevy van and a two-door Blazer; the Blazer slammed on its brakes and honked its horn. "Why me?" Bino said.

"Because they're your witnesses. Or were," Strange said. "It only makes sense, the courthouse is where the loony's going to run across the girls. To begin with, then he maybe follows them out to some joint like the Bump 'n' Run. So you're going to have files on these people, and whatever information you got on any of them is what I want to see."

"I don't have any problem with that, Mac," Bino said. "Sure, you can see whatever I've got, but it's mostly just their statements and a little background information."

Strange applied the brakes, stopping inches from the rear bumper of a Chrysler which was waiting for the stop light on Mockingbird Lane at the entrance road to Love Field. Visible on the right were a four-story parking garage and, farther away, the remote parking in front of the airport terminal. Directly ahead, a Southwest Airlines 707 lumbered skyward with twin exhausts billowing.

"Likely your files won't help us much," Strange said. "I'll grant you that, but you never can tell. More important than your files is going to be your memory. You were with these women every time they made a court appearance, right?"

"Sure. Annette Ray only made one court date, Mickey's bond hearing. Brenda Milton was down there, let's see, three times I think. Yeah, she testified on a couple of motions I filed to quash evidence, and on one of the motion hearings Goldman didn't show up. She cooled her heels in the hallway for half a day, then had to come back a week later when old Marv finally decided to grace us with his presence."

The light changed to green. Strange gave the Buick a little gas and cruised through the intersection behind the Chrysler. "Now you're cooking. Start remembering. Each time she was down there, where did she sit and who did she talk to? Did she make a lot of trips to the john? Did she park across the street, or did she go over on Jackson Street and walk a few blocks to save the parking fee? If she did, she probably would have mentioned it to you. We've got some meetings coming up, and I want you there."

Bino folded his arms. "Jesus, Mac, I'm not a cop. I got a lot to do. What kind of meetings?"

"Bullshit meetings, mostly. We're going to have the FBI's VICAP unit on the scene pretty soon, and aside from being a bunch of overbearing bastards who love to take credit for somebody else's work, those guys love to have meetings. And if you think *you* don't like the FBI, wait till Hardy Cole finds out they're coming. I've got to admit, VICAP keeps the finest statistical data on violent crime that there is, but statistical data is about all they're really good for. All that stuff about how they can climb into the killer's mind and predict what he's going to do next—that stuff is for the movies. But we're going to have to kowtow to them, you know what I mean?"

"I suppose," Bino said. "If you say so."

"I say, bullshit," Strange said. "Because I don't care who's investigating or how many latent fingerprints and dick hairs they find laying around. Nine cases out of ten are solved either by pure accident or because somebody remembers something. Now, I'm going to have my hands full playing butt-boy to these people, bringing them coffee and whatnot, while they step on everybody's toes and throw their weight around. The first meeting is tomorrow at one, at the Crowley Courts Building, conference room, seventh floor. You come and listen to these guys, and try to relate what they say to what you might remember about these girls and what they did when you had them down at the courts. Now, can I count on you?"

Bino didn't answer for a moment. Jesus, the Stanley trial had kept him out of the office for weeks, and it was true that he had a lot to do. He studied Mac's slightly round profile. The two of them did go way back.

"I never ask for much, Bino," Strange said. "And I know you've got to make a living. But this is the biggest thing we've had in years—maybe the biggest ever. Just this once, huh?" He turned his gaze on Bino, and there was a pleading look in the prosecutor's eyes.

Bino licked his lips. What the hell, he wasn't getting paid for defending Mickey Stanley, either. "Sure, Mac," he said. If you want me, I'll be there."

The gloom didn't really set in until Bino entered the reception room outside the morgue and saw Brenda Milton's mom and dad sitting there with Dodie in between them. Up until that moment, Brenda's death was just something he'd been *talking* about, and it hadn't really sunk in that, chances were, the girl who lay stone cold inside a vault just a few feet beyond the next closed door was really her. Bino led the way into the reception room and halted. Half collided lightly with Bino from behind and stopped as well. Bino wouldn't have needed Dodie's presence to tell him who the handsome middle-aged couple were. The looks on their faces told him all he needed to know.

Brenda's father was a square-shouldered man, graying at the

temples, who spent a lot of time in the sun. He wore a plaid shirt and brand-new jeans. Big-boned wrists and large calloused hands showed below his cuffs. He held a folded handkerchief in one hand, and his eyes were red. His broad nose peeled tiny flakes of skin.

Brenda Milton had gotten her build and coloring from her mom. Mrs. Milton, seated to Dodie's left on the hard bench of the county reception room, had the same clear blue eyes—misting at the moment—and sunny blond hair as her daughter, and the mother's locks were yet to show a trace of gray. Mrs. Milton's figure was still intact as well. She wore green slacks and a yellow blouse, and the fabric of her slacks molded around slim and muscular legs. The build that Bino had seen in the beach photo, the sturdy shoulders, flat firm waist, and proudly stuck-out chest, could only have come from Brenda's mom. The Miltons appeared to be very pleasant and likable folks who'd worked hard to send their daughter to college and whose reward was about to be what lay inside the morgue. Bino dropped his gaze.

Dodie, wearing the same sleeveless sweater and navy skirt she'd worn to court, got up and approached Bino. "We were just trying to save you any more problems than you already had," Dodie said. The softness around her mouth said that she meant it.

Staying upset with Dodie was impossible—she'd meant too much to him over the years. "Don't give it a second thought, Dode," Bino said. "What the hell, I couldn't have done anything about it anyway."

"Bino, this"—Dodie took him by the arm and led him over to the bench—"is Dave and Joan Milton, Brenda's parents. Folks, this is Bino Phillips, my boss."

Joan Milton nodded tearfully and averted her gaze while Dave Milton rose to his feet and extended his hand. It was apparent that the greeting took some effort on Dave's part, but his handshake was firm and genuine. Bino searched for words and finally was able to say, "I'd give anything if the circumstances were different." Dave Milton looked at the far wall as he said huskily, "Yeah."

Mac Strange had followed Half into the room and now stepped up beside Bino to say, "Mr. Milton? I'm McIver Strange, Assistant D.A. We'll get this over with as quickly as possible." Bino wondered how many times Mac had played scenes like this one. Dozens, probably, even hundreds. Yet there was a catch in Mac's voice as he spoke. This wasn't routine to Mac Strange, not by a long shot.

Mac cleared his throat and said, "If you'll follow me, please." Then he led the way through the closed door into the room where the vaults were kept. Dave Milton helped his wife to her feet and followed. In the doorway, Joan Milton sobbed and laid her head on her husband's shoulder. Dave helped his wife along with a comforting arm about her waist. Bino told Dodie and Half that they should wait in the reception room, then went into the morgue himself. He wasn't sure why he was going, but felt that he ought to be there. Anything might help.

The morgue attendant was a thin little guy that Bino had seen before, with curly hair receding from a high forehead. He was all business as he went over to roll out one of the sliding vaults. Pretty heartless, Bino thought. Then again, if he had the guy's job, he didn't know but what dead girls would become old hat to him as well. There was a sheet-draped corpse on a gurney on Bino's left. A body on a gurney was ready to roll in for autopsy. Mac had told Bino that Brenda Milton's autopsy would take place later, after the body had been identified. Get this over with, Bino thought.

The attendant stood with the vault open and touched one corner of the shroud cloth. He said, "Over here, please."

Joan Milton said haltingly, "I can't. I'm sorry, I just . . ." Dave Milton let his wife go and stand by the door while he firmed his lips and stepped forward. Bino softly closed his eyes. He couldn't look. Jesus, he couldn't. There was a soft flapping sound as the attendant yanked the shroud aside. Bino was conscious of Mac Strange's shallow breathing on his left. On his right and slightly behind him, Joan Milton uttered a sob. Bino shut his eyes even tighter.

Heavy pin-drop silence lasted for about five seconds. Then Dave Milton expelled a long sigh. "What—" he said, "what in hell are you people doing to us?"

Bino opened his eyes. Brenda Milton's father was standing by the vault with hands on hips, his jaw outthrust in anger. Bino stepped up to the head of the vault to look down on a girl with grime-streaked blond hair. The lifeless face was one that Bino had never seen before in his life.

6

Brenda Milton wondered if, before she died, she was ever going to see the world again. There wasn't any doubt in her mind that she was going to die, but she hoped for just one trip into the open air before she did. One last glimpse at the flowers and trees, was that too much to ask?

She lay naked on her back in the same position in which she'd been ever since she'd first entered this closet—except for the times, twice a day, when Mr. Numbnuts released her briefly to allow her to use the bedpan or to feed her canned corn or instant mashed potatoes which tasted more like hospital food than anything else. At least she assumed that the tiny room was a closet, because by extending her toes she could touch a wall, and by arching her neck she could brush her hair against another wall. There was a single light overhead. That much she knew because whenever Mr. Numbnuts came around the door would open, a sharp *click* would sound, and illumination would filter through her blindfold. So she knew that she was imprisoned inside a closet of some kind, and she knew that there was a light overhead. What else? she thought. What else did Brenda Milton know? Since she was powerless to *do* anything, *knowing*, she felt, was all that was left to her.

Well, the ridges digging into her fanny told her that she was locked down on coarse-grained wood. It was a table of some kind, all right, but a table built by de Sade when the old Marquis was really pissed about something. There were locking metal bands around her upper arms, wrists, ankles, and thighs, and the bands were bolted to the surface of the wood. A strip of thick soft cloth was fastened around her throat, so that she couldn't lift her head but could arch her neck to touch her hair to the wall; the strip of cloth was secured to the table as well. Spreadeagled like a captive of the Sioux. Next, she thought with a hollow laugh, the son of a bitch will put me out in the sun and cut off my eyelids.

There was a needle inserted, hospital fashion, into the large artery in her left arm, and the needle was held in place by a strip of adhesive tape. Blindfolded, Brenda couldn't see the rubber tube extending from the needle, but felt the tube's pull each time that Mr. Numbnuts let her up to eat or use the bedpan. And she knew very well the purpose of the tube, though she'd had a hard time believing it at first. *Hadn't* believed it, in fact, the first time Mr. Numbnuts had stood nearby and she'd heard the liquid dribbling into a cup or glass. It had been about the third time her captor had drawn blood from her that she had felt the unmistakable dizziness and weakness in her limbs. For some reason, little by little, he was taking her blood. *The goddam motherfucker was taking her blood. Fee, fum, foe, fie, I smell the blood of a Pi Beta Phi.* She snickered and giggled, then the giggle dissolved into a hopeless sob.

She hadn't paid much attention to Mr. Numbnuts when he'd joined the group at the Bump 'n' Run, had just figured him for another one of Donatello's crowd. Another lost soul in search of the white lady, as in, "Going out back for a piece of the White Lady's ass," which was what Donatello had called doing a line in the parking lot.

Brenda was certain she'd seen Mr. Numbnuts somewhere before that night, which was something else she'd have to think about in her process of *knowing.* She remembered thinking at the Bump 'n' Run that Mr. Numbnuts was a little weird, but what cocaine freak wasn't? Later, after she'd passed out on the daybed at Donatello's apartment, and then had awaken, groggy, locked to this bitch of a table, she hadn't even remembered seeing Mr. Numbnuts at the Bump 'n' Run. The bastard had had to remind her. Since that brief talk when she'd first regained her senses, Brenda couldn't remember Mr. Numbnuts having spoken to her at all. As though she was a laboratory animal or something, he carried her crap and her piss away in a bedpan (Bet some of you Phi Delts and Phi Gams thought that *butterflies* toted a Pi-Phi's feces away, Brenda thought), poked food down her throat, and took samples of her fucking *blood*.

What did this man want? Was it just him, or was his buddy in on it? She'd heard a few muffled conversations through the door, and though she couldn't make out what they were saying, it seemed that they were always arguing—Mr. Numbnuts and his pal—fighting over who was going to take the blood from the guinea pig. No one had visited her in her miniprison except old Numbnuts himself—she was sure of that. Not being able to see had made Brenda listen more carefully and, she thought, had even strengthened her sense of smell, and she'd grown to recognize Mr. Numbnuts from the odd shuffling manner in which he moved, and from the scent of the store-brand after-shave that he wore. Not that his buddy couldn't have worn Brut or Old Spice Regular (God, old Numbnuts, you'd never make it through Rush Week wearing that dorky stuff, Brenda thought), but the walk coupled with the odor, plus the way old Numbnuts whistled faintly between his teeth as he went about making her miserable . . . Well, Brenda would have recognized him anywhere. *Better hope they never get you in court with me as a witness, bucko, you're a dead duck if they do.*

Maybe he wanted a ransom. Well, Daddy would pay it, just like Daddy had worked his fingers to the bone to pay for that godawful tuition, and for that godawful jewel of a Mustang that was now parked back at the dorm, and that— *Oh, Daddy, help me.* Tears sprang into Brenda's eyes. She choked them back and cleared her throat, fighting her metal restraints as she did.

But Mr. Numbnuts had never even asked her name, much less how to get in touch with her parents. So much for the ransom.

Brenda didn't have any way of knowing whether Mr. Numbnuts's friend even knew that he had a captive. Donatello would have to know, of course (slimy drug-dealing mother, Brenda thought), because it had been Donatello who had invited Mr. Numbnuts along the other night. But none of the voices she'd heard belonged to the dope peddler. Actually there'd been *two* voices besides Mr. Numbnuts's, one raspy and high-pitched, the other a deep basso. Strange, but Mr. Numbnuts hadn't gagged her. He'd regret that, because the next time she heard the other voices, Brenda was going to scream her lungs out.

Sure, and then Mr. Numbnuts's buddies could come in and rape her or something. Maybe take a little blood for themselves.

So she might scream and she might not. She might . . .

The truth was that she didn't have the slightest idea what she might do, the next time he— Which was right now.

Because he was coming.

There was a rattling sound close on her right, the soft click of a latch, a slight rush of air as the door opened. She turned her face toward the sound as there was a sharp click and sudden light shined faintly through her blindfold.

He was standing there. His breath whistled faintly and there was the drugstore after-shave again. He wasn't moving, just standing there watching her. *Getting a load of the naked girl, you filthy, perverted . . . ? Well I'll give you a load, you . . .*

"What do you want?" she said in a faint voice that sounded to her like a child's. You *think* tough, Bren, she thought, but *acting* tough is something else again.

He didn't answer. The whistling of his breath continued.

"Look," Brenda said, "couldn't you just, maybe let me out of this closet for a while. I won't give you any trouble, if that's what you're . . ." She trailed off.

No sound other than his breath.

"Please." Her own voice broke into a sob.

His feet shuffled as he circled the table to stand to her left. The whistling of his breath was slightly louder now; he was no more than a foot from her imprisoned elbow.

Brenda said quickly, "Listen, if you want to fuck or something, I'm game." And then thought, What am I *saying?* I'd die before I'd let him— No she wouldn't, either, she realized, she'd do anything to get out of here.

He still didn't speak. Suddenly there were firm hands behind her neck, lifting her head, a quick tightening, then a loosening, of her blindfold. He was taking the blindfold off. He was . . .

The cloth fell away, and sudden hot light blinded her. She squinched her eyes together, then blinked, and finally turned her head to look at him. The face was the face she remembered: slim nose, regular features, pale complexion. He was naked. Her gaze lowered to his body.

And froze there. Without any conscious effort on her part, Brenda's lips twisted. His entire torso, neck to waist, was a solid mass of scar tissue. Big reddened foot-long welts, too numerous to count, criss-crossed his chest and stomach. And (*Sweet God*, Brenda thought) *his nipples were missing.* Where his nipples should have been was the biggest, most gruesome scar of all, folded-over gristle and flesh running in a line from armpit to armpit. In spite of her hatred and fear, a quick surge of sympathy flowed through her. What on earth could have . . . ?

Below the mass of torso scar tissue, his legs were visible above the level of the table from midthigh upward, and he had an erection. The erection seemed normal. *Normal?* Brenda thought. *This guy?* The hollow voice inside her said, *Well you should know, sweetheart, you've seen enough hard-ons, right?* She softly closed her eyes as a look of satisfaction crossed his face.

He leaned over her. Light reflected from one slickened welt. His hands went behind her head once more to refasten the blindfold, and for once, she was glad not to see. There was the now familiar tugging sensation in her arm, followed by the splat of liquid flowing into a glass or cup.

More blood—the bastard was taking more blood.

"Why? Why are you *doing* that?" Brenda said.

There was no answer. The tugging ceased; his shuffling footsteps moved around the table once more. The click sounded again and the light disappeared. The door closed softly, and there were more rattles as he locked it from outside.

Though she'd learned that it was useless, Brenda wriggled and struggled on the table, practically choking herself on the cloth as she tried in vain to lift her head. The metal cut into her wrists and ankles until she whimpered in pain. Finally she relaxed. Her efforts had left her breathless; her arms and legs were tingly numb. She was growing weaker and weaker.

Brenda Milton, campus beauty and Pi Beta Phi Homecoming Queen Nominee, lay in the dark and wondered how much blood she had lost.

And how much more she could lose before she died.

Patrick Quarles carried his coffee cup from the closet into his bedroom, taking the blood in tiny sips and swallowing quickly, feeling the warmth and power spread through his body. He uttered the prayer in low tones, under his breath: "This is Thy divine blood, with which I cleanse my spirit." The prayer would transform the wench's tainted fluids into an acceptable holiness, would fit the blood for entrance into his body. The prayer was important to the way of the Truth.

He went to the dresser, set the cup aside, and looked at himself in the mirror. Just as with the others, he'd let the wench gaze upon his wondrous body with her eyes, and in his soul he knew that she had wanted him. She had wanted him to fuck her, had uttered the words through her own lips. Quarles considered her desire and wondered what it would be like to have sex with her. In his entire thirty-four years of life, Patrick Quarles had never been with a woman. Had never even seen a woman naked, in fact, other than the wenches whom he'd allowed to observe his magnificence in recent months. He had seen naked women in the filthy magazines, of course, but once he'd finished with the magazines he always shredded the pictures to remove them from his sight.

Early on in Patrick Quarles's life, his virginity had been a source of shame just as the Signs of the Truth—the marks which covered his upper body—had been, but that had been before the Truth had come and spoken to him. It was a part of the Truth that Quarles had been chosen to remain clean. Now it wasn't through shame that he kept his upper body covered in public, but so that only the selected could gaze upon him. He realized now that all women would want him, would crave to touch his wondrous marks and to have him fuck them, but also realized that the privilege of physical contact with the Disciple Uziah was reserved for the lovely Rebecca and her only. He would claim Rebecca from the evil White-haired One within days, and she would rejoice to learn her true identity.

He had chosen his own name with the permission of the Truth, and now thought of himself as Uziah equally as much as he thought of himself as Patrick Quarles. When the Truth was final, he would be Patrick Quarles no longer, but Uziah the Disciple forevermore. And the name was good and fitting, taken from the twenty-sixth chapter of II Chronicles. For it was Uziah, the King of Jerusalem, who had wandered in the fields as a beast and who had suffered ridicule because of his leprosy, just as Quarles had been an object of scorn until he had learned that his marks were the Signs of the Truth.

The thought of the wench's desire for him was pleasing, even though her want could never be fulfilled. Quarles reached down to stroke his inner thighs lightly with his fingertips; since he had no nipples, and since the thick scar tissue on his upper torso was numb and devoid of feeling, his inner thighs were his source of titillation. As his fingers moved sensuously and tickled the short hairs on his thighs, his erection grew enormous. He watched his erection in the mirror, and its sight was pleasing to him. Soon he would fondle and squeeze to bring himself to climax.

The Disciple allowed his man-being to take control for a moment as his gaze roamed to the portable color TV which played on the dresser. As Patrick Quarles, he was an avid Ranger fan, and tonight's game with the Minnesota Twins was showing. As Patrick Quarles, he lived and died—ninety percent the latter— with the Rangers, and managed a dozen or so times each season to go to Arlington Stadium in person, eat peanuts and drink beer from huge paper cups, and yell the locals on. The Rangers had made a big noise in May, winning a club-record fourteen in a row, and Nolan Ryan had tossed his seventh no-hitter during the span. The team had led at the All-Star Break for the first time in history, and Quarles had been certain that the Rangers had finally gotten the lead out of their asses for good.

But now it was late September—only three ballgames left, as a matter of fact—and the critics had turned out, as usual, to be right. Four three-hundred hitters and five men slugging double-figure homers simply couldn't make up for the lack of Ranger pitching. The Twins had clinched with two weeks left in the season and, other than to die-hards like Quarles, this game meant nothing.

In the TV picture there was a mound conference in progress. On one side stood Valentine, the Rangers' handsome skipper, and on the other side hunkered Rodriguez, the squatty catcher, with his mask dangling from his fingertips and his balloon of a glove shoved underneath his arm.

In the center of the picture, head bowed, hat in hand, stood Witt, the pitcher, and just the sight of the dismal loser caused Patrick Quarles's lip to curl. Valentine was talking to his pitcher a mile a minute. Quarles had once thought that the world hinged on Valentine's every word, but lately had decided—along with a horde of sportswriters and thousands more of the Ranger fans— that the manager just might be full of shit. Quarles leaned closer to the set for a better look.

And Valentine swiveled his head, looked directly at Patrick Quarles, and said in a deep basso voice, "I am worried about your thoughts. I fear that you do not have the Truth in mind."

Quarles recoiled as though slapped in the face. The Father Himself spoke through Valentine's lips.

Rodriquez continued to paw the ground with his foot. The catcher didn't speak much English and, embarrassed, Quarles hoped faintly that Rodriquez wouldn't understand what was being said. Deep down, Quarles realized that the Father was right and realized as well that what was coming was going to be humiliating.

Now Witt tossed the ball up in the air, caught it, and looked directly at Quarles as well. Witt said in a raspy, squeaky voice, with a rural Texas accent, "You can see the guilt in his expression. He thinks only of his own gratification with the woman."

The Son. The Father and the Son as well. Quarles's throat clogged. "No. No, I don't. I work only for the Truth." His voice cracked.

Valentine raised his voice and said in decibels which shook the walls, "DO NOT DARE CONTRADICT. YOU CAN ONLY ATONE FOR SINS IF YOU ARE TRUTHFUL."

Witt ground the horsehide into the pocket of his glove. "He has been with the naked woman and has let her see his own filthy nakedness."

"Please." Quarles covered his face with his hands. Tears flowed between his fingers. "Please. I've done nothing wrong."

"Evil thoughts alone are sin," Valentine said. "He has fornicated with her in his heart."

Quarles raised his head and glared. Mucus dripped from the end of his nose. "I have not. And I will not."

Lately he had stood up to Them more often, and through his fear he was proud of himself.

In the darkness of her prison, Brenda Milton lifted her head. Mr. Numbnuts's buddies had returned. She could hear them out there, arguing with him—they were always arguing. So what if they might hurt her? Nothing could be worse than this. She opened her mouth, drew in a tortured breath, and screamed as loud as she could.

The scream, muffled by the closet door, reached Quarles's ears. He turned his head toward the sound. Did They hear her? Witt said in his rasping voice, "The harlot cries out to him. He wishes to cast his seed in the harlot's belly."

They had heard. Both the Father and the Son had *heard*. Quarles trembled as he said, "Forgiveness. Forgiveness for Thy Disciple."

Valentine appeared deep in thought. Finally he raised his voice and boomed out, "THOU KNOWEST THAT FORGIVENESS COMETH ONLY AFTER PUNISHMENT. YOU WILL ACCEPT YOUR PUNISHMENT NOW."

Quick as thought, Valentine's arm shot out of the TV set. His hand was big and firm, with large knuckles and dark hairs sprouting from the fingers. The hand wrapped around Quarles's penis, squeezed viciously and yanked hard.

Quarles held back, fighting the pain. He stumbled forward a step. They had him. Oh, They had him. For a fleeting instant it looked as though it was Quarles's own hand squeezing and pulling on his own penis, but Quarles knew better. The Truth had taken control of the TV, and now the Father was going to . . . "No," Quarles whined. "Please don't."

Witt was standing with one hip held higher than the other, and now took off his glove. "Cut it off. He must feel Our wrath."

The tears streamed down Quarles's cheeks in a flood. "Oh, please. I'll do anything."

The hand squeezed harder and twisted, sending Quarles down on his knees. "Are you going to obey?" Valentine said. "WILL THE EVIL BEGONE FROM YOUR MIND?"

"Yes . . . yes, don't."

The hand released its hold and withdrew back into the TV. Quarles's own hand came up in front of his face, and as Quarles sobbed out of control he stared dumbly at his own palm. He *couldn't* have done that to himself. It was *Them*. He had wronged the Truth, and the Truth had punished him.

Valentine's voice softened into a tone of pity. "That's better. You will suffer no harm unless you sin. Do you understand that now?"

"Oh, yes. Oh, yes, I do," Quarles said. He touched his finger-tips together beneath his chin in prayer. Tears rolled down his face and dripped from his cheeks.

Valentine's gaze softened under his baseball cap. "And do you love Me?"

Quarles bowed his head. "I love You more than life itself." His breathing was ragged and the angry welts on his upper body were the color of plums.

"He seems to have repented," Witt said. "He has one more before Rebecca."

"That is true," Valentine said, soothingly. "One more of the wenches."

Quarles's tone showed a faint hope. "The clerk?"

"Of course," Valentine said. "You must hurry. Faithful disciples of the Truth will be rewarded."

The voices faded with a soft crackle of static. Still down on his knees, the tears running down his face, Quarles looked up. Valentine retreated to the dugout while Rodriguez trotted back behind the plate. Witt was staying in the game.

Big mistake, Quarles thought. They'll hit him like they owned him. As Quarles got up and went into the bathroom, the first batter drove Witt's curveball into the corner and rounded the bases on his way to a stand-up triple. Two more runs scored for the Twins.

Patrick Quarles's name wasn't on any suspect list, and he'd never been in the service or in jail or anywhere else to have his fingerprints taken. Everyone who worked with him considered him a first-rate young man, and in a lot of respects he was. He was hardworking and dependable. Up to now, no one had had a reason to do a background check on him. If they had, their findings would have caused their jaws to drop to the floor.

His first memories were of a large and clawlike tattooed hand attached to a thin, sinewy tattooed arm, the hand raised to strike him. Even today the tattoos were burned into his mind: the writhing cobras encircling the forearm, the mammoth spider above the slogan "I am Death," the spider's web whose center was the elbow and whose stranded net spread out to both the upper and lower arm. Even the fingers and palm bore tattoos. On the back of each middle knuckle were tiny panthers and in the exact center of each palm was an inch-long centipede. In particular, he recalled the centipede as the right hand descended as if in slow motion, the many-legged insect growing larger, larger, and finally vanishing as the blow landed on his cheek or the side of his head. At times, mercifully, Patrick would black out. Usually he remained conscious until the tattooed hand had struck many blows.

And the lessons which accompanied the beatings: "Thou shalt not steal." "He that believeth and is baptized shall have everlasting life." "If thy right hand offend thee, cut it off." "Thy body is the Temple of God." Lessons spoken in a basso, East Texas rural singsong, the name of God pronounced, "Gawd-uh," as though the word had two syllables.

His memories of his mother: A thin woman with stringy, filthy hair, pipestem legs in shapeless shorts as she sat nearby and watched the floggings. Quarles's own voice, the voice of a small child as he cried out to her, "*Muh*-ver, *Muh*-ver." Her dull face impassive as she watched, her only reaction to come over and pin his arms as he tried to shield his face.

Quarles's world as an infant and small child was the interior of a two-room trailer house in Seagoville, in far southeast Dallas County. His father was a sometime bus mechanic, sometime day laborer, full-time addict, who had learned his religion in prison— had had his own flock, in fact, in the Texas Department of Corrections, Coffield Unit, where he'd used the Power of the Word to gain favor among the other inmates, to con them out of their commissary privileges, and to butt-fuck the choicest of prison punks, some of whom were the property of the prisoners within his flock.

By age seven, Patrick could quote the major scriptures, chapter and verse, and even some of the minor passages. And no wonder: When he couldn't quote the scriptures at his father's command, his father would haul the little boy to one side of the trailer house, chain him to the wall, administer a beating, and starve the boy for days.

When Patrick was five, his father left for a few months, the only period in Patrick's childhood during which the beatings stopped. It was also the only time that the boy was to see any of the outside world at all; glimpses of flat, dull Texas countryside as he rode alongside his mother in an ancient black pickup truck on the way to visit his father. Memories of the time: endless periods of waiting in line alongside other filthy children and their mothers. Finally his father's craggy face, his hair shaved to inch-long quills. Patrick quoting the Bible scripture to his father through the thick, visiting-room wire screen.

His father's eight-year sentence was over in eight months—prison overcrowding. The family reunited, the floggings resumed, with the long periods of chained-to-the-wall starvation.

And always, the lessons: "Thou shalt not commit adultery." "He that looks upon a woman to lust after her has already committed adultery in his own heart." "Thou shalt know the Truth, and the Truth shall set you free."

It was within months—even weeks, perhaps—of his release from prison that Quarles's father began to use the razor. His bearded face twisted in religious fervor, Quarles's father would chain the boy, strop the open straight blade deliberately while mouthing nearly incoherent Bible verse, slowly advance on and slash the naked child while Quarles's mother, as always, sat by and watched as though she were observing a sewing bee. The cuttings went on for a year, and it was a miracle that the child didn't bleed to death. The slashes were deep, some within a fraction of entering Patrick's body cavity. It was during the spring of Patrick's sixth year on earth that his mother sat on the bed and held the child rigid, arms pinned to his sides, while his father systematically cut off the boy's nipples because, according to Quarles's father, a man's breasts had no purpose and were the instruments of evil. During this same session Patrick's father lifted the child's scrotum and—also under the babbled theory that sex was a tool of the Devil and had no place in the teachings of the Lord—set about to castrate the boy. A two-day session with speed and alcohol had taken its toll, though, and Quarles's father passed out on the floor and saved Patrick his manhood.

The two Seagoville police officers who came to the trailer house three weeks later weren't interested in child abuse. Instead, the cops were armed with a search warrant and were looking for items taken in a supermarket burglary. On forcibly entering the trailer they did find several of the items, among which were a crated gross of razor blades. They also found, chained to a wall, a seven-year-old child who weighed twenty-eight pounds, and on whose upper torso they did not see a single square inch of unscarred flesh.

Quarles's parents' photos adorned the newspapers for a few days, and the accompanying articles were full of descriptions of Patrick's injuries. Then, like all news, the news became old and disappeared, first to the back sections, then from the paper entirely. Quarles's parents went quietly off to jail—where his father died a year later in a prison-yard incident related to a punk's affections, and his mother spent four years, got out, took up with another man, and later smothered her own newborn in its crib—and Patrick became a ward of the state.

Quarles spent the balance of his childhood and all of his adolescence at the Buckner Orphans Home on the far East Dallas boundary, just a few miles, in fact, from Bino Phillips's stomping grounds in Mesquite. Buckner Home is set in an open field, built of dullish red brick in dullish brown terrain. Quarles's memories of the home: Open-bay sleeping with forty other homeless children. Matronly women who did their best to be mothers, but whose time was divided among forty kids.

And ridicule. Children are cruel beyond imagination, especially children deprived of parental love. Patrick had been at the home for less than a month when one snaggletooth youngster, a head taller and quite a bit heavier than he, came over at bedtime and poked at the scar tissue on Patrick's chest. "Ooo," the boy said. "What're *those?*

And a second youngster, a chubby redhead glad for the opportunity to distract attention from his own portliness, chimed in. "Ooo. They're *ug-lee.*"

And Quarles spent the night in tears, huddled under a thin blanket to hide his body, certain that he was the most hideous creature on earth. His feelings about himself were to last for nearly twenty years.

As the orphans grew up together and became teenagers, Patrick's torture became more inventive. Nicknames followed one after the other: Scarry (shortened later to Scar), Pus-Bucket, No-Tits, Freaky—to each of these names Quarles at various times responded. The monicker that stuck, though, from the age of thirteen, was the brainchild of an orphan named Ronnie (last names weren't important at Buckner Home), a big athletic youth who one day came up with the name while reading a comic book. "The Heap." The Heap was a creature, colored green in the comics, created in a nuclear garbage dump. The Heap Quarles became, and the Heap he was to remain until he grew into a man. His body never saw sunlight; he wore clothing buttoned high around his neck to hide his ugliness.

In spite of his physical problems, Patrick Quarles showed himself to be an exceptional student. His ability to memorize—particularly where Bible verses were concerned—amazed his teachers at the home, and his grades were in the upper ten percent at the public East Dallas high school where the orphans attended class. His exceptional score on the SAT won him a partial scholarship, and he attended the University of North Texas in Denton where he earned a degree in English.

He also worked well with his hands, and in high school shop classes learned to build furniture. He sold his first piece, a breakfast table, when he was sixteen and paid the bulk of his college expenses selling his handmade tables and chairs.

And finally, Quarles entered society. For more than a decade thereafter, Patrick Quarles—other than his continued shame over his body, which caused him to wear high-necked shirts and refrain from dating women—lived normally and labored dutifully to make a living. At twenty-eight, he bought his own home.

And in his thirty-fourth year he first heard the voices, first realized that his physical affliction had a purpose in the Truth. One month after the voices first came to him, Quarles stole a cocker spaniel from a fenced-in yard in North Dallas and took the animal home. There he slit the dog's throat, gutted the cocker, and drank its blood. Five weeks later he shot a cow in a field and decapitated the beast. Then, using a garden spade, he scooped the brains from the cow's head and drank blood from its hollowed skull.

And four months after Patrick Quarles heard the voices for the first time, Annette Ray disappeared on her way back to the SMU campus after testifying in federal court. She was twenty years old.

Quarles took his time in the shower, letting the hot water relax his muscles, clamping his eyes tightly shut as the jet stream from the nozzle soaked his hair and sent a minitorrent cascading down over his face. He was glad that the Truth had not punished him further and realized that he had done wrong in having lustful thoughts about the wench. It would not happen again. The body of Uziah the Disciple was reserved for Rebecca alone.

He finished his bath, blew his hair dry with a yellow Clairol dryer, then wiped a circle in the mirror frost and shaved. He splashed on Old Spice Regular, indistinctive and unmemorable, a lotion that anyone might use. He patted his cheeks, liking the burning sensation of the after-shave. Quarles savored his time in the bathroom. It was here and only here that the voices never spoke to him, and he could be alone with his own thoughts. He recapped the Old Spice bottle, shoving the plunger down with his forefinger, then returned naked into the bedroom. He looked warily about. In the bedroom he must move with care because in the bedroom the voices were all around.

He went to his closet and dug through the hangers, slighting charcoal and navy blue suits, along with bright sport shirts and white and khaki Dockers. Finally he found a drab gray knit shirt, shrugged into it and buttoned the collar snug underneath his chin, and stepped into faded Levis and buttoned them as well. Then he put on blue cotton socks and black Nike sneakers and finally went over and studied himself in the mirror. His curly brown hair was cut conservatively short and his pale complexion was slightly yellowed. He used a lot of creams and oils to tone his unwrinkled skin, but the faint yellowish tint refused to go away. Even at thirty-four, dressed in T-shirt and jeans, he could have easily passed for a college kid. *Had* passed for one, in fact, the times he'd wandered unnoticed on the campus at SMU. He knelt before the dresser and opened the bottom drawer.

There were only three of the wooden spikes remaining—four-inch hard maple slivers painted with clear lacquer. The spikes represented the final marks on the wenches' bodies even as the nails in the Master's hands and feet signaled the end of His earthly existence. The three pegs wouldn't be enough; Quarles would make more. He took one spike, dropped it in his pocket, then moved the rest aside to rummage at the back of the drawer.

Finally, he stood holding a hypodermic needle and a baggie which held three ounces of Mexican brown heroin. China white gave him a better kick, but money had been tight lately, and a little Mexican brown was all he could afford. He sprinkled some of the beige powder into his palm and snorted it up his nose, then returned the heroin and hypo to their hiding place. Muted sobs came from within the closet, but Quarles ignored them. Not *his* captive, not Patrick Quarles's. Definitely, the wench was a prisoner of the Truth. He moved out of the bedroom and down the hallway toward the living room as the heroin jolted through him like rushing warm water.

In the living room he sat on the couch beside a blue Adidas athletic tote bag, unzipped the bag to reveal a heavy black one-piece jumpsuit folded inside. He dug underneath the jumpsuit and felt down inside the bag to touch the handle of the Smith & Wesson .38 revolver which nestled at the bottom alongside the claw hammer used for driving the pegs. As a man, Quarles needed the gun. Once the Truth had set him entirely free, he would have no need for man-made things.

He closed the bag, hefted it, and after a final glance around the room went through his front door and into the night. As he hop-skipped downstairs, Quarles whistled breathily the opening bars to "Fly Me to the Moon," over and over, slightly off-key. His footsteps crunched gravel as he made his way across the drive to stand beside his car. Fifty yards away was the dock; beyond the dock the *Seastork II* floated still on its moorings, and rays of light danced on the lake like thousands of fireflies. As he climbed behind the wheel, Quarles wondered briefly if next year might belong to the Rangers. He doubted it. For the Rangers to have any chance, Quarles thought, Valentine would have to go.

7

Andrea Morton had legs up to here, and in spikes and a micro-mini was flat drop-dead. Fact of the matter, Andrea hoped that the minis *never* went out of style again. She'd worn them in high school, only five years ago, even though in '86 the minis had been definitely out. In those days they'd called her a sixties chick, but as long as the guys (and more than one of the grown-up men *teachers*, she'd happened to notice) had kept on eyeing her legs, she hadn't really given a damn. She privately admitted to being a trifle short in the boob department—Andrea spent a lot of time in self-evaluation, and probably would have sprung for silicone implants if it hadn't have been for the cancer scare—and had decided sometime back that if she was going to majorly com-pete, she had to show off what she *did* have. Whatever you've got, strut it, babe, is what she told herself.

And not only did Andrea Morton have drop-dead legs, the outfit she was wearing was drop-dead perfect as well, and she spent a couple of extra minutes turning back and forth, looking herself over from all angles in the full-length mirror which she'd affixed with putty on her bedroom closet door. The skirt and loose cotton hip-length sweater were black, matching her shoes, and a few minutes earlier she'd stripped off her patterned pantyhose—they'd been tinted navy, with rows and rows of tiny black hearts, and called attention more to the pattern than they did to the legs underneath—and traded them in for nude. Her summer tan hadn't quite faded as yet (she'd spent a quick thirty minutes by the pool after work that afternoon to make sure), and the nude pantyhose made her look as if she might not be wearing anything at all under the mini. *She was a long cool woman in a black dress, long cool woman got it awwlll.*

She looked pretty good, all right, and as she confirmed the fact for the umpteenth time by turning her back, spreading her feet apart, and checking out over her shoulder the way the skirt molded taut against her thighs and fanny, she considered—also for the umpteenth time—the only part of her appearance that she was worried about. The new do. Well, not the do itself, for that hadn't changed, her hair billowing out around her head, chopped off parallel to the floor just below her ear level, the portion below the cut razored down to a smooth surface so that an outline of the do resembled the Liberty Bell. It was the color. The transformation from Andrea the Dark to Andrea the Platinum had cost half a week's U.S. District Clerk pay two days ago, and tonight was going to be the first time that the new Andrea had gone public. Worth every nickel if the hair helped her nose out the competition, but if the new blond look had the opposite effect, Andrea was going to lock herself inside her apartment and not emerge until the color grew out. She swore to *God* that she was.

The hair wouldn't help her with the younger set—the college and just-graduated crowd who swigged beer from longnecks and staggered around between the trendy bars and discos on the West End—but, then, neither would the clothes. (If she was looking for younger guys she would have worn tight jeans and Dance Reeboks.) Just recently, Andrea Morton had begun trolling for the older dudes. Older dudes had more money to spend, knew better how to *treat* a woman (none of that fuck or walk shit, Andrea thought). Older dudes were definitely where it was at.

If she'd been three or four years older like Daphne Wilson, her friend from the U.S. Attorney's office, Andrea wouldn't have worried near as much about the hair. She was picking Daphne up in half an hour, and remembering Daphne caused Andrea to check her tiny watch with the slim black suede band. Daphne's hair was light brown and worn in ringlets, and she was certainly no competition to Andrea in the leg department, but Daphne had been to college and everything and, Andrea had to admit, was pretty cool and sophisticated. *Daphne* liked Andrea's new blond do, but Daphne wasn't the one that Andrea was out to bowl over. Besides, Daphne could be lying. Daphne could be putting Andrea on, secretly thinking that the blond do was the pits, secretly glad that Andrea had changed her looks because it gave Daphne a leg up in the race. Other females, Andrea had learned the hard way, didn't always tell the truth, even if they were supposed to be your good friends.

If the blond hair didn't do the trick, Dodie Peterson was the one that Andrea was *really* going to blame. Not that Dodie had done anything on purpose—Andrea didn't know Dodie very well, and had only talked to her a few times when Dodie came over from Bino Phillips's law office to file a bail bond or motion at the clerk's office—but Andrea had noticed for a long time the way that all the lawyers and FBI Agents around the Federal Building did double-takes when Dodie went by, and had finally decided that it had to be Dodie's hair. Blonds just had more fun, that was all there was to it. As a matter of fact, Andrea had been more than a little pissed when she'd come out from under the dryer because her new color didn't exactly match Dodie's. Dodie's hair was softer and had more gold in it, while Andrea's new color, she thought, made her look more like some kind of forties movie queen. Which would be A-OK with the older dudes, so Andrea guessed that she shouldn't complain.

Bino Phillips had seemed to like Andrea's hair when he'd come into the clerk's office to look up an old record for the Stanley trial, but Bino Phillips ogled *everybody*. Not that Andrea particularly minded; Bino Phillips was a really good-looking guy around forty who drove a white Lincoln Town Car, but Bino Phillips probably would have looked Andrea over even if her hair had been fucking *green*. There was this other guy as well, a guy who worked down at the Federal Building, and *he'd* acted as though he liked Andrea's hair, but this other dude, Andrea thought, was sort of slimy and creepy. No, the real test was going to come tonight. Andrea checked her watch again and decided that she'd better get her ass in gear.

She moved around her apartment, turning off lights, making sure to leave the one in the kitchen burning, and reducing the volume on KVIL-FM on her stereo. She'd recently switched to KVIL from hard rock Y-95, but that had more to do with her interest in the older dudes. Dress for 'em and play their music, if you really want to hook 'em. She reached inside her small handbag to jingle her keys, then went out into the cooling night air and locked her apartment. Andrea hustled downstairs with her high heels clicking and her fanny jiggling under her mini. If the do didn't work, she was going to *kill* that Dodie Peterson.

Halfway to street level, Andrea paused. She allowed herself one quick glance at the breezeway across the parking lot, shuddered slightly, then continued on her way. To hell with him; she hadn't liked that Donatello guy to begin with, and thought he'd just been asking for it. Any guy going around flaunting the fact that he was a dope dealer was bound to get it sooner or later, either from the DEA or one of his customers. She briefly wondered whether old Donatello had gotten himself done in with a gun or knife; the only word out was that there'd been a murder. Tawny Willis, the chick who worked at Hooter's, and who lived right across the pool from Donatello's pad, had seen a guy climb onto the patio and go in through the sliding glass door about two in the afternoon, when Tawny had been right in the middle of reading *The Silence of the Lambs*. According to Tawny it had been a skinny dude with a mustache who'd been wearing a plaid sport coat. Well, if Andrea saw any skinny guys with mustaches hanging around, Andrea was going to scream like hell.

At the foot of the steps she hesitated again and let her gaze roam two ground-level apartment doors down the way to where Dodie Peterson lived. Though they'd been neighbors in the Corners section of the Village for a couple of years, Andrea had never spoken to Dodie away from the Federal Building, and had been thinking lately that it might be cool to get to know Dodie better. Next week, in fact, that was exactly what Andrea was going to do. *If* the blond color worked, of course; if it didn't work she might sneak down to Dodie's and set fire to the place. Andrea tossed her head, causing her hair to swirl, then *click-clicked* her way in spike heels across the parking lot to where her Hyundai sat.

She turned the key in the lock, then froze with the door open as a prickly sensation tickled the back of her neck. Damn, was somebody *watching*? She gazed around the parking lot at Fords, Chevys, and even a few Caddys and Mercedeses in the moonlight, but didn't see anybody. You dummy, you're acting like a nerd, she thought, the new do has driven you bananas. That and all the rumors of bloody murder going around. If somebody *was* watching, maybe they'd like her hair. She laughed nervously, got behind the wheel, started the engine and turned on the lights, and wheeled out onto Shady Brook Lane. Older dudes, you'd *better* like blonds, she thought. Ready or not, here comes the new Andrea Morton.

Oscar Beemish, in from Detroit for only three days and having already cemented his deal, was pretty sure he was going to celebrate with a portion of choice Texas trim. The only doubt in his mind was which of the girls he was going to pick. But for a man who'd just talked a Texas bank into loaning him two million dollars—right on the heels of the S&L fraud, when damn near every banker was diving for cover as though it was Groundhog Day and the sun was shining—selecting the right piece of trim shouldn't be any problem at all. He peeled a hundred from his roll, creased the bill, and held it between his fore and middle fingers to wave it toward the bar. "Yo, bring us another one." He raised his voice enough to be heard over the soft piano music, but was careful not to shout. A man was calling enough jealous attention to himself just by sitting in a booth between two tasty young ladies, without being a loudmouthed asshole to boot.

On his left, the brunette whose hair was done in ringlets said, "Hey, I don't know. I'm close to my limit," while pushing her stemmed glass toward the edge of the table, making it easier for the waitress to take over for a refill.

On Beemish's right, the platinum blond with the puffy hairdo (Angie? No, Andrea—Jesus, Angie was Beemish's daughter's name) said merely, "Cool." She was the one, long legs in a mini and flashy tent of hair, who'd first gotten Beemish's attention, but after sizing up the situation he'd about decided that the more conservative brunette would probably turn out to be the better piece of ass of the two. And sizing up situations was what Oscar Beemish did best of all. Just ask the boys down at Texas Bank of Commerce, Beemish thought.

The downstairs bar at the Adolphus Hotel was jumping for a weeknight, bar stools crowded, about half of the tables occupied, a man wearing a dark suit and horn-rim glasses playing steady Cole Porter on the ivories. It was the kind of atmosphere where cash brought faster service, which was one reason that Beemish had waved the hundred-dollar bill. Another reason for paying cash was that, back home in the Motor City, Beemish's wife audited the American Express bill like a pinch-breasted bookkeeper. So far Miriam Beemish, whom Oscar had married right out of high school, and had kept barefoot and pregnant for a dozen years before hitting the big time, had swallowed her husband's stories of nights watching TV in the hotel room when he was on the road. A big bar tab might change that image, and Oscar figured that he could steal enough cash out of his fourteen Egg Roll Hubba-Hubba locations to more than make up for the IRS deductions he was losing. The two million from Texas Bank of Commerce would bankroll more Chinese takeout places in Flint and Lansing, with enough siphoned from the principal for a spa and workout room at Beemish's house, and plenty left over after the home improvements to keep Oscar in strange trim while he was on the road. Things are definitely looking up, Beemish thought.

As the waitress, a slim young lady wearing a gold jacket with the Adolphus emblem on its breast pocket, hustled over to place fresh drinks all around—Cutty neat for Beemish, a whiskey sour for the blond and a pink frothy Satin Doll for the brunette—and tote away the empties along with Beemish's Benjamin Franklin, the platinum blond hiccuped and said, "When is it you're leaving town?" She wore just enough lip gloss to make a pinkish shine, and as she put away the whiskey sours a rural Texas accent crept steadily into her speech. Another plus for the brown-haired one, Beemish thought.

"Oh, two, three days," Beemish said. Actually, he had reservations on the 11:50 American in the morning, but didn't want whichever female he wound up with to think that this was a hit-and-run proposition. Oscar, you *dog*, Beemish thought. "Listen," he said, "you girls like to, maybe, make another spot or two when we finish this one?" He addressed his words to the table in general, but his eyes were cut toward the brunette.

The brunette (Daphne? Yeah, sure, the goddess of something-or-other) regarded Beemish over the rim of her glass. "I might be game," she said. "But she's driving." Daphne wore a brown pantsuit and had a filmy orange scarf around her neck—not near so flashy as the blond but more mature and definitely showing more promise. She had a pretty, intelligent, olive-complexioned face with a round, slightly pouty chin, and seemed to have her head on straight. Probably has more sense than to bug you later, Beemish thought.

"Well, I might be game, too," the blond said. "Long as you two don't make me feel like a *third wheel* or something." Her face screwed up into a petulant frown.

"Well, I'm not driving anything," Beemish said, "and wouldn't know where I was going anyway. Hey, Angie, it'd be up to you to pick the best spot."

"*Andrea*," the blond said.

Beemish felt like kicking himself. "Excuse me. What the hell, we just met."

"Well, you didn't forget *her* name." Andrea nodded toward Daphne.

"Mine's just easier to remember," Daphne said. "And he's right, Andrea. Maybe someplace else the male population is a little more dense. And a lot more with-it." As she spoke, she scooted forward and directed her words to Andrea; then she leaned back and brushed her lips close to Beemish's ear. "Just cool it, huh?" she whispered.

A girl after my own heart, Beemish thought. Wonder if she's into any kinky stuff. "Well, now you're talking," he said, brushing the lapel of his dark Armani suit. "What do you say? I'm starved. What's a good place to eat this time of night?" The waitress returned with three twenties, a pile of singles, and jingly change, and set her tip tray down in the center of the table. She walked away swinging her her hips under ankle-length black tights. Beemish made no move to touch the money.

Andrea looked first at Daphne, then at Beemish, and finally riveted her gaze on the pile of money. "Steak?" she said. "I guess I could stand a little bite myself."

Beemish sat jammed into the backseat of the little green Hyundai as Andrea steered her way down the parking garage ramp to go east on Commerce Street. Daphne tilted her head to peer over Beemish's shoulder through the rear window. "That guy was in the bar," Daphne said. She was sitting in the front shotgun bucket seat. Her left arm was draped over the seat back so that her hand rested on Beemish's knee. Each time that Andrea would swivel her head as though to look in that direction, Daphne would quickly move her hand to rest on the back of the seat.

Beemish had a problem with turning around to follow Daphne's gaze. First of all, his knees were crammed against the back of the driver's seat; Andrea had already asked him twice to move over so he'd have more room, but Beemish didn't want to scoot sideways, first of all because sliding to sit behind the shotgun seat would make it impossible for Daphne to touch his leg without Andrea noticing. Secondly, he was sitting bolt upright and sucking in his stomach, and any twisting movement might cause his belly to hang out embarrassingly over his belt in plain sight of Daphne. When the tailor had told Beemish that the pants should be let out a couple of inches, Oscar had bowed his head. Jesus Christ, he was already into 38s and was damned if he'd have them enlarged to boot. He needed to get his body in better shape to keep up with the young trim; his thick head of hair would stand the test forever so long as he kept pouring on the Grecian Formula. Beemish turned his neck as far as it would go, but was only able to see to his right, out the side window. "What guy?" Beemish said.

Andrea the Platinum's body was a whole lot more supple than Beemish's, and her knees weren't jammed against anything. She twisted around to look hopefully out the back window along with Daphne. "What guy?" Andrea said. She was fighting the stick-shift lever, which protruded from the floor between the seats, and as she turned she released the clutch pedal while the lever was between gears. The five-speed growled in protest.

The Hyundai bounced hard over the dip at the end of the drive to career to the right on Commerce, and Beemish's right-angle perspective now showed the interior of the parking garage. There was a man hustling across the ground floor, all right, though in the garage's dimly lit interior his outline wasn't clear. As Beemish watched, the man reached the side of a tan Buick—Beemish didn't know much about cars, but the Buick wasn't new by a long shot—flung the door open and dove behind the wheel. As the Hyundai moved along down Commerce, the Buick disappeared from Beemish's line of vision behind the garage's eastern exterior wall.

"Man looked to be in a hurry," Beemish said. "Probably couldn't stand it when the good-looking blond split."

Andrea giggled and returned her attention to the street in front of her, yanking the wheel to the right and barely avoiding a collision with the rear bumper of a panel truck.

Quick thinking, Oscar, giving the blond a compliment, Beemish thought. Wonder what it's going to take to get rid of her.

His belly full of mesquite-broiled T-bone, Oscar Beemish decided to bring his choice of women out in the open. Down here in the Lone Star State, he thought, they probably call it "cutting one out of the herd." He opened the passenger door for Daphne, then reached in front of her to fold the seat forward. "Sit in the back with me," Beemish said. The Hyundai was nose-on to the curb in front of Dunston's Steak House on Lovers Lane, where Beemish had just forked over eighty-six bucks plus a fifteen-dollar tip for his own T-bone, sirloin strips for the girls, and three more rounds of Cutty neat, whiskey sours, and Satin Dolls. Be cheaper to go ahead and pay for the trim, Beemish thought. Visible through the front window of the restaurant, waitresses wearing boots and midcalf western skirts carried trays of food to candlelit rough wooden tables and booths. Across the street in a shopping center, the Inwood Theater was showing *Tie Me Up, Tie Me Down*. As he glanced first at the movie's title on the marquee, then down at Daphne's rump under the smooth fabric of her pantsuit, Beemish got ideas. He showed Daphne a guarded wink as she watched him doubtfully over her shoulder. Her slim fingers twisted as she played with the scarf at her throat.

Daphne started to climb in, then paused with one foot on the backseat floorboard to shoot a questioning glance at Andrea. Daphne wore tan open-toed flats and her toenails were painted brown to match her outfit. The blond stood on the driver's side, ready to climb behind the wheel, and she flashed a porcelain smile. "Y'all don't mind me," she said. "Go ahead." Then she sat down and slammed the door with a vengeance that rocked the Hyundai on its springs. Jesus Christ, with that set of legs I don't know why she can't score, Beemish thought. Maybe it's the Daisy Mae accent. Maybe she should just raise her skirts and keep her mouth shut.

Daphne struggled into the back and scooted to make room; Beemish piled in behind her, making sure to keep his coat buttoned and his belly sucked in, then reached forward and closed the passenger door. Andrea jammed the lever into reverse and the Hyundai roared backward with a neck-popping squeal of rubber. Jesus, Beemish thought, this broad is really pissed. Gears ground as the Hyundai reversed its direction; Daphne's firm leg brushed Oscar's; as the car hurtled forward, Beemish wondered if Andrea's insurance would cover a passenger's whiplash claim. Suddenly, Andrea threw on the brakes, and Beemish very nearly rammed his head into the back of the front seat.

"Idn that the same Buick?" Andrea said. "The one the dude got into in the Adolphus garage?" Her gaze was out the window, toward a car parked a hundred yards down the way from the restaurant. Someone was behind the wheel, but in the darkness Beemish couldn't tell whether the driver was a woman or a man.

At Beemish's elbow, Daphne drew a sudden breath. "I think you're right, Andrea."

"You girls are dreaming," Beemish said. "Come on, let's go." He put his arm around Daphne and drew her close. She smelled of lilac.

As the Hyundai left the restaurant, Beemish got a better look at the parked car. He had to admit it was an old tan Buick, and he had to admit it was a dead ringer for the one he'd seen earlier. The world's not *that* small, he thought—it couldn't be the same guy. Could it? As the Hyundai fishtailed onto Lovers Lane, he blew in Daphne's ear and promptly forgot the other car.

Beemish should have known that a place known as Milo Butterfingers would be crawling with youngsters. As he bobbed and weaved among young guys with razored hair and knit Polo and oversized Rudolph Mills shirts, and chicks in baggy pressed shorts with the cuffs turned up exactly an inch, doing his damnedest to keep up with Daphne while the multiple speakers blasted "Devil in a Blue Dress," Beemish wondered if the strange piece of ass was going to be worth the effort. He wondered if *anything* would be worth all of this, his belly jiggling up and down, sweat pouring from his scalp and cascading down his forehead. He was breathing like a cardiac patient. There was a painful stitch in his side.

"We've got to give Andrea a chance to *meet someone*," Daphne had said as they'd turned south off Lovers Lane onto Greenville Avenue. "I can't just go off and *leave* her." Well, hell yes, Beemish was all in favor of giving every woman in this world a chance to get fucked, the more the merrier. But Jesus Christ, couldn't they try a piano bar? At this point Beemish was ready to slip a guy a few bucks just to take the blond off his hands. He narrowed his eyes to peer through the forest of moving bodies on the dance floor, in search of Andrea and the tall young guy who'd asked her to dance a few minutes ago. Don't let the corny accent scare you off, buddy, Beemish had thought, she's bound to be hell in the old sackeroo.

The fast dance number was at long last over. Beemish stood gasping for a moment while Daphne, fresh as new cat litter, smiled prettily at him. Jesus, I've got to have some of that, Beemish thought. He took her firmly by the upper arm and steered her through the crowd toward the four-seat tables. Christ, one more dance like that one and he could forget the piece of ass. He'd never get it up.

As he and Daphne neared their table, Beemish's heart dropped to his ankles. Jesus, there she was, all by her lonesome, the blond sitting there with long elegant legs showing to within an inch of her hip joint, morosely studying the tiny stemmed glass which had contained her most recent whiskey sour. All that remained of the drink was the cherry in the bottom, and as Beemish watched, Andrea picked up the cherry and plucked it from the stem with even white teeth. Wonder how much *this* fucking tab's going to be, Beemish thought. Jesus, what happened to the young guy? Maybe he could use a few greenbacks. Beemish narrowed his eyes and peered around through the darkened club.

As Daphne sat springily on the edge of her seat, and as Beemish sank back into his chair feeling like rehabilitation center material, Andrea said, "I think I'd better be getting home." Her vacant gaze was on her glass.

Glory Hallelujah, Beemish thought.

"Why, what's wrong?" Daphne placed a hand on Andrea's forearm.

Jesus Christ, don't *argue* with her, Beemish thought. He said, "Maybe she's tired," in a voice that he hoped didn't sound too anxious.

Daphne turned to Beemish to say, "No, I *know* her." Then she leaned nearer to Andrea and said, "What happened?"

"Maybe nothin'," Andrea said. "But you know that guy I was dancin' with? Well this creepy old dude tried to cut in. *Man,* what a weirdo. The guy dancin' with me wouldn't pay him any mind, and the dude got really nasty about it. Kind of scared the young guy away, and then I ran as fast as I could back to the table. And you know what?" She paused for breath.

Let me guess, Beemish thought. The old guy turned into a werewolf or some fucking thing and bit the shit out of her.

"Well, I think," Andrea said, "that the guy trying to cut in was the same guy in the Buick, that we've been seeing ever since downtown. Now I can't be sure. But it kind of scared me, you know?"

Beemish breathed an inward sigh of relief as the Hyundai pulled over to stop, scraping the curb with its left front tire. Andrea the blond had apparently gotten over being scared and had gone back to being pissed, either that or she was a lot drunker than she acted. Jesus, ever since they'd left Milo Butterfingers, Andrea had handled the Hyundai like a wild woman, whipping in and out among lanes of near bumper-to-bumper traffic on Greenville Avenue, her platinum Liberty Bell of hair scrunched down between her shoulders like an Indy driver's crash helmet. Beemish pushed the passenger-side bucket seat forward and struggled out of the back to stand in the street, then leaned over to offer his hand to Daphne. She took the hand and scooted toward the door, then leaned over toward the front seat and said to Andrea, "You sure you're going to be all right?"

Andrea's smile in the dim interior lighting appeared painted on. "Just dandy. Y'all go ahead." She sounded mad as hell and her speech was slightly slurred.

A ribbon of sidewalk wound away from the curb and in among two-story apartment buildings with peaked shingled roofs; on both sides of the street were more apartments, stretching into the distance as far as the eye could see. Beemish had a road pal—a John Deere salesman, also married, living up in Lansing—who called this section of Dallas "Pussy Jungle." This was the first time Beemish had seen the Village firsthand, but he decided that it definitely wasn't going to be the last. Jesus, if only half the apartments had women living in them, there must be ten thousand broads within a mile radius of where Beemish was standing. Talk about your fucking Promised Land.

"No, Andrea," Daphne said, concerned. "Tell you what, we'll ride home with you, then we can walk back to my place."

Are you out of your mind? Beemish thought. "How far is that?" he said lamely.

"Andrea lives"—Daphne pointed straight ahead with a manicured index finger—"right up there at the Corners. Not over a mile or so."

A mile? A fucking *mile*? "What's the Corners?" Beemish said. "I thought you girls lived at the Village."

"We do," Daphne said. " But the place is so big it's divided into subsections. My apartment is right up there—this is called the Gate. There's about ten sections—I can't even name them all." She turned back to Andrea. "What do you say? I'd feel better, knowing you're all right."

I swear to God, Beemish thought, if the broad pulls this stunt I'm calling a cab, strange trim or no.

"I'll be all right, Daphne," Andrea said. "Now I mean it, you two go on and let me be." Her lower lip quivered slightly.

Beemish took the bull by the horns, increased the pressure of his grip on Daphne's hand and practically yanked her out of the car to stand beside him. Daphne shot Beemish an irritated glance, but made no move to get back in the Hyundai. Instead, she leaned over and said to Andrea, "Are you sure?"

Andrea said icily, "I'm sure." Then she bent sideways to yank the passenger door closed with a thunk of metal, jammed the lever in gear and left Beemish and Daphne standing in the street as the Hyundai screeched off into the night. The tail lamps bounced up and down as the little car negotiated a dip, then disappeared around a curve in the road.

Beemish thought, Whew. Now that's over with, time to get the good stuff on. He grasped Daphne's upper arm to escort her toward her apartment building. Firm flesh moved over vibrant muscle under his fingers. Daphne resisted slightly, then smiled up at him, put her arm around the back of his waist and rested her head against his shoulder as they moved along the sidewalk in the moonlight. There was a quick stiffening in Beemish's crotch. Almost there. Jesus, almost fucking—

Auto engine noise sounded behind them and headlight beams touched them for an instant, then moved on. Daphne drew away from him and turned toward the street as the car went by, lights illuminating the pavement, one tail lamp winking off, then back on, as the car went over the dip, then continued in the same direction in which, seconds earlier, Andrea had gone.

Daphne gasped in the moonlight. "It's *him*. I swear it is."

"Huh?" Beemish squinted after the disappearing car. "It's who?" Disappointment surged in him. The hard-on he'd been building wilted like time-lapse photography.

"The Buick," Daphne said. "The guy that . . ." She put her hands on her waist and said rapidly, "473-DWJ. 473-DWJ. 473-D—"

"Jesus Christ, are you sure?" Beemish said.

"—WJ. 473-DWJ. It's *him*, I'm telling you. 473-D—"

"What the hell are you doing?"

"—WJ. His license number, you dodo. 473-DWJ. 473-D—"

"Wait a minute." Beemish dug in his inside breast pocket. "I've got a pen." He produced a ballpoint and small pad and, hunching over and squinting in the dimness, wrote down the number. He looked up. "I've got it, now can we . . . ?"

Daphne was already fifty feet away, her bottom wiggling in determination, the soles of her shoes slapping on concrete as she took off after the Buick like a marathon speed-walker

Beemish dropped his hands to let the pad and pen dangle by his hips. "Hey. Hey, where you going?"

"Andrea's," Daphne called out over her shoulder. "She's my *friend*."

Beemish looked helplessly behind him toward Greenville Avenue, trying to remember how he'd gotten into this. Jesus Christ, all he'd wanted was . . . Then, his belly flopping up and down under his buttoned coat, Beemish jogged after her. "Wait a minute," he said between ragged breaths. "Wait a minute, I'm going with you." Just until I can get to a phone, Beemish thought, then I'm calling a taxi.

Andrea Morton drove with both hands clutching the wheel and hot tears streaking her makeup. It was the hair. It was the goddam *hair*, it had to be. She looked every bit as good as Daphne. And I sure have a better pair of legs, Andrea thought, glancing down at her nylon-encased thighs—and yet Daphne, Andrea's former (underscore it, Andrea thought, as in *former*) best friend Daphne, had just gone home with the sophisticated older dude while Andrea the Platinum hadn't attracted anything but some creep who followed her around in an old beatup Buick. To hell with being blond, Andrea thought, tomorrow here comes the dye.

And the creep—god, Andrea thought, the *ugliness* of the guy, skinny face and loose floppy cheeks, dressed like some street person in filthy jeans and wornout shoes—not only had the dirty *creep* been a pest, he'd scared off the only decent chance Andrea had had to snare a cute guy for herself. It was true that the guy at Milo Butterfingers hadn't been one of the older dudes, complete with bankroll, that Andrea would have preferred, but at least he'd been tall and pretty good-looking, and making it with him sure would have beat hanging around with that bitch Daphne—the *slut*—and the older guy that Daphne had stolen right from under Andrea's nose. As soon as Andrea got inside her apartment, she was going to break things. She was sure of it.

She depressed the clutch pedal, ignoring the brakes and grinding the lever down into second gear as she squealed onto Shady Brook Lane, then a hundred feet past the intersection whipped to her right into the Corners parking lot. She brought the Hyundai to a jolting halt in a space between a Ford Bronco and a fire engine–red Trans-Am, turned the key to kill the engine, and sat for a moment. Dodie Peterson. Sure. The Trans-Am was *Dodie Peterson's fucking car*. Dodie high-ass Peterson, the one who'd gotten Andrea to go blond in the first place. Andrea pictured the steel lug wrench in the Hyundai's trunk, then pictured herself swinging the wrench like Conan the Barbarian while she smashed every light and window in Dodie's car. The image made Andrea smile, and for seconds she considered actually doing it. Then she got out of her own vehicle and clattered in spike heels across the parking lot toward her apartment, a leggy platinum blond in a black miniskirt, listing some from too many whiskey sours and mad enough to chew on nails.

At the bottom of the stairs, Andrea paused long enough to stare daggers down the way at Dodie's place. She had another quick mental picture of herself, once again armed with the tire tool, only this time she was breaking all of the windows in Dodie's apartment. Never mind that Dodie Peterson hadn't ever *told* Andrea to change her hair color—had never even discussed anything with Andrea other than courthouse business, as a matter of fact— it was still all Dodie's fault, her swinging her ass around the courthouse with all those lawyers and FBI agents leering at her. Andrea actually took a step toward Dodie's place, then paused, giddily clutching the banister. To hell with it, Andrea didn't even have her nasty old tire tool along. With a final angry "Umph!" she clattered her way upstairs with her firm bottom wiggling and her high heels tottering from side to side. She was so mad at Dodie and that slut Daphne—and so tipsy from whiskey sours as well— that she failed to notice the old tan Buick as it cruised into the parking lot behind and below her. The Buick's lights were off.

Andrea fooled with her key, finally worked it into the lock to get the door open, and stumbled into her apartment, ranting and raving under her breath. She shoved the door closed behind her with her foot before she stalked to her bedroom. The pressure of her foot was less than firm and the plunger on the door lock failed to engage.

It was *her* car, the little green Hyundai, and he knew it without even reading the license number. He had the license plate memorized, just as he had every tiny snag in the smoothness of her underwear burned into his consciousness, and he knew every dent and spot of chipped paint on the Hyundai as well. One of the screws which held the chrome letters spelling out the car's make was missing, and it was the missing screw which identified her car for him. He'd removed the screw himself, in fact, one afternoon when his obsession with her had driven him to stand in the lot across from the Federal Building and gaze at her automobile for more than an hour, and he'd taken the screw home with him and placed it on his dresser among the secret pictures he'd taken of her, the bottle of nail polish he'd stolen from the medicine cabinet in her bathroom, and the pair of her false eyelashes, which occasionally he'd put on and wear in private. Never mind that it was only a common metal screw, it was part of *her*. And tonight, finally, he was going to touch her. He pressed lightly on the accelerator, pulled his sister's old Buick around to the other side of the Corners parking lot, stopped, got out, and followed the same path which *she* would have taken only moments ago. A light warm breeze touched his cheek and, heard in the distance, a water sprinkler spit and hissed.

His name was William Erly, though everyone had called him Rascal ever since his sister had hung the name on him when he was only five. He wasn't quite a street person. Though he dressed and shuffled his feet as if he was one of the homeless—and more than once of late had spent the night, unwashed and hungry, in the Salvation Army shelter on Young Street downtown—he did have a place to live and he did have money in his pocket. The money came, as always, from his sister, just as he'd lived rent free in his sister's house—except for the times he'd been in the county jail or Texas Department of Corrections—ever since his release, at age eighteen, from Buckner Orphans Home.

His parole had been up in June and he wasn't seeing a psychiatrist, even though the prison shrink at Eastham Unit had strongly recommended that he receive as much aftercare as possible. "As possible" had translated to Rascal's parole officer as "within the budget," which at the time of Rascal's release had been zero. He'd served four months of a three-year beef in prison for fondling a child, and if beatings and gang rapes at the hands of other inmates while the guards looked the other way hadn't been enough of a lesson, Rascal's parole officer had decided, then nothing was ever going to cure him. Besides, as Rascal had told the prison psychiatrist, it hadn't been the three-year-old he'd been interested in. It had been the child's *mother*, and touching the little girl had merely been contact with something—anything—which had belonged to the object of his infatuation.

He didn't like Andrea as a platinum blond—though, God, he still *yearned* for her—and once he got to know her he would tell her as much. It had been her soft brown wealth of hair, in fact, that he'd first noticed three weeks ago when she'd brushed close to him on the street, shot him a fearful glance, and hurried on her way, and he'd begun to follow her. He'd been near her for all of her waking moments since then, except for the times she'd been at work and he'd crept into her apartment to claim a few things that were a part of her. Tonight he wouldn't wake her, God, he'd *never* do that, but he would be with her while she slept, and sometime during the night he would lay his hand against her cheek. If she stirred at his touch, he would bolt and run before she had a good look at him, for she wouldn't understand and would probably scream. To touch her, though, he would take the chance.

Rascal knew that he was ugly—and if he ever forgot his looks, he always had his sister to remind him—and his narrow face, sagging jowls, and squinty, red-rimmed eyes embarrassed him.

Though he was only thirty he'd easily pass for fifty, and had the
brutality dealt in the Texas Department of Corrections to thank
for his three missing front teeth. He'd seen the disgust in Andrea's
face earlier that night when he'd tried to dance with her, and her
disgust had made him angry, and had caused him to make a fool
of himself. He had to take better control, that much he understood, and for once he was glad that Andrea didn't know his name.
He should never have approached her, should have kept his love
for her a secret known only to himself.

He reached the bottom of the staircase and began to climb,
touching the banister every two steps or so. The wads of paper
covering the holes in his shoes made whispery shuffling noises as
he ascended. He could have gone the rest of the way with his eyes
closed, so often of late had he been to her apartment. Overhead,
two faint stars twinkled through the haze.

He grabbed for the doorknob, at the same time fishing for the
key in his pocket. He'd taken a chance in getting the key, waiting
outside the District Clerk's office in the Federal Building until
she'd gone on an errand, taking the ring of keys from her purse
and having a duplicate made, and returning the key ring without
her knowing about it. The chance he'd taken had been more than
worth it. Tonight, though, he didn't need the key; the door swung
inward at his touch with a flick of metal and a whisper of wood
over shag carpet. Rascal paused on the landing and held his
breath. No sound came from within.

He had a small thin flashlight in his pocket, and now brought
the flashlight out and switched it on. He crouched down, poked
his head inside the doorway, and let the beam probe the darkened
apartment. The beam illuminated the green imitation leather
couch and chairs, the small portable TV on its rolling stand, the
tall corked wine bottles which sat on the counter between the
kitchen and living room. Her purse was on the couch—the small
black purse she carried when she went out in the evening. Rascal
had touched and fondled the little handbag many times and once
had sat on the edge of her bed to poke his erection inside the
purse and squeeze the purse's interior around his hardness with
his hands. On the floor in front of the couch were a pair of black
spike-heeled shoes, one standing, one lying on its side. Rascal had
handled the shoes as well and a week ago had spent the better
part of an hour with his nose inside them, sniffing the fragrance

of her feet. He remained in a crouch as he entered the room, then stood upright and clicked off the flash.

He picked his way around the living room furniture with the familiarity of a blind man at home, sidestepping the couch, chairs, and small coffee table on his way to the hallway that led to her bedroom. He stopped before entering the corridor to crouch beside Andrea's spike-heeled pumps. He handled them gently, righting the overturned pump and licking the toe of each shoe in turn. Then he went noiselessly down the corridor with the flashlight's beam illuminating the carpet before him.

Outside her bedroom, he got down on his haunches and placed his ear against the crack in the door, and readied the flashlight in his hand. He could remain this way for hours if he had to, listening for the measured sound of sleep breaths, and once he was sure she was asleep he would go inside. At the same time, he was tensed to spring for the living room if he should hear her approach the door. As he listened, Rascal softly closed his eyes.

She was breathing. God, she was *breathing*.

But the breathing noises which came from within the bedroom were ragged and tortured, more gasps than breaths, and in between the breaths she uttered a series of muffled whimpers. Rascal's eyes opened wide.

Was she in orgasm? God, was she *doing herself*? Not her, surely not her, not that creature. Dare he look? As he crouched beside the door with blood pounding through his temples, it was no longer a question of dare. Rascal Erly couldn't have resisted opening that door any more than he could have sprouted wings and flown out through the living room. He climbed to his feet and, with a sigh of anticipation, clicked on the flash and entered the bedroom.

For an instant he didn't understand what he was seeing. The flashlight's beam fell at once on the bed, and there on a smooth, tanned bare leg which was bent slightly at the knee. The muscles in the leg were taut with exertion, and in the perimeter of the flashlight's beam Rascal Erly caught a glimpse of yellow rope tied around the ankle and extending to one corner of the bed's footboard. Rascal's lips twisted in puzzlement as he swept the beam the length of the supple bare writhing body, past the dark patch of hair at the crotch—God!—and over the flat stomach and small breasts with pointed nipples, to finally illuminate . . . God!

The man who was bent over the girl had his back to Rascal. He wore a black one-piece covering of some kind (an image of the jumpsuit he'd worn while in county jail flashed through Rascal's mind), and the man's face was close to her throat. The girl's hands (Rascal was certain by now that they were *her* hands, even though he was praying that they weren't. God, that harm should come to her . . .) were raised over her head and her wrists were bound in the same fashion as her ankles. As Rascal watched, the man lifted his head and looked around, blinking in the light from the flash.

The man's face appeared pasty white in the flashlight's beam, and his eyes were coal-black slits. A dark liquid dripped from his chin. His mouth was curved in a mirthless smile.

Rascal Erly believed in ghosts and vampires and always had, and Halloween stories told in the dark scared him to death. The apparition before him in Andrea's bedroom would have scared anybody, but to someone like Rascal Erly the sight was enough to cause heart failure. Dracula lived. Dracula *lived*.

But the face—Rascal had seen the *face* before, though at the moment he was too piss-in-your-pants afraid to remember where. But it dawned on him through his panic that the face was real, that it was a familiar face, and that Rascal Erly didn't personally know any vampires. This, then, whatever it was doing here, had to be a man.

And all at once recognition flooded over Rascal. Standing here before him with Andrea Morton's blood dripping from his narrow chin was . . . was . . .

It was *the Heap*.

It had been more than a decade, fourteen years actually, since Rascal had seen that face, but the face of the Heap was one he'd never forget. The tortured features were burned into Rascal's mind just as was the Heap's terrible scarred body. At Buckner Home, the Heap had been a source of constant ridicule just as Rascal himself had been. Patrick Quarles. The Heap.

Quarles hissed at Rascal—*hissed*, and for just a second Rascal's mind clouded and he thought once again that he was seeing Dracula—then reached over the girl's body to pick up a pistol and level the gun at Rascal's face.

The Dracula image vanished from Rascal's mind like lightning as he stared down the barrel of the gun. Scared out of his wits as he was, Rascal had enough sense to know that a vampire didn't go around pointing guns at people. A real vampire would have shrunk at once into a bat and swooped at him. This was indeed the Heap, and the Heap was aiming a gun at him. Dim-witted though he might be, Rascal knew to run from a man with a pistol, and run like hell. He dropped his flashlight, charged out of the room, and ran down the corridor toward the living room. As he did, a deafening blast stunned his ears and a bullet splintered the doorframe.

Oscar Beemish, huffing and puffing, was within a hair of leaving Daphne and striking out into the night on his own. He'd forgotten all about the Texas trim after which he'd been lusting, and even the sight of Daphne's firm young ass wiggling along in front of him left him cold. Bunch of lunatics was all these Texas pussies were, just a bunch of fucking—

Daphne stopped in her tracks, pointed across the parking lot, and said, "There. Over there."

Beemish stopped as well, just feet behind her, and bent over to rest his hands on his knees. His collar was soaked with sweat; he'd given up on holding in his stomach, and his belt dug into his midsection. He turned his head in the direction where Daphne was pointing. "Over where?" Beemish wheezed. Christ, these Texas women were every bit as dumb as Texas corn-pone bankers. Maybe even dumber. Dumb as a fucking—

"The car. The Buick, right over there. Come on." Daphne lowered her arm and took off across the parking lot toward the row of apartment buildings. She moved from bright moonlight into deep rooftop shade.

Jesus Christ, Beemish thought, she's not even breathing hard. He squinted toward the parked car. So what if it was a fucking old Buick. Lots of old Buicks still on the road so all the spics and niggers would have something to drive. He raised his head to yell after Daphne, "Hey, don't you think we should call somebody? Cops or something?"

She shook her head and quickened her pace even more. "No time. No time."

Beemish sighed, wiped sweat from his forehead with the back of his hand, and strode lamely in pursuit. Jesus *Christ*, this was dumb. Oscar T. Beemish the Egg Roll Wizard, charging around the parking lot in some loony apartment complex in Bumfuck, Texas, chasing after some broad who'd rather go on a fucking marathon than spread her legs. Jesus, this was—

Daphne halted at the foot of a metal staircase. As Beemish drew alongside, she said, "Up there. Andrea lives first door on the right."

Beemish leaned on the banister, gasping for breath. "Huh?" he said.

"Up there. Right up there."

"*Me?*"

She backed up a step and put her hands on her hips. "Well you don't expect *me* to go up there alone. Really."

Beemish thought, Jesus Christ, women's fucking lib. Broads wanted everything equal, okay, until it came time to pick up the tab or whip somebody's ass. He unbuttoned and removed his coat. "Hold this," he said, and when Daphne took the coat and draped it over her arm he loosened his collar and yanked his tie off. "This, too," he said, and she reached for the tie and laid it over the coat. Not much better, but at least he could breathe. He let his belly overhang his belt; to hell with it, he was too tired to suck it in. He raised a hand to her, palm out. "Just wait here, okay?" Anything, anything to get this bummer of a night over with. He grabbed hold of the banister and climbed.

He'd managed three labored steps when, up above, a muffled explosion sounded. A door opened. A man ran outside and charged down the stairs toward him. The guy wore old beatup shoes and looked like a Bowery bum, a guy in raggedy-ass khaki pants and some kind of fucking work shirt, running downstairs like a bat outta hell. Jesus Christ, a fucking hobo yet. Beemish sagged against the banister and raised a hand.

He was able to say, "Hold—"

The hobo slammed into Beemish like a strongside linebacker, and Beemish had a closeup view of sagging cheeks, narrowed squinty eyes, and a mouth gaping open like a fish's mouth. The air flew out of Beemish's lungs in a whoosh. He staggered back, keeping his death grip on the banister and very nearly tumbling head-over-heels downstairs. The bum hardly broke stride, and thundered on. He reached the bottom of the steps, dodged around Daphne—who shrank back, clutching Beemish's coat and tie to her chest—and dashed into the parking lot.

Oscar Beemish's head was swimming. He watched the retreating man's backside and churning legs until the guy disappeared behind a row of cars. What the fuck am I supposed to be doing? Beemish thought. Oh, yeah. Yeah, climbing these stairs to some nutty broad's apartment, so another nutty broad won't have to put herself out any. Regular Sir fucking Galahad run over by a wild-ass hobo. Go on up, he thought, before the bum comes back. He put both hands on the banister to haul himself upward. As his blurry gaze roamed up the staircase, his eyes widened.

Jesus Christ, who was *this* fucking guy? Somebody'd turned loose one of the Munsters, a guy in black with a pale face which seemed white in the moonlight, and blood—Jesus, thought Beemish, they're not fooling the Egg Roll Wizard, that's a bunch of fucking ketchup—running down his chin, charging downstairs just like the hobo. Only the Munster—Grandpa, Beemish thought, it's fucking Grandpa Munster, that's who it is—was waving a gun. Jesus, thought Beemish, what an end for the Egg Roll Wizard. He flinched and raised his arm to protect his face.

The running man hit Beemish with a shoulder and kept on going. This time Beemish *did* go over, arms flailing, rooftops and moonlit sky whirling before his eyes. His shoulders landed painfully on metal, then his feet came over his head as he made a perfect backward somersault, scraping his knees on concrete and winding up on his haunches at Daphne's feet. I'm filing a fucking claim, Beemish thought. Suing the shit out of . . .

Painfully, Beemish rose. His shoulders throbbed and his knees burned like fire, but at least he wasn't dead. He turned and watched dumbly as Grandpa Munster took the same path as the hobo had taken, charging pell-mell into the parking lot.

Quarles went down the steps with the voices ringing in his ears. "Catch him, you must catch him," the high-pitched raspy voice told him, and the basso chimed in to say, "He knows you."

Quarles hadn't been expecting *anyone* to walk into that bedroom, much less someone that he knew. Had the filthy weasel Rascal recognized Quarles? Of course he had. Of all the people to . . .

The paunchy man on the staircase didn't matter. Quarles had never seen the man before and knocked him aside. Ditto with the woman at the bottom of the steps; Quarles swept by her with barely a glance in her direction. The raggedy man was the only one that mattered. He had to kill the raggedy man so that the raggedy man couldn't tell, and so the voices would quit screaming in Quarles's ear.

Quarles called on every ounce of strength within him, picking up speed, practically flying as he charged across the parking lot, dodging in between parked cars with his gaze sweeping, searching for the weasely . . . Rascal, Quarles thought, Rascal Erly, the prime whiner at the orphans' home. Always the loudest in calling out Quarles's hated nickname, the Heap, the first to giggle and point when Quarles removed his shirt, Rascal directing attention away from his own pitiful self. If it hadn't been for Rascal, in fact, Quarles's life at Buckner Home might even have been bearable. Quarles halted in the parking lot to look around, his chest rising and falling rapidly. Fifty yards ahead of him, a starter chugged.

The car was an old Buick with a faded DON'T MESS WITH TEXAS bumper sticker below its license plate, and Quarles squinted to make out the driver's scraggly, unkept head of hair. It was Rascal Erly, no doubt about it. As the Buick's starter wheezed and slowed, Quarles took five long running steps and leveled the gun in both hands.

The Buick's engine caught and raced, and the car screeched backward. With the bumper sticker approaching at breakneck speed, Quarles flinched. The pistol went off with a loud crack. As the recoil sent Quarles's hands up over his head, the bullet flew harmlessly over the Buick's roof.

Quarles barely had time to mutter, "Fuck." He dove headlong to his right as the Buick's fender banged into his shin; tears of pain jumped into his eyes as he hit the pavement rolling. Miraculously, he didn't drop the gun; as he rolled over and over the .38 went off again. A hundred yards away, a window shattered.

The Buick squealed to a halt, reversed its direction, and picked up speed. As Quarles struggled up on one knee to raise the .38, the car fishtailed out of the parking lot, careened to its right on Shady Brook Lane, and disappeared behind a row of buildings.

Quarles was suddenly afraid. Rascal Erly was gone, and Rascal Erly *knew*. Rascal Erly would *tell*.

Quarles stood. His injured leg buckled; he stumbled and righted himself. He wiped the back of his hand across his forehead, then stared in shock at the streak of red on his wrist. His teeth dug sharply into his lower lip.

And across the parking lot, the paunchy man from the stairs and his woman companion stood side by side, staring at him.

Stumbling, limping, gasping in pain, running his tongue over his lower lip for the last remnants of blood, Patrick Quarles made his tortured way to the adjacent apartment building and through the breezeway into the courtyard. Beyond the courtyard and behind the building was where Quarles's own auto was parked. On his way through the breezeway he passed the apartment where Donatello the drug dealer had lived, and where Quarles had taken his—not *his*, but the Truth's—most recent captive.

Just outside Donatello's apartment, a cat rested on its haunches. The animal was black as midnight. Its tongue flashed as it licked the backs of its paws to wash its face. As Quarles limped painfully by, the cat lifted its head to meow at him.

And then the cat said, in a deep basso voice, "You have failed. Failed, *failed*, FAILED." The words followed Quarles into the courtyard and echoed from the building walls.

After the Grandpa Munster character had disappeared through the breezeway across the parking lot, Beemish turned to Daphne and said, "Jesus Christ." His coat was folded over his arm and his tie was draped loosely around his neck. Every time he tried to straighten up he winced in pain; the fall down the metal staircase was going to leave one helluva bruise between his shoulder blades. All around and above him, lights winked on. A second-floor window rasped; a hoarse male voice yelled, "What the hell is going on?"

Daphne's forehead bunched in concern. She turned to direct her gaze upward, toward the landing at the top of the stairs. "Andrea. My God, *Andrea.*" She left Beemish and started up, taking the steps two at a time.

Beemish stooped to touch his wounded knee as he watched her go. *Now* she's going up, he thought. Now that poor old Oscar's gotten himself knocked silly by the hobo and the ghoul, *now* she's going up. He took two painful strides to follow, then stopped in his tracks.

Jesus Christ, what was he thinking about? The loan documents from Texas Bank of Commerce were in his briefcase back at the hotel, the ink was barely dry on them, and the bank wasn't funding the money for thirty more days. These Texas bankers were dumb as shit, that was true, but a helluva lot of them were fucking Baptists. Fucking Bible-banging Baptists. Beemish had almost screwed up at lunch that day and ordered a drink, then had wised up when he'd seen a couple of bankers squinting at him. And if they'd get uptight about a guy having a little drinkeroo, what would they say about the Egg Roll Wizard chasing around after a little strange poontang, huh? Why, they'd cancel the loan in a heart-beat, that's what they would do. Goodbye Egg Roll Hubba-Hubbas in Flint and Lansing, and goodbye spa and workout room.

And aside from the bankers, what would Miriam Beemish think about this shit? Never mind her, though, old Oscar had been pulling the wool over Miriam's eyes for years. But those fucking Baptist bankers, they'd be hell to deal with.

As Daphne went through the second-floor entry to Andrea Morton's apartment, Beemish turned at ground level and made tracks in the opposite direction. He'd gone halfway across the parking lot when he paused again. Not this way, turdhead, Beemish thought, this is the way the Munster guy went. Beemish made a quick left face and half-walked, half-stumbled out of the parking lot onto Shady Brook Lane. He hugged the sides of the apartment buildings as he went north, peering fearfully in all directions. If he ran into the vampire guy again, Oscar Beemish was going to die on the spot. Die and go to hell, that's what the Egg Roll Wizard was going to do.

Beemish found an all-night convenience store, a 7-Eleven, four blocks north on some fucking street or the other, and used the pay phone to call a cab. Then he stood on the curb and waited, glancing occasionally through the brightly lit window at shelves crammed with potato chips, shaving cream, toothpaste, and every brand of candy bar known. Christ, did the broad know his name? Oscar, yeah, but did she know his *last* name? Beemish wasn't sure. There was a rip in his pants leg (fucking thousand-dollar suit, Beemish thought) and skinned, bleeding flesh showed through the tear. Beemish lowered his forearm until his coat shielded the tear, then raised his gaze to the sky and whistled a nonchalant off-key tune.

He rode the taxi to the Adolphus, told the cabbie to wait and reinforced his request with a twenty-dollar bill, then limped past the check-in desk to the elevator. In his room, he changed into slacks and a sportshirt, and stuffed his belongings into his foldover Wayfarer zip-up bag. Then he made his painful way back to the elevator, rode to the lobby, and checked out of the hotel. The desk clerk, a young man in a gold blazer with the Adolphus emblem on the pocket, glanced at him rather strangely and did a double-take at the clock behind the counter, but dutifully rang up his bill and handed him his credit card slip to sign.

Beemish spent the rest of the night on a hardback chair in the waiting area at DFW International, snoozing as much as he could. Around three o'clock in the morning there was a huge flash of lightning outside, streaking across the runways, followed by a giant clap of thunder. Beemish leaped to his feet as though touched by a live wire and very nearly ran out of the terminal. Then he walked to the plate glass window and watched sheets of water cascade onto the wings of parked jet airliners and rolling baggage carts. Texas, Beemish thought. *The stars at night are big and bright.* Horseshit. He stretched aching muscles and returned to his seat. The rain continued for the better part of an hour. Oscar Beemish didn't sleep any more.

At six-thirty in the morning he forfeited the return portion of his thirty-day advance purchase ticket on the 11:50, and paid full fare for a seat on the 7:00 a.m. American. The plane had a two-hour layover in Kansas City, but Beemish didn't care about layovers. He wanted the fuck out of Texas. By the time the 747 bumped to a landing in Missouri, he was snoring like a buzz saw.

8

Bino was awake when the northbound warm front from the
Gulf collided with the eastbound cool mass of air from the
Rockies, causing stampede winds and a four-inch deluge which
fell unchecked for a little over an hour. He was sitting in his
underwear at the breakfast table in his kitchenette when the rain
began. His thick courtroom file lay open, and he'd been sorting
out what information he had on Annette Ray and Brenda Milton,
but he hadn't found much that he believed would help Mac
Strange. He was tempering his bleary-eyed survey of pictures and
profile sheets with short periods of watching Cecil the Oscar fish,
who was in turn watching him. Cecil floated motionless in his
tank between waving fins, his gaping mouth opening and closing,
and his expression said that he thought a guy sitting around in
Jockey briefs in the middle of the night was nutty as a fruitcake.
"Fuck you, Cecil," Bino had muttered a few minutes before the
downpour commenced. "I'm a lawyer—what can I tell you?" Cecil
had flicked his tail, sunk a few inches lower in the water, and had
looked as though he thought that being a lawyer was no excuse
for being a moron as well.

Bino had already tried in vain to sleep, but his fitful naps had
been filled with nightmares. He'd gone to bed early, around ten,
and before he'd turned off his bedside light he'd spent a few minutes reading about the Vampire of Sacramento in the paperback

book he'd gotten from Shoesole Traynor. Jesus, the guy really *had* gutted some of his victims. Not only that, but when the cops had arrested him he'd been carrying a box filled with bloody human parts. When Bino had reached *that* passage in the book, his lips had pulled back in disgust. He'd turned off the light, tossed the paperback across the darkened room, and buried his head underneath his pillow.

When he'd finally dropped off he'd dreamed about Dracula, wakened with a start, and gone back to sleep to dream of Dracula some more. At times the Prince of Darkness had been Bela Lugosi in black and white; on other occasions in Bino's dream the vampire had been Frank Langella in living color; but in each and every dream the victim had been the same girl with flowing blond hair who'd shrunk back in terror while the fiend had sunk bared fangs into the flesh of her throat. It was in the middle of about the third nightmare that Bino realized the victim was Dodie. He'd thrown back the covers in disgust, stomped into the kitchen and plopped his thick file onto the table, and there he'd been sitting ever since.

There wasn't much warning for the rain. One minute the night outside was calm, and the late September moon was beaming down; the next minute it was dark as Injun Joe's cave, the wind was screaming through the courtyards and breezeways of the Vapors North Apartments, and a single huge bolt of lightning flashed against a background of boiling cloud. The lightning was followed in seconds by a thunderclap which vibrated the windows and rattled the glasses on Bino's drainboard, then the rain began. There weren't any light warning drops, either; the heavens opened and a Niagara of water blasted the rooftops and splatted on the sidewalks.

Bino sat bolt upright at the table and swiveled his head to stare out the window. As sheets of water ran down the pane he pictured a bat, wings flapping like helicopter props, who came crashing into the kitchen to expand like magic into a man wearing a black cape, and who had blood dripping from his mouth. As Bino pictured the vampire, he glanced fearfully through the opening over the kitchen counter into the den, at the lowslung red velour couches and chairs, at the fifty-one-inch Mitsubishi TV screen like a giant unseeing eye. He laughed nervously and said to Cecil, "No sweat. Just . . . a little rough weather is all." Cecil twisted in the water and showed Bino his tail.

He closed the Mickey Stanley file with a thump and snap of

rubber bands, then he went to the refrigerator and poured himself a glass of orange juice. He slipped from the glass as he strolled into the den, peering nervously right and left, and approached the bank of tape cassettes mounted on the wall above his stereo. Music, that always calmed him down. He randomly pulled a cassette from the rack and read the label. Jesus—Michael Jackson, *Thriller*. He quickly replaced the Jackson tape and found one by Sinatra, plugged Old Blue Eyes in, and sank into one corner of the sofa, sipping orange juice while "New York, New York" played smoothly over the speakers, accompanied by the drumbeat of rain. In six hours, Bino was due in Hazel Sanderson's court. He was going to feel like shit.

When the storm blew in over the Village, Dodie Peterson wasn't asleep, either. In fact the same bolt of lightning which scared Bino half to death illuminated Dodie, slim legs showing in Levi cutoffs, wearing a T-shirt that was a hand-me-down from Bino. The T-shirt engulfed Dodie's upper body like a tent, and featured a cartoon of Peruna, SMU's Shetland pony mascot, pawing his way out of an earthen grave, above the caption, "Mustang Football '89, Alive and Kickin'." When the lightning struck, Dodie was padding barefoot down the sidewalk toward her apartment with her soft blond hair whipping around her head like Medusa snakes in the sudden gale. Her body was bent forward to fight the wind, and under her arm she carried a big orange plastic laundry basket. The basket was filled with freshly laundered towels, size 36-C Vassarette bras—some white, some pink, others lacy black—along with petite Jockey for Her cotton bikini panties in the same three colors. When the bolt of lightning sizzled across the heavens, she quickened her pace. The blast of the ensuing thunderclap sent her into a dead run, the hem of the T-shirt billowing behind her and the folded towels rising partway out of the laundry basket as it banged against her hip.

Like Bino in his far North Dallas digs, Dodie had gone to bed early and hadn't been able to sleep. She'd tried watching Jay Leno—who she thought took some getting used to but in the long run might be as good as Carson or even better—then, when the "Tonight Show" was over and she still wasn't drowsy, had struggled through a few pages of *The Kitchen God's Wife* by Amy Tan, loving the book but not being able to concentrate on what she was reading. Finally she'd turned off the light and buried her head underneath the pillow, but that hadn't helped, either. She kept picturing the tortured looks on Brenda Milton's parents' faces that afternoon at County Medical, and her own brief glimpse of the body in the vault, who'd turned out not to be Brenda after all.

Just two days before Annette Ray had disappeared, Dodie had taken Annette and Brenda to lunch at the Blue Front Restaurant and there had gone over both girls' proposed testimony with them. Now Annette was dead and Brenda was missing. Annette and Brenda had both been blonds. Dodie hadn't missed that.

Normally, Dodie didn't let herself get wrapped up in Bino's cases. After all, most of the clients who came to the office were creeps, and while there were a few whom Dodie liked personally— her favorite was a habitual burglar named Wimpy Madrick, who was so out-and-out ugly that Dodie thought he was cute—most of them got exactly what they deserved. "Everybody's entitled to a defense," was what Bino always said, but there were a few of his clients that Dodie doubted were entitled to the time of day.

The Mickey Stanley case, though, was different. Dodie was crazy about Kit, Mickey's mother, and had to admit that Mickey, with his aw-shucks grin and unaffected manner of carrying himself, had just the kind of looks that turned Dodie on. Not that she'd ever let herself get *involved* with a client—wow, she had enough trouble with her feelings for Bino himself, and the times in the past she'd let herself go overboard with her boss—but since Bino went around ogling every female under sixty, Dodie figured that a furtive glance at a client or two on her part wouldn't hurt anything.

And aside from Mickey and his mom, there were the witnesses, Brenda and Annette, both addicts. Just as Dodie herself had been an addict—was *still* an addict and knew it, though she hadn't touched narcotics in going on ten years now—and, if Bino hadn't found her in county jail and given her a job, would have probably been in the same boat as the two coeds.

Since she hadn't been able to sleep, Dodie had gotten out of bed, dug into her change jar for a handful of quarters, gathered up her things, and headed for the laundry room. On her way she'd seen a young woman in a brown pantsuit walking toward the parking lot with a chunky older guy in a suit huffing and puffing along a few feet behind her, but Dodie had lived at the

Village for a lot of years and didn't think much about two people stalking around after midnight. In the long run, Dodie had been lucky that her laundry was done when it was—five minutes later and she'd have been stranded in the deluge.

She charged up to her door, set the basket down, and dug in the pocket of her cutoffs for her key. She paused with the key in the lock and tilted her head. Down the way, something was going on.

Visible through the breezeway, an ambulance stood in the parking lot with its rooflights flashing. On either side of the ambulance was a black and white squad car. Down the sidewalk, a crowd had gathered at the foot of the metal staircase which led to the second floor of the building. Dodie squinted to make out two uniformed cops talking to three men, two of whom were wearing suits and the other of whom wore slacks and a knit sport shirt. In the semilight and the whirling red flashes from the ambulance, Dodie wasn't sure, but the angular guy in the sport shirt looked like Hardy Cole. There was a woman standing in the group who looked like the same woman that Dodie had seen on her way to the laundry room, but Dodie wasn't certain of that, either. She withdrew her key from the lock and took one step in the direction of the gathered crowd.

The sky opened and the rain pelted down like falling silver darts. Dodie uttered a startled "Eek," swept her laundry basket up in both arms, and shouldered her way into her apartment. Her hair was damp (There goes the old twenty-five bucks at the beauty shop, Dodie thought) and so were the towels in her basket. She muttered, "Damn!" Then she slammed the door, set the basket aside, and parted the drapes to peer out through the window. The crowd by the steps had broken ranks and was running for cover. As Dodie watched, the guy in the sport shirt disappeared around the corner of the building.

In the darkness of her apartment, Dodie Peterson hugged herself. She was suddenly cold.

Hardy Cole had a hard time giving instructions with a torrent of rain beating down on his head and shoulders, so he ceased his yelling and went through a rapid series of hand signals. The good-looking girl in the brown pantsuit—Daphne, Cole thought, and I'd damn sure better be remembering her name—got the message at once, ducking into the back seat of the black and white police cruiser, lifting her feet and swinging her legs up and inside the car. The flashing ambulance rooflights illuminated her chest, shoulders, and arms. Her pantsuit was soaked in blood up to the elbows.

Cole ignored the rain and stayed on the sidewalk, moving aside while the paramedics lugged the gurney past on their way to the ambulance. There were five of the white-suited guys, heads lowered in the downpour, two at each end to carry the gurney at a fast walk, and the fifth hurrying along to one side, keeping the pressure on the platinum blond's carotid artery. Like Daphne's, the fifth medic's forearms were covered with blood. Hardy Cole didn't profess to be any kind of medical wizard, but he'd seen enough auto wreck and stabbing victims to mentally chart the odds of survival based on the amount of blood loss he observed at the scene. Cole made the platinum blond's chances to be forty-sixty against making it, give or take. He was crossing his fingers and really pulling for her.

As the medics loaded the gurney into the ambulance, Cole sprinted for his own unmarked Chevy. He reached the car's side, gave a come-on wave to Mac Strange, then dove behind the wheel. Strange had been standing, dry as a bone, underneath the second-floor landing which hugged the perimeter of the building. He now ducked his head and jogged clumsily through the rain, dodging puddles as he ran, flung open the Chevy's passenger door and half-sat, half-fell in beside Cole. Water was running down the county prosecutor's face and his sparse hair was plastered on his head. The shoulders of his dark suit were drenched, while the rest of his clothing could pass for only wet.

"If we got a next life," Cole said, "let's *me* go to law school and *you* be the cop. I don't like hanging around out in the rain while you stand under the awning. Since when did they start sending prosecutors out on homicides? Three times in a row, huh?"

Strange showed a wry smile. Dim light from underneath the dash cast shadows across his face. "Every time there's something in Park Cities the D.A.'s office gets a call. They want to make sure no bigwigs' toes get stepped on."

"Well, in case you ain't noticed," Cole said, "those are Dallas squad cars sitting over there. The city boundary's three blocks west of here. I like it that way, these Dallas boys got their shit together."

"Me, too." Strange brushed off the front of his coat, reached down and did the same to his pants legs. "But there's still the connected cases, out at SMU." He swiveled his head to look at the black-and-white, maybe thirty feet from the Chevy. Visible through the squad car's backseat window, the girl had raised her forearms to examine her sleeves. "Young lady done good, huh?" Strange said.

"Better than good," Cole said. "She called 911, then she held that artery down with her thumb till the medics showed. Any chance the blond's got she owes to her girlfriend." He thoughtfully scratched the underside of the visor with his thumbnail. His hands were wet and his nail left a trail of moisture on the vinyl. He wiped his hands on his pants legs. "Jesus, this is wearing the old man out, Mac. Last night I got three hours' sleep, tonight maybe four."

"That makes two of us." Strange used his cupped hand to stifle a yawn. He hadn't shaved. Cole tried to recall how many times in the past twenty years he'd seen Mac when the prosecutor had a stubble on his face. Hardy couldn't remember any.

"We'll get the whole skinny downtown," Cole said, "but the girl said something about a guy being with her when the perp ran past them on the stairs. The perp knocked the guy down. Brave son of a bitch ran off someplace and left the girl alone with her friend. Maybe I ain't doing so hot with finding Brenda Milton, but *that* Romeo asshole I'm going to locate. Trust me. Beginning tomorrow."

Strange lifted a hand, bent his fingers to study his manicure. "Sounds like a good idea." He fished a roll of Lifesavers from his inside pocket, extracted one with his thumbnail, and popped it into his mouth. The odor of wintergreen drifted through the car's interior. He offered the package to Cole. "Want one?" Strange said.

"No thanks. And when I get my hands on the guy I'm going to—" Cole's head tilted on his thin corded neck. "Whatcha mean, '*sounds like*'?"

Strange put the mints away and nervously cleared his throat. "Just what I said. Sounds like. But let's don't do anything till this meeting tomorrow afternoon. We're going to—"

"*Mac.*"

"—listen to some people"—the prosecutor scooted forward in the seat and propped his knee against the dash, his gaze straight ahead while rain bombarded the windshield—"who are the same people that are going to talk to that young lady downtown tonight. We won't be in on it. They're from VICAP."

"Jesus fucking *Christ* . . ."

"You know, Violent Criminal Apprehension Program, National Center for Violent Crime. A mouthful, huh? FBI, Washington. And in case you're wondering, Hardy, I don't like it any more than you do, but I'm not running the show. From now on when these people say jump, we say, 'How far?' That's the word they're giving me, and that's the word I've got to give you." Strange folded his arms.

Cole also looked straight ahead. His jaws bunched and his eyes narrowed into slits. He didn't say anything for a few seconds, then said, slowly and evenly, "Well I'll tell you something. They can call in the FBI, Secret Service, whatever. They can call in the U.S. Coast Guard and the Pony fucking Express if they want to. But this motherfucker's mine." He turned toward the prosecutor. "Book it, Mac. And tell 'em Hardy P. Cole told you, anybody wants to know."

Brenda Milton also was awake to hear the thunder, and the sound of the sudden deluge heard through the ceiling told her something new. She was either inside a one-story building or, if there was more than one floor, she was at the top. She filed the data away in her storehouse of useless information, lifted her fanny to give her flesh some relief from the coarse-grained wood, then relaxed, turned her head sideways, and closed her eyes.

Mercifully, the pelting of the water on the roof put Brenda to sleep in minutes. In her dreams a parade of homecoming floats passed by, decorated with red and blue chrysanthemums. A queen with a sparkling crown sat at the pinnacle of one of the floats, wearing a blue satin gown. The lovely face framed by the crown and wealth of luxuriant blond hair was her own. Brenda Milton stirred in her sleep, and her lips curved upward in a pretty smile.

Patrick Quarles never heard the thunder, and never knew that it was raining. He was sound asleep, lying on his side with one arm bent and his cheek resting on his hand. Most nights Quarles tossed and turned, but after he'd performed a service in the name of the Truth the voices would leave him alone and allow him to rest. He needed the sleep.

On a nearby chair a dark suit, white shirt, and tie were neatly laid out, and on the floor beside the chair sat a pair of black polished shoes. Quarles was due at work in the morning at nine. If he was late, the folks at the Federal Building would give him hell.

9

Roscoe T. Gillingham's twenty-three years with the U.S. marshal's service had taught him that the better people, if they bided their time, got the better jobs. So five years ago, when United States District Judge Hazel B. Sanderson had appointed him bailiff in her court, Roscoe hadn't been particularly surprised. That the young squirts around the courthouse—fresh-faced kid marshals without enough time in the service to amount to a popcorn fart, FBI agents who thought that Hoover's men were the only law enforcement people that amounted to a hill of beans, and just-out-of-law-school federal prosecutors who figured the government service for a stepping stone to making some big money defending the likes of drug dealers and tax dodgers—called him an "old woman" to his back, and had hung the nickname of Barney Fife on his sloping shoulders, none of this bothered Roscoe T. Gillingham one iota. Roscoe T. Gillingham was going to run this here courtroom to a tee, and anybody that didn't like the way Roscoe did things could go and talk to Judge Hazel about it. The judge would tell 'em where to get off, where Roscoe T. Gillingham was concerned.

This morning Roscoe had arrived on the job at seven-thirty—hour-and-a-half early, by God, and never asking for one penny overtime or compensatory days off for giving a little extra—and by eight-thirty he'd gone through a pot of coffee and figured his share of the civil service retirement fund down to the penny. Then he'd checked on the Stanley trial witnesses and found them all present, accounted for, and seated in the amen row. When there was a trial going on, the federal prosecutor furnished Roscoe a daily list of witnesses who were due to testify, and Roscoe by God made sure that the witnesses were there on time. Had the witnesses report by eight-thirty even though court didn't convene until nine and even instructed the snitches how to dress. Roscoe didn't have any control over witnesses who weren't under a plea bargain agreement to testify, but he watched over those who *had* made deals like a marine drill sergeant. Modest skirts and blouses for the women—none of that tight-britches, tight-sweater, dope-fiend shit—and dark suits, ties, white-sidewall haircuts, and polished shoes for the men were all that Roscoe would tolerate. If the witnesses didn't like it, by God, then they could just fall into the holding cell with the rest of the jailbirds. This morning the witnesses were all shipshape and in apple-pie order, even more so than usual. Roscoe then saw to the jurors' comforts—a fresh pot of coffee in the jury room, soft drinks in the icebox, and sandwiches ready in case deliberations were on the fierce side—then headed for the judge's chambers to make certain that things were as Hazel Sanderson wanted them. If there was one thing that Roscoe knew, it was which side his bread was buttered on, and he realized better than anyone that as long as he made certain her Mr. Coffee contained exactly a scoop-and-a-half of Luzianne, that plenty of powdered cream and little pink Sweet 'n' Low packets were on hand, and that the thermostat in her chambers was set exactly at seventy-one degrees, then Judge Hazel was going to let Roscoe continue to run this here courtroom any way that he pleased. By God.

Roscoe strolled past the courtroom's rear entrance on his way to the judge's office, a short, slightly stooped, gray-haired man in gray slacks and a navy blazer, his gaze roaming from side to side. The two young marshals had already brought Mickey Stanley over from the Lew Sterrett Justice Center and were sitting on a bench with the prisoner handcuffed between them. Right smart early, Roscoe thought, and also thought that the two wet-eared marshals wouldn't have arrived until after court had convened if they didn't know that being late would earn them a ration of shit from Roscoe T. Gillingham. The marshals wore Stetsons and cowboy boots.

One was reading the newspaper and the other a *Time* magazine. The prisoner was dressed in an expensive drug-dealer navy suit, white drug-dealer Christian Dior shirt, and red drug-dealer Countess Mara tie. He was rubbing his wrists where the handcuffs had dug into his skin and had a morose expression on his square handsome face, which to Roscoe's way of thinking was tough shit. *Don't do the crime if you can't do the time,* asshole, Roscoe thought. He nodded to the marshals and moved on. The judge's chambers were the fourth door down on the left; the door moved on noiseless hinges as he entered her reception area.

The judge's secretary wasn't there, of course—usually five, ten minutes after nine, Roscoe thought, and one day soon Roscoe was going to have a talk with the young woman, let her know how the cow ate the cabbage, by God, where the government service was concerned—so Roscoe picked up a dust cloth and did a little cleaning up, taking extra precaution with the gilt pole from which hung the giant Stars 'n' Stripes. Then he straightened the legal journals into a neat stack on the coffee table, in easy reach of any visitors who were seated on the leather sofa, made a mental note that there were only two peppermint sticks left in the jar—Judge Hazel had two sticks a day, one on her way to court and the other on her way home—and took a couple of steps toward the judge's office. He stopped in his tracks. Light was streaming through the crack at the bottom of the closed door.

Judge Hazel? No way: The judge walked through that entry at five till nine on the dot, rain or shine, and that was ten minutes from now. But who else would have the nerve to go in judge's chambers without checking with Roscoe T. Gillingham? Well whoever it was, they were fixing to get themselves a piece of Roscoe's mind. His forehead wrinkling into a frown, Roscoe turned the knob and walked briskly inside.

It *was* the judge, by God, and she was already seated behind her polished mahogany desk, wearing her robe. As Roscoe entered the judge narrowed her eyes behind Martha Washington glasses. Her loaded-for-bear expression made Roscoe just a tad nervous. Seated across from her were Mr. Goldman the prosecutor, Bino Phillips the defense lawyer, and a tall man whom Roscoe didn't know. By God, even the court reporter was in there, the young guy with the uppity manner about him and, Roscoe thought, a license to steal from the government merely because he'd been to the Texas School of Court Reporting and knew how to run a shorthand typewriter. Roscoe checked his watch. He'd set it that morning by the clock atop the Dallas County Government Center on his way to the Federal Building and knew the watch couldn't be wrong. He held his wrist close to his ear. No sir, ticking away. Roscoe cleared his throat.

"What is it?" Judge Sanderson said. "We're busy in here." She'd been reading from a small stack of stapled letter-size pages, and the thunder was in her eyes. Whatever this powwow is about, Roscoe thought, these men had better mind their p's and q's.

"Just doing my job, judge," Roscoe said, drawing up to his full five-eight. "The witnesses are here, dressed good and proper for court, and the jurors taken care of." As if anybody would have to worry about that, Roscoe thought, with Roscoe T. Gillingham on the job.

Judge Hazel resumed her reading. Her gaze on the page before her, she said, "Well, send them home. No court today, Roscoe." Behind her on her credenza, the Mr. Coffee was half full and the red light was on. Goldman had a Styrofoam cup balanced on the arm of his chair, the stranger had an identical cup to Goldman's resting on his knee, and steam was rising from the judge's big brown mug.

Roscoe spoke without thinking. He said, "But you said yesterday that . . ." Then trailed off, already regretting his words.

Her head snapped to her right as she threw Roscoe a glare that might set the drapes on fire. She removed her glasses and blinked. "I know what I said. That was yesterday. This is today. No court." She replaced her glasses on her nose and straightened the file that she was reading with a papery rattle. "That's all, Roscoe."

Roscoe practically bit his tongue to keep from telling her exactly what he thought, lowered his head, and backed out of the room. No matter what he thought, she was the judge. If Roscoe wanted to go on running this here courtroom as he pleased, he couldn't afford to be on her bad side. He softly closed the door and retreated to the corridor.

Thanks you get, by God, Roscoe thought. Bet her coffee ain't worth shit, neither.

Bino was absolutely dying for a cup of that coffee, but the old heifer hadn't offered him any and he was damned if he'd ask for it. *Goldman* had coffee, of course—old Marv, in fact, was practically waving the cup under Bino's nose every time the prosecutor lifted it to his mouth to drink—and so did Goldman's tall, rangy sidekick. Both Goldman and his buddy had been slurping coffee when Bino had come into the meeting a couple of minutes before the bailiff. So far, except for a curt nod, Hazel Sanderson hadn't acknowledged Bino's presence. Tough it out, Bino thought.

After the thunderstorm had subsided, he had spent the rest of the night in his living room listening to music, showered and shaved around six, stumbled into light gray suit, white shirt, and navy blue tie, and slapped his own face repeatedly to stay awake while driving the Linc downtown. When he'd entered his office at seven-thirty, the phone was ringing. When he'd answered, Hazel Sanderson had said, "Meeting in my chambers, Mr. Phillips, eight-thirty. Don't be late." Then she'd hung up on him. Bino had groaned, then had tilted his swivel chair and dozed off at his desk. Dodie had shaken him awake when she'd come in at eight-thirty, and he'd jogged the five blocks to the Federal Building with his briefcase banging against his leg and his tie flying out behind him. He'd barged into the meeting, huffing and puffing, fifteen minutes late. Jesus, he wanted some of that coffee. He licked dry lips with a dry tongue.

Judge Sanderson laid the papers down and regarded the court reporter. "These transcripts here. You're certain they're word for word?"

The young guy smiled. "Absolutely, Your Honor." He reached in the side pocket of his dark suit and produced a small tape recorder. "What I do is, in addition to typing in the courtroom, I'm recording the proceedings. After I transcribe, I play the tape back and compare it with what's on paper. Any corrections necessary, I make them." He turned his smile toward Goldman and Bino. "That's not for publication, by the way—I know you're not supposed to have recording equipment in federal court." He looked back to Hazel Sanderson. "Word for word, Your Honor, I'll stake my life on it."

She regarded her own folded hands. "All right, then. That's all."

The court reporter was apparently used to quick dismissals from federal judges, and didn't look fazed in the slightest. He stood, smiled and nodded to Bino, Goldman, and the stranger, and left.

When the court reporter had gone, Hazel Sanderson said, "How long of a delay, Mr. Goldman?"

Goldman tugged on his goatee as he extended his other hand, palm up, in the direction of the stranger. "I'll have to leave that up to Mr. Deletay. I'm only acting on orders from above, Your Honor."

Bino's chin lifted. "Huh? I beg your pardon, but I don't know what's going on here." He wasn't wide awake, but at least was getting his interest up.

Goldman showed even white teeth in a half smile, half smirk. "You should get up in the morning, buddy. We've already been through this." He leaned on his armrest, tilting muscled shoulders. Jesus, Bino thought, why does Goldman always look like he could step into the ring as a middleweight?

"You have a point, Mr. Goldman," Hazel Sanderson said, looking Bino up and down. "Well whose fault is it that you *don't* know what's going on? I said eight-thirty, Mr. Phillips. In your experience with me, when I say eight-thirty do I actually mean a quarter to nine?"

Bino dropped his gaze. "No, ma'am. I had a tough night."

"You act like you're wanting a tough *day*, too," Hazel Sanderson said.

Bino was getting more and more awake every second, and a slow burn was beginning to rise in his cheeks. He sat up straighter in his chair. "Well," he said, "okay. I'm late. Does that mean I'm not supposed to be let in on what this is?"

Hazel Sanderson's eyebrows raised. Bino doubted that anyone besides him ever backtalked her, except maybe a few guys as she handed them out forty- or fifty-year sentences, which likely accounted for Bino's position on Hazel Sanderson's shit list. He didn't let it worry him, though—she wasn't going to run over him. Nobody was. The judge opened her mouth to speak, but before she could say anything the newcomer cut in.

"Excuse me, judge," the stranger said in a deep, radio-announcer baritone. "But I haven't met this gentleman." He stood, leaned across Goldman, and extended his hand toward Bino. "Nelson Deletay," the stranger said, "VICAP." He pronounced his name *Deel*-tay, and he had the same expression that Bino had once seen on Roger Staubach, just before Bino had gotten up the nerve to ask Staubach for his autograph on a football. The standard I-know-you've-heard-of-me-but-I'm-going-to-be-modest look. Bino had given the ball to Half's nephew as a birthday present, and the gift had tickled the kid to death, but Bino hadn't liked asking for the autograph. He took Deletay's extended hand and shook it. Deletay's grip was too tight; not quite a bone-crusher grip but damn close, more like a politician who was getting across the message that you'd better vote for him if you didn't want the *real* muscle to come calling. Bino would have had to stand to see if Deletay was as tall as Bino's own six-six, but it would be close. Deletay looked mid-forties, with a serious, sharp-featured face and iron gray hair that was styled and sprayed. Bino didn't trust anybody whose hair didn't move. "Hi," Bino said. "Bino Phillips. "

"Nelson jetted in from Washington this morning," Goldman said. "You know about VICAP." The last part was a statement and not a question. Goldman's tone had a reverence about it, as though the Pope had come for a visit. Deletay continued to regard Bino as though Bino was one of the serfs and Deletay lived in the big house on the hill.

"Sure," Bino said. "Glad to meet you. I got a question."

Deletay glanced first at Goldman, then at Hazel Sanderson, then gave a hearty chuckle. "I'll answer if I can," Deletay said. "But don't expect someone from Quantico to have *all* the answers. We don't claim to."

"Well," Bino said, "me and Barney—Barney Dalton, he's this friend of mine—we go a lot to this place called Joe Miller's Bar. It's this place out on Lemmon Avenue, a lot of writers hang around, a few lawyers and . . . never mind, you don't need to know all that. But anyway, Barney and I are going to have a party for one of Barney's girlfriends on her birthday."

Goldman and Hazel Sanderson were both fidgeting, while Deletay's expression was one of forced patience. Bino went on.

"And we're having this band, pretty good group, plays, you name it, all the way from Willie Nelson to the Doors, and that's a pretty big spread. Well what I was wondering is, it's just a one-night deal and we're not charging any cover charge, but—" Deletay's expression was beginning to evolve from one of patient interest to one of out-and-out irritation—"they *are* going to charge for everybody's drinks. So tell me. Do we have to pay you guys anything?"

Goldman and the judge exchanged glances while Deletay frowned. "I beg your pardon?" Deletay said.

"I want to get it from the horse's mouth," Bino said. "VICAP's got a local office here that goes around collecting from all the clubs, but they don't seem to know. What they say is, if you perform live music and charge people to listen, then VICAP's got to get its cut so all the artist's copyright is protected. But on a one-time party like that, the local guys here don't have the answer." He grinned around at the room in general.

There was stony silence. Deletay's features sagged. Hazel Sanderson regarded Bino as though the big white-haired lawyer had just grown a second head. Goldman tugged fiercely at his goatee. Finally, Goldman said, "Jesus Christ, Bino. The outfit that monitors music copyrights, that's ASCAP. Nelson's from VICAP, that's the Violent Criminal Apprehension Program. National Center for Violent Crime."

Bino glanced at Goldman, then at Deletay, then leaned back and folded his arms. "Oh," Bino said. "Wrong group. I don't guess I do have a question, then."

More silence, punctuated by a noise like a deflating tire as Deletay expelled the breath from his lungs. Deletay resumed his seat, propped his elbow on his armrest, and rested his forehead on his knuckles, regarding his knees. "Ex-excuse me, judge, for interrupting."

"No apology needed, Mr. Deletay," Hazel Sanderson said. "And no more comedy, Mr. Phillips, is that clear?"

"Huh?" Bino said. "I just thought—"

"*No more comedy.*" Hazel Sanderson pointed a wavering finger. She rattled the papers before her like a circus strongman preparing to rip a phone book in half. "And since you're the defense attorney in this case, yes, you're entitled to know what's going on. And if you'll refrain from interrupting, I'll tell you. All right?"

Bino smiled and nodded. "Mind if I have a cup of coffee?"

"Yes, I mind," she said. "Now, as you know, I'm getting transcripts of these proceedings, skimpy as the proceedings are at this point, for review in ruling on the defense's motion for a mistrial. *Your* motion, Mr. Phillips."

"*His* witnesses," Bino said, pointing at Goldman. "They were the ones in the courtroom when they weren't supposed to be." Goldman rolled his eyes.

"I'm aware of that," Hazel Sanderson said. "But before I rule on *your* motion, there's a new motion before me. Handed to me last night by messenger. *This* motion: Mr. Goldman's motion." She held up the sheath of papers that she'd been studying.

Bino sat up straighter. "Wait a minute. I didn't get a copy of that. I'm supposed to have a copy of any motion the government files, unless the rules have changed."

Goldman sank lower in his own chair as he practically mumbled, "I'll see that you get one, buddy."

"Now *this* motion," Hazel Sanderson said, ignoring the interchange, "is for a continuance. The government is now wanting to stop the trial for sixty days. I want to cooperate as much as possible, but I've got to say I don't see any legal basis for delaying a trial in progress. Highly irregular."

"Sounds like a lot of motioning to me," Bino said. He looked to Goldman. "Let's cut through all the gobbledygook. How come you want a delay, Marv?"

"It's these murders," Goldman said. "People around the courthouse disappearing. You seen the morning paper?"

Bino frowned. One thing he'd caught in all the conversation yesterday with Mac Strange was that the county folks didn't want the reporters in on this. Might cause a panic. Nolan Pounds? Bino thought. The true-crime guy, maybe, shooting his mouth off? "I haven't seen much of anything this morning," Bino said.

Goldman reached down beside his chair, picked up his briefcase, and snapped it open. He reached inside, produced a copy of the *Dallas Morning News*, and handed it over. "Maybe you'd better glance at it, then," Goldman said.

It didn't take much of a glance. The headline was across the top of the front page, "AUTHORITIES FEAR SERIAL MURDERS," followed by the smaller caption underneath, "FBI to Aid in Courthouse Ritual Killings." What the hell was going on? Goldman had said that Deletay only flew into Dallas that morning. How did . . . ? Bino scanned the article. Jesus Christ. Deletay had called the Dallas paper yesterday, from his office in Quantico, and given a full-blown interview. Like a publicist calling to say that a star was coming in to promote his movie. Bino let the paper fall into his lap. "What about Mac Strange?"

Deletay lifted his head from resting on his knuckles. "Who?"

Goldman lifted a hand. "No big deal. Just the local guy that's been handling it."

"Oh," Deletay said. "We keep the local boys filled in. No cause for alarm."

"Nice of you," Bino said.

"What seems to be happening here," Deletay said, "is that the victims are being put on display. As witnesses in a drug trial, mainly, though the young lady last night worked in the Federal District Clerk's office. Our person unknown seems to be sitting back and picking his conquests like a man in a shooting gallery, watching the mechanical ducks parade by."

"Huh? Last night?" Bino said. He looked down at the paper.

"Another one, buddy," Goldman said. "Right across the parking lot from the guy they found yesterday."

Jesus, the Village again, this one even closer to Dodie's front door. Dodie hadn't said anything about— Come to think about it, though, she hadn't had a chance to say anything. The second that she'd shaken him awake, Bino had bolted for the courthouse.

"So what we're going to do here," Deletay said, "is shut down his playhouse for the time being. The only way to effectively do that is to delay this trial until our man is in custody." What *we're* going to do, Bino thought. A moment ago, Deletay had called the killer, *our* person unknown. Mac Strange wasn't going to like this worth a damn.

"All this you're wanting to do is understandable under the circumstances," Hazel Sanderson said. "But we're still in a court of law. There just isn't any precedent for stopping a trial because some murders are going on, not that I've ever heard of."

"There's more to it, your honor," Goldman said. "The powers that be are placing me on temporary assignment. Until the killer is out of circulation I'm to devote a hundred percent of my time to whatever legal matters that the VICAP people need assistance with. Search warrants, record subpoenas, or whatever. Obviously I can't work with Nelson and be in trial at the same time." He paused to lick his lips. "You'll notice I'm requesting the delay, officially, to give us more time to get our evidence in shape."

"But that's not a legitimate reason for a continuance, either, Mr. Goldman," the judge said. "The government's ducks are supposed to be in a row before they ever indict anyone."

"So it says in the book," Bino said.

"I told you, Mr. Phillips," the judge said. "No more comedy."

"Sorry, judge," Bino said. "I was just thinking out loud. But, hey, listen, what's the problem? All you have to do is, you don't even have to rule on Marv's motion. All you have to do is pigeon-hole *my* motion."

Judge Sanderson's eyebrows lifted. She wouldn't like the source, but she was getting the idea. "I hadn't thought of that," she said.

"Sure," Bino said. "You can't grant a continuance, but there's no time limit in ruling on a motion for mistrial. Just take my motion under advisement and rule on it once the guy is caught. That's all."

The judge laid Goldman's proposal aside and reached for the trial transcripts, which the court reporter had left on the very front edge of her desk. "Great idea. If you'd point your efforts more toward the practice of law and less toward levity in the courtroom, Mr. Phillips, no telling what you might accomplish."

"Well, you know, judge," Bino said. "All work and no play."

Hazel Sanderson's lips twitched, and for an instant Bino thought she was actually going to grin at him, but she caught herself. "Well, gentlemen, that's what I'm going to do. I'm taking the defense motion for a mistrial under advisement, and you can let anyone know that the ruling may take a while. How about that?"

"Right on," Bino said. He wondered if she was tickled enough so that she'd give him some coffee, but decided he'd already pushed it with her as much as he should.

Goldman leaned over and whispered something to Deletay, who nodded. Goldman turned to Bino. "There's a couple of more things, buddy," the prosecutor said.

Bino touched his fingertips together. "Why am I not surprised?"

"There's a meeting—" Goldman said, "well, I'd better let Nelson . . ."

Deletay didn't need much urging to take the floor. "I've called all the troops together, all the different law enforcement agencies that've been involved in this thing, to sort out and coordinate information. One o'clock today, the conference room over at the Dallas County Courts Building."

Bino didn't know whether or not he should tell Deletay that Mac Strange had invited him to the same meeting. He decided that he shouldn't. "Hey, great," Bino said. "That's where Mac Strange works, you two could—"

"The Dallas Police are coming," Deletay said. "Plus the University Park Police, and the Dallas County investigators. Trade information, you know?"

"*Trade* information?" Bino said. "Or *get* information, from them to you? There's a difference."

Deletay had the formula for dodging sticky questions down pat: He simply ignored them. "And I'd like to have you and Mr. Goldman attend," Deletay said.

"Why's that?" Bino said. "I'm not investigating anybody. I'm just a lawyer." His own words sounded familiar to him, and he thought a minute. Oh, yeah. Yesterday, he'd said almost the same thing to Mac Strange, while Mac was hauling him around identifying bodies.

Deletay and Goldman exchanged glances again. Then Goldman sat forward and said, "Okay, buddy, here's the deal—in a nutshell. Two out of three missing women are your witnesses in the drug trial. We're going to need whatever information you've got on Annette Ray and Brenda Milton, both from your files and the things you might remember about them." He shuddered. "Jesus Christ, drinking blood."

So the feds wanted exactly the same information that Mac Strange had asked for. Bino crossed his legs and didn't say anything.

"Additionally," Goldman said, "since it seems to be your trial witnesses our man is interested in, we'd like to see your information on the rest of your witnesses. So that Nelson and his people can determine which ones, if any, are likely future victims."

Deletay nodded.

"And I saw the big files you've got, Bino," Goldman said, "with the rubber bands around them. I mean, they were right there in the courtroom, buddy, right there in plain sight. And I could tell from the questions you were asking that you've got some background stuff on my witnesses, too." The prosecutor grinned and yanked on his goatee.

Bino was finally getting it. He pointed at Deletay and said to Goldman, "You want me to turn over my case files to him," Bino said. "To Nelson."

Goldman nodded, still grinning.

"Just to him. Not to Mac Strange," Bino said.

Goldman nodded again.

"And maybe you could help old Nelson look them over, Marv," Bino said.

"Now wait a minute," Goldman said.

"And then maybe you and old Nelson could make a few Xeroxes, huh?" Bino sat back and folded his arms. "Not without a court order, Pancho."

Goldman now looked to Hazel Sanderson, who snapped, "Don't you cooperate with *anyone*, Mr. Phillips?"

"Sure do, judge," Bino said. "I cooperate with every court order that gets served on me. I don't know what legal precedent you'd use to make me turn my files over to *this*"—he pointed at Deletay—"guy, but I'd be interested to see."

Judge Hazel looked at the ceiling. Bino had her there, and she knew it.

"But," Bino said, "just so everybody won't think I'm a sorehead, tell you what. I'll come to your meeting, Mr. Deletay. Yesterday I agreed to go over my files and give what dope I had on those same witnesses to Mac Strange. I'll come to your meeting, and if Mac gives the word, the files are yours. How's that?"

"The county guy?" Deletay said, as though he was talking about one of the street sweepers.

"That's who he's talking about," Goldman said.

"Oh," Deletay said, "that shouldn't be much of a problem."

"Don't bet on it," Bino said.

Hazel Sanderson opened her top desk drawer and dropped the trial transcripts inside. "You gentlemen are going to have to continue your battles elsewhere," she said. "I've done everything I can to help you, but I've got other matters. I think we're through." She showed Bino a defiant glare.

Deletay and Goldman exchanged more looks. Goldman snapped his briefcase closed.

"Not quite," Bino said. "There's one more issue."

Hazel Sanderson slammed her drawer with a bang, and for an instant Bino wondered if she'd broken the damned thing. "Oh, enlighten us, Mr. Phillips," she said. "What could that possibly be?"

"Bond," Bino said.

Goldman had half-risen, preparing to leave, and now sat back down. "Huh?"

"Bail. For my client. You know, the guy on trial."

"Oh, come *on*," Hazel Sanderson said.

Deletay resumed his "The Thinker" position, elbow on armrest, forehead resting on his knuckles.

"I haven't made a big deal out of this," Bino said, "because I thought we were getting on with the trial. But it's been ninety days since you last denied him bond, and he's entitled to another hearing. If you're going to take the motion for mistrial under advisement, this can drag on and on with him in jail. Mickey's lived around here all his life and I doubt that the government can show he's any kind of risk to run off. He'll be released to his mother. I think he's entitled to bond, and I think that's something I *can* show legal precedent for." He showed Hazel Sanderson a determined blink.

"But you . . ." The judge's face reddened. Her jaw puffed out. "Taking the motion under advisement to cause a delay in the proceedings, that was *your* idea."

Bino grinned from ear to ear. "I know," he said.

"Wait a minute." Goldman was out of his chair now, bouncing up and down on the balls of his feet. "Just a minute, here. This man's charged with enough to send him away for sixty years."

"Charged with," Bino said. "*Charged with*, that's all. He's entitled to bond, judge, and I wouldn't be any kind of lawyer if I didn't try to get it for him."

Hazel Sanderson's eyes narrowed, and Bino snapped that she was taking hold of herself to keep from flying completely off the handle. "I think this is a cheap trick," she said. "Suppose I don't grant him bond. Then what?"

"Well, Mickey doesn't have any money to speak of," Bino said. "His mother's paying my fee out, bless her heart, over a hundred years or something. So I guess what I'm saying is, if you don't let him have bail, then I'm going to have to buy my own ticket to New Orleans, to the Fifth Circuit Court of Appeals. I think I could get him bond from the Fifth Circuit within forty-eight hours, judge. Maybe I couldn't, but I think I could." He threw a cold stare in Goldman's direction, then returned his attention to Hazel Sanderson. He wasn't bluffing and she knew it. And, he thought, I'm stoking her fire to put it to me the first chance she gets. It was too late to back out, though—he'd already shot off his mouth.

"Bond, huh?" Hazel Sanderson rocked back in her chair, her chin moving up and down. "It's bail he wants. All right, Mr. Phillips. Bail is hereby set at two hundred and fifty thousand dollars. You just try to appeal *that*, sir. Tell the clerk to draft the order, Mr. Goldman, a bail order for a quarter of a million dollars. I'll sign it."

Bino swallowed hard. "Excuse me, judge. But don't you think that's a little excessive?"

She mockingly lifted her eyebrows. "Excessive? Why, no, I don't think it's excessive. Do you think it's excessive, Mr. Goldman?"

"Sounds low to me, your honor," Goldman said. He looked as though he'd just eaten the cheese.

"Tell me, Mr. Phillips." Hazel Sanderson grinned like Cinderella's ugly sister. "When your client gets out, does he have his own car? Or maybe he'd like to use mine."

On Bino's right, Goldman snickered. Deletay raised his head from his knuckles and blinked.

"Uh, I think I need a cup of coffee, judge," Bino said.

Bino had always thought that Half-a-Point Harrison was the mirror image of his father, and looking Pop Harrison over as Pop bailed out of his pickup in front of the Federal Building just reconfirmed the family resemblance. Same thin nose, sharp features, and even the same pencil mustache, the only difference being that Pop's thin hair and mustache were snow-white where Half's only showed traces of gray. Even when Half and Bino had been little kids in Mesquite, back when Pop used to buy them licorice sticks and Grapette soda in an old grocery that smelled of cold cuts and cheese, the other men around town would look at the two whippersnappers and say to Pop, "Boy hidy, I can sure tell which one is yours."

Standing on the curb about five feet from the pickup, Bino said, "Thanks for coming, Pop. I didn't know anybody else to call."

"Don't start that. You'll have me bawlin' and grabbin' for my hanky," Pop said. Jesus, Bino thought, he must be seventy—moves like a man twenty-five years old. "Come back here and give me a hand," Pop said. "Come on, boy, I'll get me a parkin' ticket if we don't hurry." He circled the pickup and went to its bed. Bolted inside the bed was a huge tool box with a hinged, padlocked lid. Pop went through the keys on his ring, looking each one over carefully. He lowered his voice. "Phone's ringin' off the wall. This weekend we got National and American League playoffs plus the NFL." He found the right key, held it up between two fingers and squinted, then inserted the key in the padlock.

A voice behind Bino said, "Now what's this?"

Bino turned. Goldman and Hazel Sanderson stood on the sidewalk, both prosecutor and judge watching with widened eyes. Goldman would have just delivered the bail order to the judge, and was probably taking her out for breakfast to butter her up. Bino said, "How you, folks?" And returned his attention to Pop.

Pop had the tool box's lid raised. "Here," he said. He produced a gunnysack with a rawhide drawstring. "Hold this open," Pop said. Bino spread the sack's mouth. Pop took bundles of hundred-dollar bills from the tool box and dropped them inside the bag, one at a time, with a series of soft plops.

Still on the sidewalk, Goldman said in a stage whisper, "Big real estate investment, no doubt."

Bino kept his gaze riveted straight ahead, not wanting to get into it with Goldman. Bino and the prosecutor both understood that Goldman knew damn well where Pop's money had come from, but would play hell proving it.

Pop said loudly, "Cashed in my savings bonds." Then, to Bino, Pop whispered, "Now I got to give you some smaller money. You didn't give me much notice."

The gunnysack was about half full, and was beginning to get a tad heavy. Pop dug back into the tool box and brought up huge bundles of tens, fives, and one-dollar bills. The bundles were held together with jumbo rubber bands. Pop continued to pile them into the bag, saying, "Motorcycle cop comes by I'm getting me a ticket for sure."

Bino glanced over his shoulder. He was literally staggering under his load now, and quite a crowd was gathering, men and women alike staring open-mouthed at the greenbacks as Pop dropped them into the bag. Goldman and the judge stood in the center of the mob, which now must have numbered close to fifty.

The traffic on Commerce Street had slowed to a crawl, brake lights flashing on and drivers rubbernecking as they went by.

"Now this last little dab," Pop said. "You're gonna have to excuse the shit outta me, but it's the only way I could do it. You got to give a man more notice. This last hundred, well . . ." He climbed up into the pickup's bed, bent over the tool box, and hefted up a bulging cloth sack. "It's in quarters."

Pop dropped the bag of quarters on top of the paper money. Bino's legs bent under the load, and he stumbled backward two steps before he could right himself. Behind him in the crowd, a male voice said, "Jesus *Christ*."

"Two-fifty on the nose," Pop said. He climbed down and went around to the pickup's driver's side.

Bino yelled, "Pop." Perspiration had popped out on his forehead, and he seriously thought he might be developing a hernia.

"No time," Pop said. "Son, they charging fifteen dollars for a parking ticket in this town. Send a man to the poorhouse." He started to climb into the cab, then paused. "You get me a receipt, you hear?" He got in the truck, gunned the motor, and wheeled away in moving downtown traffic.

Bino turned to face the crowd. Jesus, were his knees going to give way? The cords in his neck stood angrily out and his face was red from exertion. In among the mob, a brunette in a tight miniskirt winked at him and gave a come-on sideways jerk of her head. He looked away from her. Goldman and Hazel Sanderson looked as if they were seeing a ghost.

"Hey, Marv," Bino said between labored breaths, "help me, okay? Just up to the marshals' office to post bond. Come on, gimme a hand, willya?"

Kit Stanley, seated beside Bino on a bench outside the U.S. Marshals' office, was dressed prim and proper as usual, but her actions were anything but. She wore a simple navy business dress with medium heels and sat on the edge of her seat with her knees bent and her legs coiled, ready to spring. Each time the marshal's door would open, Kit would gasp and jump to her feet; then when the person coming out proved to be one of the marshals or a secretary from the U.S. District Clerk's office, Kit would sigh in dissapointment and sit back down. Jesus, thought Bino, like a teenager waiting for her first date or something.

There'd been a few tears when Bino had told her, upon her arrival in court, that Mickey was getting out on bond. The tears had streaked Kit's makeup somewhat, but she didn't act as though she noticed. Then, after the brief crying jag, there was this gee-whiz-where-is-he? act that was still going on. Bino himself had sore hands from dragging the money to the marshals' office after Goldman, the asshole, had refused to help. While one marshal had written the receipt, a second marshal had been on the phone to Brinks, ordering an armored car.

Finally the marshals' office door opened and Mickey Stanley emerged. He wore the same suit which he'd worn every day to court. His shirt's top button was undone, and the knot on his tie was loosened to about six inches below his collar. His thick black hair was slightly disheveled, his head was tilted to one side on his bull neck, and he blinked rapidly, probably from disbelief. His gaze zeroed in on Kit, and he showed her a weak smile.

Kit bounced up like an Elvis fan, traversed the thirty feet or so of corridor with her calves moving like engine pistons, and threw her arms around Mickey's neck. She hugged him. She kissed his cheek. She buried her face in the side of his neck and bawled. Mickey seemed rooted to the floor and appeared slightly embarrassed. Kiss her, you dumb asshole, Bino thought. She's your mother. He got up and went over to face Mickey as Kit continued to cry and carry on. Bino shoved his hands into his pockets and regarded his shoes.

Finally, Bino said, "Uh, Kit?" She kept right on hugging Mickey for dear life and crying into his shoulder.

You're going to stain the suit, Bino thought. He put a hand on Kit's shoulder and pulled her gently away from her son. She tilted her head and regarded Mickey as though she'd found God. Mickey cleared his throat and said in an aw-shucks tone, "Hi, Mom. How you doing?"

"Kit," Bino said, "I know you're going to want to get on home, spend some time with him and everything. But I got to visit with him a minute, okay? Mind waiting for us down the hall?"

Kit looked at Bino. At first she wasn't focusing, as though she'd forgotten who he was. Then she said, "Oh." She was still crying buckets as she said, "Oh, certainly. You go ahead." She squeezed Mickey's arm and took about five steps in the direction of the elevator, then turned and came charging back. This time it was

Bino she hugged, standing on her tiptoes and throwing her arms around his neck. "Oh, thank you. Thank you," she said, and then kissed Bino on the cheek as well. She released him, started away, turned to say, "Thank you," one more time, and retreated to stand expectantly by the elevators.

Bino followed Kit with his gaze, then swallowed a lump from his throat and turned to Mickey. Mickey appeared to be in a daze. Bino crooked a come-on finger, said, "Over here, Mick," and led the way to the same bench where he'd been sitting with Kit. Mickey had a seat and raised his eyebrows expectantly.

"Couple of things," Bino said. "How you feeling?"

Mickey rubbed the side of his neck. "I could eat something. I bet I lost twenty pounds on that jail food."

"I 'spect Kit'll fix that," Bino said. "Now, this is a long way from over. We talked about this before, and you understand you're probably going to wind up doing some kind of time over this. I mean, we can't get around the fact that you've been fooling with dope, right?"

Mickey nodded. "I'm ready for that. Just not the rest of my life, huh?"

"That's what we're working on," Bino said. "Now. You know about Annette Ray. Well, Brenda Milton might be in the same boat. She's missing."

"They dropped a morning paper off at the cell," Mickey said. "I read about the FBI coming to town."

"Yeah, they've made a big deal out of this, which increases the odds that some newspaper people might be coming around— also a book writer, a guy named Nolan Pounds. Now, you don't talk to any of those assholes. You send 'em to me, you hear?"

"Whatever you say, boss," Mickey said.

"Now, what I want you to do is," Bino said, "I want you to put your thinking cap on. Whoever's killing these people is probably somebody that's been at the trial. In the long run it's probably lucky you've been in jail, otherwise Goldman would be pointing the finger at you for the murders. But you know all these guys that Annette and Brenda know, and I want you to think. Anything weird about any of 'em—and I know they're all weird as hell— but any violence, any offbeat behaviour, devil worship or any of that shit, I want to know about. Capiche?"

"Sure. I can't think right now, but maybe something'll come to me."

"That's the ticket," Bino said. "Don't think any help from you won't be taken into consideration at sentencing time. Now you go on home with your mom." He gave Mickey a fatherly punch on the shoulder.

Mickey rose and started to walk away, moving like an athlete, his shoulders rotating.

"Hey, Mick," Bino said.

Mickey turned.

Bino pointed to the bench. "C'mere."

Mickey came back over and sat down.

Bino hesitated, then decided to get it off his chest. "Now, we've done a bunch of soul-searching while you were in jail," Bino said, "and I think you're on the right wavelength. But repenting in jail and staying repented on the street are two different things. Brenda Milton couldn't keep away from the dope, and you can see where it's gotten her." He pointed a finger. "So I'll tell you something. If you fuck up it's going to kill your mother, not to mention a guy I know that's put up one helluva lot of money to put you on the street. So listen close, Mick. If you screw this up, you can look for old Bino here to whip your ass for you." He winked. "Now, you're a big strong boy and twenty years younger. You want to try me on that, you go ahead."

10

There were some things about county facilities, Bino thought, that were always the same regardless of *where* the facilities were located. As though the county could build an office complex, say, right next door to E-Systems' Las Colinas supermegabuck shrine, complete with moats and waterfalls, put just as much money and frills and whatnot in their building as E-Systems had, yet you'd still know you were in a county-owned building.

Take the room where Bino now sat, for example, the eleventh-floor conference room in the Frank Crowley Courts Building, a mile or so west of downtown Dallas on Commerce Street. Bino was in a cushioned armchair with the county guys clustered together on the end of the conference table at his right, the University Park cops ganged up directly across from him, a uniformed Dallas police lieutenant and a plainclothes Dallas homicide detective on the same side as he, two chairs down on his left, and the federal troops, including Goldman, holding forth at the head of the table. Jesus, Frank Crowley Courts Building wasn't that old. They'd finished it, what, less than five years ago?

But the beige-colored walls were yellow with age, and there were ashtrays filled with cigarette butts sitting on the conference table, on the bookcases, and on the metal rolling server (which contained the coffee pot, cups, cream, sugar, and Sweet 'n' Low), even though Frank Crowley Courts Building was designated as being smoke-free. And, as Bino looked around him, no one in the room was smoking. Several of the county guys, Mac Strange and Hardy Cole in particular, looked as though they were dying for a cigarette. But nobody had gotten up the nerve to light one— not with the federal watchdogs looking on. So if nobody's smoking, Bino thought, where in hell did all the cigarette butts come from? Like part of the decoration, as if, whenever the county moved into a new building, a guy ran down to the conference room, sprayed a little yellow on the walls and set a bunch of butt-filled ashtrays around. And the county smell was there, too; stale smoke in a caldron of stale air. Maybe the same guy who sprayed on the yellow and set out the ashtrays also had a spray can labeled "LAW ENFORCEMENT CONFERENCE ROOM ODOR"—something like that. One day, maybe when he retired, Bino was going to do a study on it.

The University Park cops were easy to distinguish from the Dallas police and the county guys as well, without even reading the logos on the uniform sleeves. The U.P. captain's navy blue was bluer than the Dallas lieutenant's, the gold trim golder, the white shirt whiter, and the U.P. guys had spiffier haircuts and closer shaves. Mac and Hardy and the county guys wore rumpled suits and their collars were loosened, while the U.P. detective's navy suit was freshly pressed and his tie was spotless. In fact, the guy dressed as though he might be sitting in a director's meeting at AT&T.

One thing for sure, Bino thought, the University Park police weren't going to like the newspaper people sitting around the perimeter of the meeting, their chairs flush against the yellowed walls, pens and notepads in their hands. Out in bluenose Park Cities everything had to go through a coordinator, who'd carefully weed out the sensitive material before the reporters got their hands on it. Things were done that way to keep from stepping on any of the big-buck citizens' toes. But there they were, the reporters, admitted on Nelson Deletay's orders no doubt. Even Nolan Pounds was sitting in, the true-crime guy, with his thick legs crossed. A few minutes ago Pounds had shaken Bino's hand, and Bino had mumbled hello. He'd also noticed Pounds and Goldman in animated conversation, and Bino didn't have much doubt how the federal prosecutor was going to come across in Pounds's book.

Wonder how he's going to portray me, Bino thought. Probably make me out to be a horse's ass.

And Mac Strange wasn't going to like the reporters being in attendance, either, but for a slightly different reason than the University Park people. The county contingent didn't want the proceedings of the meeting in the papers because they were afraid panic might spread. Showed how much regard Deletay and his VICAP crew had for the locals.

The federal people were all in dress-for-power black, of course—even the young woman. She had short, fluffy brown hair which turned up at the ends and wore pale rose-colored lipstick. In designer jeans and wearing high-heeled shoes along with a smile, she probably would have been cute; stern-faced and clad in a severely cut black pantsuit, she blended right in with the rest of the feds. The girl was seated on Goldman's left. Deletay was on Goldman's right. Deletay leaned over in front of Goldman to say something to the girl and then rose from his chair.

"Gentlemen," Deletay boomed, "here's what we're to talk about." He strode casually to the blackboard that stood behind his chair and picked up a long yellow piece of chalk. The chalk squealed across the board as Deletay printed, in firm bold strokes, the word "SERIAL," underlined it, turned and said loudly, "Serial." Then he wrote, "MURDER" on the board, underlined that as well, and said, equally loudly, "Murder." He laid down the chalk and favored one and all with a pinch-browed glare. Bino glanced down the table at Hardy Cole. Hardy was about to bust out laughing. All around the room, reporters scribbled madly away.

"Now, this isn't the movies, gentlemen," Deletay said, "and we haven't stuffed any moths down anyone's throat"—smiling, pausing for a laugh, getting none, going smoothly ahead like Johnny Carson when one of his jokes fell flat—"but this is *dead serious business*. Now, I'm not going to spend a lot of time with me, because I'm not, no one person is, as important as our overall goal, which is to put this individual out of business—permanently. For those of you whom I haven't met"—spreading his hands— "I'm Nelson Deletay. We'll be working together." He smiled.

Deletay had *said* that he wasn't important, but his tone had sounded as though he thought he was important as hell. Bino shifted in his chair and crossed his long legs under the table.

"So, briefly," Deletay went on, "I'm going to try to give you the big picture, and then turn the meeting over to Sandra Nestle. She's a lot prettier than I am and knows a whole lot more about the subject." He smiled charitably at the girl, who showed a modest grin that looked as though grinning modestly was a course taught in FBI school.

"VICAP," Deletay said, folding his hands behind his back and pacing back and forth, "holds a lot of mystique for the public in general, but we're anything but a bunch of glory guys." He stopped. "Details. Hard work and details, that's what it takes to handle one of these cases, just like any other part of law enforcement. And believe me, you people have a role in this which is one helluva lot more important than anything we might do. You're the guys down in the trenches. For us to do our job, every little detail you can furnish us is going to be carefully evaluated, believe me, and anything you have, no matter how insignificant it may seem, that little detail might turn out to be the straw that broke the camel's back. Now Sandra here is going to be your main contact on Dracula Don, and you're going to find Sandra to be a crackerjack. But that doesn't mean I'm not available. My door is open to you, guys."

"Hold on." The voice came from the far end of the room. Bino swiveled his head to his right. Hardy Cole was on his feet. "Maybe I've been asleep," Cole said. "But Dracula who?"

Deletay showed a mild fatherly expression. "Dracula Don. That's our designation for this case. We've found that that giving the perp a name, though we don't know his *real* name at present, giving the perp a name makes him seem more alive to us and less like a figment of someone's twisted imagination. Less like we're chasing a shadow."

Cole seemed to deflate. "Well I'll be damned," he said, then resumed his seat. He leaned over and whispered something to Mac Strange, and Bino, looking directly at Hardy, read the county investigator's lips. Hardy was saying, "What's wrong with 'Plasma Pete?' " Bino stifled a grin and returned his attention to the front of the room. This was going to be a coordinated effort, okay. Each group was going to coordinate their efforts to keep the other group from finding out what was going on. Seated against the far wall, Nolan Pounds had already taken a whole page of notes, and now flipped his notebook to a fresh sheet.

"Now, we already know quite a bit about Dracula Don,"

Deletay went on, "a whole lot more than anyone realizes. We can tell you his approximate height, weight, and hair color, and we can give you a pretty accurate profile on who is most likely to become one of his victims. Sandra will give the details on that, but I'm making a small point here. If we have this much information in this brief span, then tomorrow we're going to have even more. And more the next day, and even more the next. What information we do have on this guy depends a hundred percent on you people. So what do you say, men? Let's get this guy." Deletay paused for effect, then said simply, "Sandra," and then sat down.

Sandra Nestle had a pile of notes, a stack of paper at least six inches high which she now produced from her briefcase and carried to the front of the room. A podium sat in one corner, and at her request Goldman and Deletay moved the podium center stage. Deletay went about his task in a businesslike manner while Goldman looked sort of pained. When the rostrum was in place, Sandra Nestle loaded her notes onto the tilted flat surface, cupped a hand over her mouth and cleared her throat.

"Thank you, Mr. Deletay," she said. "And for those of you who don't already know, my boss Mr. Deletay was being too modest. If it wasn't for him, there wouldn't *be* any VICAP. It's his baby from start to finish, and those of us who are lucky enough to work for him are proud of it."

Deletay now beamed while Nestle paused to shuffle papers, and as Bino shifted his gaze from Deletay to Nestle and back again, he mentally snapped his fingers. Jesus, he'd *thought* there was something familiar here, and now he got it. Sandra Nestle slurred her *s* words slightly, as though anyone standing near her might be in for a saliva shower bath, and she spoke in a subdued, but still recognizable, backwoodsy accent. Bino blinked. Jesus Christ, *Jodie Foster*. Not Jodie herself, of course, but the same hairdo, same accent, all of it. And Deletay. Bino shifted his gaze. Sure, Deletay, the way he walked and sat, the expressions . . . Jesus Christ, *Scott Glenn*. Bino wondered briefly whether the actors had used Deletay and Nestle as role models, or if it was the other way around, that Deletay and Nestle had seen the picture umpteen times and were imitating the actors. Jesus, thought Bino, any minute they'll wheel Anthony Hopkins in, locked up inside a

Plexiglas cage, and then Hopkins will slobber all over his cage and start playing mind games with everybody.

"For the record," Nestle went on, "my name is pronounced *Nest*-lee." She threw a brief underling-type smile in Deletay's direction. Deletay, who'd pronounced it *Nessul* when he'd introduced her, waved an apologetic aw-shucks hand. Bino made a mental note to call her *Nessul*, and him *Dell*-i-tay instead of *Deel*-tay, and then act as though he'd made a mistake when they corrected him. Just a little needle, Bino thought, won't hurt anybody. And then they could counter by calling him "Beano."

"Now," Sandra Nestle said, walking to the blackboard, sliding the board to one side on its rollers, revealing a large bulletin board with its surface nearly covered with thumbtacked pictures and maps, "for Dracula Don. Four victims thus far, three deceased, plus a fifth who's disappeared and may not be among the living. By the way, gentlemen, we believe the fifth victim, a young lady named Brenda Milton, to be alive. Temporarily. More on that in a few moments."

Nestle paused for that to sink in while she picked up a needle-like wooden pointer from the corner of the room, then leaned against the wall to one side of the bulletin board and crossed her ankles. Her profile's not bad, Bino thought, just some nice makeup and the right clothes and Sandra Nestle could be a damn good-looking woman. Nestle raised the pointer and touched its tip to one of the pictures. "Victim Number One. Annette Ray."

Bino's gaze traveled from Sandra Nestle's slender nose and soft rounded chin, down to her slim arm and across to her delicate red-nailed fingers, and then along the pointer to its tip, finally resting on the photo, and—

My *God*, Bino thought. Graphic detail, sliced-open skin revealing gray dead flesh underneath, Annette Ray's pretty face not so pretty anymore, the lips pulled back in a permanent snarl of terror, the once-soft blond hair clinging to her head like clumps of dry tangled straw. Bile rose in Bino's throat and he looked quickly away.

"Age twenty." Sandra Nestle's tone was cool and professional, like a biology lab instructor's. "Student. Cause of death, a single bullet wound in the forehead, fired at close range—the powder burns are quite prominent, you'll note—with the bullet exiting from the back of the skull. Here." She moved the pointer quickly to another photo.

Bino snuck a peek from the corner of his eye. Christ, the second picture was even worse than the first one. It was a shot of Annette's naked corpse from the rear, and a pancake-size portion of the back of her head was missing. Christ, Bino thought, oozing brains. He very nearly bolted from the room but forced himself to sit still.

"Unfortunately," Nestle said, "we don't have anything for ballistics on this one. The body was found here." The pointer moved once more, and this time its tip went to the map, resting on a small park about a mile north of the SMU campus, Caruth Park. Bino knew the place well: Back when he'd been a student he'd spent many a springtime afternoon in Caruth Park, studying on a picnic table, taking walks with Annabelle, or just hanging out with Barney Dalton and some other guys. The park held a softball diamond, playground, a rock-banked creek with plenty of crawdads in the spring and summer, and grove after grove of tall elms, sycamores, and pecan trees. If you didn't keep an eye out for the squirrels in the park, they would sneak up and steal food right out of your pocket.

"The body was submerged in a creek, for, best estimate, four or five days," Nestle said. "Dragging signs in the underbrush might indicate that the killer dumped the body here, though the dragging signs could be unrelated. The body was only feet from the creek bank, tangled in underwater bushes. Some youngsters fishing for crawdads found her. These incisions"—back to picture number one, the pointer resting first on the grisly cut on the left side of Annette's throat, then moving to the smooth lacerations on the righthand side—"were definitely made before death. The arteries were cut with a sharp, toothless instrument, and the killer used a sawing motion. Flecks of rust removed from the wound were steel. Probably a straight razor, gentlemen, not that common an instrument these days and well worth noting. Tooth impressions around the wounds, the flesh puckered outward. Suck marks, gentlemen. We have a nice model of Dracula Don's dental work, once we have him in person to make a comparison." Nestle took two cool and professional strides to the podium, checked her notes, and returned to the bulletin board. Deletay was scanning the room, checking out the faces of the listeners, while Goldman pretended to study his case file. Old Marv wasn't fooling Bino, though, the federal prosecutor simply didn't want to look at the pictures on the board. As a matter of fact, Bino thought, Goldman looks sort of guilty, sitting there with his head down, pulling on his goatee. Jesus, could *Goldman* be Dracula Don? Naw, that's silly, old Marv wouldn't suck anybody's blood. Then Bino's eyes narrowed slightly as he thought, *Would he?*

"Bruises on both breasts," Nestle said, "are finger marks. He squeezed her. Very hard. But something unusual in this case, in spite of the violence exhibited here: There are no bite marks. Not one single tooth mark on any of these victims other than around the cutting wounds. In cases such as these we've learned to expect biting. It's always there, but not with Dracula Don. Nothing on the buttocks, around the naval area, nothing anywhere on the body, in fact, that we've come to associate with these sex crimes. No semen in any body cavities, the mouth, rectum, or the vagina. Minute traces of semen on the left side of the stomach. We got a small break here, because the frontal portion of the body wasn't quite underwater." She showed a tight smile. "He dribbled on her, gentlemen." Nestle's sour expression said that she didn't like guys who went around dribbling. Wonder what she thinks about old basketball players, Bino thought.

"Our man is Type A-Positive," Sandra Nestle said, "the second most common blood type, not much use in making a concrete ID. The sperm count is low, by the way, but he's not sterile. The blood type is admissible as evidence, of course, but common enough to be virtually useless without a lot of backup material. Our work is cut out for us, gentlemen." Nestle went over to the coffee server, wrinkled her nose at one of the butt-filled ashtrays, poured ice water from a silver carafe into a Styrofoam cup, and had a sip.

While Nestle took her short water break, Bino scanned the room, looking over reporters writing like crazy, at one slender young newsguy in a green blazer and slacks who stood, squinted at the bulletin board, then resumed his seat and jotted something down. Nolan Pounds was turning to still another fresh sheet on his pad. But, Bino thought, none of the cops are taking any notes. Strange as hell, the Dallas, University Park, and county guys sitting there with notepads and ballpoints ready, but not writing anything down. Could only mean that, so far at least, Nestle hadn't said anything that the local law enforcement people didn't already know. Which made one wonder: Why the meeting? It's for the newspaper guys, Bino thought, strictly for the press. Bino would bet that the reporters were all spelling Deletay's and Nestle's names correctly. Newshounds recognized a source of information when they saw one.

Nestle set her water cup back on the server and returned to the bulletin board to retrieve the pointer. "Now for Dracula Don's trademark," she said. "The peg driven through the vagina wall." She paused and took a deep breath. She had everyone's attention now, the reporters on the edges of their seats. They want to keep the public informed, Bino thought.

Nestle went back to her pile of notes, leafed through them, and returned to the board holding a photograph. She removed a thumbtack from the corner of the board and affixed the new picture right in the center, covering portions of three of the other photos. She stood aside for everyone to have a look.

Jesus, thought Bino, this is carrying things a little bit too far. The new picture was a closeup of the corpse's crotch, silken pubic hair and all. Bino hadn't gotten to know Annette Ray very well, but he'd had a conversation with her father since her death, and the dad had seemed like a decent guy. Wasn't anybody entitled to privacy from these people? Jesus, Nestle could have just told about it, without having to show the picture. The rounded end of the spike protruded from between the lips of the vagina. The cops all kept their seats, but the reporters stood and craned their necks. Nolan Pounds was quite a bit shorter than most of the newspeople, so the true-crime guy had to edge around the wall for a better vantage point. Wonder if Pounds intends to use that picture in the center pages of his book, Bino thought. Totally disgusted now, he leaned back, folded his arms, and regarded the ceiling.

"The peg, or spike if you will," Nestle said, "is important for a number of reasons. It's administered postmortem, of course, both the striations in the flesh and common sense tell us that. The victim would have to be lying completely still. To Dracula Don it's an act of finality. He drives it in with a mallet or hammer.

"The spike is four inches in length, and it's handmade," Nestle said. "Hard maple, machined and turned, sanded and lacquered. The lacquer is important. Gifford and Tillman grade-two hard enamel. You won't buy this stuff in a hardware store, because it's strictly a commercial product, sold to professional cabinetmakers and such. Even more important"—Bino watched from the corner of his eye as she used the pointer to indicate picture number two, the backside photo showing the missing portion of the skull—"because traces of the same lacquer were found on the victim's buttocks and shoulder blades—here—and here. This is also true with Victim Number Two, who we'll get to shortly. We think that the victim was laid out nude at some point, either dead or alive, on a surface painted with the same enamel. A floor, possibly, but more than likely a table. We believe that Dracula Don is a wood-worker, gentlemen, and from the grade of the lacquer involved, he's no amateur.

"The medical examiner," Nestle said, "is relatively certain that death occurred more than twenty-four hours before the body was dumped because of the decomposition. The body's being sub-merged in water, of course, makes the exact time of death virtually impossible to tell. The corpse was relatively livid. Two days is probably the maximum time from death to dumping, and since there was no insect invasion of the body, we assume it was never left outside for any appreciable period. Also, the semen was still present, probably deposited only moments before she went in the creek." She blinked and folded her arms, causing the pointer to tilt upward. "It's our current theory that Dracula Don held this woman captive from the time of her disappearance until he killed her, then dumped the body. About two weeks in captivity. Here's why we think that."

She took the vagina picture down (Thank God, Bino thought), returned it to her stack of notes, and poured another drink of water. This time she gulped the water down and returned hastily to the bulletin board. Bino grudgingly had to admit that Sandra Nestle seemed to know her stuff.

"Needle marks," Nestle said, indicating a shot of Annette's arm, extended against a white background with her elbow facing down. "Possibly consistent with drug usage, but we doubt it. No-tice the small marks around the main puncture wound. We think it's a needle attached to an intravenous rubber or silicon tube that he inserted in her. More than likely to draw blood, and the small marks indicate unsuccessful piercing attempts. We believe—and we acknowledge that it's bizarre—but we believe that Dracula Don was using Annette as a supply source, keeping her prisoner with the tube inserted into her vein, so that all he had to do was unclip the end of the tube when he wanted a drink. This is more than mere speculation, gentlemen. New blood, replacement for blood lost through donation or injury, contains a slightly higher white count. Analysis of what blood remained in Annette after Dracula Don finished with her indicates that she'd been in a constant state of rejuvenation. When he found an alternate source of supply he simply got rid of Annette. Which brings us to Victim Number Two." Nestle quickly removed about half of the pictures from the board, leaving more pictures which were just as graphic and grisly as the others had been.

As Sandra Nestle worked, pulling thumbtacks, stacking photos in the crook of her arm, Bino slowly shook his head. Good show. Damn good show. He still thought that Deletay was a pompous jackass, and he still thought that Sandra would look a whole lot better if she'd smile occasionally, but he didn't have any doubt that both of them knew what they were doing. Bino let his gaze roam. The University Park and Dallas cops were all ears, and even had begun to take a few notes. Even Hardy Cole was attentive now, though he did catch Bino looking at him and managed to slouch and show a sardonic grin. You're not fooling me, Hardy, Bino thought, the young lady's got you by the ears.

"In the interest of time," Nestle said after carrying the photos she'd removed to stack them on the podium, "I'll dispense with a point-by-point description, only to emphasize"—touching another photo with the pointer—"the arm with the identical needle marks. There are some subtle and insignificant differences, but everything points to the fact that Victim Number Two received virtually the same treatment as Annette Ray. Victim Number Two was shot through the heart, but we believe that only shows that Dracula Don didn't like the mess he'd made with the first girl. Any close examination of the evidence you'd like to do on this one, just see me in private. Oh. There were traces of the same lacquer as on Annette Ray. Victim Number Two, incidentally, was named Edna Moore. Twenty-two. She was a hooker."

There was a rustling at the far end of the table, and Bino snapped his head around to find Mac Strange whispering a mile a minute to Hardy Cole. Cole looked mad as hell and finally stood. "Mind telling us how you knew that, Miss Nestle?"

Nestle let the pointer hang down until its tip touched the floor. "Knew what?"

"Her name. We still haven't been able to find that out."

For the first time, Nestle seemed to be stumped. She threw a hasty SOS in Deletay's direction, and Deletay now stood and faced the room.

"From the materials sent to us at Quantico," Deletay said. "There was a motel receipt made out to Sally Trent, so we checked with the motel manager, more of a pimp, really, and found that Sally Trent was an alias. We got the real name from some of her . . . co-workers, for lack of a better word."

"Sent from where?" Cole said.

Deletay frowned. "Beg pardon?"

"The materials you got. Sent from where?"

There was a pregnant pause as Deletay regarded his shoes, punctuated by the rustling of paper as Sandra Nestle pretended to study her notes. Suddenly the University Park police captain stood, fingering the gold trim on the sleeve of his uniform as he said, "We'll take credit for that. We sent it to them." He was tall and thin with neatly trimmed brown hair showing just a hint of gray in the sideburns, and wore thick bifocals encased in dark plastic frames. He nodded to Bino. "We haven't been introduced, Mr. Phillips. I'm Will Utley, University Park Police."

Bino shrugged and grinned. "Glad to know ya."

"You sent the stuff to the FBI without saying anything to us?" Hardy Cole said to Utley.

Utley squared his shoulders. "That's right."

"Neat," Cole said. "Really neat. What else did you send them?" Bino had always figured that the lean and angular county detective was just about as tough as he looked, and had wondered what Hardy would do if he got good and mad. Bino might be about to find out.

Utley did his best to meet Cole's gaze, but the U.P. cop finally lowered his eyes. "Just a blanket," Utley said.

"Just a blanket." Cole's prominent chin moved up and down. "The blanket missing from the murder scene."

"One of our people came up with it," Utley said.

Cole's eyebrows lifted, and for just an instant Bino thought that Hardy was going to come charging around the table and take a poke at Utley. Finally Cole expelled air from his lungs, said,

"Well that takes the fucking cake," and sat down and folded his arms. "Excuse the language, Miss Nestle," Cole said, but his expression didn't look as though he was sorry at all. Utley resumed his seat and sheepishly regarded his notepad. Deletay sat down as well, and looked expectantly at Sandra Nestle. Deletay's expression was a slight smirk, thin lips turned upward at the corners of his mouth.

"No problem," Sandra Nestle said, smiling. "People get worked up, we understand that. And since it's been brought up, the blanket." She rummaged through her notes and held up a single letter-sized piece of paper. "There were some grass particles, of course, common Bermuda like the grass on the campus, or any number of yards in the city. More lacquer residue, which tells us that Dracula Don is taking his prey, probably, all to the same place. Plus four strands of black hair that match the hair on the victim's head. They're not all blonds, gentlemen. The young woman last night was a brunette with a bleach job, so we doubt that we're looking for anyone with a blond fetish. We don't think the hair color is significant.

"In addition," Nestle said, "three hairs which are *not* the victim's. Two curly hairs, color brown, and from their length we're assuming they came from a man. That or a woman with very *short* hair, but in all these cases we're fairly safe to assume we're dealing with a man. We haven't been wrong as yet." As she spoke, Nestle showed a triumphant half smile, and as she finished her sentence she was looking directly at Bino. Jesus, Bino thought, I didn't do it. Wonder if she's got it in for guys.

"So in Dracula Don's case we're going to assume he's a man with short and curly brown hair. The third hair on the blanket was dark and quite coarse, consistent with a pubic hair. If it's Don's, we'll have it for comparison once he's in custody. And he *will* be in custody sooner or later, gentlemen, of that you may rest assured. The presence of the hairs just tightens the noose."

"Unless it's a cop's hair," Hardy Cole said.

Nestle cocked her head to one side. "Say that again?"

Cole stood, shrugging off a restraining hand from Mac Strange. "A cop's," Cole said. "They tell you that blanket was missing from the murder scene, that one of their own cops carried it off?" He was alternating his gaze between Nestle and Utley, while the U.P. Captain suddenly found his notes interesting as hell.

"We don't have any information on that," Nestle said.

"I didn't figure you did," Cole said. "How 'bout that custodian, a guy named Herbert Trevino? They tell you he's a witness, and that he saw the killer running off from the scene?"

Nestle fixed Captain Utley with a scalding glare. "That's news to us," Nestle said.

"I thought it might be," Cole said, sitting down. Mac Strange whispered something to his investigator, and Bino thought that Mac's lips were even easier to read than Hardy Cole's had been. Mac was saying, "Shut the fuck up, Hardy."

Nestle's expression softened, and she seemed to lose some of her confidence. She said quickly, "Perhaps we'll have to investigate further, then." Then she cleared her throat and coughed. "Edna Moore, Victim Number Two, had the same needle punctures, and might have been another of Dracula Don's blood supply sources. I say 'might have been' because she was an addict, had more needle marks behind her knees and on her ankles. The peg was present in her vagina as well.

"She was last seen," Nestle said, "on a Wednesday night, week before last. A prostitute named Barbara Wells tells us that she and Edna were working the bar at the Doubletree Inn on LBJ Freeway, far North Dallas. Edna told Barbara that she was leaving for an appointment around eleven, and that's the last time anyone—or anyone we can locate—spoke to the victim. Edna then vanished until her corpse turned up, out at the college."

"Say, wait a minute." Bino was on his feet, and was halfway through his first sentence before he snapped that he was just a visitor in this meeting and probably ought to keep his mouth shut. Too late, though, he'd already popped off. "There's been a theory," Bino said, "at least everybody's told me that this guy was somebody who was picking his victims around the federal courts. Doesn't that, the girl being out at the Doubletree Inn, doesn't that knock the federal building theory in the head?" He looked around. The cops were all looking at him as though they wished he'd shut the fuck up. Maybe I should sit beside Hardy Cole, Bino thought.

Nestle drew up to her full height. "That's a point," she said. "The trouble is that it's not a very *good* point. Edna Moore appeared in federal court on the same day that some motions were heard in the trial that you people are involved in. Edna pled guilty to some misdemeanor drug charges, and her sentencing was set for next month." Nestle arched an eyebrow. "That answer your question?"

"Uh, yeah, I guess it does," Bino said, sitting down. Jesus, Nestle acted as if Bino was one of the guys who used to stand her up on dates. Never saw her before, Bino thought. His cheeks were red in embarassment.

"That about finishes . . ." Nestle was at the podium, poring over her notes. "Oh. One more significant point. The same lacquer residue, only on Edna Moore the lacquer was on her breasts and on the front of her thighs. Interesting, what?" She looked around.

Bino didn't want to speak up again but couldn't help it. "Interesting how?" he said weakly.

She gave him the look that she probably reserved for stupid questions. "The position," she said. "The other woman, Annette Ray, Dracula Don kept on her back. Edna was a prostitute and he imprisoned her face-down, apparently. We think it says something about his regard for the victim. This becomes even more important with Victim Number Three." Nestle smiled. "Who is a man. I think we'll take a short break, gentlemen. Victim Number Three requires some preparation." She left the podium with an expression as though she was licking her chops to tell what Dracula Don had done to a man.

Nestle walked over to speak to Deletay in guarded whispers, while the cops all stood, stretched, and headed for the exit. Goldman kept his seat and seemed deep in thought. Jesus, thought Bino, I don't know if I can take any pictures of Donatello. He stood to follow Mac Strange and Hardy Cole down to the county cafeteria. On the way, he decided that he'd better not eat anything.

Over the past eight years, Dodie Peterson had learned how to handle Bino's business; in fact there were times when she felt that she knew what to do around the office better than he knew himself. When he was away—which in a one-lawyer, one-girl, one-part-time-investigator/part-time-bookmaker operation was most of the time—she never missed a beat. In fact she felt that she could do a better job of running the office when Bino *wasn't* around.

On this particular day she was glad that she had plenty to do, because keeping busy would prevent her mind from wandering to last night, would keep her thoughts on business and away from the policemen who'd been standing around in the thunderstorm near her apartment. She'd watched through her window while the medics carried the gurney downstairs and out to the ambulance. That morning a man in the parking lot had told her, while she was getting in her car, that there'd been an attack up in 214, and that Andrea Morton was in the hospital and barely alive. Dodie didn't know Andrea Morton very well, had only talked to her a few times in the clerk's office, but the thought of wild maniacs loose at the Village sent shivers running up and down Dodie's spine. Just maybe, she thought, I should take Half's advice and move.

After she'd shooed Bino off to the federal building—it wasn't anything unusual to find Bino snoozing when she arrived at the office, and she was damned if she'd given him the satisfaction of asking where he'd been all night—she spent most of the morning straightening out the correspondence files and fielding phone calls. There wasn't much to handling the calls—Barney Dalton called to find out whether Bino was dropping by Joe Miller's Bar that afternoon, and Dodie told Barney there was a pretty good chance
· of that, since Bino dropped by Joe Miller's every day that he wasn't sick or something; later, a burglar client named Wimpy Madrick called to say that he was going fishing and wanted to know if his hearing on a new misdemeanor charge could be set off, and Dodie told Wimpy that she doubted it because the case had already been postponed about a hundred times, but she'd see what she could do—but the files were a real mess. When Bino had a trial going on, they always were. During trials, Dodie spent most of her days down at the courtroom taking notes, which caused the mail to simply *pile up*, and the estimations were that Mickey Stanley's case would go for the better part of a month. This morning there'd been a stack of envelopes on Dodie's desk a foot high, and a pile even larger on Bino's sofa. Wow, she'd *never* be finished with all of this. It won't disappear by me looking at it, Dodie had thought, then had tucked her tongue firmly into one corner of her mouth and gone to work.

By one o'clock—having dashed down to Bek's Hamburgers in the tunnel for lunch and eating about half of a salad special, a total of twenty minutes away from her desk—she had the stacks of mail whittled just about in half. Both hers and Bino's wastebaskets were overflowing with solicitations for ads in the *T.V.*

Weekly—Bino thought that lawyers who advertised in magazines and newspapers were really sleazeballs, and Dodie agreed with him, not to mention that Bino could barely handle the clients he already had—million-dollar chances from Publisher's Clearing House with Ed McMahon's picture on the envelope, come-ons to call an eight-hundred number or forfeit the prize you'd already won, and requests for donations from two departments at SMU. The rest of the mail Dodie had sorted into three piles: One contained those papers which only required filing (forms from the courts giving notice of upcoming hearings and whatnot—Dodie's reasoning was that, goodness knows, the clerk sends an individual notice a couple of days before the hearing anyway, so the forms she'd gotten that morning she only had to stick in the folders without making any followup notations). The second pile held matters such as plea bargain offers which Dodie could handle on her own, giving the clients the good or bad news, as the case might be, then finding out whether the client wanted to accept the plea bargain or go on fighting the case. Finally, in the third neat pile, were those pieces of correspondence which would go to Bino for him to mull over for no telling how long before letting Dodie take care of them anyway, just as she handled virtually everything else. She was going over a letter from Eddie Nelson, a pimp currently doing three years in the Texas Department of Corrections for maiming one of his girls—not one of Dodie's favorite clients but a client nonetheless and part of the job—and wondering whether Bino would be willing to send Eddie twenty dollars for cigarette money, when the phone buzzed. Dodie picked up the receiver, cradled it between her shoulder and soft cheek, and continued to read Eddie's letter while she said, "Lawyer's office."

A man said over the line, in a not unpleasant tenor, "Why aren't you in court?" His speech was rapid and his tone excited.

Dodie hesitated. She didn't recognize the voice, but the guy on the phone seemed to know her. Of course the guy could be a *breather* or something, but breathers didn't normally make cold calls to lawyers' offices. Breathers generally looked for a female name in the book and called unsuspecting women at home. Finally, Dodie said hesitantly, "In . . . ? Gee, Bino's . . ." Wow, you dumbo, Dodie thought, don't tell him you're here alone. Why take the chance? She said, "We're not going to court today."

The man's voice lowered to a near-whisper. "That's good. You're in *danger* down there."

The nagging dread in the back of Dodie's mind doubled in size in a flash. She blinked. "I beg your pardon?" Bino had connected a small recorder to the phone sometime back, and Dodie now simultaneously depressed the PLAY and REC buttons, using her middle and index fingers. Her nails were manicured and covered with clear polish. Seen through their plastic covers, the recorder reels turned slowly.

"Not so loud," the man hissed. "They'll hear you."

"I don't . . . *who'll* hear me?" Dodie's voice quavered slightly. The letter she'd been reading slipped from her fingers and landed face-up on her desk.

"Oh, Lord. Oh, Lord God, they'll . . ." The man's speech trailed off into silence. There was a rattly, clunking sound over the line, then a deeper, huskier voice said in the background, "Do not lie to me. You are speaking to Rebecca."

Her words driven by a little anger and a lot of fear, Dodie said, "Who *is* this? Tell me right now, or I'm hanging up."

A third voice chimed in over the phone, saying first in a high mimicking falsetto, "*Tell me right now or I'm hanging up.*" Then, in a still high pitched but definitely male voice, "You're talking to *him*, you stupid woman. Who do you *think* you are talking to?"

"If this is a joke, it's *not funny.* Would you like to speak to my boss?" Dodie's blue-eyed gaze was frozen on the revolving tiny reels.

Then the deep voice said to her, "Your boss? You stupid woman, the White-haired One is at the courthouse, and has been since early this morning. So why are you lying?"

Dodie's throat constricted so that she could hardly breathe. She tried to speak, but all that came out of her mouth was a pitiful moan, like that of an injured child.

Now the original voice, in the same near-whisper, said, "They won't leave me alone. I can't *make* them leave me alone."

Then the high shrill voice said, "Leave you alone? We'll leave you alone when the Truth has its being. Then there will be no more need for you."

Dodie slammed the receiver into its cradle, and while the ringing sound died into nothingness she continued to stare at the reels.

Bino was in court. They knew that she was alone.

She jumped as if touched by a hot poker, then got up to run around her desk, slam the hallway door and lock it from inside. She was sobbing. She returned to her chair, fidgeted helplessly for an instant, then fumbled with her index finder and located the number for Judge Hazel Burke Sanderson's court, in the Federal Building. Her fingers trembling, Dodie misdialed twice, then finally punched the number in correctly. As she listened to the ringing on the other line, she released the buttons to turn the recorder off.

11

There wasn't any doubt in Bino's mind that the world was better off without the Donatello guy, a guy without any morals, hanging around selling dope to a bunch of college kids, but why did he have to cash in his chips with his insides falling out all over the place? Why couldn't the guy have had a heart attack or something? Jesus, with Donatello's deathbed picture to gaze upon over the past half-hour or so, even the hardened cops were turning green around the gills.

In fact, the only one who seemed to like Donatello's picture was Sandra Nestle, the VICAP Queen. Nestle had been walking to and fro in front of the bulletin board, waving the pointer around, indicating first the gaping hole where Donatello's stomach should have been, and then showing a tight smile as she pointed out his intestines where they lay beside him on the bloodsoaked sheets. Nestle had even come up with Donatello's real name: Horace Potts, for Christ's sake.

"So what can we learn from the condition of Mr. Potts's body?" Nestle said, resting the pointer on a section of large intestine which was gray in color with flecks of red goo on its surface. "That Dracula Don hated the man, of course. All men, that's our theory. He hasn't cut any women open, at least so far. The women he's more gentle with, at least to his way of thinking—though the women involved might not agree." She chuckled, then leaned her back against the board so that Donatello's gaping belly wound was directly over the top of her head. *Look at me or the picture, boys. Your choice.* Bino riveted his gaze on the tip of Nestle's chin.

"What we're looking for, gentlemen," Nestle said, "is a man with terribly misguided affections. You'll find that he was a child abuse victim—that you can count on—and that the father, or stepfather as the case may be, was the abuser. His mother may well have participated, but he is convinced that everything unpleasant that happened to him was his father's fault alone. He'll be between thirty-five and forty-five. His schizophrenia will have remained dormant for years, only recently triggered, and very likely he'll show a veneer of normalcy. We're talking a professional man in many instances, a doctor, accountant,"—she looked directly at Bino and smiled—"or even a lawyer." Then, to the room in general, a grinning Sandra Nestle said, "Anyone know what you get when you cross a lawyer with Don Corleone?"

The cops all looked at one another with puzzled expressions.

"An offer you can't understand." She broke up laughing, her shoulders heaving as she walked to the podium for a brief glance at her notes. Deletay doubled over, slapped his knee, and favored Nestle with a boy-is-that-ever-rich expression while all the detectives and uniformed policemen continued to shoot quizzical looks at one another. Bino shifted nervously in his chair. Nestle returned to the bulletin board, leaned against it, and folded her arms.

"And remember, I said *many instances*," Nestle went on. "The point is that most of these people have very high IQs, a psychological makeup, actually, consistent with an actor or a college professor. Often drugs are involved, less often alcohol. The mental makeup must be there first, of course, but drugs can act as the catalyst which puts it all together for him. Oh. The drugs and alcohol are, of course, consistent with the symptoms for any adult child abuse survivor, but only a minute percentage of those people are psychopaths. There must be something else. Usually it's a physical disfigurement, probably as a result of the abuse, or even a birth defect of some kind. We had a case in Maine where the abnormality was something as small as a nearly unnoticeable speech impairment.

"In Dracula Don's case, as most of you know," Nestle said, "we suspect that it's someone who's been spending a lot of time in federal court of late. That seems to be the connection between all of the victims. We're going over the federal employee roster, and anyone who fits the criteria of a suspect will be evaluated, background gone over, and each will be asked to submit voluntarily to physical examination, donate hair samples and whatnot. Undergo fingerprinting, I suppose. How many prints have we found so far?" She looked expectantly around, like a teacher who'd just thrown out a question for the class at large. "Anyone," Nestle said.

Hesitantly, the Dallas homicide detective rose. "Only two that we can't account for. A partial latent thumbprint from Donatello's bathroom. That's . . . Mr. Potts. The guy up there in the picture. Another from the kitchen. The rest of the prints were his—Mr. Potts's." He sat down.

"Very good," Nestle said. "Oh. We're only doing male profiles and fingerprints of course, and for starters we're only talking civilian employees. No federal law enforcement people or judiciary the time being, though I'll tell you we're perfectly ready to take a look at any and everybody in order to come up with our man. So. Exclusive of females and government agents, Mr. Goldman, how many Federal Building employees does that leave?"

"Four hundred and twenty-one," Goldman said. His head was down and he was looking at his case file.

"Okay," Nestle said. "And oh. For those with prior criminal records, the fingerprinting won't be necessary. We'll already have prints on those people. So now, how many are we talking, those who require fingerprinting?"

Goldman raised his head, glanced quickly at Bino, then stood and approached Sandra Nestle. The federal prosecutor mumbled something which apparently was for her ears only, then resumed his seat.

"Excuse me," Bino said, partially rising. "I didn't hear him."

"I said, 'four hundred and twenty-one,' again." Goldman raised his voice and pointed a finger. "But I'm opposed to limiting it to federal employees. What about the defense witnesses in the Stanley case? Those people have been to the courtroom a lot."

Bino rolled his eyes. "Oh, Jesus, Marv. Yeah, okay, you got it. I got three witnesses left. One is the defendant, Mickey Stanley. Until two or three hours ago he was in jail. Another is Mickey's mom, and I doubt she's even had a parking ticket. The third witness I got is my own investigator, Horace Harrison. He's been to trial once, for bookmaking. And he got acquitted, and since you were his prosecutor you already know that. So now, while we're on the subject, what about *prosecution* witnesses? There's about fifty of those people, and they've been to court just as often. How many you got, Marv, that don't have rap sheets?—that they'd have to fingerprint."

Goldman dropped his gaze. He fumbled with his file. He cleared his throat. "None," he said.

Bino sat down and dropped his knee against the edge of the table. "That's what I thought," he said.

Nestle's gaze darted back and forth between Bino and Goldman, and it was obvious that she was trying not to smile. She strolled over to the podium and looked at her audience over her stack of notes, taking her time, like an actress about to deliver one cliff-hanger of a line. She cleared her throat. "Dracula Don may very well have an accomplice. It's not unheard of in cases like this, though it's not common, either."

Bino took his knee down from the table's edge and sat up. Nestle damn sure had *his* attention, and all around him there were rustling noises as the city and county cops twisted in their chairs.

"The most recent attack," Nestle said, "last night. The victim, Andrea Morton, not involved directly in the current trial, by the way, but very close to it. She works in the district clerk's office, two floors down from the courtroom, but she routinely delivers mail and other routed materials to the judges' chambers. She's in and out of the courtrooms several times in a day. She's alive, gentlemen. St. Paul Hospital lists her as critical. We haven't been able to talk to her as yet.

"She was out on the town with a girlfriend, and sometime during the night the two of them took up with a man." Nestle wrinkled her nose as though taking up with men was way up there on her list of no-no's, rustled a couple of papers, and then went on. "The trio made several nightspots, then Andrea dropped the man and the girl friend off at the girlfriend's apartment—just down the street from Andrea's, by the way, also in the Village complex— and then Andrea proceeded home alone. The attack occurred within moments after she entered her apartment. The assailant or assailants were either waiting for her or followed her inside.

"According to the girlfriend, someone had been following them in an older-model Buick," Nestle said, "and when Andrea let her and her . . . *friend*"—Nestle wrinkled her nose once more—"off, the Buick trailed Andrea away from the girlfriend's place. The man-friend copied the Buick's license number down."

"Well, maybe we're getting somewhere," the Dallas lieutenant said, looking up from his notepad. "What's the number?"

"That's a major problem," Nestle said. "Neither of the women knew the male companion. This was a common pickup. The man went with the girlfriend to Andrea's place, and the two of them encountered not one but *two* men who were running from Andrea's. One was Dracula Don, we're certain of that. According to the witnesses, there was blood on his face." Nestle twisted her mouth as if to say, "Oh, *gross*," and then went on. "Our man Don seemed to be chasing the accomplice. There was gunfire. This was confirmed by other residents who heard it, and a shell has been retrieved from a nearby apartment. One of the bullets broke the window. It's a .38, gentlemen, the same caliber used in Donatel—Horace Potts's murder. Ballistics has it now and we're hoping for a match. If we get one it's the first physical evidence we'll have to tie Dracula Don to both attacks. After the two assailants had fled, the girlfriend went in to administer to Andrea, and the . . . *man*-friend tucked his tail and ran away himself. We can only surmise that he panicked. For whatever reason, he hasn't been located, and he's the one with the license number." Nestle wrinkled her nose again, and Bino thought that if Nestle wasn't careful her features might freeze and she could go through life with a wrinkled nose.

"What about the guy's name?" the Dallas plainclothes detective said. "Anybody get that?"

"Only his first name," Nestle said. "Oscar. And we know he's from out of town. According to the girlfriend, he had a northern accent, and we know he met the two women downtown at the Adolphus Hotel. We don't even know for sure he was staying there, but we're having it checked out even as we speak. If our man wasn't in fact staying at the Adolphus, we've got real problems in locating him."

"Jesus Christ." Now it was Goldman who spoke, the federal prosecutor's own nose wrinkling, and Bino thought that maybe Nestle and Goldman should have a contest. "I mean, really," Goldman said. "All these women running around town picking up these guys, it's a wonder there aren't more killings than there are."

"We're really not here to moralize," Nestle said. "But I can't disagree with you. All these kind of cases, if women would be more careful . . ."

"Damn right," Goldman said, standing. "Let's face it, they put themselves in a spot where, if there's a loony in the neighborhood, it's like falling off a log for him. Andrea Morton, yeah, I know her, wanders around the courthouse making eyes at everything in pants. She's out with a girlfriend looking to pick some guy up, and wham. Ten to one the girlfriend's some bimbo herself." The federal prosecutor looked around, pulling at his goatee.

Sandra Nestle coughed nervously and regarded her pile of notes. Choked laughter sounded on Bino's right. Down at the end of the table Mac Strange and Hardy Cole were smirking at one another like a couple of schoolboys who were acting up in class.

"Well, what's so . . . ?" Goldman was staring daggers in the direction of the county guys. "What's so funny?" Goldman said. "Bunch of women getting gored and you guys giggling about it."

Strange and Cole exchanged glances, then Mac climbed slowly to his feet. "That's not what's funny, Marv. It's what you said about the girlfriend being a bimbo."

"Well, let's face it," Goldman said. "That's probably what she is. Women going around looking for a night in the sack with some guy they don't even know. Let's call a spade a spade here."

"You can call it whatever you want to call it, Marv," Mac said. "But the girlfriend you're talking about, she's a federal prosecutor. Works right in the office with you. Daphne Wilson. You know her, too, huh?"

"What I know about serial killings," Bino said, "I've learned in the past two days. And tell you the truth, I don't have any information in my files about any of these people, I don't think, that Marv doesn't have. It's the principal of the thing, people ordering me to give my records to somebody."

"Well, let's see what you *do* have," Nelson Deletay said. He was behind Mac Strange's desk, leaned back in Mac's swivel chair. Sandra Nestle was also in Mac's office, across from Deletay. Mac and Goldman were on the sofa with one empty space between them. Deletay had originally announced that he was only "sitting in in an advisory capacity in case Sandra needs me," then had promptly taken charge once the troops were assembled. Bino wasn't sure but thought that Nestle's back was slightly arched over the interference from her boss. A few minutes ago Hardy Cole had wandered in, but at Deletay's request Mac Strange had asked the county investigator to leave. Bino suspected that at the moment Cole was right outside in the hall, seated on the edge of one of the straightbacked chairs and doing a slow burn.

"Look, Nelson," Bino said. "I got no stake in this other than I'm a lawyer involved in defending his client. As far as your blood-drinking guy goes I'm just a concerned citizen. I told Mac Strange I'd surrender my records to him, and as far as I'm concerned that's what I'm going to do. If Mac gives the word, they're yours." He swiveled his head to zero in on Mac.

Mac's legs were crossed and he was regarding his knee. "I think you'd better do what the man wants, Bino. I've got enough problems keeping Hardy Cole in line. Hardy wants to go charging off on his own and to hell with everybody else. We've got orders on this. Mr. Deletay here is the man."

Bino studied Strange for a moment, noted the deep lines at the corners of the county prosecutor's mouth, realized with a jolt that Mac was getting old. Bino himself had been practicing law over twenty years, and both Mac and Hardy Cole had been veterans when Bino had been a shaver fresh from law school, working for Richard Bigelow. Ten years ago, anybody trying to take over one of Mac's cases would have had a fight on his hands. Bino shrugged. "Whatever you say, Mac." He reached down, got his thick folder from the floor and laid it on the desk in front of Deletay. "All yours," Bino said.

Deletay made no move to touch the folder. "Have you been over these?"

"With a fine-tooth comb," Bino said. "We've been making a lot of noise, a lot of stuff going back and forth between Marv and me"—he jerked a thumb in Goldman's direction—"but the truth is that I don't think there's much in there that'll help. I've got Annette's and Brenda's phone numbers and mailing addresses, and a little background sketch. I don't think there's anything in there that you don't already know."

"What about your personal recollections?" Deletay said. "Anything you've remembered about either of the young ladies' activities on the days you went to court with them?"

"Nothing so far," Bino said. "Tell you the truth, when they had those hearings I was pretty involved in what was going on in front of the bench. Dodie, that's my secretary, Dodie Peterson, she's the one that sat with the girls. I haven't had a chance to talk to her about it." Bino looked around—at Deletay watching him over folded hands, at Sandra Nestle sitting primly forward on her chair, her legs crossed, her lips slightly parted.

"Well, she's someone we'll definitely have to interview," Deletay said. He reached in his breast pocket to withdraw a slim black pen with a gold clip. He uncapped the pen and slid the cap onto the reverse end. "What's your secretary's full name, Mr. Phillips?"

Bino drew a shallow breath. It wasn't that he minded the question, it was Deletay's delivery that set him off. Irritation crept into Bino's tone as he said, "Dora Annette. She's been with me eight years."

Deletay scribbled on a notepad. "Some of the banter between you and Mr. Goldman, in there in the meeting, intrigues me." He held the pen between a thumb and forefinger and tapped Bino's file with the pen's blunt end. "In addition to the victims, is there also information in here regarding your other witnesses? The ones besides Brenda and Annette."

Bino didn't look at Goldman, kept his gaze across the desk, speaking to Deletay. "Yeah, sure, they're in there. Won't do you much good, though. Look, the only reason I'm even in this case is because of the defendant's mother, Kit Stanley—I knew her in college. She tutored athletes for extra money. Mickey—that's the defendant—Mickey was a baby then. His father was a guy I sort of knew, a basketball player four years older than me. He left Kit while she was pregnant, and I'm not sure whatever happened to him. Probably he's in jail, tell you the truth. What I do know is, Kit raised Mickey on her own, and there's a lot of credit due her for that. Mickey got a football scholarship, otherwise she could never have put him through school. He needs his butt kicked for what he's put his mother through the past few years, but you'd have a hard time putting any of the killings on him since he's been in jail. Anyhow, take care of my stuff, willya?"

"We'll do that," Deletay said. "They're all yours, Sandra."
Nestle bent forward to scoop the files onto her lap.

Bino stood. "I'd appreciate it if you'd copy what you want and
let me have the originals back. I've still got a guy to defend." He
felt suddenly tired, and not all of it was from a lack of sleep the
night before. Looking at those grisly pictures he'd seen in the
meeting would wear anybody out. "If you're through with me,"
Bino said, "I think I'll go."

No one answered. Bino moved to the door, raised a hand
toward Mac and Goldman on the sofa, and went out into the hall.
He'd been right about Hardy Cole. The county investigator was
seated near the door and looked ready to chew nails. Bino nodded
to Cole and continued on his way. He had to go back through
the conference room to retrieve his briefcase, and as he grabbed
the handle and hefted the case his gaze fell on the bulletin board.
Donatello's picture was still hanging there, the dope peddler on
the bed with his head thrown back, a gaping wound in his midsection. Bino averted his gaze and hustled through the door and on
downstairs to the parking lot. Once inside the Linc, he sat for a
moment and let the motor idle. He leaned his head against the
steering wheel and tightly shut his eyes.

12

Bino decided not to go directly home even though he was so tired that it was an effort to move and his eyelids felt as though they weighed a hundred pounds apiece. It seemed like years since he'd entered the meeting at Lew Sterrett Justice Center, but it was now only a little past two in the afternoon. If he went to his apartment right now, Bino reasoned, he'd fall into bed and snooze for ten or eleven hours, then wake up at midnight and wander around listening to music until dawn for the second night in a row. Tough as it might be, he'd be better off to wait until after sundown to cop any z's.

Besides, he needed a few laughs, something to take his mind off all these killings and disappearances. Jesus, what a string of downers. What he'd do, he'd drop by Joe Miller's Bar for a couple of drinks and see if any of his friends were hanging around. Likely Barney Dalton would be through with his golf game for the day, and would be holding forth at Joe Miller's, firing off a few one-liners. Ever since college, ever since he and Barney had played basketball together, whenever Bino needed a few chuckles all he had to do was look up his old buddy. Always had done the trick and likely always would.

So he steered the Linc onto southbound Stemmons Freeway, whipped through the figure-eight mixmaster of highways southwest of Reunion Arena onto I-30 going east, skirting the southern edges of downtown Dallas, and finally edged into the northbound lanes of I-45. There wasn't a cloud in sight; the sky was a brilliant blue above its smoggy lower edges and the late September temperature was in the lower nineties. Bino set the a/c fan at middle speed, plugged a vintage Elvis tape into the wraparound, and drummed his fingers on the padded dash in rhythm to "Blue Suede Shoes." Jesus, he felt better already.

Midafternoon traffic was sparse, and by the time he'd followed I-45 north to the Lemmon Avenue exit, and had made the ninety-degree turn onto westbound Lemmon, he'd shaken his blues and his head was bobbing up and down to the music. Elvis had pounded through "Blue Suede Shoes" and "Return to Sender," and was now slowing the pace as he moaned tearfully into "I Was the One." The Linc bounced into Joe Miller's parking lot as Bino sang loudly, "The waayy she kisses you *now*-ow," and came to a halt between a green Nissan Maxima and a yellow Ford Bronco. The Bronco was Barney Dalton's current transportation, Bino thought, and the set of golf clubs visible through the Bronco's rear window confirmed it. Hey, old Barn was here. Things were definitely looking up. Bino cut the Linc's engine, stripped off his coat and tie and tossed them into the backseat, and practically skipped through the parking lot to bump the door with his shoulder and enter the bar.

He paused for a moment as his vision grew accustomed to the dimness. Finally the tables and booths were visible enough to him so that he felt he could walk through the club's interior without tripping. So he picked his way over to the bar. There Barney was holding court. He was on a barstool with his thick brown hair bobbing up and down and his rust mustache wiggling as he talked nonstop to a cute brunette in jeans and T-shirt who was seated on his right. Bino slid onto the stool on Barney's left and propped his forearms against the foam padding on the bar.

Barney was saying, "—and it's like I was telling the guys on the course, what's life without a few kicks, huh?" He was drinking a dark liquid from a beer mug, and so was the brunette, and so were maybe five or six men and women who were scattered up and down the length of the bar. "Always time for a party, I always say," Barney said. The brunette giggled cutely and sipped from her mug. A half-full pitcher was next to Barney's elbow.

"Hey, Barn," Bino said. "What's goin' on?"

"Bino." Barney swiveled on his stool and grinned from ear to ear. "Hey, buddy, it wouldn't be the same without you. Glad you could make it. Man, we haven't had a good Bloody Mary party in months." He leaned over to grab an empty beer mug, filled it from the pitcher, and set the drink in front of Bino. "Bottoms up, buddy," Barney said. "Plenty more where that came from, they're all on me today. Made five birdies on the back nine."

Bino's features sagged. Jesus, it *was* a Bloody Mary, thick red liquid swirling around, thick bloody . . . *Jesus.*

"Well, drink up, buddy," Barney said.

Bino gagged. Beads of sweat popped out on his forehead. "I think I'll . . . I think I'll pass, Barn," he said quickly, then ignored the stares all around him as he got up and retraced his steps through the doorway and out into the parking lot. Once he reached the Linc he leaned unsteadily against the fender while the pavement beneath his feet tilted dizzily and the pulse in his temples pounded like drums. It was a full five minutes before he could climb in and start the engine.

By the time Bino had taken I-45 north to LBJ Freeway, then headed west to Dallas Parkway and pulled into his numbered space at the Vapors North, the pounding inside his head had subsided to a dull roar and he was weak as a kitten. Between charging off to the courthouse at the crack of dawn and then sitting in the meeting at Lew Sterrett Justice Center for several hours, he hadn't eaten a bite all day. Now, to top it all off, Barney Dalton had offered him a Bloody Mary to drink. He climbed slowly from the Linc and literally staggered through the breezeway to the courtyard where his apartment was located. He skirted the pool, fumbled his key into the lock, and entered his silent digs.

Cecil looked hungry, so Bino dutifully ladled a minnow into the Oscar fish's tank, then turned quickly away so he wouldn't have to watch Cecil run the darting little bugger down and swallow him whole. Normally he enjoyed watching Cecil commit murder and mayhem, but today things were different. Today Bino stumbled over to the refrigerator, hoping to choke down a peanut butter sandwich and then fall into bed. He'd just spread Peter Pan Smooth and Creamy onto a piece of buttered split-top wheat bread, and was screwing the top back onto the peanut butter jar, when something in the living room caught his attention. He went over and peered through the opening over the kitchen counter. On the table beside the sofa, the red light on his answering machine blinked rapidly. He slapped the lid onto his sandwich and carried it into the living room, munching thoughtfully as he sat down and pressed the playback button.

There was a sharp click, followed by the silent noise of rewinding tape, then Dodie's soft voice said, "Bino, I've been calling all over for you." There was urgency in her tone, and fear as well. He swallowed sticky peanut butter and sat up straighter. Dodie then said on the tape, "I've gotten this really creepy phone call down at the office. I'm really scared, and since I can't get you I'm calling the police." There was a disconnecting click followed by the sound of the dial tone, then the machine switched automatically back to the answering mode.

Dodie wouldn't have made that call unless things were serious. She just wasn't the type to fly off the handle. He picked up the phone and called his office. After two rings a male voice answered, saying, "Hello, lawyer's office." It wasn't Half's voice, and aside from Dodie, Half should be the only one picking up the line.

"Who is this?" Bino said.

After a second's pause the male voice said, "Well who in hell is this?"

"This is Bino Phillips. That's my office you're in."

"Yeah. Yeah, Mr. Phillips, this is Detective Warren with the Dallas Police. I think you'd better get down there. You got real trouble, it looks like to me."

If Nelson Deletay wanted to take over Mac Strange's office, that was between Deletay and Strange, but taking over Bino's office was something else again. Bino said, "Excuse me, Nelson, but you're in my seat." His tone was calm, but he made sure that his look told Deletay that the big white-haired lawyer wasn't fooling around, and might be just a little bit crazy to boot.

Deletay's eyebrows lifted just a fraction and he opened his mouth to speak, then he looked Bino over and apparently changed his mind. "Sure thing," Deletay said. He got up and moved around to sit on the couch beneath the old basketball photo along with Sandra Nestle. Nestle was still wearing her black pantsuit. Her lower jaw dropped in surprise as she looked at Bino, then at Deletay, and back to Bino again. Bino doubted if Nestle had ever heard anyone confront Deletay before. If Deletay continued to throw his weight around in Bino's office, she was likely to hear it again.

Bino sank into his cushioned swivel chair. The padding gave softly under his buttocks and thighs to remind him just how beat he was. He said, "Thanks. Now. You've done *what* with the cassette from my tape recorder?"

"Sent it for voice analysis," Deletay said. "Won't hurt it, and we'll give you a receipt."

"They didn't even ask, Bino," Dodie said. "They just took it." Dodie had worn a pale blue summer dress with shoulder straps today, and her blond hair was tied back into a ponytail. There were dark circles under her eyes as though she hadn't been getting much sleep, and Bino knew the only time that Dodie ever tied her hair back was when she hadn't had time to wash it. A lot of women would have looked like hell in that condition, but Dodie appeared merely a little less wonderful than usual. Bino had hugged her when he'd first come in, and she'd been quivering slightly. From fear, Bino had thought, but from the sizzle which now emitted from her clear blue eyes, he supposed that was quivering from anger as well. "Just marched in here and didn't say squat," Dodie said.

"Tell you what, Nelson," Bino said. "You can give me a receipt, then you got five minutes to get my stuff back to me."

"It won't be long," Deletay said. "Take it easy. Our goal is more important than anybody's personal feelings." Visible beyond him, through the open doorway, the plainclothes Dallas cop was still at Dodie's desk, answering the phone. When Bino had come in, Nolan Pounds, the true-crime guy, and another man who'd introduced himself as a syndicated columnist, had been wandering around in Bino's office as well. Bino had curtly invited the writers out, and they now sat side by side on the sofa in the reception room. Mac Strange was also in Bino's office, seated on the windowsill with the mirrored western wall of Becker Tower and the pointed spire atop the old Mercantile Bank behind him in the background. Mac's lips twitched as though he wanted to laugh.

"Oh?" Bino said to Deletay. "Well, what *is* your goal?"

"To stop these killings," Deletay said.

"I agree that's what it *ought* to be," Bino said. "But it looks to me like your goal is to get as much of this as possible into print.

Well, I'm not one of your hired hands. If you want something out of my office, you call up and make an appointment like everybody else."

Deletay hesitated and glanced at Nestle before saying, "In the future we will."

"In the future you'd better," Bino said. To Mac Strange he said, "You hear the tape, Mac?"

"They played it over," Mac said. "It sounded like three guys, maybe, but it could have been one guy changing his voice. One time the voices seem to change right in the middle of a sentence."

Nestle spoke up for the first time. "If it's Dracula Don, and right now we're assuming that it is, then I suspect voice analysis will show that it was only one man. You remember these people hear voices? A lot of the time they assume the different personalities and say the words themselves. It's pretty common."

"Plus," Deletay chimed in, "what he had to say pretty well firms up that we're dealing with someone who's been in federal court. He knew that you were were gone to the Federal Building. And"—he glanced at Dodie—"I don't want to frighten you, miss, but you fit the victim profile perfectly."

Dodie shuddered and hugged herself. Her gaze lowered.

"Well you *are* scaring her, Nelson," Bino said.

"She's an attractive young woman," Deletay said. "Like the rest, except for the drug dealer."

"I don't care what she is." Bino stood and pointed. "That's the door, folks. Now get out of here, I want to talk to my secretary." Reason told that he might be biting off more than he could chew, bearding Deletay this way, but at the moment Bino was too fed up to care.

Deletay rose from the couch. "Hmm. Well, I guess I can tell when I'm not wanted."

"Glad you're that observant," Bino said.

"We're still going to interview her at length," Deletay said, pointing at Dodie. "It's still my investigation. Let's don't be forgetting that."

"Yeah, well you've investigated around here all you're going to for today," Bino said. "Out."

Deletay balled his hands into fists. "I don't want to have to put pressure on you."

"I'd think twice about that, Nelson. I'll tell you something.

You're standing in my office and I don't see that you've got any warrant on you. I asked you to leave. If you don't I may put a little pressure on *you*, such as with my foot against the cheek of your ass."

"*Bino*," Dodie said. Her tone was reproachful, but she looked as though she wouldn't have minded giving Deletay the boot herself.

Deletay said, "Hmm," then looked at Nestle and said, "Hmm. Come on, Sandra, we've got more to worry about than this guy."

"You ought to have," Bino said. "And I'm not that worried about the tape. What, three bucks? The tape's yours, but my files are something else again. You get them copied and back to me."

Nestle rose and looked at Bino as though she thought he was nutty as a fruitcake, but her gaze held a certain respect as well. She went out into the reception room with Deletay close on her heels. Mac Strange hoisted his fanny off the windowsill and started to follow.

Bino said, "Mac."

Strange paused. Deletay turned to peer into Bino's office.

"Close the door, Mac," Bino said.

Strange appeared hesitant, then said through the doorway, "Just a second, Nelson. I've got to calm this lunatic down." He softly closed the door, shutting out Deletay from view. "Yeah?" the county prosecutor said.

"You know that what I'm telling that guy doesn't go for you, don't you?" Bino said.

"Tell you the truth, you might have more guts than sense," Strange said. "Like him or not, Deletay's conducting a pretty damned important investigation. Plus the guy can make it tough on you."

"I know that," Bino said. "And I know that sending the tape for analysis is the right thing to do. I just don't like these federal people barging in and taking over. You were in that meeting today. Three or four hours, the girl didn't tell a thing that every cop in there didn't already know. The whole thing was for the newspaper guys. If you ask me, these Quantico folks are in the way more than they're helping—not that the investigation is any of my business. As a citizen, though, I'd just as soon that the guy doesn't go around drinking everybody's blood any longer than necessary."

Strange spread his feet, folded his hands near the bottom of

his coat, and looked down for a moment. When he raised his
head there was a gleam in his eye. "Some of us might feel the
same way," Mac said. "I just go about it a little differently. Yelling
at these people won't get you anything but sore vocal cords."

"Yeah?" Bino said. "Well, just what is it that *you're* doing
about it?"

Mac scratched his own chin. "Bino, you and Hardy Cole got
a lot in common. Both of you are old enough to know better, but
you still pop off a lot, you know? These feds went over to the
Adolphus Hotel today, to try to find out about the guy that's supposed to have written the license number down. The hotel manager stonewalled 'em. He told 'em if they want to know anything
about any guests of the hotel they're going to have to get a court
order. Deletay said he didn't want to make any waves, says he
knows some guy in Washington that might have some stroke with
the Adolphus people. You know what Hardy says to me? Says
Deletay's full of shit—excuse the language, Dodie—says Deletay's
full of it and that Hardy P. Cole could get the information in a
New York minute."

"And?" Bino said.

"And so I pretended I didn't hear old Hardy. Come to think
about it, Hardy might be over at the Adolphus this very minute.
I don't know for sure, though, I haven't asked anybody where
Hardy's gone, and neither has Deletay. What Deletay doesn't know
can't hurt him, right?" Mac opened the door, paused, and gave a
broad wink. "You cool it, Bino, you hear? Don't get your blood
pressure in an uproar, it's not good for you." He left.

When Strange had gone, Bino said, "Well, I'll be damned."

"You do do a lot of yelling around, Bino," Dodie said. She
rested her forearms on the armrests of her chair and crossed her
legs.

Bino went around behind his desk. "Maybe I do. How you
feeling?"

"I *feel* all right. But, wow, if you could have heard the guy
on the phone."

Bino scratched his forehead. "Where's Half?"

"Out at the farm, with Pop," Dodie said. "He called in and
said that if you needed him you know where to look."

Bino sighed inwardly as he studied her, her earnest expression,
the dark circles under her eyes. The times in the past he'd needed

her, she'd been there for him, and often over the years he'd wondered if he might be in . . . Hell, no, not old "Hardrock" Phillips.

"Let's go, Dode," Bino said.

One blond eyebrow lifted and her head tilted to one side. "Go where?"

"By your place, for you to pack a few things. You're going to stay with me, at least for tonight. As soon as he's available you can go to Half's if you want, but no way am I letting you stay at your apartment with this nutso running around."

There was hesitation in her look. Sure, Bino thought, she's thinking the same thing that I am. About one night on her birthday we got sort of, caught up in each other, and another time when I was down in the dumps right after Winnie Anspacher died. Once more as well, just before Christmas one year. Dammit, Bino thought.

Dodie said, "Gee, Bino, I . . ."

"On the couch, Dode. Or *I'll* take the couch, whatever. Better than somebody drinking your blood, isn't it?"

She smirked, then her face lit up in a Tinkerbell grin. "Oh, I guess it is," Dodie said.

13

Hardy Cole was in fact at the Adolphus Hotel that very moment, and Hardy was getting the runaround. "So what you're telling me," Hardy said, "is that you're not giving up your records to law enforcement people, regardless. We can get a court order, you know that, but it's a drawn-out deal and a pain in the ass, tell you the truth."

"Be my guest," the hotel manager said. He was a natty little man wearing a dark blue suit, a starched shirt with a narrow blue pinstripe, and a solid navy tie. His dark hair was too perfect, and Hardy suspected that the guy was wearing a hairpiece. "I'm telling you the same thing I told the FBI agents yesterday," the manager said. "They were from right up the street at the Dallas FBI office, but they confided in me they were taking orders from somebody in from D.C. It's like this. We cooperate a hundred percent with the police, no question about that, but what you people are wanting is out of line. We have security, you know? Any specific guest record you're welcome to, but just to go bulling through our records for someone named Oscar? Uh-uh. Now, though, if you bring a court order in here I've got no choice but to give you the records, and when someone sues us I've got the order to fall back on—that's the way it was for the FBI, and that's the way it is for you."

They were standing in the lobby, off to one side of the check-in desk, near a waiting line consisting of men in business suits and women in tailored fall clothes with groomed hairdos, stepping up in turn and presenting American Express, Visa, or MasterCard for confirmed reservations. The carpet was deep red, crystal chandeliers tinkling softly overhead, the oldest hotel in Dallas refurbished to look the way it had in the Roaring Twenties. Cole was wearing brown slacks, a plaid sport coat, and a tan shirt with the collar undone. His expression showed neither full house nor busted flush, and his jaw worked slowly on a wad of Wrigley's Spearmint.

"Look," Cole said, "you know we're talking pretty serious stuff here. This isn't some guy walking his hotel tab."

"It wouldn't matter if you were after the Boston Strangler," the manager said. "It's our policy to protect our guests' privacy." He nodded and smiled to a couple in their forties, a blond woman and a bald man who had just left the check-in line. "Glad to have you, folks," the manager said.

Cole shrugged and spread his hands, palms up. "I guess I'm wasting my time, huh?"

"That's about the size of it. You've got your job to do, we've got ours. I could get in big trouble if I deviated from policy."

"Yeah," Cole said. "I see what you mean. Well, as long as everybody's doing their job . . ." He held up one finger. "Just a minute, huh? Be right back with you."

Cole left the manager and took two long strides after the man and woman whom the manager had just greeted. "Hey, bud," Hardy said loudly. "You, too, honey. Y'all wait a minute."

The man stopped and turned, showing an irritated grimace. The woman, wearing a charcoal-gray tailored suit and medium heels, muttered, "Well, I *never.*"

"Yeah, hon, I never, either," Cole said, stopping before the couple, fishing in his back pocket, flashing the shield. "Detective Cole. I'll be needing some ID from you two."

The man scratched his bald head and glanced at the manager, then glared at Cole. "What in hell is this, officer?" the man said.

"Easy, bud," Hardy said. "This here your old lady, or she a hooker?"

"Jesus, it's my wife. Twenty-three years."

"Okay," Cole said. "You two show me some ID proves that, or I'll have to take you in."

The hotel manager had left the check-in desk and was suddenly at Cole's elbow. His cool, all-business expression had been replaced by one of near-panic. "What in the world is going on here?" he said.

"I'm asking for ID to see if this gal's a hooker," Cole said, jerking a thumb toward the well-groomed woman. She was slightly pale, as though she might faint dead away.

"You can't . . ." The manager looked at the man and woman and forced a tight smile. "Excuse us, folks. I'll talk to the policeman over here." He started to lead Cole back over to the check-in desk.

"Well, you'd damn sure better," the man said. "Ten years we've been staying in this hotel."

"Yeah, sure, bud," Cole said loudly. "You and the little lady stay right where you are. Don't try running off, you hear?" He was speaking to the couple over his shoulder as he followed the manager.

The manager leaned an elbow on the counter. "Just what the fuck are you trying to pull, detective?"

"Hey, no use to start cussin' me." Cole held up both hands, palms out. "Just doing my job, same as you. State law, voted in last November: Any time we suspect prostitution we got a right to ask for ID. You want to call your lawyer, have him look it up?"

"I know about that," the manager said. "I *voted* for the law. Yeah, in some fleatrap out in South Dallas, but not in the *Adolphus*, for Christ's sake."

Cole shifted his gum from one cheek to the other. "You could be right, maybe I should call my supervisor. But hey, I read those new laws pretty carefully when they come out, and I don't remember anything about any 'fleatrap.' Said just 'hotel' best I remember." He looked toward the check-in line, where men and women alike now glanced nervously in his direction. Cole said to the manager, "And, you know what? Every one of those women over there looks like a hooker to me. Guess I'll have to ID 'em, huh? Like you said, your job, my job. I could get in real trouble if I start ignoring what the law says. Somebody might think I'm on the take or something."

"Jesus Christ," the manager said breathily, and again said, "Jesus Christ."

"Tell you what, though. If I had those records to look at I wouldn't have time to check anybody's ID."

"You son of a *bitch*."

"Hey, I don't got to take that," Cole said. "I'm going back to do my duty." He headed for the couple whom he'd questioned, and who appeared ready to bolt and run.

"Wait a minute," the manager yelled.

Cole stopped and turned.

"Just a minute," the manager said. "The records—I'll get them sent over to my office. You wait here." He went behind the desk and talked a mile a minute to the clerk.

"Hey, nice of you," Cole said. He grinned toward the waiting couple and raised his voice. "Just a little joke, folks. You all go ahead. Have a nice stay in Dallas, huh?"

14

Patrick Quarles checked the bubble on the level and decided that the California redwood needed more sanding. He set the level aside and hoisted the wood from the twin sawhorses onto the workbench, grunting slightly with the effort, and then flipped the switch on the electric sander. The machine whined; its rotor became at once a blur of motion. Quarles lifted his cup and drank more blood, his eyes shifting warily right and left, right and left, as he surveyed the furniture shop over the cup's rim. The blood had cooled to near room temperature and had coagulated into thick reddish-brown curds which coated the inside of the cup. It was easier to swallow the blood when it was warm. He set the cup aside, adjusted his safety goggles down over his eyes, lifted the sander, and applied the spinning rotor carefully to the wood. The motor's whine increased in volume as sawdust flew, and the sweet smell of the redwood wafted into his nostrils like incense. At eighteen, he wouldn't have needed the level and would have had the wood perfectly aligned on the first attempt. Sixteen years of part-time-only woodworking had weakened his eye.

Until recently he'd done cabinet and furniture construction on weekends, on a referral basis only, but the time had long since passed when he could make more than pocket change at it. He'd paid his way through college building furniture, but that was before assembly-line manufacturing, coupled with runaway inflation, had made the handbuilt items too expensive for retailers to stock. So Patrick now built furniture only when he wasn't busy with his job, though the hours spent in the shop were still his favorite time. *Had* been his favorite, that is, until the Truth had come into his life. Now he had no place to relax, not even inside the shop. Even in the shop, the voices told him what to do. The project he was now working on was Theirs, of course, and in a way he was glad that Judge Sanderson had suspended the trial until further notice. Now he could finish the project and not have to listen to the voices complain about his laziness.

Quarles was shirtless, wearing worn and faded jeans with holes in the pockets and Reebok sneakers that had once been snow-white but now were a dirty gray. He wore no socks. A wide cloth belt of pouches and loops encircled his waist; the pouches contained four different grades of nails, wood screws of varied lengths with both wide and narrow threads, and large tacks with springloaded expanders on their ends. Hammers and chisels dangled from the loops, their handles bumping softly against Quarles's hips and buttocks as he moved about. A fine coating of sawdust clung to his belly and shoulders, and nestled among the sparse hairs on his chest like flaking dandruff. His scars, also coated with sawdust, stood out on his torso like raised snowcapped mountain ranges. The lenses of his safety goggles were coated with with an off-white dusty film as well.

The shop occupied the entire ground floor of Quarles's house and was open on the side nearest the lake; as Quarles worked, he glanced occasionally down the slope toward the calmly rippling water. More fall thunderstorms were in the forecast. Quarles was absolutely terrified of thunder and lightning, and tonight as the wind and rain whipped the lake into a whitecapped fury he would tremble and bury his head under the pillow. The slope leading from the house to the shore was bare black dirt for the most part, dotted with scrubby mesquite trees and weedy patches of Bermuda grass.

Quarles had built the boat dock during the first summer after he'd bought the house by the lake. He had kept the dock in perfect repair until he'd become Uziah, Disciple of the Truth; the pilings beneath the dock were now covered with slime and barnacles and its surface wood rotting and cracking. A month ago, his foot had fallen through a hole while he was walking on the dock; the swelling in his ankle from the fall hadn't completely receded and he still moved with a slight limp.

He hadn't had the equipment to build the *Seastork II*; he'd had the hull constructed by the Hundlee people down in Lewisville the year after he'd built the dock. Quarles had done the boat's interior, though; the oak paneling, the cabinets, and cushioned window seats. The *Seastork II* was eighteen feet in length and powered by twin Chrysler engines, and until the Truth had come, Quarles had kept the *Seastork II* spick-and-span and running like a charm. But his work as a Disciple had stopped the boat's upkeep as well. Like the dock's pilings, the boat's underbelly was now coated with slime; its white hull had yellowed, and the paint was flaking in places. Quarles couldn't remember the last time he'd started the *Seastork*'s motors, and he doubted seriously whether the engines would run if he tried. A Disciple of the Truth had no time for foolish water sports.

The shop itself also reflected the change in Patrick Quarles's habits since the voices had assumed control. Once spotless, the floor was now coated with sawdust. Piles of unfinished furniture lay along the walls, underneath the workbench, and in the corners: a tabletop here, a chair arm there, a complete breakfast table with one leg carved into the shape of a lion's paw and the other legs blunt and scarred by the chisel—all projects that Quarles had begun and never finished because of the Work of the Truth. The tools of his furniture-making trade—offset hammers, wood chisels, Phillips and flathead screwdriver—once in neat-as-a-pin order, now lay scattered about on the workbench and on the floor.

A month ago he'd connected a recording machine to his phone. He now refused to answer in person, sitting mute by the cradled receiver until callers identified themselves, because most of the calls came from irate customers who'd placed deposits on furniture with him and then never received their orders. In fact, he would have had the phone disconnected altogether if it hadn't have been for his full-time occupation; often he wondered when he would quit work entirely and devote a hundred percent of his time to serving the Truth. Only when the Truth was complete could he discard his man-existence altogether.

There was a steel overhanging door for closing off the open end of the shop in winter, and near the open end stood three space heaters. He hadn't bothered to store the heaters the previous spring; it was too late to store them now because winter would be coming again in a couple of months. The drill press, punch, and wood lathe stood side by side with thick coats of dust on their surfaces.

Quarles turned the sander off, lifted the redwood from the workbench, and placed it carefully on top of the box that he'd built. The box was in the shape of a six-sided coffin—was to be a coffin of sorts, in fact—and the lid which he'd been sanding was a perfect fit. He checked the slots and picked one of the hinges off the workbench and tried it. The hinges would do. There were two openings in the lid, both rectangular, one at the place where the intended occupant's head would lie and the other just below the middle of the box. There would be a hinged door over the head opening, both for feeding and for punishment purposes. The other slot was smooth, with beveled edges, and would remain open at all times so that Rebecca's pubic area would be visible. Bolted to the inside bottom of the box were four sets of steel shackles. It was a good job, and Quarles was pleased with his work.

The high-pitched voice said without warning, "How much longer? Don't you know you must hurry?"

Quarles's head jerked upward as he looked frantically around. Usually they spoke through other objects; through the television, sometimes through animals. In the shop, though, their voices emitted from empty space, from the corners and walls themselves.

Then the deep basso voice said, "And the Arrows of Truth. Have you prepared more?"

His lips drawn back in fear, Quarles indicated the workbench. "Over there. They're . . . over there." And they were; perfectly machined and varnished, four hard maple spikes like board-game pegs.

"*Four?*" the high-pitched voice said. "Only four?"

"But with her in the box, will there be need for more?" Quarles whined. "I thought . . ."

"IT IS NOT FOR YOU TO THINK," the deep voice said. "The Servant of the Truth need only to act and to follow the Way."

Quarles's nose was running; he wiped his upper lip with the back of his hand. "I'm almost through."

"He's almost through," the whiny voice said, mimicking. "What about the Windows of Truth? Are they ready?"

"Just as I was told," Quarles said, his eyes narrowing slightly, being careful to give credit for the slots, *Their* idea and not his own.

"They must be perfect," the deep voice said. "Her angelic face through one window, the Portals of Evil through the other."

Tears of humiliation leapt into Quarles's eyes. "Her . . . *pubic area*. Yes. Yes, that's what you said." He spoke in a near-whisper, then picked up a hinge and set it in place to show them his handiwork.

" 'THE PORTALS OF EVIL,' I SAID." As the deep voice became enraged, Quarles cowered and covered his face. The voice continued, more softly but still sternly, "It is the Way. Tomorrow night you will take her."

Quarles recoiled as if slapped. "Tomorrow night? I can't. I—"

"YOU CAN. YOU WILL DO AS YOU ARE TOLD." The basso voice was so loud that the walls vibrated. Then, softly and quite gently, "I can see your work, and it is good. Once Rebecca is ours, we will be One. She will partake of the blood of the Truth."

Quarles lifted his head as wonderment crossed his features. Praise? He'd never received praise before. "One? We will be One?"

There was no answer, only the faint crackling which told him that they were through speaking to him for now.

One. They would be One.

It was the Way. It was a Sign.

Quarles's fear left him in a rush and he smiled. It was Time. Oh, it was Time. He swiftly set the hinge in place, reached into his waist pouch for screws, withdrew a screwdriver from one of the loops, and worked to affix the hinge to the outside of the box. As his fingers moved rapidly, he lifted his voice in song, his not-unpleasant tenor going through the first two verses of "Going Afar Upon the Mountain." When he'd been very small it had been his father's favorite hymn, often sung as his father used his fists to beat the child senseless.

The sound of the electric sander coming from directly beneath her didn't disturb Brenda Milton very much. She didn't move a muscle, and the fluttering of her eyelids was a reflex, nothing more. The sound which vibrated the floorboards and bounced from the walls inside her tiny prison was an angry buzz, but to her it was muted and far away, like dream noise. She hadn't heard much over the past twelve hours, and the sounds that she did hear were barely penetrating her consciousness. Consciousness, such as it was.

Her eyes were open in the darkness, but her pupils were twin points as though she stood in brilliant sunlight. One of her eyelids drooped while the other was open wide as she stared at nothing.

Her skin was naturally fair, but the summer hours at the beach, pool, and tennis court had turned her the shade of butternut ice cream. Since the beginning of the fall semester she'd used a sun-lamp in her room to retain her golden color. Brenda tanned easily without burning, and all of her life her complexion had caused other blonds to green with envy. No longer. Over the past four days her skin had lost its lovely sheen and was now as white as chalk. The large artery in her arm had withered until it was barely as big around as the needle that was inserted into her flesh. On the skin around the needle was a mottled purple mark the size of a quarter. Her heart rate, normally a well-conditioned sixty beats per minute, fluttered now, racing pell-mell to a hundred and eighty and then slowing to near forty, only to speed up again.

When Patrick Quarles had last come to her, less than an hour ago, he'd found that she had soiled herself and the table beneath her buttocks. He'd cleaned her with paper towels and carried most of the runny waste into the bathroom to flush it away, but he hadn't been particularly thorough. The closet in which she lay smelled of drying feces. The stench didn't matter to Brenda; odors meant no more to her than sounds.

No longer did she fight or strain against her shackles, and no longer did she attempt to lift her head. Any thoughts that she had were vague and fleeting, and any will which remained in her was directed to only one purpose.

Brenda wanted to die.

Quarles worked all night, and put the finishing touches on the box at sunup. His work was perfection. The openings in the lid were octagon-shaped with neatly beveled edges, and the door covering the face-slot fit as though it were a part of the lid. The cherrywood stain finish he'd applied would dry in half a day, and the box would be ready for use by afternoon. An achy tiredness flowed through Quarles's muscles as he stood beside the shop's only window to drain the last remnants of blood from the cup.

The predicted thunderstorm had come and gone during the night, though Quarles had been so intent with his work he'd barely noticed it, and the outside air was crisp and clear. The sun sent its early morning rays dancing over the surface of the lake in a series of quick red flashes. Quarles swallowed and turned for a final glance at his handiwork. Not even *They* could complain. At last he could rest.

He ascended the steps and went down the hall into his bedroom, used an old Bunsen burner to melt Mexican brown heroin in a spoon, then injected the syrupy liquid into his arm. A muffled sob came from within the closet, but he ignored it. He stretched out on top of the covers and intertwined his fingers behind his head. His eyelids grew heavy. Soon he would sleep.

And tonight, they would be One.

As Quarles had worked tirelessly through the night, the Father's meaning had come to him in a flash. Quarles had been confused about the Truth. The second voice, the high-pitched voice, was not the Son and never had been. Uziah the Disciple was only a temporary existence, a transitionary state. The high-pitched voice belonged to the third member of the Trinity, the Holy Ghost.

They would be One. Patrick Quarles's father was The Father.

And Patrick Quarles was Christ.

15

At about the same moment when Patrick Quarles was watching the sunrise through the window of the furniture shop, Bino Phillips woke up stiff as a board. He'd been sleeping on his living room floor between the sofa and the fifty-one-inch Mitsubishi TV, having rolled off the couch four times during the night and having finally decided that a night on the floor was better than a broken arm or leg from falling off the sofa. He struggled to his feet and grumped into the kitchen, shirtless and wearing the bottom half of an ancient SMU basketball warmup with a large hole in the knee. Cecil was drifting motionless in his tank, his mouth slowly opening and closing, and he now regarded Bino with an Oscar fish's version of a condescending smirk. As Bino turned the faucet on to half fill the Mr. Coffee pot, then sloshed the water around and dumped it out in the sink before filling the pot to the brim, he paused long enough to give Cecil the finger.

As Bino listened to the hiss of the Mr. Coffee's water heater and the dribble of the thin brown stream trickling into the pot, there was an urgent throbbing in his bladder. Jesus, he had to go to the toilet. He padded barefoot down the hall and partway opened the door to his bedroom.

Dodie sat on the end of the king-size, wearing thin cotton panties and a bra. She had a pair of jeans by the waistband and was lifting one pretty leg to put the britches on, and now gave a startled "Eek!" and raised the jeans to cover her chest. "Don't come *in* here," Dodie said.

Bino leaned on the door frame and regarded the ceiling. "Look, Dode. I got to use the bathroom, okay? It's not like I've never seen—"

"*Out.*" Dodie got up and crossed the room, then held the jeans up in front of her with one hand while she placed her other palm in the center of Bino's chest and shoved.

He backed up a step and spread his hands, palms up. "Dodie, I'm dying."

"*Out.*" She used her shoulder to slam the door in his face with a solid thunk.

"Jesus Christ," Bino mumbled, then went back to the living room and said loudly to Cecil, "Jesus *Christ.*" Bubbles rose in Cecil's tank, and Bino supposed that Cecil was snickering. Well, fuck Cecil. Bino slipped his feet into Reebok sneakers, shrugged into the top to the warmup suit with "SMU BASKETBALL" stenciled across the chest, then went outside and down the sidewalk to Tilly Madden's apartment. Tilly was the manager of the Vapors North, and hell to look at in the morning, but if Bino didn't get some relief he was likely to rupture his bladder. He rang the bell and waited impatiently on the porch, first on one foot and then the other. A soft wind blew on his cheek. The sun peeked out over the apartment house roof, and a flash of light reflected from the gilt doorknob.

Tilly opened the door the width of the chain latch and peered outside with curlers in her hair. "You leaving or just now coming in?" she said. "Cute *outfit.*" In her office Tilly generally wore thick red lipstick, mascara, and pantsuits with padded shoulders, along with huge dangling earrings, and in her war paint and business dress she was pretty intimidating. Bino thought that in her pink bathrobe, with curlers in her hair and her face pale and grainy, Tilly could stop an eight-day clock. Her husband, a skinny little guy, had been working nights of late. Squinting at Tilly over the taut chain lock, Bino thought he understood why.

"Tilly, I need a favor," Bino said. "I need to use your bathroom."

"Yours not working? Damn plumbers, no telling when I'll get one out here."

"Naw, it works fine. It's just . . . there's a young lady in my room."

"Congratulations," Tilly said.

"Jesus, it's my secretary. I'm letting her stay there for her protection."

"I'll bet. Well, who's—"

"Christ, Tilly, I'm about to pop."

"—going to protect her from you?"

He didn't feel as though he could hold it for five seconds more. "Tilly, *please.*"

"Just a sec." She closed the door, rattled the chain lock, then opened the door wide. "Hurry," she said. "My husband's not home, you know. I don't want the neighbors talking." Tilly stuck her head out to look up and down the sidewalk.

Bino went past Tilly and took two-for-one strides through her living room. "Me too, Tilly," he said painfully, over his shoulder. "I don't want anybody watching us, either."

Bino urinated while looking at a picture of Buddy Madden in his Pee Wee Football uniform, hanging on the wall behind the commode. Tilly's middle boy had later grown into a blocky towhead who'd once pelted the Linc with mud balls as Bino was leaving the parking lot. Three years ago, while Bino had been defending a federal judge, he'd let Buddy use the Linc for a date while Bino himself borrowed Tilly's pickup for undercover duty. Later, Bino had found a package of rubbers under the seat of the Linc. Buddy had turned out all right, though, and was now a sophomore at Harvard. Time flies, Bino thought. He finished, pulled up the bottoms of the warmup, flushed, washed his hands, and went back out into the living room.

Tilly was on the sofa reading the *Dallas Morning News.* "Look both ways before you go," she said, "and if anybody's coming, duck back inside. We have to practice a little discretion."

"Yeah, right," Bino said. "Thanks, Tilly." He headed for the exit, but as the front page of the newspaper flashed in the corner of his eye, he stopped in his tracks. He'd caught two words in the headline: "Deletay" and "Silence." Jesus, there damn sure wasn't anything silent about Nelson Deletay. Bino thought he'd better take a closer look. "Lemme see that, willya," Bino said. He retreated and lifted the paper from Tilly's lap.

The headline read in full: "FBI'S DELETAY MODEL FOR 'SI-LENCE OF LAMBS.' "

Bino muttered, "Jesus Christ," and began to read. Apparently Deletay had given a full-blown interview after all of the cops had left yesterday, during which the VICAP bigwig had hinted—without coming right out and saying—that the character in the movie was based on him. The newspaper headline writer had stretched the truth slightly, but that's what headline writers were for. Dumb, Bino thought. If the wacko killer was reading this, which he more than likely was, it was going to boost hell out of his ego to think that the government had its top gun in town. Be better, Bino thought, to make the nut think that no one was paying any attention to him. The story was continued on page 12A. Bino flipped through the paper to find the second portion.

Tilly snatched at the newspaper. "Hey. I was reading that."

Bino turned away from her, positioning his body between Tilly and the paper. "Just a minute, okay?"

"Don't you get the paper at your place?"

"I used to," Bino said. "But I wound up with a bunch of unread newspapers scattered around. Now when I want one I just go buy it at the 7-Eleven." He found page 12A, rattled the pages, and spread the paper out to finish reading the story. Jesus, it was all there; the bit about suspecting somebody at the Federal Building, a list of the victims—including a few gory details, of course—the "Dracula Don" nickname, the whole ball of wax. Why didn't they just draw a diagram, so the killer would know where to strike next to keep from getting caught? Directly underneath the story was a photo of Deletay and Sandra Nestle seated at a desk (Mac Strange's desk, Bino thought—I'll bet Mac is going to love this), frowning as they went over what looked to be a stack of evidence. They should make a new movie called "Baah-ing of the Goats," Bino thought.

"Gimme that," Tilly said. "Get your own paper."

Bino finished the story, folded the paper, and offered it to her. "Why would I want to buy one?" Bino said. "I've already read it."

Bino was seated at his own breakfast table, drinking coffee, when Dodie emerged from the bedroom. She'd tied her hair into a ponytail and wore a midthigh gray skirt, white cloth blouse, and charcoal-gray heels. Bino had practically given himself a hernia carrying in all of the clothes she'd moved over from her apartment. Dodie looked fresh as a daisy and smelled nice.

"The bathroom's all yours," Dodie said.

"Thanks, I'm out of the mood," Bino said. "Coffee?" He got up and dug a fresh cup from the dishwasher while Dodie sat at the table and primly crossed her legs.

Dodie rested her elbows on the tabletop and her chin on her intertwined fingers. "I like sleeping in your bed."

Bino was pouring coffee and nearly dropped the pot. She'd never before been in his bedroom that he could remember. He'd been in hers twice, though, once five years ago on an evening that had begun as a birthday lark; another time after Barney Dalton had helped him dispose of a dead guy named Winnie Anspacher whose wife had shot him. The thought of the nights he'd spent with Dodie sent little tremors up his backbone. Neither of them had mentioned it since, but the sparks were still there occasionally. More than occasionally where Bino was concerned. He often wondered how Dodie felt about it. "Thanks, Dode," he said. He replaced the pot on the Mr. Coffee hotplate, then set the cup on the counter to add sugar and powdered cream.

"Wow, it's big enough to get lost in. Did you pick the flowery bedspread yourself?"

He stirred her coffee and set the cup in front of her. "Why, what's wrong with it?"

Her gaze was across the breakfast table, out the window. "Nothing. It's sort of feminine." She sipped coffee and made her it's-too-hot face.

He sat across from her. "That's because a woman picked it out for me. It was—"

"I wasn't *prying* . . ."

"—my aunt, my mother's sister Lucy. She lives in Mesquite." He pictured his Aunt Lucy, wearing a flowered dress and thick bifocals, frowning as she looked over the giant Mitsubishi screen, and pursing her lips over the row of bottles in the liquor cabinet. Aunt Lucy had matched Cecil, fishy eye for fishy eye, and Bino had to admit that his bachelor digs were a long way from what his aunt was used to in Mesquite. It was a knockout of a bedspread, though—nice and quilty and a pretty good comforter when the weather was really cold. Bino had lost his mom in a traffic accident while he was still in high school, his dad four years later, and

Aunt Lucy was the only family he had left alive. She was a long way from a mother, but still the next best thing.

Dodie looked at her watch. "I guess I'd better get a move on."

"I don't know if I like that," Bino said. "You being in the office alone."

"I'm not crazy about it, either, boss. But it beats staying here by myself while you're running around. Besides, I've got a lot of work left to do. There's people around, the guy's not going to come to the office." She stood. "Is my car all right where it is?"

Bino pictured her old Trans-Am where she'd left it yesterday, across the apartment parking lot from the Linc. "For one night, yeah. It looks like you'll be staying awhile, though. Tonight you better leave it in a numbered slot. Use 24, two spaces down from me."

"What if that's somebody's parking place?"

"It isn't," Bino said. "24 is actually for the laundry room. Tilly lets her friends park there. I'll tell her about it."

"Okay," Dodie said, rising. She went into the living room, retrieved her big navy blue purse, and turned to look at Bino through the opening over the counter. "Will you be coming in today?"

"Sure, later," Bino said. "I've got to go back to the county courthouse. They've got my Stanley case file down there, making copies."

"I think they're barking up the wrong tree," Dodie said. "The guy over the phone sounded like a real creepo, not like someone with a steady job with the government."

"I don't agree with you," Bino said. "If all the weirdos running around *looked* like weirdos, they'd catch them all in a heartbeat. What I think is, it's somebody working around down at the Federal Building that blends right in with the furniture. He picks out his victim, stalks them around town, and then when they least expect it, *bam*. Yanks them right in off of—" Bino halted in midsentence. Dodie's mouth was suddenly twisted in fear, and there were worry lines on her forehead and around her eyes. "Sorry, Dode," Bino said. "Open mouth; insert foot. Listen, if anybody lays a finger on you they're going to have to go through me."

"That's a comfort." Dodie shifted her purse from one arm to the other. "I'll see you this afternoon, boss." She turned on her heel and marched out of the apartment, slamming the door behind her.

Now what'd I say that for? Bino thought. Jesus, what a yo-yo. Shaking his head ruefully, he picked up the coffee cups, placed them in the sink, and went in to take a shower.

16

Eliminating law enforcement agents, females, and judges from the list might have cut down on the Dracula Don candidates, but you certainly couldn't tell it from the mob of suspects now gathered in the county conference room at Lew Sterrett Justice Center, right in there among the butt-filled ashtrays. Jesus, thought Bino, I wonder how they're operating the Federal Building today. There were seats for about half the suspects—with the chairs around the perimeter filled by reporters, of course—while the rest of the men, all wearing brown or blue suits, or slacks along with short-sleeved shirts and ties, milled around, sat on the edges of the conference table, and grumbled angrily to one another. Aside from three of the reporters—two young brunettes and a fortyish redhead—Sandra Nestle was the only woman in the room. She was seated at the head of the table alongside Goldman, who was thumbing through a thick file folder. As Bino watched from out in the hall, through the partially open doorway, Nestle stood and loudly cleared her throat.

Nestle wore a black pantsuit which looked identical to the one she'd had on yesterday, and Bino wondered if VICAP sprung for uniform allowances. Nestle said at the top of her voice, "Have your attention," and then as the jumble of voices died into silence she said more sedately, and quite professionally, "We won't take up any more time than necessary, but most of you know what this is about and know it's very serious. We're limited as to space, so we've got to hurry through this and bring the next group on in. So far, no one has failed to respond to our request. That's a plus, because if someone wasn't here they'd be Number One on our list. That's something to keep in mind in case we have to do this more than once." She paused for a moment to let that sink in, then held up four fingers. "We're doing this in four phases, and to make things orderly we've got four different rooms set up. You'll go through them one at a time. In the first room they'll need a sample of your pubic hair. Next is a blood sample. The third room is where they'll need semen samples. Some of you guys may enjoy that." She lowered her head and looked at her notes while the group before her shot nervous glances at one another. "The last stop," Nestle said, "is the interview room. They're going to want to know, among other things, your whereabouts on certain nights. If you were shacked up with someone you weren't supposed to be with, tell them with whom. If you were doing drugs, tell them where and with whom. Mr. Goldman has agreed that nothing you say in the interview can be used against you"—the expressions on Nestle's captive audience were incredulous—"and in case you don't believe that you can just make up your mind whether you'd rather fess up to using dope or be the prime suspect in a string of murders. Everything you say in the interview is going to be verified."

As Nestle went through another examination of her notes, Bino decided he'd seen enough. He backed up, turned the handle and clicked the latch softly into place, then went as quietly as possible down the hallway to Mac Strange's office.

Bino'd say this for Mac Strange; The county prosecutor kept a cool head on his shoulders. If Nelson Deletay had taken over Bino's office the same way that he'd taken over Mac's, Bino probably would have gone to jail for punching out the federal guy. But Mac was taking it in stride, sitting calmly on the small couch alongside Nolan Pounds, the true-crime writer, while Deletay talked on Mac's phone and used Mac's initialed pen set to make notes on Mac's personalized notepad. Bino stood in the entry and shot a questioning glance in Mac's direction. Mac raised a hand in a come-on-in gesture. Bino closed the door behind him and had a seat in one of Mac's visitors' chairs. Deletay kept the receiver pressed to his ear and gave Bino a nod. Bino nodded back.

As he listened over the phone, Deletay used his palm to smooth his iron-gray hair. Finally Deletay said, "Well, how long are we talking about?" Then he listened some more, looked disappointed, and finally said, "Well, do your best, Sam. I'm sitting on a powderkeg here." He hung up and said to Mac Strange, "Damn. Three days."

Mac uncrossed his legs on the sofa and recrossed them. "If it's the best they can do, it's the best they can do," he said calmly. He wore a dark brown suit. His coat was open and his potbelly overhung his thighs.

"Damn hotel won't cooperate," Deletay said. "The U.S. Attorney says he can't get us a court order until he can free up a man to get it drawn up. Mr. Goldman could do it, but he's helping Miss Nestle with the suspects down the hall. Delays. Delays." He nodded curtly to Bino. "What is it, Mr. Phillips?"

Bino hooked one arm over the back of the chair and fingered the lapel on his own blue suit. "Well, I thought I'd pick up my files, if you're through copying them."

Deletay glanced at Mac, then back at Bino. "What files?" Deletay said.

"You know, the ones I left down here yesterday," Bino said. "You were going to Xerox them."

Deletay folded his hands on Strange's desk and blinked. "We're not through with them. When we are we'll let you know. Glad you're here, though. That phone call to your office brings up some more ideas. Our boy Dracula Don could be one of your clients, somebody that knows your little secretary. How many clients have you got?"

With a little effort, Bino thought, I could really hate this guy. "I couldn't tell you on the button," Bino said, sliding his rump forward in his chair and crossing his legs. "But four, five hundred. Ones that aren't doing time right now, maybe a third of that. I think I see what you're getting at, and I need to let you in on a couple of things. Number one: Furnishing you information I've got on victims is okay and makes sense, but turning over my files on my other clients is something else. What's in those files is attorney-client privileged information. And so you'll know, I represent a lot of guys you wouldn't want to go to dinner with, but I got no real wackos unless maybe you're talking about a couple of them that won't be seeing daylight for a lot of years. I'll save you the trouble on my clients' files. I won't turn them over and they wouldn't help you if I did."

"Oh?" Deletay drummed his fingers. "Where did you get your psychiatry degree?"

Bino's jaw dropped. He didn't say anything.

"Everybody's got a theory," Deletay said, "from the janitor up to the mayor. The trouble is that none of the theories are based on any experience. That's what VICAP's for. You're not qualified to decide if someone might be a potential serial killer. We are, Phillips—it's that simple."

Bino wondered where he rated on Deletay's list, between the janitor and the mayor. Probably on the lower end. "Well, I confess I'm just a lawyer," Bino said, "and not a psychiatrist. But I do know my clients, and you're just not going to find this blood-drinking guy among them." He folded his arms in finality.

"Well, thanks for your analysis, Dr. Phillips," Deletay said. "I suppose in addition to a court order for the hotel records, I'm now looking at getting one for your client files." He shifted his attention to the sofa where Mac Strange sat along with Nolan Pounds. "Sorry for the interruptions, Mr. Pounds. Where were we before I had to get on the phone?"

Pounds, who had been scribbling furiously during the exchange between Deletay and Bino, now looked up and blinked. "Lot of good material here," the writer said. "Let's see, Nelson— I think you were talking about the Kansas City Creeper." He backtracked a couple of pages on his legal pad, checked what he'd written, then flipped to the current sheet.

"Oh, yes." Deletay tilted Strange's swivel chair back as far as it would go. He inclined his head slightly forward, squinched his eyes closed, placed his elbows on the armrests, and used his fingertips to massage both sides of his forehead. "We were out at the farmhouse, right?"

Pounds checked his legal pad once more. "I believe so."

"I was a lot younger then," Deletay said, his eyes still shut, his fingers pressing in and rotating in little circles. "Twenty-two years, to be exact. It's hard to describe the feeling—you'd have to experience it yourself. But once I was alone in there and the quiet closed in around me, I could *feel* him. No—more than that—I *was* him. As I moved from room to room I could actually sense the victims' presence, even though their bodies had been moved days ago. I could smell the odor of them, hear their anguished screams."

Bino's jaw dropped as he looked to Strange. Mac's gaze was vacantly on the floor, and his lips were twitching. Nolan Pounds never missed a beat, writing as fast as his fingers would move.

"And all at once it came to me," Deletay said. "We'd thought it was the men who'd died first, but that wasn't the way with that bastard. It was the women who were first to go. He'd forced the men to watch him kill the women."

Bino rolled his eyes, motioned to Strange, and indicated the door. He rose quietly. Strange did the same, and the two of them started toward the door.

Deletay's eyes popped open. "Where are you going?"

Bino halted in his tracks. Jesus, maybe the guy *was* psychic. "I was just—" Bino said, then licked his lips and said, "I thought maybe Mac could get my files, and then I'd help him copy them so I could take the originals with me."

"All right with me," Deletay said. "But say, Mr. Strange, before you go. We've had a complaint from the hotel manager at the Adolphus, something about one of your investigators down there throwing his weight around. We can't have stuff like that going on. Cole, that's the investigator. Let's get him in here—I need to have a talk with him."

Mac's gaze flicked at Bino, then shifted back to Deletay. "Hardy?" Mac said. "I can't contact him. He called in sick today." The county prosecutor shrugged round shoulders and smiled. "You think it's something going around?"

As Strange left the room with Bino on his heels, Deletay shut his eyes once more, and Nolan Pounds eagerly assumed his writing position.

17

Hardy Cole, wearing a summerweight sport coat and short-sleeved shirt, thought he was going to freeze to death if he didn't get into the taxicab. He was bent forward against the howling frigid wind off Lake Michigan; his tie had blown free from his coat and stood straight out from his neck in the gale like a flag at Tiger Stadium. In Dallas, it was going to be ninety degrees that day; Hardy hadn't checked Michigan weather reports but doubted if it was over fifty-five outside Detroit Metro Wayne County Airport, and the windchill factor must have been twenty degrees lower. The cab driver, a portly, fortyish guy wearing a thick windbreaker and and a billed cap that somehow stayed on his head in the wind, opened the rear taxi door and stood aside. Cole dove inside like a gopher headed for cover. The driver slammed the door, went around and got behind the wheel, pulled the lever to start the meter clicking, and said in a thick northern accent, "Where to?" He turned to look at Cole through a clear bulletproof partition. The sound of his voice came through a slot that was maybe three inches by six.

"Just a minute, I . . ." Cole said, then fished inside his coat, pulled out several small pieces of paper and looked at them, one at a time. The first item was a wallet-sized driver's license photo that he'd gotten over the fax, a picture of a bullet-headed guy with thick black hair. Cole transferred the photo to the bottom of the stack, then squinted to read his own writing on the second piece of paper. "Three-seventeen Michigan Avenue," Cole said.

"Downtown Motown," the driver said. The cab pulled from the terminal curb into bumper-to-bumper traffic, stopping and going under skies the color of factory smoke. "You just in for the day, huh?"

Cole was busy with returning the slips of paper and photograph to his inside breast pocket. His fingers were slightly numb from the weather, and he rubbed them briskly on his pants leg. "Why you ask?" Cole said.

"You got no luggage."

"Oh," Cole said. "Well, yeah, I hope so. Depends on whether I can see this guy. Listen, what's the fare from the airport to where I'm going?" Cole had withdrawn a thousand dollars from his personal savings, and his airline ticket, a guaranteed seat with no advance purchase, had cost him eight hundred. Mac Strange had told Hardy over the phone that he'd do what he could as far as the expenses went, but he couldn't guarantee anything. Cole was really pulling for Mac to get the cost of the trip past the county travel people. If he can't, Cole thought, then the kid's orthodontist is going to have to wait a while.

"Be, maybe, twenty-five bucks," the driver said. The cab left the airport grounds to turn right on a busy four-lane street with an island in the center. Cole read a streetsign over the taxi's yellow nose; the sign read, "WAYNE RD.," and beside it was another sign reading, "TO I-94," with an arrow pointing north. The driver said, "We take 94 up there, catch the Ford Freeway and stay on it to the Jeffries, then south on the Henry Cabot Lodge Freeway all the way to Michigan Avenue. It's"—he shot his windbreaker cuff, rolled a thick freckled wrist to look at his watch—"ten-thirty. You're talkin' a half hour this time of day. You'd come in two hours earlier it'd be an hour, give or take. You from Texas, huh?"

"You figure pretty good," Cole said. He sat back and folded his arms as the cab angled to the right and onto a freeway access ramp. Up ahead on the interstate, cars and trucks moved east and west like passing bullets.

"It's the accent," the driver said. "Plus I know it's about time for the American flight to come in. So, you up here in Michigan much?"

"First trip. Look, where's Farmington Hills?"

"Shit, northwest Wayne County. Long way from where you're goin', out Lodge Freeway from downtown. If you're going to Farmington Hills you better figure on being here more than a day." The driver hit the gas, accelerated into moving freeway traffic. A green and white sign suspended above the freeway stated that the exit for the Henry Ford Museum was three miles ahead. The landscape on both sides of the interstate was green going to fall orange, red, and brown, leaves blowing from tall trees onto swampy northern land.

"I hope I don't have to go there," Cole said. "This guy I'm looking for, that's where he lives. I'm trying to catch him at his office."

"Must have money, he's got a home up there," the driver said.

"That I wouldn't know," Cole said. "I never heard of the guy before yesterday afternoon, tell you the truth."

The driver had understated the time, and the trip took close to forty minutes. He'd understated the fare as well; as the cab pulled to the curb in downtown traffic the meter clicked to show $29.80. Cole handed a twenty, a ten, and three singles through the slot in the partition, then said, "If I get hungry, is there a good restaurant in walking distance?"

"I don't eat downtown," the driver said, peering at Cole through the inch-thick bulletproof plastic. "But a block down there they got a Day's Inn, if you can stand hotel food. At least you're not likely to get poisoned. Coupla spots near Renaissance Center, some more near Cobo Hall and the Joe Louis Arena, all of them six or seven blocks, just south of the loop. But I wouldn't be walking too far downtown on my own, unless you got a gun. Ain't safe even this time of day." Visible beyond him, a young brunette crossed the street, wearing a light fur jacket and hunching her shoulders against the wind. As Cole watched, her skirt whipped up to show the thickly knit portion of her pantyhose.

"Well, thanks," Cole said. "And keep the change, you hear?" He exited the cab and hustled across the sidewalk to enter the office building, listing to one side and fearing that the cold wind might blow him out of his shoes.

The logo on the door was a cartoon, a grinning, slanty-eyed Oriental character wearing a chef's hat and green running shoes, charging along top-speed with a platter of steaming eggrolls balanced on his upraised hand. The gilt lettering under the logo read, "Egg Roll Hubba-Hubba, Inc." Beneath the corporate name, also in gilt lettering, "Detroit," "Lansing," and "Flint," were in a column, one directly under the other. The names of the final two towns were in letters slightly brighter than the rest of the sign, as though they'd just been added to the list. Cole went in and told a trim lady of around thirty-five, seated behind a huge receptionist's desk and wearing a beige sweater, that he was here to see Mr. Beemish.

"Your name?" she said, reaching for her phone.

Cole was leaning on his hands, which were gripping the edge of her desk. "It's a personal matter."

She withdrew her hand from the phone and let it drop into her lap. "I'll still need your name."

Cole thought that one over, then decided, what the hell. He was fifteen hundred miles outside his jurisdiction, had no authorization for being here—so what could a little lie hurt? Beemish wasn't voluntarily going to see any detectives from Dallas County, Texas; the egg roll king had made that much clear yesterday over the phone. "Tell him it's Dave Rylie," Cole said. "Texas Bank of Commerce, up from Dallas."

She eyed him as though she thought this lean and angular guy in a sport coat didn't look much like a banker, then told him to have a seat as she picked up the receiver. Cole went over to a leather couch and sat beside a man in a tan suit who was balancing a briefcase on his lap. Cole's brown hair was wind-whipped; he reached up and did his best to comb it with his fingers. He crossed his legs, looked upon a framed architect's drawing of a free-standing Egg Roll Hubba Hubba restaurant—a one-story building with a bamboo roof and a sign out front featuring the same cartoon logo that Cole had seen on the office door—then shifted his gaze to check out abstract art in the form of a cluster of stainless steel balls, and a potted tall green fern. Visible in the corner of his eye, the receptionist was talking a mile a minute into her receiver. She finished and hung up. In seconds, a door at the rear of the reception area opened and Oscar Beemish came out.

It was Beemish, all right, Cole didn't need to check the picture in his pocket. He'd studied the photo on the plane and would have known Beemish anywhere. Stumpy, big-bellied, fat-faced guy of fifty, coal black hair that Cole would give odds was dyed, a charcoal soft cloth suit that was seven hundred bucks off the rack before you hauled it to the tailor to have it fitted. Beemish's walk was more of a swagger, a guy-in-charge type, but at the moment with a worried look. Beemish approached the couch, his gaze shifting from the guy with the briefcase to Cole and then back again. "Mr. Rylie?" Beemish said. His voice was tenor and slightly hoarse and carried the same northern accent as the cabdriver's voice.

The guy with the briefcase stood and offered Beemish a white business card. "Dan Loman, Mr. Beemish, Morgan Restaurant Equipment. Got a minute?"

Beemish glanced at the card and stuffed it his breast pocket. "Not now. Later, okay?" He offered his hand to Cole. "Since one man's eliminated, that leaves only you. Oscar Beemish, Mr. Rylie. Come on in."

Cole shook hands. Beemish's palm was slightly damp and between smiles he was glancing at Cole's sport coat and open-necked summer shirt, doubtless wondering, just as his receptionist had, why this Texas guy wasn't dressed like a banker. Cole didn't speak, just fell in step on beige flat-weave padded carpet as Beemish led the way past the receptionist and an open paneled door into his own office.

Beemish's office was about the size of a half-court basketball layout, and his carpet was pale green. His desk was polished dark oak and would easily make two of Cole's desk, back in the cubbyhole in Dallas County. There was a credenza, bookcases filled with leatherbound volumes, and a photo of a politico type standing by grinning while Beemish, wearing a suit, broke ground with a shovel. Behind the desk, a telescope on a tripod pointed out the window toward a city skyline topped by smog and soot-colored clouds. Beemish stood aside and gestured grandly; Cole followed Beemish's direction, sat down in a leather-upholstered armchair, and crossed his legs.

Beemish went around behind his desk, then sat in and tilted a high-backed swivel chair, and folded his hands at his midsection. "Listen, I hope there's nothing wrong with the loan documents. I went over them with my lawyer two or three times. Must be something important for you to come all the way up . . ."

Cole snapped his wallet open and flashed the shield just below eye level. Beemish suddenly had the look of a man who'd swallowed a red Chinese pepper, thinking it was a piece of tomato, and had just realized how hot the bastard was. "Zero for two," Beemish said. "You're not Rylie, either."

"No, but I'm the guy that said he was Rylie."

Beemish leaned forward and extended a hand across the desk, palm up. "Mind if I have a look at that?"

Beemish had just thrown a doozy of a curve. Not one citizen in a thousand would ask for a closer look at a badge, and Cole had been planning to let Beemish think his visitor was Michigan heat. A guy like Oscar Beemish, though, probably held the gift horse's lower jaw wide open while he went over the animal's teeth, one at a time. Cole handed the wallet over and racked his brain to think up a good one.

Beemish squinted at the wallet, and his face lost its scared expression in a hurry. "What's this Dallas, Texas, shit? Listen, I already talked to a guy down there, told him I'd love to help out, but I really don't have any information. Why don't you follow up with . . . ?" Beemish reached out and thumbed through a stack of phone messages that were impaled on a gilt spike.

"Detective Cole," Cole said. "Me. I'm the guy you talked to on the phone. Yesterday afternoon late, and what you said was that you didn't know shit from shinola about any attempted murder in Dallas, and that if I didn't quit bugging you you'd have your fucking lawyer on my ass. Then you hung up on me." He showed Beemish his standard cop's shit-eating grin.

Beemish's eyelids dropped warily to half-mast. "Well, maybe I did put it a little differently." He tossed the wallet over on Cole's side of the desk with a soft leathery plop. "Aren't you a little out of your territory? Tell you what—I think I'll ask the Detroit P.D. what authority you've got up here." He picked up his light green telephone and pressed the button to turn his speakerphone off.

Cole slid forward in his chair and rested his forearms on his thighs. "Look, Mr. Beemish, I'll make you a deal. You don't fuck me around, I won't fuck you around. Detroit P.D. would shit a brick if they knew I'd come over here without checking with them. So would a lot of the people in my own department. There's just some things that I don't have time for. We've got a lunatic running around down in Dallas killing people, and every minute I waste might mean he's killing somebody else. I got to cut a few corners."

Beemish withdrew his hand from the phone, a man more confident now, his expression saying that he knew he had the upper hand. "Sorry about your problems. The trouble is they're not *my*"—he touched his own chest with his fingertips—"problems. Look, so I was in Dallas. A lot of people were in Dallas." His forehead wrinkled. "How come you to say you were from Texas Bank of Commerce? You pull that out of your hat?"

"No," Cole said. "And so you'll know what I know, I got your address from the register at the Adolphus Hotel. Also in the hotel record was a phone message to you from a guy named Weems at TBC. So I talked to him. TBC's loaning you two million dollars, which ain't hay, especially the way things are with banks these days."

Beemish pointed a fat finger. "Listen, if you fuck up my loan . . ."

"I'm not trying to do anything to your loan. What I'm trying to do is keep one sick bastard from killing people, and if that fucks up your loan . . . well, it does." Cole was within inches of going around the desk and having a real heart-to-heart with the guy.

Beemish reached for a pen and notepad. "Who's your supervisor?"

Cole sighed and studied Beemish, the loudmouthed fat guy making a killing in Chinese food and thinking he could run over everybody. Finally Cole said, "Okay, Mr. Beemish, you want my supervisor? First you'd better listen. Number one: You're a material witness in an attempted homicide and one of the only people who's seen a dangerous killer face-to-face. And don't bother with the I-don't-know-from-nothing bullshit, because I know better. You wrote a license number down the other night that's probably the key to finding our man. I want it. You can probably get me run out of Detroit, but I'll guarantee you that as soon as I get back to Texas I'll have a judge issue a bench warrant and writ you down there to talk to me from the county jail."

Cole paused for a short breath. Beemish's confidence was fading; he was looking uncertain now, doubtless wondering if this cop from Texas could really do all that he was saying, and thinking that the horse's ass of a cop probably could. Cole raised two fingers in the boy scout sign and went on.

"Number two: I got your first name from a young lady named Daphne Wilson, whose pants it was you were thinking about getting into the other night, just before you ran off and left her alone with a girl who'd just had her neck slashed open. Pretty slick, using your first name only, you sly cockhound, and if you'd picked her up someplace other than the hotel where you were staying I never would have found you. You oughtn't to shit where you eat, you know? Something else you did wrong—you didn't ask the young lady what she did for a living."

Beemish's features sagged. "Daphne Wilson? I don't know any—"

"Bullshit. What the young lady you claim not to know does— well, she's a federal prosecutor. Right, you sly cockhound, she works in the U.S. Attorney's office, and she don't like you so much. I can't understand why, tell you the truth. She ought to be slobbering for some of your dick after the way you treated her, right? But anyway, she works in the white-collar crime section and her specialty is bank fraud. Now, you think if she felt like it, she could come up with a false statement on your loan application at Texas Bank of Commerce? I bet she could. False statement to get a loan, that's a two-year federal beef. And if you don't come up with that license number you wrote down in one helluva big hurry, we're damn sure going to find out if little Daphne could come up with something on you."

Beemish's eyes lowered and were suddenly misty. "I'm a married man. Twenty-eight years, the same woman."

"Well, I'll borrow your line." Cole touched his own chest with his fingertips. "Not *my* problem. I've had my wife twenty-six years myself, only I don't run around after no strange poontang. Maybe 'cause I can't afford it, but I don't. Now let's quit wasting time, and you get me that license number."

Beemish expelled air from his lungs in a long wistful sigh. "I dropped that suit in a pile in my closet, to take to the cleaners. Come on, I'll have to drive us out to my house. Not a word around my wife, you hear? You say one word around my wife you can forget me giving you anything." He stood. "Jesus Christ, that good-looking broad's a *prosecutor?*"

"Card-carrying," Cole said. "You need to watch out who you're feeling up, you know?"

Hardy Cole stood on shag pile carpet up to his ankles and used the phone. He was in Oscar Beemish's cavern of a den, feeling slightly envious as he alternated his gaze between the Canadian moose head mounted above the seven-foot fireplace and the grizzly. The grizzly's jaws were open wide, showing teeth that had to be six inches long, and the bear hung directly across from and snarled silently at the moose. Jesus, Cole thought, look at the size of those antlers. Cole had never particularly wanted to be rich, thought that rich guys had to compromise a lot of principles to make money, but he'd always wanted once in his life, just once, to hunt big game. The closest he'd come had been whitetail deer, little animals with big soft eyes that just broke your heart to draw down on. As he listened to the rings on the other line, Oscar Beemish stood behind him in the entry hall at the foot of the stairs, explaining to his wife why the guy from Texas was so uptight about a few notes that Beemish had left at home. Cole didn't have the slightest idea what line Beemish was feeding her and really didn't care. After the fourth ring, Mac Strange picked up his receiver and said hello.

"I got it, Mac" Cole said. "I got the motherfucker."

There was a second's hesitation before Strange said, "Hi." Then, muffled probably by Strange's hand over the mouthpiece, "It's for me, Nelson. My wife."

Cole let the small square writing pad containing the license number dangle by his hip. "You got something to write with?"

There was a rattling noise on the phone. "Okay, yeah, a dozen eggs. What else?"

Cole lifted the pad and squinted. "The first numbers are four-seven-three. Now this paper got a little wet and this writin's smeared. Four-seven-three, and the rest is either D-W-J, Dork-William-Jackoff, or D-M-J, Dog-Mary-Jasmine. Check 'em both, Mac."

"California oranges?" Strange said. "Last week they had Floridas on sale for sixty-nine cents a pound."

"Huh?" Cole scratched his head. "Oh, I gotcha. Texas. Texas plates. Now, I got a flight back in two hours, land DFW at seven-oh-eight. You have somebody meet me. And tell 'em if I don't get off the plane to come aboard and wake me up. If they don't I'm liable to sleep clear through to Mexico or some fucking place. If we ever get through this, I'm going to hibernate all winter."

18

Patrick Quarles had read the newspaper, but was determined to keep its contents a secret. As he backed his GMC Supercab pickup up to the open end of the shop, he sang country and western songs; oldies, portions of "Your Cheatin' Heart" and "I'm So Lonesome I Could Cry" by Hank Williams, a few stanzas of "Settin' the Woods on Fire," all songs that Quarles absolutely despised, songs to which his father used to listen over the radio. Anything, Quarles thought, sing any lyrics that you can remember, anything that pops into your head, anything to keep them from reading your thoughts. Until this day was over and he had become One with them, he didn't want them to know about the newspaper article. The newspaper stated that Patrick Quarles—not calling him by name, of course, for the Way of the Truth was much too clever for men to ever find him out—was insane. Why, Patrick Quarles was *not* insane, but only a man, and as a man had no understanding of the Truth. Only Uziah the Disciple understood, and used the man-body of Patrick Quarles to do the bidding of the Way. Further, if *They* were to learn of the FBI's presence in town, of the Great Chief of VICAP himself, They might even postpone his taking of Rebecca, and he was determined that nothing would stand in the way of his becoming One with Them.

He used a two-wheeler to load the box into the pickup's covered bed, backing up to the tailgate, scooting his rump on hard ridged metal, grunting as he hauled the dolly and its load up behind him. Had to be careful with the box. The box must remain perfect in order to receive the perfection that was Rebecca. Once he'd rolled the dolly snug against the front of the bed, he carefully draped the box with a thick furniture mover's blanket. Then he crawled around on all fours and closed the louvered windows in the bed's cover. His chest and underarms were damp with sweat and he was breathing hard, but he didn't dare stop to rest.

Quarles continued to shout inane hillbilly lyrics at the top of his lungs as he climbed down to the ground and slammed the tailgate, and continued to sing as he warily looked around the interior of the shop. He was dressed in pale blue coveralls, regretfully so, because the covering of his upper body shielded the Marks of Truth on his chest and stomach. After this day had passed and he was One with them, Quarles would never cover his upper body again.

His athletic tote bag, carrying the black jumpsuit and pistol, lay near the bottom of the steps leading up into the house. He'd carried the bag down earlier, right after he'd gone into the closet to draw more blood from the woman. He wasn't sure whether the girl upstairs was alive or dead; the stream of blood was down to the barest pulsing trickle. As he'd halfway filled his cup, she hadn't moved or opened her eyes.

He hoisted the tote bag, dropped it onto the floorboard inside the pickup, got behind the wheel, and started the engine. As he pulled away from the shop and through the yard, he turned on the radio and flipped the SCAN button until he located a country and western station, then raised his own voice in off-key harmony with the singer on the radio.

His tan four-door Olds sat at the end of the gravel drive, near the place where the driveway entered the woods to wind down to the public road. He seldom used the pickup anymore and drove the Olds to work. He skirted around the parked car, entered the woods and bumped along in the deepening shadow of the trees, keeping a steady fifteen miles an hour. The pathway through the woods was dotted with crater-sized potholes, and more than once in the past he'd come within a whisker of breaking an axle. Quarles hunched his shoulders and shifted his gaze from side to side. *They* were all around him, in the passenger seat, on the dashboard, crawling on the padded ceiling like invisible insects. He turned the knob to play the radio even louder. Their presence pressed in on him like deadweight; he was scarcely able to breathe, bouncing around inside the cab as the pickup rattled onward.

And suddenly he was out of the forest, the road smoothing out as he covered the final two hundred yards of property before turning onto the narrow highway. He braked to a stop, waited while a yellow school bus passed followed by a Dodge station wagon, then left the gravel and turned left onto the asphalt, picking up speed. A quarter-mile ahead was I-35, the north-south Dallas to Denton freeway; Quarles gunned the engine until the speedometer needle reached forty, then maintained a steady pace behind the station wagon and school bus. *They* were no longer with him; the weight lifted from his shoulders and he swallowed huge gulps of air.

There was a traffic light at the freeway entrance; the bus stayed in the center lane with its lefthand turn signal flashing while the station wagon nosed up behind the bus and signaled a left turn as well. Quarles eased the pickup to the right, pulled up alongside the station wagon, and flipped on his own right turn signal; the bus took up a lane-and-a-half, preventing Quarles from easing forward to turn right on red. A portly woman showing thick reddened legs in thigh-length shorts was driving the station wagon with a little girl of around five in the passenger seat beside her. Quarles's spirits lifted in hope. *They* had left him, they really had. No presence was in the passenger seat, nor on the dashboard, and nothing unseen scuttled across the ceiling. Maybe now they would never know the words written in the newspaper.

On his left, the little girl was grinning at him through the station wagon's window. Her brown hair was tied into doggy ears, and her two front teeth were missing. Midafternoon sun glinted from the window and partially obscured her image. Quarles smiled and waved at the child, and she waved back at him. *They* are gone, Patrick Quarles's pitiful man-being thought. *Oh, Jesus H. fucking Christ, They are—*

The tenor voice screeched suddenly, coming from the radio speaker. "He thinks he can hide the words of the Quantico man."

And the basso followed within a fraction of a second, shouting, "YOU ARE A FOOL TO THINK THIS. AN UGLY AND DIS-

GUSTING FOOL TO THINK YOU CAN HIDE ANYTHING FROM THE TRUTH."

Quarles's hands trembled and his spit dried up. "I was going to *tell* you. As soon as we are One."

"One with *you?*" the basso voice said, then, with so much rage that Quarles very nearly bolted from the cab. "ONE WITH YOU? WHEN YOU HIDE THINGS?" There was a pause and then, more evenly, "Tell me who you are."

Quarles gently closed his eyes and said in a very small voice, like a child's, "Patrick. I am Patrick."

The tenor voice now laughed. "Not *that* foolish name. Who are you?"

Quarles's grip tightened on the wheel. "Uziah," he said rapidly. "Uziah, Disciple of—"

"NOT THAT NAME," the basso voice howled. "SAY YOUR NAME RIGHT NOW."

Tears streaked Quarles's cheeks as he bowed his head in humiliation. "I am the Heap."

"That is what you are," the basso voice said. "A hideous, ugly, scarred heap. And if you continue to hide things, a heap is what you will remain. Now, ACCEPT YOUR PUNISHMENT, you pitiful heap."

Quarles's throat constricted in fear. He pounded on his own window. In the station wagon, the child's grin melted into a look of concern as Quarles shouted at the top of his lungs, "*Help me. They're going to kill me.*"

"The child will not help you," the tenor voice said. "And neither will the FBI, you stupid heap."

Quarles's eyes rolled in fear. "Will, *too*. Will, too, help me, and if you don't leave me alone right now, I'll call the number in the paper and tell on you. I really will."

The basso voice uttered a vicious laugh. "Don't you know that no one will believe you? The FBI will lock you up for life if you tell. Now. Accept your punishment."

With tears rolling down his cheeks in a torrent, Quarles pounded once more on the window. "They've got me. Oh, They're going to kill me, I know They are."

A huge invisible hand clamped onto the back of Quarles's neck. A force like moving steel yanked his head backward, then smashed his forehead into the steering wheel. Once, twice, three times the force banged Quarles into the wheel, until his teeth rattled and he screamed at the top of his lungs.

Within the station wagon, the little girl turned to her mother in terror. "Mommy. *Mommy.* That man is *hurting himself.*"

Her mother leaned over to squint through the window at the pickup truck. The truck's driver was indeed banging his head violently against the steering wheel, drawing back, and smashing into the wheel again. The man's lips were twisted in pain.

The mother grasped the little girl by the arm. "Stop looking at him, Debbie," the mother said. "Ignore him, it's not our problem. So many nuts running around, it's a wonder we're not all murdered in our beds."

Quarles had done wrong and knew it. Never, ever, should he try to hide anything from the Truth, no matter what the consequences might be. If only his transgression did not prevent him from being One with Them!

Breathing like a cardiac patient, tears drying on his cheeks, Quarles steered the pickup south on I-35, then took the up-and-over ramp and bore east on LBJ Freeway. He maintained a white-knuckled grip on the steering wheel and kept the speedometer needle on fifty-five, ignoring the cars and trucks that whipped by on both sides to leave Quarles in their wakes as though he were standing still. He couldn't take the chance of going one mile over the speed limit. If he should run afoul of a traffic cop, the policeman might discover the box in the pickup's bed, and then Quarles would have to kill the policeman.

He turned to the south on Central Expressway, slowing in bumper-to-bumper traffic as he moved steadily along between construction barriers and read the signs which told him that the renovation project on the old freeway was well under way. Quarles couldn't remember any time in his life that Central Expressway *hadn't* been under construction, and he wondered dully if he'd ever live to see the day when the renovation project was finished. Then he realized with a laugh that it didn't matter. Quarles's man-being would cease to exist once he became One with the Truth, and the Truth would have no need for freeways.

He continued onward, trooping along with the stream of cars and trucks past Northpark Shopping Mall, and underneath the

Northwest Highway overpass, to exit at Caruth Haven Lane and halt at the stop sign. As the pickup idled and the steering wheel vibrated under his fingertips, Quarles looked to his left across the expressway. As far as he could see in the distance, sunlight cast gridlike shingle-shadows on the gray rooftops of the Village. Two joggers, a man in white T-shirt and shorts and a woman in blue-and-gold spandex, loped side by side along the sidewalk and turned to run in among the apartment buildings. Only two blocks away was the apartment in which Rebecca lived. The thought that he might harm her caused Quarles's bowels to churn, but if he must hurt her to make her a part of the Truth, he would do so.

Quarles's nose was running; he wiped his face with his sleeve. Behind him, a horn beeped impatiently. His determination firm, Patrick Quarles put the truck in gear and turned left to cross the freeway toward the apartments.

The two-wheeler *bump-bump*-ed unevenly over the expansion joints in the sidewalk, and Quarles reached up to steady the box underneath the quilt. He continued to think of it as a box. Just a harmless oblong box, sanded and stained, that he'd made in the furniture shop. If he thought of the contraption as a prison—as *her* prison—his resolve might fail him.

He was rolling his cargo away from the parking lot and between two-story apartment units of brick and redwood paneling. Sweat oozed from his palms as he approached the stairway leading up to the clerk's apartment, the place where he'd encountered Rascal Erly. It had been *Them* who had attacked the girl, of course, but Rascal Erly had seen only Quarles. And someday, Rascal Erly was going to *tell*. He made a ninety-degree righthand turn and pushed the two-wheeler parallel to the building, on toward Dodie Peterson's apartment (his man-being continued to think of her by her human name even though his Disciple-self knew better). He moved slowly and deliberately, a clean-cut, if slightly sallow-complexioned, young man in pale blue coveralls who obviously had his act together—only a workman delivering a new piece of furniture, nothing to cause alarm. He passed two girls in short white pleated dresses who were carrying tennis rackets. They smiled at him. He returned the smiles and continued on his way.

When he reached his destination he turned around, backed up the dolly, and wrestled the box up the one step to *her* porch. In addition to *Their* presence all around him, he now felt *hers*. Right here, this was where she came after work, did a little hop-step up on this very porch, inserted her key with well-formed hands, and tripped lightly in over the threshold. Around five-thirty, that's when she would arrive. Two hours from now, plenty of time to prepare himself to receive his Rebecca into the Truth.

The passkey in his pocket had belonged to Donatello the drug dealer. "Like falling off a log, man," is what Donatello had told him. "I just went over and told the manager I'd locked myself out and she loaned it to me. Had me a duplicate made. Dude can't pay me, I just loan him the passkey, tell him to see what he can find in one of them apartments might be worth something. They want to get high, man, they come up with it." Donatello had been Quarles's source for the Mexican brown heroin. Now he'd have to find a different supplier. Quarles fished in his coveralls for the key, turned the key in the lock, pushed with his shoulder. The door moved inward with a swishing noise over green shag carpet. Quarles glanced right and left, then grabbed the handles of the two-wheeler and slowly backed his load in over the threshold. The hum of a refrigerator motor reached his ears and the odor of rose petals drifted up his nostrils.

He righted his load, closed the door, and paused to catch his breath while he looked around. Her sofa and chairs were chrome frames with flowered cushions, sturdy and inexpensive; a table model TV sat on a small table that was draped with a flowered cloth, and sat alongside a component stereo. Everything was dusted and neat as a pin; tiny rose-scented sachet pillows were in a bowl on top of the TV. Quarles smiled. He'd known her apartment would be clean; it was the only way that *she* would live.

He left the box standing upright on the dolly and quickly left the apartment, retracing his steps along the sidewalk past the staircase, doing a fast column left and moving toward the parking lot. The pickup was backed up to the curb with its tailgate open. He slammed the gate, climbed into the driver's seat and moved the truck to an empty space across the lot, then left the truck carrying his athletic tote bag and headed back for the apartment unit. Halfway across the lot, he paused. Someone was watching.

It was the same two girls in tennis clothes whom he'd seen earlier. One was a redhead with short hair, the other a brunette. The brunette was sitting inside a small foreign sports car (an

MG?—Quarles didn't know one from the other) while the redhead stood outside the car and talked to the brunette through the car's window. The redhead was talking rapidly to the other girl, but the redhead's gaze was on Quarles, and she was smiling. Was *flirting* with him—no doubt about it—and words couldn't describe how *uncomfortable* was the sensation that now gripped Patrick Quarles. He couldn't *stand* for women to look at him that way. His head lowered, his neck flushed in embarrassment, Quarles resumed his fast walk and hurried on between the buildings. The redhead made a sour face at him as he went by.

Once back inside Rebecca's apartment, Quarles felt better. Just being in the place where he could sense *her* presence calmed him. He set the tote back aside, rolled the dolly and its cargo carefully into her bedroom, then returned to the living room for the bag. Back in her bedroom, he dropped the tote bag on the floor and sat on the end of her bed.

The bed was a queen-size, with a white cotton spread spotted with yarn tufts like rabbit's tails, and the mattress was firm. Quarles wondered what she wore when she slept. White, he thought, something white and clean, a shortie gown perhaps. Did she sleep with panties on? No, she wouldn't. She'd slide long firm legs in between the sheets, and her gown would cling to the sheets and ride up around her midsection, revealing . . . there was a quick tightening in Quarles's groin. His breath quickened as his gaze roamed around her bedroom, paused momentarily on the open bathroom door and the spotless green tile beyond, then came to rest on her dresser. His upper lip curled.

There were three framed pictures on the dresser, and she was in all three, perfect lips curved to show perfect teeth in a smile, her long blond hair like ruffled silk. In one photo she was alone, wearing jeans and a western shirt, leaning against a wooden corral fence with bare dirt and a barn in the background. The second picture showed her in the office, perched on the edge of a desk, wearing a green business dress and white high heels. Behind the desk sat the strange thin man, the one whom Quarles had seen outside the courtroom with her. In the picture, the thin man wore a white shirt and tie, and he looked uncomfortable. It was the third photograph which caused Quarles to sneer.

The third photo showed a golf course in the background, rolling fairways, a green on the left with a flag hanging limply from the pin. *She* was wearing blue shorts and a white knit shirt; she had her perfect ankles crossed and her lips in a cheesecake pout and was leaning on a big pro-line golf bag with gleaming irons and woods sticking up from within. And behind the bag—Goddam *bastard*, Quarles thought—was the tall white-haired lawyer. God, but the man was smug, smiling confidently into the camera, wearing tan golf slacks and a pale blue knit shirt, his snow-white mane slightly wild, his skin deeply tanned. Quarles's man-self *hated* the White-haired One, while his Being in the Truth felt only contempt. How could she stand to *be* with him? Quarles couldn't bear to *look* at the smug son of a bitch. He shifted his gaze, stared unblinking into the bathroom.

The tenor voice said without warning, "Why are you waiting?"

Quarles cringed, and his eyes widened in fright. No matter how often They came to him, Their voices always shocked him nearly senseless.

The basso voice was louder than the tenor had been. "Why indeed. Do it."

Quarles hunched his shoulders, hugged himself, squinched his eyes tightly closed. He had to. Oh, Christ, *he had to*. He stood, averted his gaze from the photos, and exaggerated his limp as he crossed over to the dresser. He slid the top drawer open, gazed dully at bracelets and earrings inside a velvet-lined jewelry box, closed the drawer, slid another one open. Christ, there they were, white, yellow, and black cotton panties folded alongside white, yellow, and black cotton bras. He gingerly touched a white pair of the panties, then picked them up, turned, and spread them out between his hands.

"This?" His voice quavered. "You want this?"

And the tenor voice answered him in a mimicking falsetto. "*This? You want this?* Just do it. They are part of her."

Tears of frustration sprang from Quarles's eyes and ran down his cheeks as he hurried back over to the bed and sat down. He laid the panties across his knees, reached over and unzipped the tote bag, rummaged inside, and lifted the small red suction bulb. He'd filled the bulb from his cup just before he'd left the furniture shop. He uncapped and shook the bulb; the liquid inside sloshed thickly around. Quarles sobbed pitifully as he lifted his face to the ceiling. His tone was a whining beg as he said, "Please. Do I *have to?"* Always, he thought, always They will humiliate me until I am One with Them.

And the same mimicking falsetto answered, *"Do I have to? You must, and you know you must."*

Sniffling, Quarles lifted the panties, put his hand inside the leghole, spread the soft cotton crotch across his palm. He pointed the bulb downward and squeezed. Thickening red liquid ran from the nipple, soaked the cotton, spread outward to wet the palm of his hand. Disgust spread over Quarles's features as he tossed the bulb away. It bounced softly on the carpet and rolled over. A drop of blood soaked into the green shag. Quarles raised his face once again and closed his eyes.

"Do it," the tenor voice said, and the basso voice shook the walls as it shouted, "DO IT."

Whimpering, the tears rolling down his cheeks, Quarles lifted the panties to his mouth and sucked at the crotch. His lips puckered and he lapped the blood like a thirsty mongrel cur.

Quarles bent close to the bathroom mirror and turned slightly sideways to examine the left side of his torso. He needed more oil there so that the Marks of the Truth would glisten. He quickly uncapped the plastic bottle and spread coconut oil thickly over himself. That was better. He spread the remainder of the oil over his upper thighs and rubbed it into his crotch. His flesh shone like a bodybuilder's in competition; the scars on his torso stood out in marvelous bas relief. Rebecca would be pleased with him.

He was naked, having showered, toweled himself, and dabbed on some of her body powder. He could not touch her if he had body odor; he must prepare himself for Rebecca even as he must prepare her to become a part of the Truth. He used the same towel with which he'd dried himself to wipe down the inside of the shower, being extra careful in the corners to clean off all of the soap residue; her quarters must be as spotless as he'd found them. Finally he dropped the towel into the dirty clothes hamper on top of her jeans, T-shirts, panties, and bras, and returned to the bedroom.

He'd laid the black jumpsuit carefully out on the bed; it was the garment he would wear to transport her once he had claimed her. For now he must remain naked to show her the glory of the Marks of Truth. The box, lid open and ready, was laid out flat on the carpet; once she was inside the box, it was going to be a job to lift his cargo back onto the dolly. He would need the strength found only in the Way. His Smith & Wesson .38 lay on the bed; he picked it up. The blood-soaked panties were in the wastebasket; he averted his gaze from them and went into the living room to wait. The clock over her mantel said fifteen until five. Three-quarters of an hour left before she tripped lightly through the door. He wished that she would smile and embrace him but knew that could not happen. He must force her to learn the Way even as *They* had forced him to learn.

He carried a straight-backed chair from the kitchen, placed it near the front door, and sat on it, laying the pistol gingerly across his naked thighs. The sun outside cast parallelograms of light on the drapes covering the front window. Quarles nervously crossed his legs, uncrossed, and recrossed them again.

How would he take her? He thought he knew. He thought he would hide behind the door and, as she entered, take one step forward, clamp his hand over her mouth, and hold the gun against her temple. "Please don't say anything," was what he would tell her and would want to add 'I'm not going to hurt you,' but he was not sure that he wasn't, and he must not lie to her. Lies were instruments of men; in the Way there must be only Truth. Truth is the Way, Quarles thought and smiled secretly to himself.

Quarles's chin lifted slightly as footsteps scraped on cement just outside the window and a shadow appeared on the drapes, moving from left to right. Someone was coming.

Oh, Christ, someone was *coming.*

A woman. The shadow was a woman's shadow, slender and supple, hair bobbing around her head, and the scrape of shoe on concrete was the light step of a woman.

Perhaps the woman would pass. Perhaps she would go away.

The footsteps clicked onto the porch, and then the door chimes sounded, a quick, hollow *bong-bong.* Quarles sat stiff as stone, unmoving, not even breathing. It couldn't be *her.* It was too early for *her,* and she wouldn't be ringing her own doorbell. If the woman outside thought that no one was home, she would go away. Of course she—

The door chimes sounded again.

Quarles left his seat and got down in a crouch. Slowly, silently, he crept over to sit on his haunches by the hinged side of the door. If the door were to open it would hide him from view. He glanced at the inside knob. The plunger was sticking out; the door was unlocked. It's *unlocked*, he thought. He hadn't pushed the button in when he'd carried in the tote bag.

The door chime sounded a third time, followed by a series of sharp rapid knocks.

Resignation flowed through Quarles as he tensed his muscles and readied himself to spring. If the woman didn't go away, he was going to have to kill her. If he were to allow her to live, the woman would interfere with the Way.

Kit Stanley was fit to be tied, even though she was madder at herself than she was at Mickey. It was her own fault for weakening, her own fault for handing him the keys to the car last night and standing docilely by while he went out. All of Mickey's troubles had been Kit's fault, to her devoted mother's way of thinking, beginning twenty-seven years ago when, as a greenhorn college freshman, she'd lifted her skirts in the backseat of a Pontiac GTO (My *God*, Kit, one foot touching the ceiling and the other in between the bucket seats, rooting around in the parking lot behind the basketball arena with the lights of Central Expressway glowing on the horizon) and gotten herself pregnant. That she'd spent the last twenty-seven years trying to make up for it didn't matter. That she'd held down a department store job plus tutoring athletes to work her way through college, that she'd turned down dates on which she was absolutely dying to go, just to be with her baby, that she'd worked her fingers to the bone in order to raise Mickey, that she'd even forsaken her maiden name of Boston for that bastard Teddy Stanley's name, so that Mickey wouldn't feel out of place—not one iota of all that mattered. Her mistake had been a doozy, and she simply wasn't ever going to live it down.

"Just for a little while, Mom. You don't have to worry about me," Mickey had told her last night. God, how could she be so dumb? Just as dumb, she thought, as she had been to look the other way when the silly game of football had taken control of Mickey's life; just as she'd been dumb enough to pretend that his college football scholarship had mattered so much, when in fact playing football had turned her son into just another slab of beef on the hoof. And when life between the goal lines was over, baby, it was over, and all that was left was the hollow echo in the cheering section. That and drugs. Sweet mother of God, Kit thought, how could I have been so absolutely fucking *dumb*?

"Just for a little while, Mom. You don't have to worry about me."

But worry she had, and worry she should have. When Mickey hadn't returned in two hours she'd begun to pace the floor. She'd still been wearing a hole in the carpet at four in the morning when the car had pulled into the driveway with a squeal of brakes, and she'd been standing at the door in her robe, hands on hips and doing a toe-tap, when Mickey had stumbled in. And stumble he had, fumbling endlessly with his key to insert it in the lock and bumping the door frame with his shoulder as he'd crossed the threshold. His eyes had been so bright they'd practically glowed, and Kit hadn't needed to turn on the light and examine the redness under his nose to know what he'd been up to.

He'd turned his charmer of a grin on her, of course, just as he always did, and his big shoulders had canted at an angle as he'd spread his hands to her, palms up. "Hi, Mom," he'd said. "Boy, you'll never believe what happened."

That's when Kit had slapped him.

Sweet God, she had—had raised her small hand and slapped her own son right across the mouth. Her baby, she'd slapped him even though his problems weren't his fault. Were *her* fault and always had been. She hadn't hurt him, of course—Mickey was too big for her to *really* hurt—but the hangdog look that had crossed his face would live with her for weeks. Today, she'd let him sleep until an hour ago, until nearly four in the afternoon, and when he'd gotten up he'd been *so* sorry for what he'd done. He'd even cried some and told her that he knew he was going to prison for a while, but once that was over he was going to make it up to her. She'd see.

Kit's first impulse had been to ignore what had happened and keep it to herself. But, she'd decided, ignoring Mickey's problems in the past was what had led to this: Mickey headed for prison with absolutely nothing that his mother or anyone else could do about it. Mickey needed help and, if his mother had anything to do with it, help was what he was going to get.

She'd never be able to repay Bino Phillips for what he'd done, and Kit knew it. Bino had really stuck his neck out to have Mickey released on bond, and now Mickey was saying thanks for the favor

by taking dope on his first night of freedom. Not that it was Mickey's *fault*, of course.

And then there was Dodie. Kit didn't know what she would
have done without Dodie. People like Dodie Peterson came along,
Kit thought, about once in four lifetimes. Having once been ad-
dicted herself, Dodie understood about drugs. Sweetheart that he
was, Bino was sort of a hothead at times, and if he found out that
Mickey had slipped last night, the big white-haired lawyer might
fly off the handle. Dodie, though, Dodie would fix it if she could.
Dodie was pure aces.

So, to Kit's way of thinking, the solution to the problem was
simple. Dodie would understand and would take Mickey to some
sort of group meeting where he could get help. Bino *wouldn't*
understand and might even have Mickey's bond revoked and have
Mickey put back in jail.

Which was the reason Kit Stanley was at the moment ap-
proaching Dodie Peterson's apartment in the Village while
Mickey, shaky but remorseful, waited in the parking lot inside
Kit's four-door Nissan sedan. She was going to tell Dodie what
had happened and hope against hope that Dodie could help.
Someone *had* to help; otherwise Kit was going to lose her son.
Which, of course, would be Kit's own fault and not Mickey's.
Never Mickey's.

Kit hurried down the sidewalk between the apartment units
with a purpose, a compact woman in her late forties with hair the
color of a raven's breast, looking fifteen years younger than she
was, firm buttocks and trim legs moving under pressed white cotton slacks. Though she'd had very little time for men in her life
(other than Mickey, of course—God, Mickey *was* her life) Kit was
still a head-turner. In addition to the slacks, she wore a blue long-
sleeved man's shirt, the tail flapping loosely around her hips, and
low-heeled black patent leather shoes. Her eyes were almost as
black as her hair, and only the small crow's feet at the corners of
her eyes gave away her age. She reached Dodie's apartment and
stepped quickly up on the porch and rang the doorbell.

And waited. And rang the doorbell and waited some more.
And finally knocked loudly, and then waited even longer.

Damn, she thought. She'd been so caught up in trying to find
help for Mickey that Kit had never even considered that Dodie
might not be home. Dodie came straight to her apartment from

work nearly every day. Kit checked her watch. Damn, *damn*, she thought, it's not even time for her to be here. Another, what, half hour to forty-five minutes?

Well, she'd gotten Mickey this far, and she wasn't about to let a little wait stop her. That's what Kit would do—just go back out to the car, and she and Mickey would wait until Dodie came home. Kit nodded to no one in particular, left the porch with her shoes scraping slightly on concrete, and retraced her steps toward the parking lot.

As the woman's steps retreated, Patrick Quarles stood out of his crouch and moved nearer to the window. The woman's shadow passed over the drapes, the slim girlish shadow walking briskly, swinging its arms, moving right to left and then disappearing from view. She was gone. The woman was *gone*, thank Christ, and now Quarles at least didn't have the unknown *she* to worry about. A sigh of relief escaped his lips as he returned to the chair to sit down and lay the pistol across his lap. He nervously squeezed his own bicep and shuddered.

As she stepped quickly down the sidewalk, a thought came to Kit Stanley which stopped her in her tracks. God, another problem yet. This wasn't someone's house, where she could wait in the driveway and be certain that the someone would see her. This is the *Village*, dimwit, she thought, the be-all and end-all of luxury apartment living, a maze of complexes, parking lots, and court-yards surrounding swimming pools, and Kit didn't have the slight-est idea from which direction Dodie would come, where Dodie would park her car, or down which sidewalk Dodie would ap-proach her digs. She had to leave Dodie a note of some kind, a message telling Dodie that Kit (and Mickey?—should she tell Dodie she'd brought Mickey along?—No, Kit thought, I'll explain all about Mickey when I see Dodie alone) was waiting, and exactly where Kit's car was parked. Chuckling at herself, shaking her head, Kit turned on her heel and walked toward Dodie's apartment once more.

And stopped once more in her tracks.

Leave a note with what? Kit thought. You don't even have your purse with you, yo-yo, much less paper and pen. She'd have to find something with which to write in the car. Maybe Mickey had a ballpoint she thought, then remembered that Mickey hadn't even carried writing materials when he'd been in college. But somewhere in her car there'd be a pen and pad—there always was. Kit spun and headed once more for the parking lot.

And halted after two firm steps.

Could Dodie's place be unlocked? she thought. I know good and well that *Dodie* has something to write with inside—she works for a lawyer, doesn't she? The odds against the place being unlocked were a hundred to one, but why walk all the way to the parking lot, then come back to find that Dodie's place was open all along? Dodie certainly wouldn't *mind* if Kit went on it, Dodie was such a godawful *caring* person. May as well give it a try, Kit thought.

She hustled back to Dodie's, walked up on the porch, firmly gripped the doorknob, turned it and pushed . . .

Quarles couldn't believe it, the same brisk, slightly scraping footsteps returning, the same lithe shadow passing across the drapes, the quick hop-step onto the porch. He jumped as if touched by a live wire, then crept over to get down by the hinged side of the door. There was a slight rattle as the doorknob turned. Patrick Quarles shut his eyes and held his breath.

. . . and the knob turned easily and the door moved inward. Kit at first smiled, then frowned in concern. She hadn't expected that she could just walk right in, and now that she could she wasn't sure whether to like it or not. She couldn't believe that Dodie would leave her place unlocked on purpose, and Kit decided that, once inside, she was going to be careful—keep an eye peeled and both ears open—and at the first sound or sight of anything out of place she was going to leave, lickety-split. Kit stepped into the apartment, backed into the door to close it, heard the faraway noise of a refrigerator motor, was aware of the fragrance of rose petals—

And was suddenly face to face with a naked wildman. Her heart came up into her mouth and her breath ceased at once. A man, it was a man, dear God, a few inches taller than she, standing only feet away, a man whose face was the color of pale death, and whose body (my sweet God, Kit thought, what could have . . . ?) was a mass of grisly scar tissue (dear God, *he has no breasts*, Kit thought), and whose flesh glistened as though soaked in perspiration. Was this a joke? It *had* to be a joke, some young friend of Dodie's, hiding, jumping out to scare the bejesus out of—

The creature uttered a guttural snarl, raised a pistol from its side and pointed the gun at her. A *snarl* my God, a snarl just like in—

The man's (*creature's*, Kit thought, he's more of a creature than he is a man) lips moved to form words as he said in a high tenor voice, "Don't *shoot*, you idiot, someone will hear you."

An accent like a country preacher's.

Kit backed away a step and raised her hand to cover her throat. "I won't. I promise I won't, I don't even have a—"

"And don't just stand there, you fool." The creature's lips moved once more, and one more a hillbilly preacher's voice came out, but now it spoke in a deep basso. "Do it."

And strangely, Kit was thinking that there was a ventriloquist in the room, someone hiding behind a chair or table and throwing their voice, making this creature sound like two different people. That at any second Edgar Bergen would appear, grab the naked man, set him on old Uncle Edgar's knee, and the creature's mouth would move, but Kit would know all the time it was really Edgar Bergen tossing off those snappy little one-liners, and when it was over she and Edgar Bergen would have this big laugh, and— *Oh my God*, Kit thought, *I've seen this naked man before, I really have. Where have I . . . ?*

These thoughts came to Kit just as the man reversed the pistol, gripped it by the barrel, and grunted slightly as he raised the gun and brought it smashing down against her jaw. Then there was the soft pop of bone ringing in her ear, followed at once by the numbing pain, suddenly the room spinning before her eyes as she tumbled to the floor, the absolute certain knowledge that her jaw was broken, and finally the absolute certainty that she was about to die as the man uttered an eerie, high-pitched scream and raised the gun once more . . .

Mickey Stanley's remorse lasted for as long as it took his mother to disappear from sight among the apartment buildings. Mama was really uptight, huh? Had even slapped him. Mickey touched his own cheek where her palm had landed. Had stung some but hadn't really hurt, but had let him know that Mama thought his doing drugs last night was really a big deal. Well,

Mickey didn't think it was a big enough deal to warrant all this carrying on. Just like the few little drug transactions he'd been involved in weren't a big deal, and just like the time in jail he'd done wasn't all that much to raise a fuss about. Once his lawyer Bino Phillips had finished cutting through all the bullshit, Mickey was going to be free to go and do what he did best, which was to play a little whup-ass fuckin' football. So what did doing a few lines with his friends last night have to do with anything?

Mickey laid his muscular arm up on the windowsill in his mother's car and flexed his bicep. No way was Mickey Stanley going to any federal penitentiary. Who was going to believe a bunch of lying snitches? Anybody could see with one eye closed that those people weren't telling the truth up there. At least, *Mickey* could see that they were all lying, but Mickey had access to a few facts that the jury didn't. It hadn't occurred to Mickey as yet that maybe the jury couldn't tell that the snitches were lying. Woe to Mickey if the jury didn't happen to see it his way.

But what the hell, he'd always been able to get out of any trouble that might come along. Like the time when he was in college and the University Park policeman had caught him red-handed driving down Hillcrest Road, right beside the SMU campus, with two grams of nose candy in his glove compartment and a coed in the passenger seat so stoned that it was all she could do to lift her head. Nothing to it, baby, just tell that old cop that you were fixing to whup some orange and white University of Texas ass come Saturday, and any kind of charge he was about to hang on you went flying out the window.

To Mickey's way of thinking, selling a few drugs was just something to do while he was taking his short vacation from professional football. So far, he hadn't had the breaks. The Kansas City Chiefs, who'd drafted him in the second round and paid him a pretty good bonus, had cut him in his rookie year just because he'd let one receiver beat him on a post pattern in a preseason game. And each and every one of the four additional ballclubs who'd cut him in the past five years had had their collective heads up their collective asses. One more tryout, that's all it would take, once he got this little federal drug trial out of the way.

He'd seen enough of pro ball to know that it wasn't as juicy as amateur ball, but once amateur ball was over a guy just had to learn to roll with the punches. College ball had been a dream come true; meeting a guy in a five-hundred-dollar suit every Thursday night to pick up an envelope containing two-fifty in cash, tooling around in a yellow Corvette, going to class when he fuckin'-well pleased, getting one humdinger of a blowjob whenever he wanted from Sylvia Martel, whose daddy lived over in Tyler and was in the truck and trailer bidness. Colleges knew when they had themselves a real honest-to-goodness whup-ass defensive back and knew just how to treat a guy.

So, Mickey thought as he watched a redhead climb out of a white sports car and amble across the parking lot, what am I doing here? Letting Mama talk him into coming over to spill his guts to this Dodie Peterson, what had Mickey been thinking about? Mickey could think of a number of things he would like to do with Dodie (such as having her sit on his face, for example) but puking all over her about how he was hooked on drugs damn sure wasn't one of them.

So instead of planning to tell Dodie how he needed help to kick the habit, Mickey was trying to figure out a way to keep from telling her anything at all—was wondering, in fact, whether he could get out of the Nissan, hustle up there among the apartment buildings, and intercept his mama before she had time to say a word to Dodie. Playing good solid whup-ass football had taught Mickey to act on instinct—if a guy spent too much time thinking things over, he was likely to be plowing up Astroturf with his nose while the wide receiver took off for the flag without a defender in twenty yards—so, without considering his options any further, Mickey climbed out of the Nissan and jogged up the sidewalk. He was wearing jeans, gray Adidas running shoes, and a gray workout T-shirt with "PROPERTY OF THE HOUSTON OILERS" stenciled across the chest. The late afternoon sun beat down to warm his arms and the back of his neck. He reached the shadow of the buildings, followed the walk in between two brick apartment units, then paused to catch his breath and look around.

Directly in front of him the sidewalk ran for two hundred feet or so, then made a right angle left in front of an iron staircase and headed off, Mickey supposed, toward more apartment units, swimming pools, and parking lots. On his left was a laundry room with gleaming porcelain coin-operated washers and dryers standing in rows inside. Just ahead and to his right, an air-conditioner compressor chugged. Mickey had spent quite a bit of time around the Village—who in Dallas who liked to drink beer, snort dope, and maybe pound a little airline hostess pussy every once in a while *hadn't* been to the Village at one time or another?—but the place was so strung-out with sidewalks, tennis courts, and whatnot that most of the times he'd been to the huge apartment complex he hadn't had the slightest idea where he was going, and his problem was intensified at the moment because he didn't know where Dodie Peterson lived. Which was an inherent danger to being a good solid whup-ass football player and acting on instinct most of the time—after you'd acted on instinct you wound up not knowing in what fucking direction you were headed. Mickey was scratching his head through his thick black hair and just about to give up and return to the Nissan to wait when he spotted his mom.

There she was, standing on a porch about a hundred and fifty feet ahead of Mickey and on his right. As Mickey cupped his hands over his mouth to call out to his mother, Kit turned the knob, applied a shoulder to the door, and disappeared from view as she stepped inside. So much for stopping her before she talked to Dodie Peterson, Charlie Brown.

Mickey dejectedly hooked his thumbs in his pants pockets and took a couple of steps toward the parking lot. He'd had it, now, and he was going to have to sit, listen, and sorrowfully nod his head while his mama watched him with damp black eyes and Dodie Peterson told him how the cow ate the cabbage where taking drugs was concerned. The problem was that Mickey didn't *give* a shit how the cow ate the cabbage. What Mickey was interested in was where he could get his hands on a few grams of Bolivian coke and how Dodie Peterson would look wearing nothing but her underwear—those two things, along with which NFL club was currently interested in one good whup-ass defensive football player.

After two listless strides, Mickey paused. What was the point in returning to the parking lot? Mama would just come out there and haul him back to the apartment unit to listen to the say-no-to-drugs spiel. As long as he was here, Mickey might as well go on down to Dodie Peterson's apartment and take his medicine. Besides, Mickey thought, brightening, there was always the chance that Dodie Peterson had been getting undressed after work when Mama had happened by. The thought of hearing the say-no-to-drugs spiel from Dodie Peterson wearing nothing but a terry cloth robe, and maybe having the robe fall open occasionally to reveal a patch of luscious soft skin, damn sure beat the thought of hearing the same pitch while sitting cramped in the back seat of Mama's Nissan. Mickey reversed his direction, quickened his pace, and covered a hundred and fifty feet of sidewalk to step up on Dodie Peterson's porch and ring the doorbell.

And heard at once a muffled *thump* from inside the apartment, followed by a soft whimper of pain. Mickey frowned, stepped nearer the door and flattened his ear against the wood. Another *thump*, accompanied by a male voice saying something in a deep hoarse basso that Mickey couldn't understand.

Mickey yelled, "Mama?"

There was now the sound of a female moan and a rapid series of thumping noises.

Mickey grasped the knob, turned it, and threw open the door. The door slammed into the wall beside the frame and Mickey stepped inside. Ten feet from where he stood, Kit lay face-up on the floor. Her head was turned to the side, facing Mickey, and blood gushed from several lacerations on her face, from the inside of her mouth, and from her nose. A smallish, wiry, naked man stood over her. The man held a pistol by its barrel and was slowly raising the gun to strike. As he tensed to bring the pistol crashing down, the naked loon said in a deep guttural basso, "Harder, you stupid heap." Mickey was vaguely conscious of the scent of rose petals.

The entire scene assaulted his eyesight—his mother on the floor, the crazy man, naked as a jaybird, about to brain her with the butt of a gun—And once more, Mickey acted on pure instinct. His right foot moved instantly backward a quarter of a step; his knee bent slightly, flexed and nearly locked. His left forearm came automatically up in the shiver position. He pushed off of his right instep, took one running stride with his left foot, and launched himself, and two hundred and twenty pounds of hurtling whup-ass defensive back rammed into some fifty pounds less of stark naked madman with a force that would have rung Barry Sanders's bell on the best day the all-pro running back ever saw, and then some.

Mickey's leveled forearm hit the pistol-wielding man squarely between the shoulder blades. Mickey was conscious of a dull pop as the man's head rocked backward on his neck. Spittle flew from the man's mouth and lightly sprinkled Mickey's cheek. Then both men were tumbling, head over heels, over the single carpeted step which descended into the apartment's living room. Mickey landed on his side with a soft grunt; the wildman kept going, flailing his arms, and fell headlong against the table which supported the television set. The bridge of his nose collided with the table's edge; the TV overturned and the picture tube exploded. Shards of glass tinkled and flew. The pistol thudded to the carpet as the naked man rolled over to face Mickey. Blood flowed from the pale-skinned nose, ran down the painfully twisted lips, and dripped from the narrow chin onto the floor.

Even as he fell, Mickey's feet moved and his legs churned, gathering themselves under him as he prepared to spring once more. The lunatic's eyes widened slightly; his blood-flecked lips opened and he emitted a piglike squeal. The squeal was reminiscent of faraway slaughterhouse noise, and froze Mickey in his tracks.

It dawned on Mickey that he'd seen the naked man somewhere before.

As the eerie squeal faded into nothingness, the naked man scrambled to his left across the carpet and reached for the pistol. His eyes, framed by pale cheeks and forehead, were wide, frightened black holes. Mickey came out of his frozen state and lunged.

And watched the naked man, stretched out on his belly, bring the pistol up from the floor as though in slow motion and extend it in both hands. And drew desperately nearer to the naked man, and stretched out his arms, and felt the slightest twinge of fear as the realization spread through him that he wasn't going to make it.

A blast shook the room like cannon in an echo chamber as the pistol bucked and pointed toward the ceiling. Strangely, the only pain was in Mickey's eardrums, shooting pain that opened his jaws and traveled instantly down his neck. The slug which tore into Mickey between his breast and shoulder bones didn't hurt at all, and not even when his collarbone shattered did Mickey feel pain. Then he was drifting in air, floating slowly away from the hideously grinning naked man, and only vaguely conscious of the collision as his shoulders hit the bottom edge of the sofa. He lay unmoving, sprawled out with his head and shoulders propped against the sofa, as the lunatic labored to stand up unsteadily, and Mickey grinned weakly as the naked man, covering his bloody nose and mouth with his palm, lurched sideways, climbed the one step up into the foyer, skirted Mickey's fallen mother, and limped his way through the front door and out of the apartment.

Mickey didn't want to move. It would be too goddamn hard to so much as lift a finger. Even when the scrambling noise reached Mickey's ears, only his eyes moved in his head to seek out the source of the sound.

It was Kit who made the noise as she crawled painfully out of the foyer and down into the living room with her own blood streaming from her mouth and from the cuts on her face. Her jaw was already swollen, and puffed out more and more by the second. She reached out to Mickey and croaked, her voice barely above a whisper, "Son, are you . . . ?"

The sight of his mother reaching out to him was the last thing that Mickey would remember, before his head fell back against the sofa cushions, and he passed out cold.

Patrick Quarles ran with a side-canted limp down the sidewalk, his nudity forgotten. His back and shoulders were numb, and the taste of his own blood was strong in his mouth. A woman and a man, wearing identical navy jogging suits, blocked his path on the walk; Quarles lowered his head and bulled in between the couple, left them in his wake as the man yelled angrily, "What in the hell are you . . . ?"

Quarles charged on across the parking lot, sparse flesh jiggling on his bare thighs, the rough pavement scraping the soles of his feet. He arrived at his pickup, flung open the door, and dove behind the wheel. The keys dangled from the ignition; he'd left the keys in the truck intentionally in anticipation of a quick getaway. A getaway minus his clothes and minus his Rebecca was something that the Disciple of Truth hadn't counted on.

Tears streaming down his cheeks to mix with his blood, Quarles started the engine, jammed the lever into reverse, and backed out of the space with a squeal of rubber. He reversed the truck's direction and sped out of the parking lot as fear clutched at his heart. He had failed the Truth, and the Truth would punish him.

19

Bino's collar was slightly damp and so were his cuffs.

When his beeper had sounded, he and Dodie had been walking slowly toward his apartment, cooling down, after jogging a mile and a half around five-thirty in the afternoon. At least *Dodie* had jogged a mile and a half, her supple legs working smoothly in green running shorts and her blond ringlets bouncing around her head in rhythm with her stride. Bino had made it for less than half that distance; then he'd walked, head down, huffing and puffing, for nearly all of the rest of the way, finally managing to run again for the last two hundred yards. Dodie had been waiting at the finish line—which was the junction of two sidewalks near the Vapors North apartments—and had showed Bino a rather disdainful wrinkle of her nose as he'd thundered past. For the past six months, Bino and Dodie had had this pact: a mile and a half each afternoon when they arrived at their respective homes, and he'd been telling her all along that he was jogging religiously. Now she knew better. Dodie *had* been jogging religiously but Bino hadn't, and his lies had caught up with him.

The beeper had been clipped to the elastic band around Bino's wrist, and his cuffs and collar were presently damp because he hadn't had time to shower before he'd taken off for the hospital. He'd returned the call from Hardy Cole, in fact, while Dodie was showering, and after learning what had happened, and *where* it had happened, Bino had decided to tell Dodie a little white lie. Not to be confused with his stories about his daily jogging routine, which were *big fat* lies, the little white lie had to do with where he was going when he'd left the apartment. He'd told her that he was headed downtown to have someone released from jail on bond.

All of which were the reasons that Bino was wearing a pale gray suit, red tie, and white shirt whose collar and cuffs were slightly damp. He supposed that he smelled like a horse, and resisted the impulse to pull his coat lapel forward and bend down and sniff his armpit. Sniffing at himself would be a dead giveaway that he hadn't showered.

Sitting here in the intensive care unit at Presbyterian Hospital looking at Kit Stanley, Bino was glad that Dodie didn't know yet what had gone on at her place in her absence. Kit's left eye was swollen shut and her jaw was wired together. There was a purple and sickly yellow swelling which extended from a couple of inches below her jawbone up to the midpoint of her cheek, and if Bino hadn't known that someone had beat the living hell out of Kit, he would have sworn she had the mumps. Her slender nose wasn't slender at the moment but was swollen and swathed in gauze and adhesive tape. The lid of her one good eye was red and drooping. A few minutes ago, in the hallway, Kit's doctor had introduced Bino to a second doctor and told him that the second guy was a plastic surgeon. Bino had wondered briefly if the hospital switchboard had a special button hooked up to a buzzer in the plastic surgeon's home, and if every time a broken nose wandered into the hospital emergency room, the plastic surgeon received a signal telling him to hustle down to the hospital and drum up some business.

Just seconds ago he'd reached over and squeezed Kit's hand. Her grip had been weak. So weak, in fact, that he'd barely felt the pressure. "They told me just a few minutes," Bino said softly. A rolling cart sat beside the bed. The cart held a blood pressure gauge, a stethoscope, and probably a dozen rubber-topped serum bottles, some full, some half full, some nearly empty. A drape separated the immediate area from the rest of the intensive care unit. The drape was beige and was suspended by hooks from a circular chrome curtain rod.

Kit's one good eye didn't seem to focus very well. "Mickey?"

It was a faint whisper, and Bino had to strain in order to hear her at all.

"In surgery." Bino hesitated, not sure how much to tell her, then decided she'd want to know no matter what. "According to the doctor they're going to have to pin his shoulder. The bullet didn't hit anything vital."

Her lips formed a pained grimace. "Bullet?"

"Yeah, gun—you didn't know?"

"I heard." She seemed to drift momentarily, then said, "Big boom."

"You used the phone, too. I guess it was you—unless it was the crazy guy. Somebody called 911, but the emergency operator didn't get a voice. When the police got there the phone was on the floor beside you." Bino winked. "You, Kitso, you're the killer. Want me to read you your rights?"

"Face," she said. "White face."

"Me? Yeah, I—"

"Him. No, him."

"The guy?"

"Him. Face. Pale face." Her good eye closed and her breathing slowed and evened out. "I've seen his face."

Bino reached over to the aluminum cart and picked up the nearest serum bottle. Demerol. Kit was going to be in and out of it for a while. "So it wasn't a black guy," Bino said.

Her eyes remained closed. "No, white. *Really* white."

Bino cocked his head. "Like he'd been sick or something?"

Kit's lips relaxed into a smile that looked as though it pained her. Probably it did hurt her to grin. "Bingo," Kit said. "I can't remember, but I've seen him." She still hadn't opened her eyes. "Somewhere," she murmured. "The son of a bitch."

"So Teddy did it," Bino said. "Your ex." He bowed his head. "Bad joke, huh?"

Kit's chest rose and fell rapidly, and it took just a second for Bino to realize that she was laughing. "Hurt . . . laugh," she said, and then said dreamily, "More Dracula," and then composed her lips to say like a sigh, "More like Dracula," before she was gone completely, her breathing slow and even as she slept a deep sleep.

Goldman fidgeted as he yanked on his goatee. Nelson Deletay was stone-faced, his iron-gray hair sprayed and immobile, his lips set in a fearless-vampire-killer line. Mac Strange's suit was rumpled and he appeared about to yawn. The three were perched on a cloth waiting-hall sofa like crows on a fence. Bino sat in a chair adjacent to the sofa, as a white-uniformed female orderly went by, pushing a food cart. One ivory-colored stocking was wrinkled around her ankle.

"You can't talk to her," Bino said.

Goldman uncrossed his legs and put both feet on the floor. "You're running the hospital now? Glad to know it."

One corner of Bino's mouth twitched. "No, Marv. I'm not running the hospital. The *doctor's* running the hospital. And the doctor says no more visitors."

"Well, *you* saw her." Goldman's jaw thrust slightly forward.

"Kit *asked* to see me," Bino said. "And while we're on the subject, what are you doing here, Marv? I thought you were just the temporary legal advisor. You joined VICAP or something?"

Goldman sat back, folded his arms, and stared straight ahead.

"Marvin's—" Deletay said, then cleared his throat and said, "We need a coordinator from the U.S. Attorney's office in all these investigations. Marvin's coordinating. Mr. Strange here"— "extending a hand, palm up, in Mac's direction—"is coordinating on behalf of Dallas County. Does that clear it up?"

"Sort of," Bino said.

"And we need to talk to the lady as soon as possible," Deletay said.

"Suits me," Bino said. "Like I told you, the doctor . . ."

Deletay patted the top of his own head. His hair didn't even wiggle. "Maybe you won't mind telling us what she said to you. Without violating any client confidence, of course."

"Kit's not my client, Nelson," Bino said. "*Mickey's* my client. Oh, and by the way, what goes for Kit *doesn't* go for Mickey. If you talk to him—once he gets out of surgery—if you talk to him, I'm going to be there as his lawyer. Particularly if Marv's involved." He glanced toward Goldman.

"We'll remember that," Deletay said. "But you didn't answer me."

Bino blinked. "Answer what?"

"Whether you'd tell us what Mrs. Stanley said to you."

"I don't guess I have any problem with that. She told me what you probably already know. It's apparently the same guy, the one

the lady prosecutor saw on the stairs the other night. What you
don't know is, Kit's seen him before."

Deletay sat slightly forward. "Christ. Where?"

Bino shrugged. "She doesn't remember. Maybe when the dope
they're shooting her up with wears off, but for now she doesn't."

"Christ, that makes it all the more important that we talk to
her," Deletay said.

"I don't guess I can argue with that. But like I said, it's up to
the doctor." Bino now leaned forward to address Mac Strange,
who was seated beyond Deletay and Goldman. "You been out to
Dodie's, Mac?" Bino said.

Strange sighed and regarded his knees. "Yeah. And it ain't
good. Looks like somebody butchered a hog in there. Prints all
over the place, but—"

"Hold on, now." Goldman reached around Deletay to put a
restraining hand on Strange's arm. "Hold it," Goldman said. "He's
not involved in any murder investigation."

"Oh, Jesus, Marv," Bino said. "That's a big problem here,
everybody's more worried about who's involved in what than they
are about catching the fucking guy."

Goldman kept his hand on Strange's arm while locking gazes
with Bino. Deletay reached forward, firmly gripped Goldman's
forearm and returned the federal prosecutor's hand to his side.
"Go on, Mr. Strange," Deletay said. Goldman dropped his gaze.

Mac dusted off his own sleeve. "Prints, like I said. Some of
which match prints at the drug dealer's, and also match prints of
the clerk's apartment, Andrea Morton. None of which match any
prints that anybody has on file. Us, the FBI, anybody. One bullet.
Ballistics has it, and it may match the one from Andrea Morton's,
which does, incidentally, match the shell and casing we got from
Donatello the dope peddler's. The very same .38. Which leaves
us with zero unless we find the guy, and unless when we do find
him he still has the gun.

"We're really making a lot of progress here," Mac said. "None
of the guys, the federal employees, nobody's pubic hair or jism
matches shit. What we're getting is a morgue full, not to mention
a *hospital* full of people, and us sitting around with our fingers up
our asses. We got the guy on tape, the call to Dodie at your office,
but we got nothing to compare that with even." Strange glanced

toward Deletay. "There was a coffin out there at Dodie's, Bino,"
Mac said. "I guess you should know that."

Bino's forehead wrinkled. "What the hell are you talking
about?"

"A coffin, just like I said. A homemade box, damn professional
job, with all kinds of shackles and shit inside. What it looks like—
it looks like the guy took the coffin out there intending to carry
somebody off. Mickey Stanley and his mom just happened by."

Bino pictured it, the guy slobbering for blood as he lugged a
coffin around. And had another mental image, Dodie helpless
inside the coffin, screaming at the top of her lungs. Bino pinched
his forehead. "Jesus Christ. Listen, I know you're going to want
to talk to Dodie."

"Of course," Deletay said. "To find out what's missing from
her apartment, if nothing else."

"Yeah, okay," Bino said. "That makes sense. But do me one
favor. Let me tell it to her first, huh? Dodie's a lot tougher than
she looks, but Jesus Christ, all this happening to her at once. I
mean, how would you like to have this blood-drinker guy stalking
you?"

Mac nodded while Deletay exchanged glances with Goldman.
Finally, Deletay said, "We don't have any problem with that.
Perhaps we could interview Miss Peterson late tomorrow after-
noon. Around five, say. That should give you time."

"It should," Bino said. "Oh. None of my business, I guess,
but since we all seem to be getting mixed up in this, what about
the license number? The one Mr. Unknown from out of town
was supposed to have written down."

Deletay cleared his throat. "I'm supposed to get word from the
Justice Department on the court order for those hotel records no
later than tomorrow."

Bino was listening to Deletay, but out of the corner of his eye
he was watching Mac Strange. Mac had leaned back slightly and,
unnoticed by Goldman and Deletay, was throwing Bino a series
of rapid winks.

"Well, good luck, Nelson," Bino said. "Those court orders can
take a while. A lot of red tape involved—and believe me, I know.
I'm a lawyer, remember?"

"And by the way," Deletay said, "as long as you're going to
talk to Miss Peterson, you might let her know that I'm going to

spend some time alone in her apartment this afternoon. I want to lay my hands on the killer's clothing, touch the same things that he has. I might pick up some of his thoughts."

As the VICAP man spoke, Bino alternated his gaze between Deletay's mouth and eyes, looking for a sign that the VICAP man was putting him on. Deletay was as serious as cancer. Bino wondered briefly if Nolan Pounds, the true-crime guy, would go out to Dodie's with Deletay and maybe pick up a few vibes of his own. Bino said weakly, "Clothing?"

Mac Strange leaned forward to say, "The guy was stark naked in there, hiding. Left his clothes and stuff scattered over Dodie's bed. Don't tell her this, Bino, but there was a pair of bloodsoaked panties in a trash can, and we think they're Dodie's. The guy escaped by running across the parking lot in his birthday suit. A couple of joggers saw him."

"Jesus," Bino said, then drummed his fingers on the arm of his chair while saying, "Jesus," again. He stood. "Well, I guess I can figure out what to tell her and what not to tell her on my own." He started to walk away, then paused and turned. "Oh, and Nelson—Dodie borrowed a couple of my Waylon Jennings tapes about six months ago. She's misplaced them somewhere. As long as you're going to be out there, see if you can pick up some vibes on where my tapes might be." He laughed nervously and waited for Deletay to get the joke.

Goldman favored Bino with a scalding glare. Mac Strange's lips twitched as though the county prosecutor was about to laugh.

Deletay's brows knitted into an I-know-something-that-you-don't expression. "I'll see what I can come up with," the VICAP man said thoughtfully.

20

Texas license plate four-seven-three-Dog-Mary-Jasmine was attached to a 1989 Pontiac Firebird registered to a Mr. Alton K. Ridley, who was a part-time convenience store clerk and part-time student at Tarrant County Junior College, over near Fort Worth. On the night that Andrea Morton had gotten her neck artery slashed, Mr. Ridley had reported for work at six p.m. and had stayed on until midnight closing time—which didn't give Mr. Ridley an alibi, since Andrea's cutting had happened sometime after two in the morning. What *did* clear Mr. Ridley, though, was the statement from the North Richland Hills, Texas, police officer who had observed Mr. Ridley returning to work through the back door at one a.m. The same cop had stopped Mr. Ridley a few minutes later as Ridley exited the store carrying a bag of candy bars and Ding-Dongs, such contraband allegedly intended to assist Mr. Ridley and his roommate through a long night of study. Upon their face-to-face encounter, the office had forthwith escorted Mr. Ridley to the North Richland Hills City Jail for a long night of practical education. Exit Alton K. Ridley from Hardy Cole's personal suspect list.

Texas license tag number four-seven-three-Dork-William-Jackoff, however, was a different story entirely. This plate identified a 1979 Buick Electra registered to Miss Coralee Erly, age 47, with an address on Beacon Street in Southeast Dallas. Miss Erly was a spinster who had inherited the house from her father. Her younger brother William resided at the same address. William Erly had done two different stretches in TDC, one for burglary and the other for molesting a child. Hardy Cole learned that the burglary beef had been a reduced-charge plea-bargain deal, and that, in fact, William Erly had been climbing in a bedroom window where a six-year-old girl was sleeping when the law had dropped the hammer on him.

The information re the younger brother living at Miss Erly's house came from a very secret bank of FBI computer files in El Paso, Texas. The files, an offspring of a system originated during J. Edgar Hoover's regime, contained information on every person in the United States who had, as a relative closer than a second cousin, family who'd served any time. The Privacy Act specifically prohibited the use of, or even the *existence* of, such a bank of computer files. The Federal Bureau of Investigation didn't give a rat's ass about the Privacy Act or the horse it rode in on. Only certain FBI officials even knew that the files were in use.

Hardy Cole knew that the files existed because one of the computer bank's operatives, who'd transferred to El Paso from the Dallas office, owed Cole sixty bucks from a football bet. Cole thanked his deadbeat gambling buddy, then hung up the phone and scratched his nose.

Item one: The license number that Oscar Beemish had recorded at the Village either was, or was very similar to, the license number of Miss Coralee Erly's automobile.

Item two: Miss Coralee Erly's baby brother was a dyed-in-the-wool, card-carrying short-eyes. "Short-eyes" was a penitentiary term which meant the same thing that screenwriters and other assorted squarejohns were trying to say when they referred to a person as a baby-raper.

Hardy Cole thought, Hmm.

The neighborhood on and around Beacon Street had been upper-middle-class at the time of the Korean War. Its decline had begun in the early sixties, and most of the houses were now divided into one- and two-room apartments which shared bathroom and kitchen facilities. Runny-nosed, shirtless, and barefoot kids now rolled old worn out tire carcasses over the same lawns where ladies and gentlemen had once played croquet.

Miss Coralee Erly's house wasn't as run-down as her two next door neighbors' houses. Miss Erly's place was a one-story wood frame with paint that was only yellowed instead of completely flaked away, and there were even patches of grass in her yard. The place to the east had a rotting front porch with a ten-degree cant toward the front, and the two-story on the other side of the Erly house had three broken windows.

Hardy Cole pulled his gray county-owned four-door to the curb just at sunset, at about the same time that Bino Phillips sat down in the waiting hall at Presbyterian Hospital. Cole wore khaki pants along with a golf shirt, and a summer-weight plaid sport coat to cover his nylon shoulder rig. Three black teenagers—two boys with the sides of their heads shaved and their hair on top waxed and sticking straight up into high-top fades, and a girl with straightened hair who wore skintight jean cutoffs—who stood in front of the sagging porch to the east of Miss Erly's, seemed to be just hanging out and probably didn't figure Cole for the law. Cops generally traveled in pairs, while a lone honky at sunset was likely the repo man. Repo men carried very little cash and were often armed. The teenagers quickly looked the other way.

An old tan Buick with license number 473-DWJ sat on bald dusty tires in Coralee Erly's drive.

And Hardy Cole thought, Hmm, once again.

The front windows of the house were covered by burglar bars. Cole went up on the porch and pressed the doorbell button. Nothing happened, so he bent his knuckles and rapped loudly on the wooden wall. In a few seconds the door snapped open the width of the chain lock, and one dull brown eye peered out through the crack. "Yes?"—a mature woman's voice, low-pitched and a bit raspy.

"Miss Erly?"

"Yes?"—slightly louder, some suspicion in the tone.

"Police." Cole had his wallet open and exhibited the shield for the dull brown eye's benefit. Officially he should have said, "County Investigator Cole," but had learned from experience that most people thought a county investigator was either doing a land survey or bringing a dependent-children support check. "Can I come in?" Cole said.

"Why?"—flat now, resigned.

"Just looking for information, ma'am." Straight from Joe Friday.

The door closed. The chain rattled. The door opened wide. "I ain't got much time," the female voice said.

Cole stepped across the threshold into a sitting room containing furniture with sheets draped over the cushions, likely to cover upholstery tears. There was a faint odor of grease-cooked meat. "Just a few minutes," Cole said. He turned.

Coralee Erly had never been pretty, and middle age wasn't improving her looks. She was buck-toothed, with a sloping chin, and the cords in her neck were beginning to sag. Her hair was thin and mouse-colored. She had narrow hunched shoulders and wore a tight purple long-sleeved sweater. Her cheap cotton pants had a cherry-blossom pattern, and her belly sagged. She was barefoot, and now padded over to sit on the sofa and cross her legs. On a brown table by her elbow was a cigarette burning in an ashtray. She took a drag, exhaled, and coughed into her cupped hand. Cole sat down in a padded rocking chair whose springs creaked.

"If it's about Rascal, he ain't here," she said.

"Rascal?"

"My brother, William."

"Do you think it's about Rascal?" Answer a question with a question—professional interrogation procedure—usually worked with innocent people. Thieves and pimps would laugh in your face.

"Well, ain't it?"

"Do you think it should be?"

Miss Erly twisted around to stub out her cigarette. The butt smoldered and smoke continued to rise. "I don't know. Should it?" Her complexion was the color of window-glass putty, and she'd heard the question-with-a-question routine before.

"Sure it is. I'm investigating a burglary," Cole said. He fished in his pocket for William Erly's mug shot and looked the picture over. Same buck teeth and sloping chin as his sister in the side-angle view.

"Rascal ain't no burglar."

"That's not what his record tells me," Cole said. "Plus he's been identified." Actually, when Cole had showed the mug shot to Daphne Wilson, the federal prosecutor who'd seen the suspect on the steps leading to Andrea Morton's apartment, Daphne had said, "Gee, it could be." Not enough for a warrant, but enough for a probable-cause arrest if you stretched the point.

"Well, I told you Rascal ain't here," Coralee said.

"When will he be here, Miss Erly?"

"Can't never tell. Sometimes he stays here, sometimes he don't."

Cole sighed and rocked back in the chair. So much for the professional interrogator routine. "Let's quit beating around the bush, Coralee."

"I *ain't* beating around the bush. Rascal ain't—"

"You read in the paper about Dracula Don?"

She froze with her mouth open, then slowly closed her mouth and reached for a crumpled pack of Pall Malls. It took her three attempts to light one with a butane disposable that she held tightly in her hand while the lit cigarette dangled from one corner of her mouth. "Rascal ain't no lunatic."

"You keep saying what Rascal ain't," Cole said. "I'm wanting to know what he is."

"He's a poor boy that's had his problems," she said. "He's been to therapy."

"Uh-huh."

"We're poor people. Ain't got no money for fancy hospitals and such."

"Uh-huh." Cole mentally kicked himself. The noncommittal "uh-huh" routine was designed to make suspects nervous, and usually did. Miss Coralee Erly, though, wasn't at present a suspect. Damn near thirty years on the job and Cole still got the routines confused—which was why he preferred the straightforward approach.

"But Rascal ain't into drinkin' no blood, I'll tell you that much." She removed the cigarette from her mouth and wagged a finger.

"Well, if he's not," Cole said, "then he doesn't have any problem. Tell you what, Coralee, he's not charged with anything. If he could drop by to see me in the morning we could short-circuit all this."

"That's what they said the last time. He didn't come back for six months, nearly."

"Well, I won't lie to you," Cole said. "If he turned out to be the guy, he probably wouldn't ever be back." He stood. "I won't take up any more of your time, Coralee. I'll be in tomorrow from eight o'clock on. I'll give your brother until ten-thirty, and then I'll be looking for a warrant." He handed her a business card. "Eleventh floor," Cole said. "Turn to the right off the elevator." He mentally crossed his fingers. Getting a warrant on Daphne Wilson's gee-it-could-be statement would be next to impossible.

Coralee Erly read the card over, then dropped it on the table beside the ashtray. She picked up her cigarette and puffed. "I guess he'd need a lawyer, wouldn't he?"

"Might be a good idea," Cole said.

21

When Bino got home, he showered and changed into his old basketball warmup while Dodie fixed green beans, sautéed onions, and corn on the cob. When he asked if there was any meat, she wrinkled her nose at him. He drowned his beans and corn in butter while she took hers plain, and he had to admit that the vegetables tasted pretty good.

After supper, they stood close together while they loaded the dishwasher, Dodie going on and on about how he shouldn't eat so many eggs and cheeseburgers and whatnot, that all that stuff caused heart attacks and cancer. Before either of them realized it, they were very close together, and as Dodie looked up after dropping a plate into the bottom portion of the washer, her face was scant inches from his as Bino bent over to load a saucer in. She only paused slightly in her healthy-diet discourse, and the quick flash of her tongue as she licked her upper lip was probably only a pause as she gathered her thoughts to say more. Bino backed up a step and reminded himself, just as he did a hundred times every day, that she was one crackerjack of a secretary, and that both of them would be better off if they didn't upset their business relationship. At least he *tried* to remind himself that they were boss and employee, but a mental image kept getting in the way of his concentration: a picture of Dodie the last time they'd spent the night together (Jesus, Bino thought, three years?), the softness of her hair as it lay on his shoulder, the warmth of her bare thigh as she slid her leg in between his.

He quickly turned away from her and fixed himself Johnny Walker Red over ice in a rock glass. She twisted the knob and, as the dishwasher gurgled and hummed, poured herself a glass of grapefruit juice. They went into the living room. Bino plugged a Bette Midler tape into the stereo and sat down beside her on the couch. He stretched long legs and crossed his ankles on top of the coffee table. "I need to tell you something."

She took off her sneakers, curled her feet underneath, and sat on her ankles. Dodie was wearing baggy thigh-length shorts and an oversized purple T-shirt. On the front of her shirt was a clipped-nail yellow moon surrounded by twinkling stars, over script writing which read, "A Little Night Run." (The Little Night Run was an annual Fort Worth Youth Orchestra benefit held in May, and this year he'd agreed to go the three miles with her. Then he'd backed out because he hadn't been jogging like he'd told her and didn't want her to know how out of shape he was.) She sipped juice and didn't say anything.

"I didn't tell you the truth tonight," Bino said. "About getting somebody out of jail."

"I know," she said.

He frowned. "How?"

"You left your briefcase. All the bond stuff, notary seal, and whatnot, they're in there."

"Oh."

"Also you wouldn't have gone yourself, you'd have called a bondsman and then had the client come and see you when he got out of jail. The take-two-aspirins-and-call-me-in-the-morning routine. Wow, Bino, you don't have to go through that with me. I'm not your—"

"Dodie."

"—keeper or anything . . . What?"

He moved his glass in a circular pattern and watched the ice swirl and tinkle in amber liquid. "There was some trouble this afternoon. In your apartment."

The tensing of her body vibrated the cushions on the sofa. "Oh?"

"The . . . guy. He came to your place."

She set down her drink and hugged herself. "I can't handle

much more of this. I mean, I'd like to be really tough and everything, but I just can't."

Bette Midler was reaching a smooth crescendo on "Wind Beneath My Wings." Bino let his gaze rest for an instant on the
roughened brick fireplace, then moved his eyes to look at the giant
blank screen on the Mitsubishi TV. "Dode."

Her soft mouth trembled. "Yes?"

"Think. It's somebody you see at the courthouse, somebody . . .
You notice any men, maybe guys that stare at you a lot?"

"I don't pay any attention to that kind of stuff."

She didn't. Bino had known maybe two or three beautiful
women in his life who weren't conscious of their looks, and Dodie
was one. When his ex-wife Annabelle had gone to a party where
every man in the place hadn't stumbled over his own feet doing
double-takes in her direction, Annabelle had gone into a snit that
might last for days. Bino said, "Here's my thinking. It's not any
of the obvious people you'd suspect. I mean, there's druggies and
there's druggies. Yeah, nearly all of these weirdo killings, there's
dope involved, devil-worship, you name it. But Mickey Stanley's
bunch is mainly just college kids, or kids just out of college. Those
Kilbourne brothers are older, but those guys aren't crazy. Slime-
balls, yeah.

"So what I think is," Bino said, "it's somebody that blends into
the background. Somebody you'd never notice, sits around down
there at the Federal Building and picks his victims like ducks in
a shooting gallery. Might be somebody with a wife and two kids.
Somebody staring at you, that might be a clue."

Dodie suddenly grinned. "Well, there's you. You go around
staring sometimes." The grin faded at once. "There are more star-
ers in this town that there are automobiles."

Bino rolled his glass across his forehead. "Well, then, who's
been at the trial everyday?"

"Mr. Goldman. You. The judge and the court reporter. Then
there's all those clerks that wander in and out all the time, plus
certain lawyers that just seem to be hanging around."

"That makes a broad field," he said. "Hell, I'm no detective."

She picked up her drink and sipped thoughtfully. "Did he tear
up my things much?"

"Huh?"

"The guy. You said you were over there. That when you told me you were going to the jail, you were really going . . ."

"No, not to your apartment. I went . . ." He studied the worry creases in her forehead. "I was at the hospital."

She swiveled her head to look at him. Her chin tilted.

"Kit Stanley and Mickey came by while he was in there, in your place," Bino said. "And he sort of . . . messed them up."

She softly closed her eyes. "God."

"Oh, they'll be all right," he said quickly. Then his shoulders sagged and he said, "Eventually, they will. Look, Dode, you don't want all the gory details. I don't have all of them myself." He thought about Mac Strange, and the coffin they'd found. No way would he tell Dodie about that. Not tonight, anyway, but she'd have to know before the FBI got hold of her. "Deletay," Bino said, "the FBI Washington guy, he want to interview you tomorrow. They don't have any way of knowing what's missing from your place unless you give him a list."

"I couldn't possibly remember off the top of my head," said Dodie. "I'd have to go over there."

"I think that's what he wants, maybe us to meet him at your place around five. I haven't seen it myself. They say there's some blood. You'd better get ready for it." He absently stroked the red velour surface of the couch with his palm.

Her long lashes moved down as she studied her lap. She shifted her position; one foot came down to touch its toes lightly on the carpet. "Bino?"

"Yeah. What is it?"

"Are they hurt really badly?" There was a slight catch in her voice.

He sighed. "Kit's beat to hell and her jaw is broken. The guy had a gun, and Mickey got shot. They had to pin his shoulder together."

She held her glass in both trembling hands. "What time was this?"

"I'm not really sure."

"Yes, you are. It was around the time we went jogging, wasn't it?"

He shrugged. "It could have been."

"Which means he was waiting for me to get home from work."

He licked his lips and regarded the ceiling.

"My sweet God," Dodie said. "How did he get in?"

"Dodie, I don't know all that. They'll tell us all that tomorrow afternoon."

"For all I know he could have been peeking through my window every night. Or even hiding right there in the apartment with me."

"Speculating on things like that—"

"Right in my own *closet*."

"—isn't going to do anything except drive you up the wall. There's nothing easy about it, babe. I'll do everything I can to make it easier on you, but I've got some idea how much good it'll do. They'll get this guy eventually. They always do."

"Oh, goody. Maybe he'll just drink so much of my blood he'll pass right out on the scene of the crime or something." A tear rolled down her cheek, streaking her light blush makeup.

"You're just tying yourself into knots, Dode." The Bette Midler tape ended, followed by silence, and then by a series of clicks as the machine prepared to play the album again. Bino reached into an end-table drawer, found a box of Kleenex, and offered them to Dodie.

She set her drink down, snatched a handful of the tissues, and turned her face away as she wiped her cheeks. Then she blew her nose. "Bino?"

"I'm right here, babe."

She laid the wadded tissue beside her glass on the coffee table and wrung her hands. "I don't exactly know how to say this."

"Well, try," Bino said. Jumpy music emitted from the speakers, followed by Bette Midler's voice in two different octaves as she did a duet with herself. "Boogie-Woogie Bugle Boy of Company B."

Dodie sniffled. "Did you mean what you said?"

"About what?"

"About doing anything you could to make it easier on me."

He leaned forward. "Sure."

"Well,"—she folded her hands in her lap and studied them—"I don't want to sleep by myself in that big old bed tonight." She lifted her head to squarely meet his gaze.

He swallowed. He hadn't expected this.

"Now, before you say anything," Dodie said. "We've never talked about the times we've been to bed together. Have we?"

"Not that I can remember."

"Well, I think you'd remember it if we had. And this isn't an invitation for sex, I'm scared to death is all. Do you think you could . . ." Her shoulders lifted and dropped, and she smiled a little smile. "Do you think you could sleep close to me in that bed, just be there for me? Without . . . you know."

He reached out to take a long pull from the Scotch, then set down his glass. "I'd be lying if I said it'd be a piece of cake." He patted her leg. "But for you, babe, yeah. For you, I guess I could."

22

Hardy Cole went to his office at eight the next morning, then twiddled his thumbs for an hour before Rascal Erly showed up, an ugly-as-sin guy with red-rimmed eyes and a sloping chin, dressed like a street bum. Miss Coralee Erly came with him, wearing a shapeless flowered Sunday dress that had to be twenty years old and black lace-up shoes. Also accompanying Rascal was a lawyer named Peter Carlos, whom Cole already knew. Carlos represented the three members of the El Diablo street gang in a suit against the Dallas Police Department, three individual officers, the sheriff, and the Dallas County Jail. "Hey, man, them poleez beat the living chit outta us and now these county pipples make us sleep five inna fockin' cell. Ain't no consitooshon, man." So, Cole thought, if the Erlys are poor people and can't afford no fancy hospital, how are they paying *this* fucking guy?

"There's a little conference room over here," Cole said. He wore a plaid shirt, yellow tie and suspenders, and was carrying two thick file folders. Then, to Peter Carlos, he said, "There's no charges pending. This is strictly an informal question-and-answer session."

"No problem," Carlos said. "I'm just along to observe." He had thick blue-black hair, wore a navy suit with a light-reflecting sheen, and had a diamond mounted in florentined gold on his right ring finger. Cole made the stone to be a carat and a half, minimum. In the courtroom, Peter Carlos would shed the rock, wear a J.C. Penney's suit which was a couple of sizes too big for him, and walk around with his shoulders hunched. All during trial the lawyer would maintain a permanently confused look like Seve Ballesteros' after a double bogey. The strategy worked too often to suit detectives like Hardy Cole.

Coralee Erly kept her seat in the waiting room while her little brother followed Cole into the small conference room with Attorney Carlos bringing up the rear. Rascal Erly shuffled his feet and sobbed pitifully every couple of steps. There was a hole in the toe of his left shoe. His shirt was the top half of a pair of army fatigues. So far he hadn't spoken. Cole sat at the head of the table with Rascal on his right and Carlos on his left. Carlos smiled and cocked his head. Rascal watched the surface of the table. Cole lifted a small recorder from a drawer.

"Keeps me from having to write things down in longhand," Cole said. "Any objections?" Rascal Erly wasn't under arrest, which meant he wasn't entitled to a Miranda warning. Carlos glanced at the recorder and continued to smile. Neither lawyer nor client said anything. Cole switched the recorder on. Tiny reels turned under clear plastic.

"Detective Hardy Cole here." Cole leaned nearer the recorder. "It's nine-oh-seven a.m. on Friday, September 27, 1991. With me is Mr. William Erly, and also with me is Mr. Erly's attorney, Peter Carlos. Mr. Carlos is going to listen in while I am asking Mr. Erly some questions, and I'll begin by asking Mr. Erly if he remembers his whereabouts on Monday night, which was September 3, from around eight-thirty until three in the morning."

Carlos said, "That's Tuesday morning."

"Right, Tuesday," Cole said. "Now, Mr. Erly, if you can remember—"

"What does this concern?" Carlos said.

Cole cleared his throat. "Well, I'm investigating a break-in which occurred at the Village Apartments, which are located on—"

"Southwestern Boulevard," Carlos said. "I'm familiar with the place. Excuse me for interrupting."

The back of Cole's neck was suddenly warm. "No problem. Now, Mr. Erly, could you answer my question?"

Rascal mumbled something.

"I beg your pardon?" Cole said. "Speak up, please."

"I was home," Rascal said.

"You were home." Cole opened one of his files and pulled out two letter-sized pieces of paper which were stapled together. "Mr. Erly, I've got a statement here from—"

"Could I see that, please?" Carlos said. He extended a mani-cured hand, took the papers, and continued to smile as he said, "This isn't a statement. These are your notes."

"Well, I was about to say," Cole said, "that these are my *notes* concerning a statement from a Miss. Daphne Wilson, who says you were on a staircase at the Village shortly after two a.m. And that—"

"Does Miss Wilson know Mr. Erly?" Carlos said. "Mr. Erly, do you know this woman?"

"Ain't never heard of her," Rascal said.

"How did she identify Mr. Erly?" Carlos said. "Was there a lineup?"

Cole reached over to press a button. The reels halted at once. Cole drew a breath. "You want a lineup? You want a fucking lineup? If you want to play it this way I'll give you a fucking lineup. I'll get the D.A. in here and we'll read Mr. Erly his rights and get the good shit on." For the most part, Cole was bluffing. At the moment Mac Strange was down the hall in his office, keeping Nelson Deletay and the VICAP folks occupied, and Cole couldn't call Mac into the meeting without Deletay finding out that Dallas County had thumbed its nose at the feds and maybe cut a few corners in their investigation. Also, Cole would look pretty silly conducting a lineup where witness Daphne Wilson tilted her pert chin and said, "Gee, I don't know. It could be."

Peter Carlos propped his elbows on the table and made a pyra-mid with his fingers. "Off the record, what are you getting at? You've had no lineup, and you've got no signed witness statement. You're wanting my client to speak into a recorder without the benefit of his Miranda protection. If you're talking burglary, or any kind of felony, he's subject to the habitual statute. As a two-time loser, he's looking at twenty-five to life."

Cole scooted his rump forward in his chair and propped his knee against the edge of the table. "To cut through the bullshit, and since you'll already know this from talking to his sister, we're not talking *just* a burglary. And we're not talking *just* your client. There was another guy."

"Your notes," Carlos said, tapping the stapled papers, "talk about someone allegedly seeing someone who resembles my client on a staircase. I don't see anything from any witnesses which places him inside anywhere."

Cole blinked.

"Now if we were talking misdemeanor trespass here," Carlos went on, "that would be a different cloth altogether. No habitual enhancement."

Cole lifted a retractable ballpoint from his shirt pocket and chewed on the ballpoint's end. To hell with procedure here. He'd already kicked procedure in the ass, and knew good and well that he didn't have enough admissible courtroom evidence to convict Rascal Erly of blowing his nose. "Tell you what, Mr. Carlos," Cole said. "How 'bout if we were talking letting your client walk altogether, keep wandering around town doing whatever he gets his kicks doing? How about that? Listen, I got to have a name. I'm pretty sure your client knows the fucking name. If I don't get the name, if somebody doesn't get the name and goddamn soon, then there's going to be more people getting killed. Truth is, Mr. Carlos, you probably got me by the balls. So you want to fuck me around, you go right ahead, but I want to be sure you under-stand what all this legal bullshit is going to cause to keep happen-ing." Cole briefly pictured the medical techs as they'd borne Andrea Morton on a gurney in the rain. He mentally held his breath.

Carlos looked at his client, who was still dully regarding the table. Carlos then played with his diamond ring, spread his fingers, and examined his manicure. He lowered his hand and said to Cole, "Can we have a minute?"

Cole softly closed his eyes. Jesus Christ, he was beat to shit—too tired, almost, to think. "Take five, Mr. Carlos. I just got to have the name, okay?"

Bino came into his office and greeted Dodie as though they hadn't just spent the night together. "Hi, Dode. Anything goin' on?" She'd left the apartment a half four before he had, pausing by the door to stand on tiptoes and impulsively kiss his cheek. "Thank you," she'd said. He'd rehearsed over and over what he was going to say when he saw her as he drove the Linc downtown. "Hi, Dode. Anything goin' on?" was the best he could come up with.

She used a brass letter opener to slice into an envelope. The mail she'd already opened was in two piles on her desk, while the yet unopened envelopes were off to one side in a small neat stack. "Couple of things: 'Weedy' Clements is coming by at eleven." She met his gaze for an instant, then looked quickly away. Dodie was having a little trouble dealing with it, as well—pretending that he hadn't turned onto his side at some point during the night to find her lying on her stomach, her face turned slightly toward him, regarding him silently through one wide blue eye. Her other eye had been pressed against the pillow. Her hair had been waving slightly in the draft from the a/c vents, and moonlight slanting through the open window had illuminated her slim bare shoulders. She'd sighed and come to him (or he would liked to think it had been her coming to him, but in truth it might have been the other way around) and then she'd whimpered softly as her mouth moved against his, gently at first and then more urgently, as she lifted her leg to straddle his waist—both of them now pretending that their lovemaking hadn't really happened, both of them telling themselves it was only the heat of the moment, a release from the pressure, both of them vowing that it wouldn't happen again, just as they'd vowed the same thing on the other occasions over the years when they'd—

"Damn, old Weedy, huh?" Bino said. "When'd he get out?" Weedy Clements had received five years on a plea-bargain deal the day before the feds had indicted Judge Emmett Burns. Bino marked a lot of time around the Burns case, noting that this or that happened just before he'd defended the judge, or just after he'd defended the judge. Jesus, had it been three years since Weedy had gone on his little vacation? Bino supposed that it had, even though it didn't seem like it. It had also been slightly more than three years, until last night, since Bino and Dodie had made love. Seemed like a lot longer, though.

"I'm not sure," Dodie said. "I think he's more worried about going back in. Says his parole officer is bugging him."

"What's he want *me* to do about it? The last time I tried to talk to somebody's parole officer I damn near got locked up myself."

Dodie blinked. "Well, maybe that's what you should tell

Weedy. Don't ask me—I don't *have* a parole officer. He'll be in at eleven."

He shrugged. "Okay. What about Half?"

"Don't look for him for three or four days." Dodie glanced toward Half's little cubbyhole of an office. "He says he spent so much time on Mickey Stanley's case that he's got a lot of catching up to do."

"Catching up on what?"

"Use your imagination," Dodie said. Her tone was light and airy; both he and Dodie were being light and airy and humorous as hell. Like a couple of teenagers who were embarrassed over groping one another while sitting in a darkened movie theater.

"I don't have to imagine," Bino said. "What else?"

"This." Dodie was holding out a thick brown legal-size envelope. The return address of the United States District Court was in bold black in the upper lefthand corner.

Bino took the envelope; his hand dropped slightly under the sudden weight. He blew into the slit end; the sides of the envelope parted to reveal a book-size stack of papers. "What is it?"

"Don't ask," Dodie said.

"That bad, huh?" Bino shoved the heavy envelope underneath his arm. Then he stepped inside the supply closet, squeezed between the wall and the Xerox, and poured himself a cup of coffee. The Mr. Coffee was on a small table by the window, between two upright metal filing cabinets. Normally Dodie brought him his coffee, but this morning he didn't want her running in and out of his office any more than necessary, since every time he looked at her he'd get this guilty feeling as though he'd taken advantage of her because all this stuff with the blood-drinker guy had made her vulnerable. Not me, Bino thought. I'd never do anything like that. Besides, she had a lot of work to do herself, and probably wouldn't even notice that he'd poured his own coffee. He carried the Styrofoam cup back into the reception area. Steam drifted up from the surface of the hot black liquid.

Dodie glanced at the cup in his hand, then looked quickly away. She'd noticed, all right. Jesus, he felt about an inch high. He lowered his head and, carrying the cup in one hand and the envelope tucked under his arm, trudged toward the door to his own office. "Hold my calls awhile, Dode," Bino said.

*   *   *

Bino thought, The *nerve* of the old heifer. He tossed the stack
of papers onto his desk with a solid *thump*, then got up and removed his coat. He hung the coat on the hall tree beside the
window, then paused for a moment to gaze down on Main Street,
at a stream of cars and trucks going back and forth far below, like
workers in an ant colony. The *nerve* of the old heifer, Bino
thought again. He turned and, hands on hips, glared at the stack
of papers on his desk.

The envelope which Dodie had handed him contained an
order from Judge Hazel Burke Sanderson. An original had been
sent to Bino with a duplicate original forwarded over to Goldman's
office. Old Hazel wanted briefs. *Briefs*, on top of all the other shit
that Bino had to do—by next Wednesday.

The briefs she was ordering had to do with Bino's motion for
mistrial. The motion he'd made (a hundred years ago it seemed) in
open court, right after Kit Stanley had pointed out that Goldman's
witnesses were sitting in the courtroom. Followed closely by Goldman's motion for continuance when Nelson Deletay had hit town,
which old Hazel couldn't find any legal precedent for granting.
For her to sit on Bino's motion for mistrial instead of ruling on
Goldman's motion had been Bino's own idea. Jesus, all she had
to do was sit there. *Briefs*, the old heifer wanted.

With Mickey Stanley now in the hospital, it would be a simple
matter just to continue the trial, but old Hazel wanted her rear
end covered. What she wanted was, she wanted to be certain that
nobody could point the finger at her for slowing down the trial.
So, to give her something to pretend to mull over—while in fact
she was running around town doing the shopping malls—she
wanted both sides, prosecution and defense, to drag out every
single case in the Federal 2d's which had to do with mistrials,
mark them all down, and present their arguments as to whether
the mistrial should be granted. Then, if somebody at the Fifth
Circuit Court of Appeals questioned why the judge took so fucking
long to rule on the motion, all old Hazel had to say was, "Gee,
look at all these briefs I had to consider." Jesus fucking Christ,
Bino thought.

Of course the briefs wouldn't be any problem for Goldman.
No way: All old Marv had to do was ring up one of the ten million
or so law clerks that the feds had on the payroll and tell the clerk
to drag fanny over to the law library. Only Bino didn't have ten

million law clerks to boss around. What Bino had was Half and Dodie, and according to Dodie, he wasn't going to have Half for several days. Which left Bino to do the fucking brief himself. Left Bino to go over to the county law library (Naw, Bino thought, I'll do it at the law library out at SMU—a whole lot better-looking fannies to watch out there), drag out about four hundred law books that weighed a ton apiece, and look the cases up himself. Jesus, Bino *hated* legal research. Absolutely despised fucking . . .

He sighed and lowered his hands to his sides. What the hell, there was nothing he could do but do it. He took resigned steps back over to his desk, straightened the papers into a neat stack, and sat down. He fixed his gaze on his old basketball picture (Jesus, why didn't I try pro ball? Bino thought—my ankle might have held up after all), then pressed the intercom button on his phone and lifted the receiver in preparation for buzzing Dodie. He needed for her to bring him his . . .

Files.

Files on the Mickey Stanley case.

Jesus, he didn't *have* his files. Nelson Deletay had his files. The federal guy.

Jesus, Bino's life was cluttered with federal guys. He absolutely *hated* fucking federal guys.

He hung up the phone and drummed his fingers.

Okay, get ahold of yourself, Bino thought. What did he need? The motion for mistrial hinged on whether the witnesses who'd been sitting improperly in the courtroom had heard any testimony that was likely to affect their own testimony when it was their turn to get on the stand—which meant that, in order to do the brief, Bino needed a copy of the trial transcript, the written record of what each and every witness had said so far—

Jesus, which he had to buy from the court reporter. Another nice little racket, Bino thought. The feds indict a guy and then make him pay for a transcript of his own trial in case he wants to appeal or make a motion or— To hell with it, Bino thought— I've got to pay the court reporter for a copy of the transcript.

Mickey Stanley didn't have any money, of course, and Kit had already donated her life savings to the cause. So Bino would have to pay for the transcripts out of his own pocket. Jesus, how much money was he already out on this deal? Now he *really* had a reason not to like the court reporter, the mild-mannered young guy who'd sat in on the conference in Hazel Sanderson's office the other day, the guy who'd assured the judge that the transcripts were correct because the court reporter had recorded everything even though, officially, he wasn't supposed to have a recorder in federal court. Bino pictured the young guy, smiling confidently as he'd held up the . . .

Tape cassette. Jesus, Bino thought, wait a minute. There's something here that . . .

Jesus Christ, *voice prints*, Bino thought.

Nelson Deletay had a tape recording of the blood-drinker guy's voice, when the guy had called Dodie at the office.

The court reporter had a tape recording of everybody who'd testified so far in the trial. The recording would also contain samples of the bailiff's and the judge's voices, along with the voices of various clerks and other judicial employees who'd wandered in and out of the courtroom and said things to the judge or court reporter.

Bingo.

Maybe old Hazel wasn't so bad after all. Bino quickly checked his desktop phone index and called a number. After two rings there was a click on the line and Mac Strange said, "Strange."

And Bino said, "I think it's strange, too."

To which Strange replied, "Fuck you, Bino."

"You must not have your shadow with you," Bino said, "talking that way on the phone."

"Hardy? Naw, he's up in—"

"Not him. Deletay."

"Oh. *That* asshole. He and Goldman went for coffee. Jesus Christ, I can't even sit behind my own desk when they're in here."

"I noticed," Bino said. "Listen, Mac, I may have something."

"Somebody needs to have something."

"That tape recording. You guys going to make those trial witnesses give a voice-print sample?"

"Working on it," Strange said. "Trial witnesses, all the federal employees, anybody who's been anyplace around that courtroom. Trouble is, it's not like the physical evidence, jism and whatnot. Deletay has to get another court order. No telling—"

"I think I can help."

"—how long that'll take . . . How's that?"

"Look," Bino said, "I got to get a copy of the trial transcripts in Mickey Stanley's case. Has to do with briefs that old Hazel's calling for. Now, this can't be spread around, but the court reporter in the trial. Guess what? He's been recording all the testimony."

"Jesus."

"That's what *I* said. Now, the odds of the ghoul being one of the people on the court reporter's tape, which is going to include the judge, bailiff, and a few of the clerks from across the hall, those odds are a hundred to one against."

Mac's tone was suddenly hopeful. "I don't care what the odds are. What are the odds of all this horror-movie shit happening to begin with? If he's got a tape of anybody that might be a suspect, I want it."

"The good part is, the witnesses who've testified include everybody involved in Mickey's case that I think could possibly be the sicko. Both Kilbourne brothers plus those two pilots. The kids involved, Jesus, Mac, it can't be one of them."

"You'd think not. When can we get ahold of this court reporter?"

Bino expelled a sigh. "No way, no way is the guy going to give his cassette to you or Deletay. You or Deletay couldn't get him to admit he's been taping the trial. But I think I can. I'm private, see—nobody that could get him in trouble over his job. Plus, I'm going to be buying a copy of the transcript from him."

"Jesus, if this would only work," Strange said.

"I'm going to call the guy right now, Mac. If he'll give the tape up, I'll have Dodie drop it by your office. She'll like doing that. Jesus, if anybody's got a stake in getting this wacko off the street, it damn sure's her."

Getting through to the court reporter wasn't as easy as Bino had thought. First of all, the guy had taken the day off, and Bino had to call him at home. Getting the home number from the district clerk was like pulling teeth, and only after Bino threatened the clerk with getting Judge Sanderson involved—it was her order Bino was trying to satisfy by getting the transcripts to begin with—would the clerk cooperate. Then, when Bino finally *did* get through to the court reporter, the guy didn't want to admit he even had the recording. Who, me? It's forbidden to have a tape recorder in federal court, don't you know that? The only way the reporter finally agreed was if Bino would pay for the transcripts, kick in an extra fifty bucks for the tape, and give his solemn word that if any heat came down, it was Bino Phillips and not the court reporter who'd sneaked the recorder into Hazel Sanderson's courtroom. Which might put the old heifer into shock, Bino admitting to anything.

Living within the system is a bitch, Bino thought.

But Bino agreed to everything—making a mental note to hit Mac Strange up for half of the fifty bucks which the court reporter was extorting—and wrote down directions to get to the court reporter's house. When he hung up, Bino was whistling. Maybe, just maybe, somebody was about to get somewhere.

When he strolled into the reception area, still whistling, Dodie said, "Wow, I don't know what there is to be so happy about." She had a stack of files on her desk, had one folder open and was making notes from the folder's contents as fast as she could write. There was a pile of pink call slips an inch high impaled on a gilt spike in front of her.

Bino ducked into the supply room, shot a Xerox of the notes he'd made while talking to the court reporter, stuck the original in his pocket and went back in to say to Dodie, "Look, Dode, I want you to run an errand." He sat on the corner of her desk.

She laid down her ballpoint. "I don't have time to run any errands. I've got to—"

"For this, you'll take time." Bino grinned. "It might lead to ending your problems with the wacko."

Her expression was suddenly serious and even a little bit fearful. She folded her hands and expectantly lifted her eyebrows.

"Here's the deal," Bino said, walking around to her side of the desk, laying the copy he'd made on Dodie's blotter and reading it over her shoulder. "These are the directions to the court reporter's house. You know, the reporter in Mickey's trial. Now, he's going to give you a copy of the trial transcripts and a tape cassette. You give him"—Bino fished in his pocket, dropped two twenties and a ten on her desk—"this fifty bucks in cash, and he's going to bill me for the transcripts. On the way back, stop in and drop the cassette off at Mac Strange's office."

Dodie picked up the money and brightened some. "What's going on, boss?"

Bino expelled a breath. "Maybe nothing at all, Dode. But it

might be a tape to match the recording of the wacko's phone call to you. Mac's people will do a voice-print analysis."

She showed the beginnings of a smile. Jesus, but I hope this works, Bino thought. I love to watch Dodie smile—hope I'll never see fear in those beautiful eyes again.

"Now if you should get lost," Bino said, fishing a ballpoint from his own pocket and underlining some numbers beneath the directions, "this is the court reporter's phone number. He's expecting you. And right down here"—Bino now circled two words on the copy, below the underlined phone number—"this is the guy's name: Quarles, Patrick Quarles. He lives up by Garza Little Elm Lake—shouldn't be hard to find at all. Now, it's a beautiful day and a beautiful drive, so take your time, Dode. Ought to take your mind off all the bad stuff that's been happening."

23

Hardy Cole barged into Mac Strange's office without knocking and didn't bother to close the door. The door banged into the plaster wall and rebounded. Mac was seated behind his desk, eating a tuna salad sandwich from the county snack bar. The sandwich was wrapped in a waxpaper napkin and had far too much mayonnaise mixed in with the tuna fish. Cole walked rapidly up to stand before the desk. "We got him, Mac. His name is Patrick Quarles. Probably he works someplace around the federal courts."

"Got who?" The question came from Nelson Deletay. He was on Strange's couch, eating a ham and cheese on rye. Beside him sat Marvin Goldman, who was digging cantaloupe and pineapple out of a Styrofoam cup with a plastic fork. The cantaloupe was browning around the edges. The couch was positioned against the back wall, hidden from Cole's view as the county detective had come charging in.

Cole turned around to face the federal men as Strange washed down a big bite of tuna fish with Coke. Cole hesitated, then said, "Jesus. To hell with it. The guy."

"I'll handle it, Hardy," Strange said, then said to Deletay, "I think he means your serial killer."

Deletay pointed a finger at Cole. "You're Hardy? Detective Hardy Cole, right?"

Cole nodded.

"One thing you'll learn in these investigations, Detective," Deletay said, "is that everybody's going to have a theory, and that every other person you meet is going to know who the killer is. At least they're going to think they do. Going off half-cocked after every lead does nothing but hamper the investigation, and what you've got to do is keep a cool head and follow procedure. Those things, the grace of God, and a pile of luck." The VICAP man took a bite of his sandwich. "Hard work and forensics evidence—there's no substitute for them. So you'll know, while you've been going your own way in this, I've been to the scene and worked up a complete psychological profile. And while we're on the subject, I've got a complaint about you, Detective."

Cole regarded the floor.

"The management over at the Adolphus Hotel," Deletay said. "You don't get anywhere stepping on people's toes, Detective. Who authorized you to—?"

"I'll take credit for that." Mac Strange sat up a little straighter in his chair, and was wondering what his share of the county pension fund might be, in case he got fired. "I knew Hardy was going over to the hotel."

Deletay glared at Strange, then at Cole, then once again at Strange. Goldman balanced his fruit cup on the sofa's arm and looked as though he'd just swallowed a whole jalapeño pepper. "Jesus Christ," Goldman said. "You guys are overstepping your bounds a little, aren't you?"

Strange wadded sandwich and waxpaper together and tossed the whole lumpy mess into his wastebasket. The sandwich wasn't worth a damn anyway. Strange said, "We were—"

"Fuck it, Mac." Cole raised a hand and stepped toward the federal men. "Mac didn't know a thing. I did it on my own. Now after we catch this guy, you can do whatever you want to about it." He turned back to Strange. "Get on the horn, Mac."

Strange ignored the stares from Goldman and Deletay and picked up his phone. He told the operator to get him the U.S. district clerk in one helluva hurry. Deletay rose, carrying his sandwich, and took a couple of steps forward. He said with his mouth full, "Now hold, hold on. You can't go upsetting everybody in the courthouse over what somebody just runs in here and . . . hang up." Strange replaced the phone in its cradle, after which Deletay said to Cole, "Where did this information come from,

Detective?" Deletay was wearing a pale blue shirt with tiny red pinstripes, a solid red tie, and the pants to a charcoal suit. His hair looked as though it was sculpted from iron-gray marble.

Mac Strange knew what was coming and rose halfway from his chair. Before Strange could open his mouth, Cole stood nose to nose with Deletay. The county cop's hands hung by his hips and were balled into fists. "I've got about ten seconds to say this," Cole said. "So listen up. I just let a guy walk to get this information, a guy that's probably going around molesting little kids and God knows what else. I hate that so much I'm ready to throw up. You know why I let this guy walk? I let him walk because I happen to think that a guy molesting little kids is better than a guy going around killing people and drinking their blood. I ain't particularly happy right now, but now that I've done this shit, Mac Strange is going to get on the phone and find out where this guy is." He held his own stiffened index finger under Deletay's nose. "And Mr. Deletay," Cole said, "if you say one more fucking word before Mac finishes his phone call, I'm going to throw you out of here. And if Mr. Goldman over there tries to say anything, I'm throwing him out, too." He turned his back on Deletay and faced Strange. "Get on the horn, Mac."

Strange decided that if his own job was in jeopardy, Hardy Cole's job was pure history. Deletay's mouth was agape, showing a disgusting wad of masticated ham and cheese. Goldman's eyes were narrowed, and he yanked desperately on his goatee as if he might pull the triangular beard off of his face. The two federal men continued to stare at Cole while Mac Strange picked up his phone and got the operator back on the line.

"Ain't nothing to doing the time," Weedy Clements said. "In fact, if it wadn for the street income you're losing while you're up there, man, it would be nice and restful. What I did, I was the clerk in Unicor. That's the prison industries, got all these federal contracts to make cable and brooms and shit. What they mostly do is, the inmates and the hacks both, they sit on their asses. Two hundred a month it made me, and you know what? Two hundred in the joint is like twenty thousand on the streets." He was seated on the couch beneath the basketball photo. His legs were crossed. Weedy had thinning hair combed straight back, a bullet-shaped head, and rubbery features that he could bend into all kinds of comical expressions. He was wearing a beige cotton sweater with a long pointy collar, open to the third button, a gold medallion around his neck, brand new stretch denims, and gray sharkskin boots. He looked like a Frenchman's idea of a wild West outlaw.

Bino stifled a yawn. "Dodie said you had problems with your parole officer." Jesus, he'd heard so many stories about the federal joint from his clients, he felt as though he'd done time himself. And in a way, he thought, he had, putting up with all these guys.

Weedy puffed on a cigar the size of an Oscar Mayer frank. He inhaled, then expelled bluish smoke. "Yeah, I got some problems. The guy's always checking on me. Once a week I'm visiting the guy, once a week he's visiting me. Ties a guy down, you know?"

Bino's eyeballs stung. Most people he'd have told to put out the cigar, but not Weedy. Weedy would spend so much time arguing over his right to smoke that he might never leave. "I can't file a bitch with the parole people based on that, Weed," Bino said. "Keeping tabs on you, that's what a parole officer's supposed to do." Sometimes Bino actually enjoyed Weedy, but today wasn't one of the times. Today Bino had too much else to think about.

"I got to make a living," Weedy said. "To make this living I got to fly to Miami, okay? I can't fly to no Miami if the guy's watching me all the time."

"Jesus Christ, Weedy, you're not supposed to leave town without permission. That's a parole violation in itself."

"So they tell me. I got these boots, you know? Big wide fuckers, can fit a kilo bag in each one, walk right on the plane and sit down like Wall Street Willie—you understand what I'm telling you? You got any idea how much money I'm talking, this parole guy is fucking with me?" Weedy rolled the cigar around between his thumb and four fingers.

"Now I don't want to hear about," Bino said, "I don't want to hear about why you want to leave town. I don't want to know anything about that. If your parole officer's really being a horse's ass—"

The telephone buzzed. Bino depressed the flashing button and reached slowly for the cradled receiver.

"—that's one thing. But if you're just trying to get away from the guy so you can fuck around smuggling dope from Miami, that's a horse of a different color. Just a minute, Weed." Bino picked up the phone. "Lawyer's office."

Mac Strange said over the line, "You're by yourself. Dodie's already left, huh?" There was an odd tension in his voice.

"Sure," Bino said, glancing at Weedy, holding up a just-a-minute finger, then dropping his gaze. "Almost two hours ago. She ought to be by your place in—"

"*Jesus*, Bino, *he's the guy.*"

Bino's forehead wrinkled. "Huh? Who's what guy?"

"The court reporter, Quarles. He's our killer. Hardy's been talking to—hey."

Bino had already dropped the phone and was halfway around the desk, his thoughts a jumble, the back of his shirttail hanging out. He yanked his office door open.

"The fuck is going on?" Weedy had the cigar clamped between his teeth, and its end wiggled up and down as he spoke.

Bino froze with one foot in the reception area. He backed up, moved over to stand in front of Weedy, and extended his hand, palm up. "Gimme your gun," Bino said.

"Jesus, what're you talking about? I'm a felon on parole—I can't be carrying no piece."

Bino leaned over, grabbed the front of Weedy's shirt, and jerked the squatty dope smuggler to his feet. The lit cigar flew out of Weedy's mouth and bounced on the carpet, throwing sparks and pieces of gray ash. Bino said, "I got to have it, Weed, and I don't have time for any bullshit. If you don't give me your gun right this minute, I'm taking it off you." His slender nose was about an inch from the end of Weedy's broad flat nose.

Weedy said, "Jesus Christ," and then said, "Jesus Christ" a second time as he reached behind him, lifted his shirt, and dug a pistol from his waistband. The pistol was a Lasermont 9mm, an automatic made of blued steel with a pearl grip. Bino released Weedy's lapels, took the gun, slid out the clip to find five stacked shells, banged the clip home with the heel of his hand, and left through the waiting room at a dead run.

Weedy stood with his mouth open until Bino had left, then dusted off the front of his shirt. He bent over to pick up his cigar and shoved the soggy end into his mouth. "Jesus Christ," he said to the empty room. "Fucking lawyers going around mugging people. A guy's safer in the joint, you know?"

24

When the man at the station where she normally bought gas had told Dodie that her old Trans-Am needed shock absorbers, Dodie had thought, Oh, pooh. Another mechanic trying to take advantage of a single girl. Well, she'd been driving her sporty, fire engine–red car for eight years—and, wow, would probably be driving it for *centuries*, unless some miracle allowed her to pay off the revolving charges at Sears and J.C. Penney's, in addition to her one snooty high-brow account at Lord & Taylor's which she used every six months or so—and she knew a whole lot more about the Trans-Am than the mechanic suspected. After all, Dodie hadn't spent all that time in her grodies, crawling around underneath the car's belly with a wrench, draining the crankcase into a two-gallon metal pan, and winding up sure as pie with oil spots on her cheeks and nose for nothing. She guessed she knew when her car needed something, and as long as it was running okay, she'd use her money somewhere else.

But now, having left the blacktop in accord with Bino's written directions, and moving cautiously along the road through the woods on the way to the court reporter's house, Dodie wasn't so sure that her car *didn't* need shocks. The hood bounced madly up and down with each bump in the road, and three different times her car's underbelly had scraped on dirt. Dodie clung determinedly to the steering wheel, set her chin firmly in a California-

or-bust expression, and nursed the Trans-Am along at a hesitant creep.

Bino had been right about the weather. It was one of those days in late September that Southern Californians took for granted and people in Texas prayed for—temperature in the mid-seventies, not a breeze stirring, sky the color of Dodie's own eyes—and during the drive up on I-35 she'd managed to get herself in a pretty good mood. The thought that there was actually someone out there who might be stalking her, plus her feelings over what had gone on last night between her and Bino (which she was never exactly sure of—her feelings about him—hot one day and cold the next) had made Dodie's morning a terrible bummer. But by the time she took the exit from the freeway, her Trans-Am zipping along and responding like a dream to her foot on the gas pedal or the slightest movement of the steering wheel, she was humming along with the rock music over the radio. That was all before she left the blacktop to enter the woods.

The forest of scrubby mesquite and tall elm trees was positively spooky, the branches so thick overhead that they blotted out the sky. The Trans-Am inched its way along in shadows like gathering dusk. Dodie wondered about the road. There were stretches that were smooth and even, but for the most part, the path was more of a trampled horse trail, as though at one time someone had carefully maintained the road through the woods, then at some point had given up and let nature take over. If the guy's planning to live up here for long, Dodie thought, he's sure got some work cut out for him. After a couple more years of heavy spring and fall rains, there would be no road at all.

There was a growing patch of sunlight up ahead which had to be a clearing of some kind. The Trans-Am dipped and bucked; branches like a gang of car-wash brushes dragged upward over the windshield, scraped their way over the car's roof, and all at once she was free of the woods. She pressed on the brake pedal and looked around.

She'd stopped nose-on to a four-door tan car, a late-model Olds or Buick (both makes looked the same to Dodie—she couldn't tell the difference without reading the car's make on the fender or trunk) parked about fifteen yards in front of her. There were tire tracks leaving the road to skirt the parked car and then returning to the narrow path again. The gravel path beyond the parked car continued for a hundred yards or so, where it seemed to vanish as though whoever had built the road had just said to hell with it and ended their work right there. At the end of the path a second vehicle was parked. This one was a truck, a large pickup with a covered bed and louvered windows around the perimeter of the cover. Sun glinted from the pickup's roof. Fifty yards or so beyond the pickup was a house.

It's a strange-looking house, Dodie thought. The house was built on a slope, and its front portion was two stories high. The rear of the house contained only one level, though, with two high steps up to a concrete back porch. There was an open overhead door at the end of the two-story portion, and inside the doorway stood three upright machines. Dodie didn't know squat about machinery, but the thin jagged blade visible to her told her that at least one of the machines was some kind of electric saw. Piles of wood lay here and there inside the doorway. Some kind of shop, Dodie thought—the last thing she'd expect to find at a court reporter's house. Dodie wasn't sure what she *would* expect to find at a court reporter's house; she supposed that she'd really never thought about it.

On the drive up she'd tried to pull up a mental picture of the reporter in Judge Hazel Burke Sanderson's court, but she'd drawn a blank. It was strange, but Dodie couldn't recall the court reporter's features in a single court in which Bino practiced; it was as though the court reporter was as much a part of the scenery as the jury box or the spectator pews, things that were in every single courtroom in the world but which one never really saw in detail.

On Dodie's left the slope ran down to the water. The lake today was as calm as the weather. The trees on the opposite shore reflected with barely a ripple to distort their images. There was a wooden dock extending from the shore nearest the house, a dock with sagging and rotting boards. A small cabin cruiser was tied to the dock. The boat floated still as a painting. On its deck were uneven piles of rope and overturned beach furniture.

Queerer and queerer, Alice, Dodie thought. She turned the Trans-Am's wheel, pressed lightly on the gas pedal, skirted the parked car and pulled up to stop alongside the pickup truck. She cut the engine, got out, slammed the door, and approached the house. The dirt beneath her feet was loosely packed, and she was glad she'd worn her brown topsiders to the office instead of the heels she usually wore. In addition to the shoes, she had on a tan knee-length skirt and dark brown cotton short-sleeved blouse. She'd gotten up early that morning—hadn't slept a wink after the lovemaking, as a matter of fact—and had taken the time to wash and fluff-dry her hair. She was glad of that as well, since she was about to see someone she didn't know.

Dodie climbed the two back steps to stand on the porch. The door was wood, painted beige, with inset glass panes. Curtains were drawn over the insides of the panes. Dodie searched for a bell button, found none, and rapped sharply on the glass with her knuckles. She folded her arms and crossed her ankles to wait.

In just seconds, there was shadowy movement beyond the curtains. The lock rattled. The door swung inward with a slight creak. A dimly outlined figure within the house said, "Yes?"

Dodie squinted in the sunlight, made out a slender man a few inches taller than she. "Mr. Quarles?"

"Yes?" A not unpleasant male alto, a tone that was slightly tense.

A muscle twitched at the base of Dodie's neck. "Bino Phillips sent me—about the transcripts and the tape recording?"

The man said, "Yes," a third time, added, "Certainly," opened the door, and stood back.

There was the barest instant, just as her foot crossed over the threshold plane, when Dodie had a gripping sensation, an urgent *impulse* to turn around and run as fast as she could. Run from what? She didn't know. Then she was inside and the door swung closed behind her. She turned. The man put something in his pants pocket. To Dodie's relief, the guy didn't look anything like a monster. He was really nice-looking, in fact, with short and curly brown hair and square shoulders like an athlete, wearing a Texas Rangers baseball shirt buttoned all the way up, along with navy shorts. Nice-looking legs, too, long and lean, though his skin was pale as if he could stand to spend some time in the sun. Dodie smiled.

"I'll be just a . . ." Quarles appeared confused. "I'll be just a minute. Wait. Wait here." He brushed past Dodie and walked quickly away from her. Near the entrance to a hallway, he turned, raised a hand to say, "Wait here," again, then vanished down the corridor.

Dodie's uneasiness returned. Don't be a nerd, she told herself, you're just too geeky. He's only going to get the transcripts and recording.

She wandered a few steps into the house and found herself in a room with a bare wooden floor and a small straw throw rug. There was a two-seater divan in the room, with a low table in front of it. On the table was a lamp, bulb glowing, and some photographs. All of the curtains were drawn; the sunlight barely filtered through. Dodie went casually over to the table and glanced down at the pictures.

And froze.

Her pulse racing, she bent to pick up the top photo, turned it around to be sure. Her breath caught in her throat.

The picture was of herself. *Me*, she thought, *Dora Annette Peterson*, standing in tight white shorts in the Village parking lot, squirting water from a hose to wash her car. Quickly, she picked up the entire stack and went through them. They were all of her. *Every single bleeping picture was of her*—jogging at sunset, doing her laundry, sunning by the pool in her bikini. The last one was a nighttime shot—infrared lens? Dodie thought—with her, clad in cotton panties and bra, on the floor by the foot of her bed, doing situps. From the angle, the picture could have only been taken through her bedroom window.

Somewhere at the back of the house, a door closed.

Dodie dropped the pictures as if they were on fire and retreated to the foyer, walking on tiptoes, fighting the impulse to run. She reached the door, turned the knob and pulled. The door didn't give, not so much as a fraction.

She touched the lock; there was no key there. The key, that's what the man had been putting in his pocket when she'd turned to him. *My God*, she thought, leaning her forehead against the door, *he's locked me*—

Behind her, something breathed. *Hissed*, actually, a sound like that of a coiling snake. Then a high-pitched tenor male voice said, "Get her, you foolish heap. It is Rebecca." It was the same voice, the very same voice that Dodie had heard when she'd gotten the call at the office. *The Very. Same. Voice.*

Her self-control completely gone, Dodie yelled at the top of her lungs and pounded in futility on the unyielding door.

Bino sat bolt upright behind the steering wheel, kicking the Linc in the butt as he herded her north on I-35. Visible in the rearview mirror, the downtown Dallas skyscrapers grew shorter with each passing second. A Niagara of wind roared by outside the window. The snow-white Lincoln was six years old, and the speedometer showed eighty miles an hour to be its top speed. Bino had never pushed the car to the max before, but he was now doing eighty and then some. Autos and trucks whizzed past on both sides as if traveling in reverse. The freeway expansion joints rolled underneath the Linc's belly like runway markers.

Weedy Clements's Lasermont 9mm lay on the padded velour seat by Bino's hip. Bino's own gun, a German-made Mauser pistol, was at home in his bedside drawer. He'd never in his life fired a Lasermont—had only fired two or three different guns of any make, as a matter of fact—and was only familiar with the gun because of what more than one of his clients had told him: "Best in-and-out piece there is, man. You go in with the motherfucker, blow a coupla beer coolers into South Houston while the clerk stands there watching you. After that nobody gives you no shit, man. Then you out the door with the bread before anybody say fuckin' Jack Robinson." Two problems: The gun had a tendency to jam easily if it wasn't cleaned and oiled pretty often, and Bino had one hijacker client who was missing a thumb as a result of failure to properly maintain his weapon. The client's name was Waldo Jones, and he was currently doing a fifteen-year hit after the law had surrounded him in a supermarket parking lot as Waldo held his mangled hand and cussed a blue streak at his Lasermont. Problem number two: Weedy Clements was an even bigger slob than Waldo Jones, and Bino couldn't imagine Weedy taking the time to clean anything.

Far ahead and on the right, a Texas Department of Public Safety patrol car had a motorist pulled to the side of the road. The Linc approached cop vehicle and offender at bullet speed. For once in his life, Bino was glad to see a highway bull. Fast as the Linc was moving, the cop was bound to give chase, and Bino definitely needed help. He'd lead the cop to the wacko's house, and then . . . Jesus, Bino thought, come on, Mr. Policeman.

He passed the patrol car. The motorist was a young redheaded female with long flowing hair. The cop was leaning on the driver's side door and didn't even have his ticket book out. Bino blasted the Linc's horn as he zipped by, traveling at breakneck speed and even careening from one lane to another in order to attract more attention to himself. The cop ignored him and continued to grin at the girl. Bino gritted his teeth and returned his attention to the road.

He lifted his rump to pull out and unfold the directions he'd written down over the phone, and checked a passing highway sign. His exit was Raintree Boulevard, which according to the sign was a mile and a half ahead. He moved to the right into the exit lane, whipped quickly to the center to pass an ancient pickup loaded down with grain bushels, then jerked the wheel to return to the exit lane once more. He went the mile and a half in something like a minute; then he was on the down-slanted off ramp, the Linc fishtailing its way onto the access road. The light at the Raintree Boulevard intersection was red. Bino ran the light, closing his eyes as he barreled around the corner, making the lefthand turn under the freeway overpass feeling as if the Linc was riding on its two inside wheels. Raintree Boulevard was a winding blacktop; no other cars were in sight ahead. A sign on his right advertised minnows, four dollars a bucket, two miles down the way. Bino floored the accelerator and continued on.

By the time he'd gone four miles on Raintree Boulevard, skirting the northern shore of the lake while late-season water skiers threw double foamy wakes across the surface of the water, he'd slowed the Linc to a twenty-mile-an-hour crawl. He absolutely hated the snail's pace, but the directions called for a dirt road on his right which he would miss if he wasn't careful. Bino kept one eye on the asphalt in front of him and the other on the right side of the road.

And suddenly, there it was, a hardpacked dirt trail which left the blacktop at a ninety-degree angle, continued for a couple of hundred yards across an open field, and disappeared into a dense forest of elm and mesquite trees. Bino made the turn and sped up; according to the directions it was a straight shot through the woods to the house on the other side. He passed the last plowed row in the field as the speedometer needle touched fifty, and drilled on into the woods.

And very nearly gave himself a concussion as the Linc hit the first of the forest chugholes. The top of his head banged into the car's roof; the Linc rocked hard on its springs. Jesus, it hurt; he furiously rubbed the top of his head. Bino slowed, then slowed even more as the second chughole came into view. He lifted the

Lasermont, held the pistol in one hand and steered with the other, and proceeded on through deep shade. He hit the button and the electric window hummed down. Far away on his left, a cow bellowed.

The trip through the woods consumed a quarter of an hour. Bino fidgeted in his seat as he pictured Dodie's bloodless form laid out on a cold stone slab. He shut his eyes tightly and shook his head to clear the image from his mind. A thick tangle of limbs brushed the windshield and then scraped their way down the roof, and suddenly he was in a clearing. A tan four-door car faced him from twenty yards away; he drove around the auto, then slammed on his brakes. Up ahead, near a GMC pickup with a covered bed, sat Dodie's Trans-Am. Dodie's sweet old Trans-Am, the one she wouldn't part with, no matter what. Bino killed the engine and, pistol held ready, alighted at a trot and headed for the house up ahead. His necktie flapped in the breeze and his shoes made dusty scraping noises.

There were two ways to enter the house, either through a glass-paned door at the far end or a yawning garage-type entryway which led into what looked to be a woodshop. Inside the big entry, a band saw and a lathe sat beside a standup electric sander. Bino made his decision on the run. It was too easy for someone to see him through the back door, and on the concrete porch he'd be a sitting duck. As he reached the near corner of the house he veered to the left and entered the woodshop. He halted. His chest rose and fell with his rapid breathing.

Patrick Quarles let the curtain fall back into place over the kitchen window. He had known that the White-haired One would come for her, would have known even had the voices not told him as much. It was good. Quarles knew now that his union with the Truth could not be complete until he had faced the White-haired One, for until he'd dealt with the White-haired One, Quarles could not be One with the Truth. Naked, his scarred body glistening with coconut oil, Quarles tightened his grip on his Smith & Wesson .38 and crept slowly to the back of the house.

There was no light on inside the shop, so Bino widened his eyes in order to see more clearly. The concrete floor was covered in sawdust and littered with partially completed furniture, a chair-leg here, a tabletop there, a breakfast table with its legs unfinished in the far corner. Sandra Nestle, the VICAP queen, had said the guy was a woodworker. Bino took two hesitant steps forward. On a low table to his left sat three metal cans with with a dried substance around the edges of their lids, as though they'd been opened and then resealed. The odor of varnish hit Bino's nostrils. He picked up one of the cans and read the label: "GIFFORD AND TILLMAN GRADE TWO HARD ENAMEL." So far, Nestle was right on the button. Bino's mouth twisted violently as he set down the can and peered further into the shop. He continued cautiously.

Twenty feet ahead were wooden steps leading upward to a second-story landing. A rickety banister ran up the lefthand side of the staircase; the right edges of the steps were flush against the wall. Bino ascended one hesitant level at a time, pistol ready, his gaze warily on the landing overhead. The combined odors of paint and sawdust drifted up his nose. There was sudden movement near the ceiling. Bino ducked down and raised his weapon as a rapid fluttering of wings sounded. A sparrow left its perch in the rafters, dipped and dove, and whipped outside like a darting gray paper airplane. Bino swallowed hard and moved on.

He reached the top step and climbed up on the landing. The landing ran to his left for twenty feet or so, and on it was a stack of pointed wood fence slats. Beyond the slats was a door made of thick oak planks. There was a taut coiled spring with one end attached to the door and the other end attached to an eyebolt which was screwed into the wall. Bino walked slowly around the pile of wood to push on the door; the door moved easily inward with a loud rasping noise from the spring. Bino took a deep breath and, holding the Lasermont ready, stepped inside the house. The door closed behind him with a dull thud. Somewhere, a faucet dripped.

He stood at one end of a long corridor. At the far end, maybe fifty feet away, the hall opened out into a foyer. Visible in the foyer was the door which Bino had seen from outside, curtains drawn over the glass panes, sunlight filtering through the curtains. Between the rear entry where Bino stood and the foyer were four closed doors, two on either side of the hall. Other than the dripping of the unseen faucet and the sound of his own breathing, Bino heard nothing.

He stepped cautiously away from the entry and proceeded

down the corridor to the first closed door on his left. He held the pistol cocked beside his ear. A board creaked underfoot. Bino tried the doorknob; it turned easily with a soft click from the plunger. He twisted and shoved. The door flew inward and around to bang against the inside wall while Bino flattened against the door frame in the corridor.

There was no sound from within. Bino tensed, held the Lasermont in his right hand, clamped his left hand firmly onto his wrist, and sprang through the doorway. He went into a crouch, gun hand extended. He relaxed and stood erect.

He was inside a bedroom. There was a double bed with two side tables, a dresser with a small TV on top. Four picture frames hung on the walls. Three held cheap prints (flying geese in one; hunters in a blind, shotguns ready in a second; hunting dogs in the third) while the fourth frame surrounded a diploma awarded to Patrick Warren Quarles from the Texas School of Court Reporting. The TV was playing with the sound turned off. On the screen, a young man gazed lovingly at a young woman, then the pair clinched and fell onto a sofa, writhing sensuously against one another. The scene changed at once into a Tide commercial.

Leaning against the dresser was a baseball bat, a blond Louisville Slugger with signatures dotting its surface. Bino picked it up. Jesus, the autographs were from the Rangers: Rodriguez, Brown, Gonzales, Sierra. Bino carried the bat with him into the adjoining bathroom, stood and gazed around at a filthy porcelain sink, a toilet with a black ring at the water's edge, a combination tub and shower with soap scum clinging to the walls. He returned to the bedroom to stand for a moment in front of the remaining unopened door, which he assumed to lead to a closet. He shoved the bat under his arm, gently turned the knob, and pushed the door open.

There wasn't much doubt that the cubicle had once been a closet, but now the hanging rods were all gone. A rough table was inside, and on it lay a naked girl. Thin pale legs extended down to shackled and bruised ankles. His stomach churning, Bino reached around the jamb, fumbled for a switch, clicked on an overhead light.

It was Brenda Milton, or what was left of her. Her wrists were also shackled, and there was a cloth strap around her neck. A needle—Christ, Bino thought—was inserted into the vein in her left arm and attached to a rubber tube. The flesh around the needle was black. Bino remembered her as a robust athletic blond. Her hair was now greasy and stringy and her limbs thin as white pipe cleaners. She was either asleep or dead. Bino stepped forward and pressed his fingers into the side of her neck. The flesh was warm and there was a faint erratic pulse. He held his palm in front of her nose. Her faint breath warmed his hand.

Bino stepped out of the closet, yanked the spread from the bed, used the spread to cover Brenda. His eyes narrowed. His jaw bunched. He carried the gun in one hand and the bat in the other, and crept through the bedroom and back out into the hall.

And felt rather than heard the movement on his right. Air swished close to his face, then something belted his right forearm. His fingers stiffened into slivers of wood; the Lasermont clattered and slid across the floor. As Bino turned toward his attacker, the baseball bat—Jesus, Bino thought, it's another fucking bat just like the one I'm carrying—rose high, then descended again. This time the blow was aimed at Bino's head.

He was barely able to raise his own bat for protection. Hard maple slammed into hard maple with a noise like a gunshot. Both bats fell to the floor where they rattled and rolled. The force of the collision put Bino instantly on his knees. He raised his gaze and his mouth opened like a flytrap.

He was on his knees in front of a stark raving naked lunatic— Jesus Christ, skin white as typing paper, thin lips twisted in hate. And it was the court reporter, all right—Bino recognized the face, but . . . Jesus, Bino thought, a stark raving . . . His gaze fell on Patrick Quarles's upper torso.

Jesus, Bino thought, almost with pity. Jesus H. Christ, what could have happened to the guy? Scars (welts, really—big raised welts) covered Quarles's belly and chest. The guy had no breasts, only a huge raised welt running from shoulder to shoulder. Bino swallowed as sour bile rose into his mouth.

The creature peeled back its lips and uttered a hiss that raised goosebumps on Bino's neck the size of spider eggs. Then it spoke in an eerie high-pitched tenor. "Shoot him, you stupid heap."

Bino was able to say in a stunned voice, "Shoot who?" And then think, Hell, I'm no stupid heap.

Quarles spoke again, this time in a deep basso, and said, "It is the White-haired One. Kill him."

The creature that was Patrick Quarles raised its hand. In the hand was a pistol. The hammer aired back with a solid *click-click*.

Bino acted on pure instinct. He lowered his head, drove off his right instep, and belted the lunatic squarely between the numbers. Quarles flew backward with a startled "Oof!" The pistol flew from his hand, banged into the wall, and fell to the floor. Then Quarles, with Bino's head thrust solidly into his midsection, hit the wall as well; the solid crunch of bone vibrated through Quarles's chest and into Bino's scalp. Bino rebounded from the collision and landed on his rump, jarring his spine. Quarles tumbled sideways, fell to the floor, and began to squeal.

The squeal was earsplitting in the close quarters of the hallway, like the terrified bellowing of pigs in the slaughterhouse. Quarles started to rise, fell again, finally climbed to his feet. His squeals rose to a crescendo as he pushed away from the wall and took off down the corridor at a half-run, half-stagger. As Quarles neared the door through which Bino had entered the house, Bino scrabbled crablike across the floor and got his hands on the Lasermont 9mm.

Bino aimed and steadied the pistol. Quarles, the bony cheeks of his ass quivering with the effort, threw open the door and stepped through. Bino squeezed the trigger; the gun went off with a deafening roar. As Quarles disappeared through the entryway the bullet crashed into the door frame.

Hardy Cole figured that he had a ten-minute head start on the caravan. He'd planned it that way. As Mac Strange, Nelson Deletay, and Marvin Goldman had taken off for the Crowley Courts Building parking garage—after Deletay, of course, had made certain that a herd of squad cars were on the way as backup and that the reporters and television people had all been alerted—Cole had gone in the opposite direction. He'd parked his unmarked Chevy downstairs in the spaces reserved for jurors, which made for an easy getaway onto Commerce Street, and he figured that he'd been headed north on I-35 before the others had reached the parking garage. Finding the Raintree Boulevard exit from I-35 had been a piece of cake; locating Patrick Quarles's lake house had been a different story entirely. Cole had stopped for directions in a bait shop near the lake. Fortunately the bait shop's owner had known Quarles and had known exactly where he lived—had remarked to Cole that Quarles was a little weird and had told Cole to watch himself.

The county Chevy bounced out of the trees and into the clearing, and Cole threw on the brakes to stop in a cloud of dust. Bino's white Lincoln Hardy knew; the tan Buick, the pickup, and the little red Trans-Am were vehicles he didn't recognize. Cole got out of the Chevy and hit the ground running, digging under his jacket for his service revolver. He'd just cleared the pistol when a stark naked man came running out of the shop entrance, squealing at the top of his lungs.

For an instant, Cole froze. Could he be seeing things, a buck-naked guy, his sallow-complexioned face contorted, nasty scars covering his upper body, limping painfully, uttering a series of mind-bending screams? Jesus Christ, the guy was . . . Never mind, Cole thought as his blood turned to icewater. This is the guy.

Cole dropped to one knee and aimed his revolver. Warn him, his law-enforcement training said, caution the guy, and if he doesn't stop, then fire a warning shot over his head. At the same time, Hardy Cole's inner self told him, Blow the fucker away.

The first shot tore into Patrick Quarles's shoulder and spun him around. The second slug blew a large portion of his skull away. The eerie squeals died in Quarles's throat. He fell on his side in the dirt. His feet lashed out convulsively.

Cole stood, let his revolver hang by his side, and slowly approached the corpse. He rolled the body over with his toe. The eyes were wide and staring, the mouth slack. Blood mixed with syrupy brain fluid oozed from the head wound to turn the dirt into reddish-brown mud.

"Stop," Hardy Cole murmured to himself. "Stop, police."

Bino found Dodie in the sitting room just off the foyer. She was naked, sitting upright in a straight-backed wooden chair. Her ankles were lashed to the chair's front legs and her wrists were tied to the chair's rear legs, her arms straight down at her sides. More rope encircled her chest, pinning her upper body to the chair back. Tissue was stuffed into her mouth and secured by strips of tape. Her blue eyes were open wide. Her thigh muscles rippled as she struggled against her bonds.

"Jesus, babe," Bino said. "Hold on. Jesus."

Her clothing lay on the two-seater divan in a pile. Bino went over, dug through the clothes, found her tan skirt, carried the skirt over to cover her nakedness. He held the garment up underneath her chin. Dodie turned her head to look at him as she continued to struggle. "Mmmm," she said. "*Mmmm.*"

Bino let go of the skirt to reach for her gag. The skirt tumbled off her and fell to the floor. He grabbed the skirt and held it in front of her with one hand while he pulled at the tape, stripped it from her mouth, and pulled out the wad of tissue. "You okay?" Bino said. "Jesus, Dode, are you all right?"

Her eyes flashed fire. She licked her lips. "Will you please *untie me?*" she said. "I can dress myself, Bino. Wow, we spent last night together. You going around acting embarrassed because I don't have any clothes on is just a little bit silly, don't you think?"

By the time Dodie had dressed and Bino was ready to accompany her outside, the medical techs had already taken Brenda Milton away in an ambulance. Bino had gone out to find them preparing to haul Quarles's body away, and had told them that there was a girl in the house who was still alive but in pretty bad shape. The medics had sprinted through the shop into the house, had cut Brenda loose with a hacksaw, and had gotten her into the ambulance in record time. With Patrick Quarles, they didn't need to be in such a hurry.

Dodie was now dressed in her skirt, blouse, and topsiders, and ready to face the world. Bino escorted her to the back door with his arm about her shoulders. Just before they stepped over the threshold, she smiled up at him and he kissed her forehead.

They walked slowly across the dirt yard toward the Linc. Patrick Quarles still lay where he had fallen, with a heavy blanket covering him. Nelson Deletay spoke to a group of reporters while cameramen pointed minicams at Deletay, at Quarles's body, at the lakeshore, and at the house. Nolan Pounds the true-crime writer was among the reporters, madly taking notes. Mac Strange and Sandra Nestle stood off to one side, talking in whispers. The papers tomorrow will have Deletay written up as the hero, Bino thought. Bet on it.

Hardy Cole slouched against the fender of his county Chevy. Cole showed a crooked grin as Bino and Dodie went by. Bino reached out and patted Cole's shoulder. "What is it they say?" Bino said. "The halfbacks get the headlines and the linemen get the headaches, something like that?"

Cole's grin broadened as his gaze moved to Deletay and the reporters, then rested once again on Bino. "Yeah, something like that," Hardy Cole said. Bino and Dodie continued on.

They reached the Lincoln's side. As Bino held the door for Dodie, Nelson Deletay yelled, "Phillips. Mr. Phillips. We're going to have to interview her. You, too. Don't go away."

Bino waited until Dodie had sat in the passenger seat and crossed her legs, then he slammed the door. He retreated to meet Deletay halfway.

Deletay put his hands at his waist. "It's important we get the details, for future reference."

"Nelson," Bino said, then licked his lips and said more softly, "Look, Nelson. I know it's important. Just . . . later, okay? We're both sort of tired right now." What the hell, Bino thought—I'm too whipped to get into it with the guy. He left Deletay standing there, got in the Linc, and drove away through the woods. As they neared the blacktop on the other side of the trees, Dodie buried her face in the hollow of his shoulder. Finally, she was crying.

25

On October 25, 1991, Mickey Stanley copped to a max of a nickel. It had taken some doing, but Goldman had finally stood still for it. An editorial in the *Dallas Morning News*, telling about Mickey's adventures in saving his mother from Patrick Quarles, had more than a little to do with Goldman's cooperation, Bino thought. Goldman dropped the original charges, and Mickey agreed through his lawyers to waive indictment on the new beef and plead guilty to an information: Importation of Marijuana, one count, five-year maximum. Mickey stood up beside Bino, pled guilty like a little man, and told Judge Hazel Burke Sanderson that he was sorry. Mickey was wearing a cast which covered his shoulder and extended all the way to his wrist. His arm was bent and supported by a sling. Mickey also waived his presentence report. His sentencing hearing was held on the spot.

Kit testified for the defendant, of course. Her facial cuts had practically healed and her nose was only slightly puffy. In her testimony she said that nothing he'd done had been Mickey's fault because he'd been raised without a father, and that his mother hadn't had the time to train him properly. Her time on the stand was delayed twice because she burst into tears.

Bino testified as well, said that Mickey was a good boy, but from the way Judge Hazel looked at him Bino didn't think he'd helped very much. Later, he would decide that he'd made a mistake by getting on the stand at all. After Brenda Milton's testimony, nothing else mattered.

Brenda appeared in a plain navy dress with a sailor collar. Her blond hair had regained its sheen. She was still weak as a kitten, and told her story in a voice so soft that the judge had to ask Brenda to speak into a microphone. She said that Mickey had never been the brains behind the dope-smuggling ring, and that he hadn't even known about most of the drug deals. After she'd testified, on her way from the witness stand to the spectator section, Brenda stumbled and righted herself at just the proper moment. After Brenda's appearance, even Judge Hazel was reluctant to let the hammer down.

Judge Hazel sentenced Mickey to six months, to be served in a camp without a fence around it. After the sentencing, Mickey grinned from ear to ear. Kit ran past the marshals at the railing and hugged her son for dear life.

Bino hoped to hell that Mickey had learned his lesson, and for the first time in his legal career wondered if maybe the judge shouldn't have given his client more time. Bino wasn't sure. He'd have to think about it.

On the day of Mickey's sentencing, Hardy Cole was in an East Dallas park playground, hidden behind a tree. Twenty yards away, Rascal Erly sat on a bench. Rascal was talking to a little girl. The little girl was around nine, wore her hair in a long brown ponytail, and had on jeans and a Six Flags Over Texas T-shirt. She chewed bubblegum and occasionally blew big pink bubbles. As Cole watched, Rascal Erly put his hand on the child's arm.

Quick as thought, Cole emerged from his hiding place and cuffed Rascal to the bench. "That's it," Cole said. "That's it, you're under arrest."

Rascal's ugly features twisted into a snarl. "Ain't done nothin'. Whatcha hasslin' me for?"

"How 'bout it, honey?" Cole picked the little girl up. "The man bother you?"

"Sure did, Daddy," the child said. She wrinkled her nose and blew a bubble in Rascal's direction. "Dirty ole child botherer," the little girl said. "I'm gonna tell the judge about it, too."

For Bino, the story ended two weeks later, on the day that he returned to the office from a bond hearing to find Dodie convulsed

in laughter. It was the first time since he'd rescued her from
Quarles's place that Bino had heard Dodie really laugh. She had
a paperback book open on her desk. Half was reading over her
shoulder and was snorting and giggling as well.

"What's goin' on?" Bino said.

Dodie's smile was ear to ear. "You see this? You *see it?*" She
held up the book with the cover facing Bino. Half hooted and
pounded on her desk in glee.

Bino leaned forward and squinted. The book was titled, in
flaming red letters, *The Pursuit of Dracula Don.* Patrick Quarles's
high school yearbook picture was on the cover beside a grisly photo
of Annette Ray's corpse, frontal view with the pubic area blacked
out. The author was Nolan Pounds.

"I heard about it," Bino said. "Jesus, they barely get the guy
to the morgue and the book's already out."

"But have you *seen it?*" Dodie was laughing so hard that her
face was crimson.

Bino took the book from her and turned it around. It was open
to the center pages where the pictures were. A scowling Nelson
Deletay was in one photo, a demure Sandra Nestle in another.
On the opposite page was a picture of Goldman, scowling from
his seat at the prosecution table. Beneath Goldman's photo was
Bino himself, a courtroom action shot of the big white-haired
lawyer making a closing argument. Bino thought the picture was
around ten years old.

He looked at Dodie and frowned.

"Read," she giggled. "*Read.*"

Bino now looked at the inscriptions underneath the pictures.
Goldman's photo bore the caption: "Attorney Bino Phillips ponders
a question." Under Bino's own picture was the wording, "U.S.
Attorney Goldman makes a point." Jesus, Bino thought, no wonder Pounds has never had a blockbuster, the guy can't even remember which lawyer is which.

Bino looked up from the book. Dodie continued to hoot while
Half doubled over and held his midsection.

"What's so damn funny?" Bino Phillips said.

About the Author

A. W. Gray is the author of the critically ac-
claimed novels *Prime Suspect*, *The Man Offside*,
In Defense of Judges, *Size*, and *Bino*, all published
by Dutton. A life-long Texan, he lives with his
wife and family in Fort Worth.